SKERRYMOR BAY

Francis Essex

NEW ENGLISH LIBRARY

This book is dedicated to RICHARD and SARA STONE
in gratitude for 30 years of friendship and advice.

A New English Library Original Publication, 1984

First NEL Paperback Edition May 1984

NEL Books are published by
New English Library,
Mill Road, Dunton Green,
Sevenoaks, Kent.
Editorial Office: 47 Bedford Square, London WC1B 3DP

Made and printed in Great Britain by
Richard Clay (The Chaucer Press) Ltd, Bungay, Suffolk

British Library C.I.P.

Essex, Francis
  Skerrymor Bay.
  I. Title
  823'.914 [F] PR6055.S/

  ISBN 0–450–05671–6

SKERRYMOR BAY

The fisherman was chopping firewood outside his back door when they arrived. Morrison decided to take the bull by the horns.

'I think I might have some good news for you by the end of the week.'

The old fellow replied calmly enough. 'Well, I'm glad to hear that, Mr Morrison.'

Morrison's curiosity overcame his good sense.

'Did you – er – receive any other offers, by the way?'

'Aye, there was one but I'd already given you my word.' He gathered up some sticks and rose to his feet. 'And we're all gentlemen around these parts.'

The old fisherman and his wife moved out one Thursday in February. Morrison and Biddy saw Mr and Mrs Ferguson stand in their front doorway and hold hands as they looked back into their home for the last time. The moment came to say goodbye to MacGregor and as the frail old lady stooped down the collie put both paws on her shoulders and licked her face in fond farewell until her husband began to walk him towards the boathouse.

Inside he said to Morrison with quiet dignity, 'I pray the house will give you the same happiness it has to Marjorie and me over forty years.'

Biddy sat on the ground hugging MacGregor and when she and her father looked at each other there were tears in their eyes. . . .

AUTHOR'S NOTE

I spent five happy years living and working in Scotland between 1964 and 1969. It was then I met Biddy who, of course, is grown up now and remains as I have described her only in the memory which itself has become enhanced by time. The supporting characters are pure fiction and even if one or two reflect faint echoes of persons I may have met at one time or another it was not in Scotland or anywhere else I could specifically name. They, as well as the incidents related, are as fictitious as the map showing roughly where all this took place.

My thanks are due to Rhoddy MacCleod not only for his hospitality and a crash course on coastal salmon netting at his fine fisheries in Fascadale, Achateny in Argyll, but also for correcting technical detail in the manuscript with the generous thoroughness so typical of him.

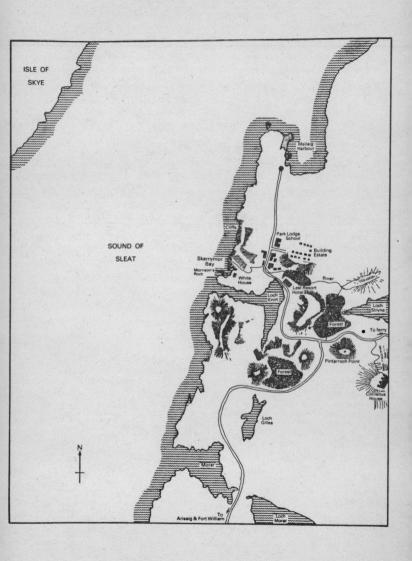

PROLOGUE

THE FRONT door opened and a school satchel hurtled into the hall having been thrice whirled around the head to provide momentum. It was followed at equal speed by a ten-year-old child sliding across the polished floor on her bottom. In the small kitchen Morrison heard the thunderous crash of small body against hall table and knew his daughter was home from school.

'Hey,' he called. 'Now put all that back the way it was.'

No reply came but quieter sounds indicated she was complying with the instruction. He turned from the stove as she entered the kitchen, pulling off the green velour hat to display a riot of naturally curly golden-red hair. The tie was knotted somewhere round the back of her neck, socks down by the ankles, both shoes scuffed, and during the day her blouse had lost an encounter with an ink bottle.

'Can I have a glass of milk?'

He slid a couple of slices of bread under the grill and gave a stir to some baked beans in the saucepan. 'Can't you wait?' he asked.

'Is tea nearly ready?'

'Just about.'

'Are you having some?'

'Yes.'

'Then I'll have a glass of milk now and another one with you.'

'Help yourself.' Morrison poured boiling water into the teapot while she crossed to the fridge and took out the milk. 'What happened today?'

'Not much. What do you expect would happen in school apart from classes and things?'

'You look like you've been through a war.'

'We got our end of term reports.'

'What did they do, fire them at you?'

She drank down the glass of milk, holding the bottle poised for further supplies, before putting both down on the table and running into the hall to retrieve her satchel. Morrison turned the toast as she returned and tiptoed herself on to a kitchen chair.

'Shall I read it to you?'

'You're not supposed to have opened it.'

She grinned up at his back, mischievous green eyes sparkling from a freckled face. 'Do you want to hear it or not?'

'Yes, of course I do.'

She slid the report from its envelope and began to read from the very top of the page. ' "Saint Elizabeth's School for Girls. End of term report, dated fourteenth of December. Form 2B. Number in class, twenty-seven." '

'I don't need to hear all that. Let's go straight to the nitty-gritty.'

'This is the best bit. "Number of times absent, one." When was I absent from school?' she asked him.

'You came with me to the clinic – I wouldn't have been home in time, remember?'

'Oh yes. That was a *terrible* day.' Her eyes drifted down to the comments on classwork and she paused doubtfully. 'I hope you're ready for this.'

'Try me.' He was buttering toast before spooning on the baked beans. She scanned the sheet searching for favourable comment.

' "Nature Study. Excellent. Bridget shows enthusiasm and ready understanding." That's pretty good isn't it?'

'It's wonderful,' her father agreed. 'Do they put Nature Study right at the top of the list? Or something a bit more important – like Arithmetic or English?'

'Nature Study's my best subject. It begins to fall away after that.' She gave a slightly uncomfortable wriggle. 'All right then, Arithmetic. "Eight." '

'Eight?' He placed the plate of beans in front of her. 'Eight out of what?'

'Does it matter?'

'Of course it matters. Eight out of ten would be jolly good. Eight out of twenty would be disappointing. Eight out of fifty would be catastrophic.'

She looked hard at the report. 'I don't know how to tell you this. What does per cent mean?'

'Eight out of a *hundred*? Oh Biddy!'

'Well, numbers and me just don't get on together.'

'But eight out of a hundred, for heaven's sake. What's it say about English?'

' "Bridget has her work days and her dream days," ' she read.

'This is the worst report I've ever heard.'

'You'll like this one. "Art. Bridget concentrates at the top of her voice." That's funny.'

'Here, give me that.' He took the report from her, preferring to read the rest for himself. The girl tucked into her beans at the same time as she studied his face for early-warning signs of genuine annoyance. 'Did you read what the headmistress says at the end?' he asked. ' "A poor exam result arising from inattention in class. This pupil must try harder next term." '

She was about to put up a spirited defence when something in her father's expression silenced the words before they were uttered. She had an instinct for his moods and a sixth-sense tipped her off when enough was enough.

'This report is just awful, Biddy.'

'I'm going to try harder next term.'

'Yes, well, that's something I need to talk to you about.'

She watched him collect his own beans and pour a cup of tea. He glanced across at her, pointing an enquiring finger at the milk bottle. She shook her head and waited.

Morrison gave her a watered-down description of his visit to the clinic for the final check-up. The specialist had recited typically impractical advice, spelling out a diet of fresh air, gradually increasing physical effort, and a healthy

11

job wherein he could make his own hours. Afterwards he took a bus to the factory and listened to a weak-faced man from Staff Relations explaining that the required reduction of workforce, combined with his extended sick leave, rendered him a natural choice for redundancy. He was sure Morrison would understand this whilst at the same time realising how much the company appreciated work he'd performed for them in the past. He understood all right; in a climate where the only secure jobs belonged to union leaders and company negotiators, he had nobody but himself to rely on.

Which meant, put into its simplest terms, that he had a daughter totally reliant on him, and he was out of work. It didn't take a degree to figure out his bank balance but the apartment was worth something and there would be a redundancy payment of sorts. If they were to be a fighting team it was as well that each was in possession of the facts so he gave Biddy the bare bones of the story, colouring it with light-hearted confidence. The child interrupted only once for a clearer explanation of 'redundancy'; for the rest she ate her beans, poured herself a second glass of milk, and watched him with serious, attentive eyes.

He looked pale. The prematurely grey hair over a young face lacked its normal sheen and, of course, the long illness had left him a great deal thinner. Most of all his eyes betrayed the sadness of a suddenly lonely widower, brightening only in brief flashes, usually a result of something Biddy had said or done. He tried hard in front of her and a faint hint of adult responsibility caused her to attempt an intelligent response, but all in all it had been the most dreadful year.

Morrison's wife had died when he was thirty-two. It was a shattering blow and the night after the funeral he looked down on the sleeping head of Biddy and wondered what he should do. His in-laws were too old to cope with a spirited grand-daughter, his own parents were long divorced, and, besides, he adored his tomboy daughter and never seriously considered the thought that anyone but he should bring her up.

12

Six months after his wife's death he had been taken seriously ill and that was when things became really rough. Biddy stayed with her grandparents, there was no other option, but for nine weeks that kid made the bus ride to the hospital every single day. Seated on the upper deck she would pass the interminable half-hour describing lurid details of her father's operations to some unfortunate passenger. She chose a different part of his body each journey and her vivid descriptions of teams of surgeons fighting to save him would move most people to advise on the importance of bravery through times of adversity, and just a few to press fifty pence into her hand. Of the two types she preferred the latter. Sometimes she spoke to them in French; not that she *knew* any French, but then neither did they. On one occasion she tired of illness altogether and painted an entirely original word-picture of her father's absence from home, until the passenger, with tears in her eyes, interrupted to say they'd reached her stop. Biddy got off the bus and didn't tell that story again – it was a long walk from the prison.

In all the stories her father was a hero figure and, on his discharge from hospital, she returned with him to the apartment where incredibly she helped look after him almost without faltering throughout his convalescence. It was during this period that Morrison and Biddy became an indestructible partnership.

'So there it is,' he concluded. 'We're on our own again, you and me. I have to find a job, you have to do better in school, and we both have to make the best of it.'

She was spreading jam on bread. 'I don't know how you could go on about my schoolwork, because yours must be the most *awful* report anybody ever had!'

The headless men were approaching down a long alley. The wall was against his back so further retreat was impossible. He tried to merge into the shadows but still the men came forward. He reasoned that surely without heads they wouldn't be able to see him even when it became obvious they were aware of his presence. He wanted to cry out but no· sound would come and the men were running at him now. He gave a scream of fear and this time it worked – the sound of it woke him.

'Daddy, Daddy, you're having a nightmare. Come *on*!' Her small hands shook him into consciousness and he began to laugh with relief. He always laughed when he came out of a bad dream, helpless, infectious laughter which used to cause Wendy to join in, and they would hug each other tightly, laughing together at nothing at all. Now Biddy was there shivering after the run from her bedroom and giggling along with him. 'What was it?'

'I can't remember.'

'You were making dreadful noises. Real scary.'

'I was frightened.'

'What *of*?'

'I don't know.' They laughed again. 'You're cold. Jump in and I'll cuddle you warm.'

She slid in beside him and within minutes was asleep again. He lay still, wide awake now, listening to her breathing. The day came flooding back, then the entire miserable year. He had tried everything he'd ever heard about to lessen the feeling of utter desolation. He'd wept, got drunk, sought solace from other women, but nothing penetrated sufficiently deep to alleviate the pain. He missed Wendy so acutely that he knew only time would come to his aid. Meanwhile he would bring up their daughter as best he could and, wherever Wendy was, she would watch him and know he was faithful to their memory.

One thing, though. He would clear out of the apartment and live somewhere else. There were too many reminders of their life together; he'd welcomed them at first but now they were proving irksome, accentuating his loneliness. Besides, he could no longer afford the mortgage whereas he could use the paper profit brought about by the increased value of the block of flats.

But where could they go, he and Biddy? What was he going to do? He was not a greedy man and circumstances

14

had long since smothered youthful ambition. He was normally energetic, good with his hands, loved the sea, the countryside, the wind and rain. He had no fear of hard work. In all of this it was only his confidence that had been shaken; give him a lucky break and he would be on top of the world again.

He allowed a succession of random thoughts to float in and out of his mind. Around four o'clock something important happened; he found himself thinking about Wendy and for the first time since her death he did not shy away from the pain her memory evoked. Rather he studied deliberately the visions conjured up and he saw her laughing face look round to him as she stood knee deep in the river expertly playing the hooked salmon. Her Irish beauty had been of such range that throughout their married life a new facet would catch him by surprise, sometimes a grave loveliness of relaxed contemplation, then a wild tempestuous excitement when she knew her teasing was arousing him, or her stunning entrance wearing the long green dress which matched her eyes, with her red hair falling gently around her shoulders. She had been an outdoor girl and uppermost in his mind was the picture of her lending grace even to oilskins as she took the helm of their sloop in a stiff breeze and sailed the boat to windward amidst bucketings of spray.

At six o'clock, when the street noises began their fourteen-hour shift, he fell heavily asleep to wake two hours later feeling thick and muggy. Biddy was already out of bed and he could hear her voice through the open front door as she raced around the building with the lad from the next apartment. A man's voice topped their shrieks sternly calling to the boy to come in for breakfast, and a distant door slam provided a full stop to the racket. A few moments later she returned carrying a couple of letters and a magazine.

'What was all that about?'

'I went downstairs to see if there was any post.'

'Old Turner sounded pretty bad tempered.'

'Maybe 'cos nobody wrote to him today.' She tossed the

mail at him and scampered out of the room. He climbed out of bed, pulled on a dressing gown, picked up the letters, and went into the kitchen. Biddy was precariously carrying a brimming bowl of cornflakes and milk from sideboard to table.

'What are you doing? I was going to cook a proper breakfast.'

'Go ahead. I'll eat it after I've finished this.'

He took eggs from the fridge and broke them into a basin. Behind him she spooned on sugar and opened his letters. 'Leave those alone.'

'This magazine's got Mr Turner's name on it. There was something for him after all.'

'Go bang on his door and give it back.'

'There's a picture of where we went on holiday with Mummy.'

He carried the basin to the table and looked over his daughter's shoulder as he beat the eggs. 'We never went to Scotland in our lives.'

'Where did we go then?'

'Devon, but you're looking at a picture of Mallaig.'

'Where's Mallaig?'

'I haven't a clue. Somewhere in Scotland.'

She read the caption. ' "The fishing fleet sails out of Mallaig." It looks yummy, doesn't it?'

After she had left for school, the last day of term, he read the magazine from cover to cover before slipping it under Turner's front door. It had to be pre-destined. Why else would she pick up accidentally the neighbour's angling magazine within a few hours of his own tumultuous flow of thoughts through the night? As he read an idea began to take shape in his head.

He spent the day dredging up a limited knowledge of Scotland, born solely out of song, story and hearsay. Mental images of swinging kilt and flaming red hair, brandishing claymores, of aggressive Scottishness by a people convinced they have been exploited and betrayed, of wild weather in a rigorous climate, and of wide-ranging music from the Highland ceilidh to the melodious colloquial dialect of Argyllshire. Perhaps a job on trawlers, fishing the lochs and coastal waters beneath brutal cliffs, or further afield in northern waters tossed by waves and raw fresh air. Wasn't it precisely the kind of life indicated by that fool of a specialist? On the other hand how was he going to find work in a howling wilderness of unemployment? Did not the abandoned Isle of St Kilda die of its own accord when the young people left for the mainland? What right did he have to remove Biddy from city and school-friends to wild desolation? Surely not simply because she made passing comment about a magazine photograph looking yummy?

As doubts threatened to gather momentum he pulled a firm handbrake on himself. It was possible to agonise to the point where nothing would be achieved. He spoke aloud in the empty room. 'I'm taking the kid to Scotland, Wendy. Keep an eye on us, darling.'

It was the last time he spoke to his wife; he never forgot her, but talking to her felt like standing still.

He and Biddy spent Christmas with her grandparents. It was not a successful few days. His mother-in-law displayed such outrage at his plan that, strangely, her anger aided rather than hindered his determination. In a dramatic movement she threw a possessive arm around Biddy and asked, 'How will Patrick and I watch our grand-daughter grow up?'

'By coming to see us,' he countered gently, 'and by our coming to see you.'

'From Scotland?'

'It's not the end of the world.'

'It is.' The woman spoke with sudden viciousness. 'It's the edge of nowhere. You're dragging a little girl into total obscurity.' From the crook of her arm Biddy threw her father a humorous wink which calmed his irritation and enabled him to respond quietly.

'I think that's pitching it a bit strong. Wendy and I were keen anglers, I know something about the fish, the sea, and the countryside and, according to her school report, a deal of this has rubbed off on to Biddy. Everything that's happened during the past year has made most of my decisions for me and, with the doctor warning that my life in the smoke is doing me no good at all, it seems a logical step to take.'

'And what of her faith? Where does that come into your scheme of things?'

'They have churches in Scotland. They're quite advanced really.' He regretted the sarcasm because her face instantly snapped shut.

'I mean the *Catholic* church, David. You made a solemn promise before the priest and I'll not allow you to forget it.'

'Yes, well, Wendy and I –' he began hesitantly.

The woman knew what he was going to say and interrupted by kneeling and appealing to her grandchild. 'You wouldn't want to go, would you dear? You wouldn't want to leave your poor old granny and go and live alone in the cold, selling nasty fish?'

'Yes please,' said Biddy.

Morrison and Biddy caught the train to Glasgow passing the journey with card games, sandwiches, and countless excursions along the corridor. She befriended another little girl who, prior to encountering Biddy's reprobate persuasions, had sat in well-behaved virtuousness for two hundred miles but now tore among the passengers with tireless aggravation until one elderly spinster threatened to call the guard.

The two children then disappeared to the far end of the train where they discovered to their delight the door leading into the guard's van had been left unlocked. Inside they found three dogs, tied up for the duration of the journey, and well distanced from each other. Two lay in a bundle of sacking but the third, an Alsatian, tugged crossly at its bond. He growled nastily when he saw the girls whereupon Biddy crossed to him unhesitatingly.

'Esserkersayker le matter voo stupido chien?' she enquired in her top-of-the-bus French. 'Jerswee un ami.' The animal cocked its ears at the child standing firmly before

him with hands on hips. 'Si voo jouez votre cards a la droitè·
Je could fix voo un bon repas.' The dog tilted its head to one
side – this was a language he hadn't come across before.

Minutes later the kitchen staff of the dining-car were
faced with two politely innocent faces pleading for a few
scraps to feed their pets in the guard's van. Busy as they
were, and contrary to regulations, they found time to
oblige them, and Biddy and her friend carefully carried two
plates heaped with meat back to the end of the train. The
three dogs and the two girls were soon good friends and
romped playfully for seventy miles or so leaving the passengers to doze in merciful peace.

Approaching Carlisle the scenery took on a new look.
Morrison must have dropped off for a few minutes because,
when he looked out of the window again, it was as if some
heavenly scenehand had dropped in a new backcloth.
Hundreds of square miles of rolling green and brown
countryside, short-cropped rounded hills some wearing
grey stone tiaras, shapeless soft-edged splodges of white
cumulus racing across blue sky causing their shadows to
race over the land as if in competition with the train. In
years past someone had collected the grey stones and, with
a patience that defied reason, had constructed mile after
mile of drystone walling to divide one field from the next
without apparent purpose because fat contented sheep
pulled at the grass on both sides. Graceless crows walked
among their feet feeding undisturbed, a farmer had
swerved his plough at the edge of a field to spare a small
shrub and then continued his crooked path for row after
row until sixteen acres of turned soil bore the blemish like
an operation scar. Later the land flattened out in the fore-
ground and distant mountains carried a dusting of snow
whilst trees, brought up in the teeth of a prevailing north-
westerly, bent their backs against the icy fingered wind and
spread thin branches southwards in a mute appeal for
warmth.

As they approached the Border country he marvelled
that an island shown as a tiny splodge of red on a world map
should offer so many miles of unspoiled landscapes seen

from a train window. He was being transported through a history of violence where the occasional ruins of a castle bore witness to the burnings and sackings of centuries-past Border raids. For endless years Borderers endured the consequences of the long quarrel between England and Scotland when a man's life expectancy depended heavily on the skill and strength of his arms and no woman felt secure when her man was away.

The battles were waged not only between Scots and English but among Highland families who fought for religious or political mastery. The scenic beauty is only skin deep in the sense that beneath the surface lies a fundamental blemish etched deeply by struggle and strife. Today the sons of long-lived families find little profit or joy from crofts and, further north, even the Gaelic language struggles feebly through its death throes. Now the English invade as tourists to meet hosts who need the trade but resent the loss of independence and pride that accompanies it.

Morrison was roused from his musings when he became aware of a strange man glaring down on him.

'They could all have been poisoned, sir,' the man declared with controlled dignity but lack of clarity. 'I will take up the inefficiency of British Rail in another place and at another time but I feel you should be informed that your daughter is the most badly behaved little girl I have ever met in my life.'

'I'm afraid I have no idea what you're talking about,' said Morrison who was at once annoyed by the stranger's pomposity.

'Therein lies your problem, sir. Children should not be permitted to roam unsupervised in my view.' At last came the precise complaint, 'Your daughter has been giving food to my Alsatian who, I might add, is supposed to be a guard dog.'

Morrison looked down from his face to Biddy in shocked enquiry. The girl tried a crooked smile but something told her it wasn't going to be enough.

In Glasgow they rested for one night scarcely drawing a breath of city air before finding themselves on a second train winding their way along a single-track railway past Helensburgh, through Fort William, and on to Mallaig. Now the two of them gazed out on rolling farmlands, fruit-laden glens, streaming burns and majestic seascapes. They saw the Gareloch and the incongruous bedfellows of the nuclear submarine base and its immediate neighbour the breaking-up yard where, on occasions, the newest submarines of the Royal Navy glowered with blunt shapelessness as an elderly ship would sail through Rhu Narrows on the high tide and proceed up the loch, dressed overall, firepumps projecting skywards, acknowledging the signals and hoots of other vessels with the dignity of overwhelming sadness before mooring alongside the wharf of its final resting place.

At Gareloch Head, Morrison and Biddy saw the start of the Highlands of Scotland, a mountainous tract of crystalline schists and granite rocks, massive and flat-topped. Then they were taken through the intersecting line of the Great Glen before rejoining the coast which now presented an almost uninterrupted succession of deep indentations and bald rocky cliffs and headlands. When they reached the Inner Hebrides, the chain of islands known as the Western Isles which stretch from Mull to the Butt of Lewis, their journey was nearly complete.

At Mallaig they heaped their cases on the platform whilst Morrison engaged a creaking old Dormobile taxi owned by its creaking old driver. They were taken to The Last Resort, a hotel chosen by him only because its name seemed to admit a sense of humour. By the time they checked in, Biddy's enforced inactivity over two days of travel threatened to explode in a display of wild spirits, so they left the cases in their room unpacked and went out for a walk. For nearly an hour they strode side by side along the coast road, continuing until they had not heard a single man-made sound for fifteen minutes. Then they stopped to look across the Sound of Sleat to Skye, with the vague shapes of Rhum and Eigg to the south-west and the fishing trawlers of Mallaig to their right. They watched the cat's-paws of a squall dance flecks of white across the grey water and felt the wind place drops of rain on their cheeks. Biddy stood close up to her father and he laid an arm across her shoulders, both experiencing a sudden surge of excitement and sharing total confidence in each other.

They didn't know it then but, below them, lay Skerrymor Bay.

CHAPTER ONE

THE LAST Resort nestled on the fringe of a forest of Scots pine trees where it opened out into a small clearing overlooking the innermost reaches of the loch, according the principal bedrooms situated at the front of the hotel an uninterrupted view of a stretch of water curving away until it became lost behind the softly undulating hills on either side. It was built from large blocks of grey stone topped by a roof of black slate tiles and the sombre effect was relieved by splashes of white where a wooden porch had been added to a door or a bay to a window. At the end of an uncared-for drive a large sign proclaimed its presence but several strips of wood had been nailed haphazardly to the supports which announced other services as they became available. Thus, with the bays and the porches, the overall effect was of a hotel existing from day to day on afterthoughts. Its land spread behind the building for several acres but, apart from several patches immediately alongside the walls where rhododendrons had grown gloriously rampant, there was no attempt at cultivation and the property merged effortlessly into the countryside beyond with only a board nailed to a treetrunk indicating it was private.

A river flowed a meandering course for several miles inland obstinately ignoring a number of tempting shortcuts into the loch itself, preferring to continue independently before spilling out into the sea three miles further on. Where it passed through the hotel's ground the water burbled busily through shallow rockfilled stretches but paused in moments of dark stillness where depth gave dignity. The river made its entrance and exit through trees

23

with an air of mystery, giving the impression that the property was larger than in fact it was, and immediately beyond the boundary could be heard tumbling down the vertical face of a waterfall where a determinedly patient watcher might be rewarded by the summer sight of a salmon arching into the air, with sparkling droplets of water cascading from its glistening leaping body, as it neared the end of its search for the source.

It was from the tourists who stayed in the hotel to fish these waters that Alistair Macleod scraped a precarious living.

Macleod was a big man, grey hair well brushed but grown long through forgetfulness, strong clean-shaven face, alert eyes darting periodically from the face behind the fisherman's tale being directed at him across the bar. He wore the kilt with an open-necked check shirt and thick-knit pullover which remained his uniform throughout the year with only the pullover being discarded on the rare hot days of summer. On an evening there was nothing he enjoyed more than taking a glass of malt whisky with his guests and reminiscing imprecisely on a past history with a Highland Division. He was fiercely patriotic, deploring issues of the day, comparing them inaccurately with incidents in Scottish history, whilst illustrating his point with singularly inept quotations from Rabbie Burns.

He had furnished his hotel as generously as funds would allow, starting by covering the entire ground floor and staircase with a bright red, green and white tartan carpet. The quality diminished with elevation, the furniture being solidly sensible, the pictures on the walls were insignificant in size and artistry, and the ceiling paper adhered by a prayer. The residents' lounge was long and narrow like a railway carriage, ten armchairs with floral loose covers faced each other and at the end of the room a well-used fan heater moaned tiredly as it blew a lukewarm gust. Beside the fireplace a gas pipe emerged from the floor but from the nozzle beyond the large brass tap there emerged, surprisingly, an electric flex which climbed straight up the wall and disappeared through the ceiling. The bedrooms offered twin beds, dressing table, wardrobe, washbasin and cane chair within bare walls, and a single central lamp. Throughout the hotel the ceilings were low and Macleod was able to stride the rooms flicking a duster at mirrors, pictures and lampshades with the result that nothing hung straight.

He had adopted a somewhat unusual attitude towards those who spent their holidays in his hotel. Basically, if they were English, he treated them as enemies and the object of his seasonal war was to part the invading forces from their money. He set about this in a manner which, he thought, was tactically superb and fiendishly clever; *he ensured that his guests enjoyed themselves.* He fed them well, the beds were comfortable, the rooms clean. At the end of two weeks the enemy invariably paid up willingly and departed happily, inevitably attempting a further invasion the following year whereupon they would retreat once more, leaving their money behind them.

On their first evening, Morrison and Biddy found him behind the bar berating an old man wearing a shabby kilt and battered leather hat who glared into his glass with taciturn stubbornness. 'Will you tell me by what God-given right you wear the Gordon tartan?'

'Why shouldn't I?' muttered the man belligerently.

'You know full well there's no a drop of Gordon blood in your veins.'

'No, but it's the only one I could pick up for ten quid and you'll no find a better reason than that.'

Macleod gave a mild splutter of indignation before catching sight of the newcomers. He came over to them. 'It's yourselves. Will you take something to drink?'

'Thank you. I'll have a whisky and –' Morrison was about to request Canada Dry but feared it might make a bad impression and amended it hastily to 'a drop of water.'

'And what about the young lassie?'

'I'll have the same, please,' requested Biddy firmly.

'You'll do no such thing,' said Morrison.

'Oh, a wee drop will no harm her.'

'She doesn't like whisky. She *loves* lemonade.'

'Is that right?'

'I'm mad about it,' Biddy declared unconvincingly and with a resigned shrug.

Macleod drew Morrison a tot from the line of inverted bottles. 'He has no right to the Gordon tartan,' he continued, as if they'd been part of the previous conversation. 'No man is entitled to wear a tartan except the family tartan he inherited. Except I doubt Cluny ever *had* a family.'

He turned to place Morrison's whisky on the bar in front of him when his attention was attracted towards the window behind them and to a car drawing up outside. He forgot his argument with the old man and absently pushed across a lemonade bottle and water jug for Morrison and Biddy to help themselves. Moments later the door opened to admit a mature, well-built man accompanied by an extremely attractive girl in her early twenties.

'Good evening to you, Mr Cornelius,' greeted Macleod with a distinct note of respect. 'Are you up for the weekend?'

'Yes, we just got in.' The new arrival's quiet voice was surprising in that his clothes were positively loud. He wore a highly coloured dress kilt, expensively tailored and with all the accessories whilst his young companion was dressed in a long tartan skirt, lace blouse, and a fine silver shawl. They looked like an advertisement for a society ball put out by the Scottish Tourist Board. The man went on, 'Here I am with ten house guests and not a drop to drink in the house.'

'We can quickly put that right for you.' Macleod's eyes went to the girl. 'Will you take something now?'

'What'll you have, darling?' Morrison tried to place the accent. It sounded like a cross between Geordie and Cockney but obviously it had been ironed out by determined self-education.

'Dry martini, please,' the girl responded.

'It'll be straight from the bottle,' Macleod warned her with a smile. 'I'm no a man for all that shaking business.'

'That'll be fine,' she said.

'I'll have the same and pour one for yourself.' Mr Cornelius turned politely to Morrison and added, 'As well

26

as your guests here.' He introduced himself as Bruce and his girl-friend as Debbie from Teddington. Morrison was given a firm handshake before finding himself looking into the cool, brown eyes of Debbie. She smiled faintly and for two seconds her attention was concentrated on him.

Her hand felt good inside his. He tried to think of something devastatingly witty to match her sophistication but the best he could manage was, 'Where are you staying?'

'Bruce has a place outside the village. Haven't you seen it? It's very large.' Her voice was soft, melodious, and well educated.

He shook his head. 'Biddy and I arrived this afternoon.' Debbie looked at the child perched on the barstool.

'Hello,' she tried.

'Hello,' said Biddy, very unimpressed.

Bruce Cornelius gave Macleod a long order of spirits, wines, and soft drinks which the hotelier wrote down before gathering the bottles into a carton. It seemed to Morrison that the bar's out-of-season weekly turnover was about to be doubled by one customer and this would explain the sudden display of respect.

'Call in and have a drink with us,' invited Debbie. 'Would that be all right, Bruce?'

'What's that, darling?'

'If Mr Morrison called in over the weekend.'

'Of course.' The warmth was genuine. 'If you can spare the time you'll be more than welcome.'

'That's very kind.'

'It's open house at weekends. We don't *do* anything, know what I mean? Just mess about, eat and drink, maybe run a movie.'

Morrison could feel a warning glance from Macleod and was about to make a politely non-committal reply when they were interrupted by the surly old Scotsman in the corner. 'Will you tell me where you picked up that tartan?' the man demanded.

'Hold your noise, Cluny, will you?' said Macleod quickly.

'You were objecting to my tartan as they walked thru'

the door,' the man persisted, 'but I notice you've no said a word about the fancy clothes *he's* got on!'

'This?' said Bruce Cornelius, completely unoffended. 'I had it made in Harrods.'

'Which is owned by a Scotsman,' added Debbie, 'so that makes it all right.'

'The Scots take the kilt very seriously,' Morrison interposed as he saw the old man about to take issue.

'It's a game, laddie,' said Macleod. 'It's funny to think a length of cloth with coloured squares can stir pride and passion in the heart of a nation, but it does.'

'Can you think of two things more worthwhile exporting than whisky and the tartan?' asked Bruce Cornelius. 'You won't see the Russians and Chinese getting worked up by such decadence, but Scotland makes a fortune from it.'

Debbie said, 'You see women all over the world wearing some tartan or another.'

'Mockery, nothing less than mockery.' It was not easy to converse with Macleod because whenever one agreed with him he changed his argument. 'The kilt is male attire and always was. Right from the days the first clansman wrapped himself in six yards of it to sleep and then pleated it in a great lump inside his belt next morning. That tube o' cloth kept him warm twenty-four hours a day whilst allowing him freedom of movement, if you see what I mean. Until, for reasons best known to themselves, the English government banned it after Culloden.'

'They *banned* it?' exclaimed Morrison in surprise.

'That they did, laddie. Of course, the Scots took no notice. The history of Scotland ignoring the English dates back to 1746.' It was said without aggression, as if he was stating a fact everyone already knew. Morrison looked up to find Debbie's eyes on him, sparkling with amusement.

'Who is that man?' asked Biddy suddenly.

'Who? Oh, Cluny,' Macleod told her as he completed packing the drinks into the carton. 'That's just Cluny. I don't think he ever had another name.'

'What does he do?'

'As little as possible for as much as he can get.'

Cornelius paid cash for his drinks order and Macleod carried the carton out to the car. While her host held the door for her Debbie turned back to Morrison. 'Are you staying here?' she enquired.

'Yes.'

'Maybe we'll see you later?'

'I'll try. Thanks.'

Debbie smiled briefly and left. Neither she nor Cornelius had touched their martinis.

Macleod returned to his place behind the bar, a look of disapproval on his face. 'You want to watch that one, laddie,' he advised Morrison.

'Which one?'

'Both. Or you'll be winning yourself a reputation you could live without.'

He would not be drawn further but whatever his views, Morrison thought, they had not prevented him taking some sixty pounds of Cornelius's custom.

Later in the small dining-room Morrison and Biddy ate dinner cooked by Margaret Macleod. She was a striking woman who in the autumn of her life carried still the echoes of midsummer beauty. All the tables were laid up but only one was occupied as they entered the room, a grey-haired middle-aged lady and a younger woman sat near the fireplace and looked up curiously as Mrs Macleod showed them to a table marked 'Reserved'.

'Will you be staying long, Mr Morrison?' enquired Mrs Macleod as she placed two bowls of thick vegetable broth before them.

'We really don't know, to be honest,' he replied. 'The hotel will have to be a shortlived luxury but if we can find suitable digs we might be in the area indefinitely.'

'You mean you've come here to live?'

'That rather depends on whether I can find work,' he replied with a frank grin.

Mrs Macleod leaned over the table confidentially. 'I hear Mr Cornelius was in the bar. I can't imagine what you must think of our little village.'

'He seemed a quiet enough man, and his companion was

charming.'

Mrs Macleod raised a pair of shocked eyebrows at this and left the dining-room without another word. Biddy looked across at her father and waved her spoon warningly. 'You want to watch that one, laddie!' She'd been in the country less than twenty-four hours yet she had caught perfectly the intonation and her mimicry of Macleod was perfect.

'May one enquire what your line is?' The question was put by the middle-aged lady who Morrison could now see wore a shirt and tie beneath a heavy-knit cardigan.

'I'm not sure I have one at the moment,' he began doubtfully.

'My father can do anything,' interjected Biddy stoutly. 'He ran a big factory almost by himself before he was ill.'

'That'll do, Biddy.' Then to the lady, 'Basically I'm an engineer but I've given up my job due to circumstances slightly beyond my control. I – er – was wondering about the boats – fishing . . .'

The lady threw back her head and gave a deep laugh. 'I think you'll find the Mallaig crews put their names down for a place on the day they're born.' Then seeing his face cloud with disappointment, 'Perhaps not quite as bad as that, but certainly there are many families who work together.'

Biddy interrupted again. 'You know the little bay at the foot of those cliffs . . . over there!' She pointed her spoon towards the window.

'Where's that, child?'

'About half an hour's walk,' explained Morrison, quietly guiding his daughter's spoon back to its correct use. 'Steep, shelving, stony beach, practically enclosed by rocks on three sides.'

The younger woman spoke for the first time. 'He means the wee bay, Janet. That will be Skerrymor Bay.'

'Ah, Skerrymor Bay. That's where the Fergusons have their place.' The lady rose to her feet. 'By the by, my name's Janet Mahoney and this is Caroline Kelso.'

'How do you do? I'm David Morrison and this is my daughter Bridget.'

Janet Mahoney nodded briskly. 'I wish you well, Mr Morrison. Life isn't easy in these parts and there's little use hoping things will improve.' She gave a grim smile. 'They can say what they like about Bruce Cornelius but at least he provides a measure of employment, and brings some spending money when he comes here.'

She crossed to the kitchen door and called through to Mrs Macleod for her bill. The younger woman, Caroline Kelso, was still gathering handbag and gloves but now she stood and addressed Biddy. 'As a matter of fact, there's a rock off Skerrymor Bay that covers at high tide about six cables out to sea. It's called Morrison's Rock. Isn't that a coincidence?' She glanced briefly at Morrison and he gained an impression of tightly drawn fair hair and grey eyes.

'That settles it!' declared Biddy.

Mrs Macleod brought in two plates of roast beef with vegetables in serving dishes. The others paid their bill and bade their goodnights leaving the two alone in the room.

As they disappeared through the door Biddy commented to Morrison in a stage whisper. 'Funny thing about this hotel, everyone joins in everybody else's conversation!'

He thought he heard the younger woman laugh.

They looked into the bar before Biddy said goodnight to find Macleod in full cry. He stood centre stage, firmly clutching a glass of malt whisky, holding forth on his favourite topic. 'Will you look at Scotland now?' he asked, looking around the assembled faces. 'A small country stuck up at the rotten end of Britain, politically exploited by Westminster, suffering from impossible terrain and even worse weather, and yet decade after decade we come up with revolutionary advances for mankind. The steam engine, penicillin, television, tarmacadam roads – dammit, it even took a Scotsman to come up with logarithms.'

He was interrupted suddenly by Cluny, seated alone in the corner of the room bored by Macleod's familiar monologue. Now his voice topped that of the landlord. 'Awa ae oo he's atween wind and waa and is aff the gleg to gang agley.' The man looked up, declaiming with a raised finger of warning. 'He'll part the cauf hintra and coup the cran to dee a fair strae daith in deid o the year.'

'What's he saying?' asked Biddy.

'He's saying nothing, lassie,' Macleod told her. 'That's the drink you're listening to.'

'Isn't it Gaelic?' enquired Morrison naively.

'Gaelic? It's gibberish. Drunken gibberish,' said Macleod in disgust.

Biddy looked with interest across at the man and walked over to his table. Macleod explained that when sober Cluny would give unwilling but completely reliable advice on weather prospects, tidal streams, wild life, when the salmon were running, or feeding grounds for the wild deer. He undertook most jobs with dour ingratitude and would accept employment from the hotelier as gillie, gardener, or handyman; from the National Trust as part-time warden, from landlords as temporary gamekeeper, or from anyone at all who required ferrying to Muck. For lengthy periods during the winter nobody employed him at all. 'At which times,' Macleod finished, 'it's customary to turn a blind eye towards his habit of poaching. Beneath the laconic exterior lies a sensitive soul and the outraged sulk which follows his being caught isn't worth the trouble.'

In the background Cluny's voice continued declaiming in sonorous gobbledegook 'Gaelic' and, glancing over his shoulder, Morrison saw his daughter seated in front of the man, head cocked slightly to one side, absorbing every nonsensical word as if it was a State pronouncement. 'His principal failing,' continued Macleod, 'is his appallingly misplaced sense of humour which results in a series of pranks, mainly directed towards myself, which are singularly unfunny.'

'Oh dear,' grinned Morrison. 'Such as?'

'Such as Hogmanay,' declared the landlord with some heat. 'I laid on a special evening, incredible value for money if I say so myself. Apéritifs, dinner, wines, favours, and a ceilidh. The place was packed with Scotsmen drinking their way to oblivion with single-minded dedication until about half past one the idiot Cluny led them a Conga all over the shop. He danced them out of the dining-room, across the bar here in a long line, through the kitchen and into the car park, where they pissed off in their cars without paying the bill.'

'That's terrible,' said Morrison, scarcely able to conceal his amusement.

'You can laugh. They mostly turned up to pay the next day but not until after I'd had a sleepless night.'

'They *mostly* turned up?'

'Aye. All except one wee fella who I'll recognise again if it takes me to my dying day. When our paths cross I can promise you he'll wish they hadn't.'

The two men became aware that Cluny had fallen silent and, turning, they observed he was listening intently to Biddy who, her head close to his, was confiding something of considerable importance. The old fellow nodded several times before picking up a point she'd made and speaking seriously but quietly. As Biddy replied with great earnestness Morrison and Macleod edged across to overhear what was being said. When they drew within earshot it was to discover that Biddy was talking top-of-the-bus French while Cluny continued in his gobbledegook 'Gaelic', both supremely contented. They talked on for a full half-hour until the Scotsman rose to bid his young companion a polite goodnight.

'I'll no tae a bowster-cup, I've a drappie in the ee. I need aa ane's back teeth the morn's mornin to knock me pan out.'

'Mays wee, et vrai que tu si parle. Ellayvuzett vec suite dreamayys,' she answered. Whereupon, with considerable dignity, he gave a small bow before leaving the bar without a word to anyone else.

Biddy returned to her father and looked up at Macleod, commenting, 'I'm terribly tired. When's closing time?'

'October,' replied the landlord briefly.

The next morning was dry but a high grey cloud filled the sky from one horizon to the other, rubbing away highlights and shadows, giving a matt appearance to the landscape. Morrison and Biddy began a thorough exploration of the area, starting with the village itself. The stone and slate, relieved by white-painted wood features, seemed a common building material and, with the grass a lifeless green, the grey rock, tarmacadam road and bare trees, they felt as if they were walking through a monochrome photograph. It wasn't a pretty village, like those in England, rather it gave the impression of dwelling places erected to match the climate and offer no more than a haven of rest at the end of the day.

Rounding a bend they came across a more modern estate in which the stonework was imported fake and the roof slates manufactured bright green. The bungalows were identical squares set within a larger square, neatly bisected by straight service roads leading to a small supermarket in the centre. The village seemed more attractive after they'd seen this.

After an early snack lunch Mrs Macleod offered to drive them into Mallaig. They browsed among the immaculately maintained fishing trawlers tugging restlessly at their mooring warps, whose skippers handled them with the skill and panache of a London taxi driver. There seemed so many that Morrison could not believe there wouldn't be a crewman's job for him on one of them although it struck him at once it must be a tough way to make a living in the depths of winter. It grew dark early and they found a small café where they drank tea and listened to Mrs Macleod relate some recent history of the Highlands – a recital more precise than the whimsies of her husband.

Throughout the day Biddy was engrossed with her new surroundings and unusually well-behaved. She bombarded Mrs Macleod with a constant flow of questions but listened to and absorbed the answers. On the Sunday she suggested she and Morrison went to church and this was so totally out of character that he began to suspect some ulterior motive. She sat quietly through the sermon and joined in angelically with the hymns. Morrison received nods of recognition from Janet Mahoney and Caroline Kelso together with a smile of approval from Mrs Macleod who, after the service, waited outside the church to introduce him to some of her friends. One of these was a very large lady called Mrs Burgess.

'Fancy your choosing to come and live here when most of us are dead set on seeing the back of the place,' this lady commented.

'Stuff and nonsense,' interjected Janet Mahoney briskly.

'It's all right for you, Miss Mahoney, with your holidays abroad each year, but there are some who would seem condemned to live and die here.'

Mrs Macleod explained that Mrs Burgess was tied to her home by a practically bed-ridden husband who had been retired early by ill health, but Janet Mahoney would not be put off.

'You must try not to sound defeatist, dear, and look on the bright side.'

'But I do, Miss Mahoney, I do. I dream of the day I can escape from this purgatory on earth; is that not looking on the bright side?'

Janet Mahoney sniffed and turned away. Morrison asked quickly, 'Where would you go, Mrs Burgess?'

'Away,' the woman replied. 'I'd take a cruise if I had the money, and just see where I ended up.'

'Back here, dear,' barked Janet Mahoney. During the exchange her younger companion had not spoken a word but had twice caught Biddy's eye. The second time she had given the smallest of winks and the child had grinned back.

That afternoon Biddy elected to climb the steep hill immediately behind the village and, because his daughter had been too good for too long, Morrison agreed to accompany her. In no time he discovered he was still far from fit but decided that physical tiredness in pure fresh air was quite different from the exhaustion he'd experienced in the environment they'd left. Nonetheless, he was grateful to return to The Last Resort.

Biddy changed into a dress for dinner and now he *knew* something was going on in her mind. It was not until halfway through the meal he remembered for the first time the girl Debbie's invitation to join them for drinks. By now it was too late. He looked thoughtfully at his daughter seated opposite him and in that moment her eyes came up to look directly into his. He knew that this had been her ulterior motive; and she knew that he knew.

Morrison dug deeply into his fast depleting resources and wrote a cheque for a secondhand Morris shooting brake. Running a car in remote areas was more expensive than in a city but, by the same token, wheels were one of life's necessities.

His idea back in the London apartment had been to purchase the salmon fishing rights on a stretch of coast and set up his own business whilst in the meantime finding some work on the trawlers. It was a long time before he had anything resembling a lucky break, and even then it came in a completely unexpected form.

Biddy brought it about as a result of instantly endearing herself to anyone she met (they didn't have to suffer her twenty-four hours a day, thought Morrison), and it was only Mrs Macleod who realised the full terror of a ten-year-old tomboy rampaging round every corner of a family hotel. She wondered whether the small return they were earning from their two resident guests was worth the effort of controlling the girl while her father was away job hunting, but then those laughing green eyes would look up at her, accompanied by the cheeky attractive grin, and she was at once disarmed. After all it was out of season and she could spare the time to help people in trouble.

Macleod himself developed a love-hate relationship with the child. When she was good he would ply her mischievously with wee tastes of exotic liquors but when she was no more than marginally naughty he gave vent to such extravagancies of verbal castigation that she quickly learned to ignore them.

At night, as soon as he had locked the door behind the last customer, he sank into a chair to read the paper before retiring to bed, preferring to clear the glasses and clean the bar in the morning. One day he descended the stairs to find the job done for him. He was amazed by the thoroughness with which the task had been carried out. The glasses and ashtrays had been washed, the floor swept, and the tables dusted. Then behind the bar he came across a large bucket filled brimful with the dregs of unfinished drinks. Floating on the surface were slices of lemon and he dared not think what else.

'I wasn't sure whether you put it back in the bottles or threw it away,' explained Biddy. 'It smells a bit but I didn't like to waste all that money.'

'Mercifully it's not my money we're wasting,' said Macleod as he carried the evil concoction out of the door.

Cluny was another who succumbed to her charm and Biddy spent hours in his company enjoying his tales about wild life, and exciting true stories of the waters surrounding the coast. Cluny talked as he walked, striding the heaths, hills and beaches with kilt swinging, and feet set so far apart that were Scotland to tip up suddenly he would be the only person to remain standing. He took Biddy to wonderfully mysterious places opening her eyes to enthralling under-standing of natural history. The man remained constantly dour, no smile ever cracked the downward lines of his features. At regular intervals he would drift into a brown study and nothing Biddy could say would provoke any kind of answer. On one such occasion the girl left him to his own thoughts and ran up a short hill to investigate an outcrop of rocks at its summit. As she scrambled to the top her feet slipped from beneath her into a narrow fissure and she fell to the ground wrenching her ankle badly. For a while the pain was quite agonising and she could not stop herself from sobbing like a baby. In a flash Cluny was by her side. He picked her up in his arms, clapped a mighty hand around the tiny ankle and, contorting his face into a caricature of anguish, he cried out at the top of his voice, `Eee-ow-ee, the pain. The 'orrible ex-croo-shiating pain!' Biddy looked up at the clownlike old face grimacing towards the heavens and laughed through her tears, whilst the pain seemed to dissolve away under the warmth of his grasp.

There came the day when they were exploring the beach

and came across a collection of fishing tackle in a near-derelict stone building. There was a heap of tangled and torn nets, rusty seized up equipment, but in the corner, chocked up and protected by the wall, a thirty-foot clinker-built workboat.

'This would float,' said Biddy.

'Oh aye, she's seaworthy right enough. Ferguson's boat will last longer than he will.'

'Can we go out in it?'

'That we cannot. And ye'll no come down here by yourself, d'you understand?'

'Yes.' She rummaged among the rusting treasures for several minutes whilst the old fellow kept a wary look-out through the open door. 'What was all this used for?'

'Fishing.'

'I know *that*, silly. I mean, what sort of fishing?'

'Ferguson used to net salmon in the season. He made a reasonable living out of it for many years.'

'I thought they caught salmon in rivers with rod and line.'

'So they do, but that's more for the sport than profit. Mr Macleod will blether on about pitting the skills of man against the strength of a cunning fish but that's because he earns his livelihood from the guests who try to do it in his river. The salmon is really a sea fish. It enters the rivers to spawn, like the sea trout does, and there's not much we don't know about its life in fresh water, but its life at sea is a closed book. Salmon shoal in schools near the surface and are sensitive to propeller noise, so trawlers are the least of their problems. When they return from the sea they are fat and lusty – they need to be if, before they spawn, they're to survive dangers the like of which you never heard of.'

'You mean Macleod's fishermen? That kind of danger?'

'Och, they're *nothing*. No, I mean diseases that sap their strength whilst they're battling up-river against currents and waterfalls. They enter the river infested with sea lice but these die off in the fresh water. Only to make room for all manner of other parasites. Worst of all if it suffers the slightest scratch, like banging up against a rock or the like o' that, then the wound can grow a fungus like cotton wool and the flesh turns soft and rotten. It's a hard life being a salmon.'

'Why can't I come down here by myself?' asked Biddy with her habitual knack of changing the subject.

'Because there's something goes on in that house at night when normal beings should be asleep.'

'Which house?'

'Up yonder.' Biddy came to the door and looked up at the small, ugly white cottage perched high above the beach.

'Who lives there?' she asked.

'Ferguson. The one I'm telling you about. He and his wife have remained locked up in that house since he gave up the fishing business.'

True enough the windows and doors were tight shut but Biddy could see a wisp of smoke coming from a chimney before it was swept away by the fresh breeze. 'So what's the mystery?' she wanted to know.

'The place is haunted. Everywhere around here.' Cluny turned and faced the sea. 'When Ferguson took the dinghy out to the workboat his dog would always come with him, standing athwart the bow planking like a figurehead. He loved the excitement of it – you could almost see him laughing from sheer pleasure. His balance was good and Ferguson never worried. Then, one Tuesday, the wind was in the north-west and freshening up to a gale when Ferguson went out. The dog came with him as usual but for reasons nobody ever understood, the fisherman lost control and an oar was carried away by the sea. They began to swing in the tide, spinning in the race, until they fetched up against Morrison's Rock. Ferguson crushed his hand trying to fend off and when he looked up the dog had gone.'

Biddy listened with rapt attention as the old fellow continued to reminisce. 'He never saw what happened or what became of the dog. He was near enough drowned himself by the time the waves cast him and the wee boat to the shore about six miles along the coast. So he never fished again. He and Mrs Ferguson just barricade themselves in their house and bemoan the loss of their dog. But late at night, when the wind blows from the Kyles, they say the beast walks the beaches and comes looking for its master. Many have heard its howls, and some have even seen its black shape as it runs back and forth in its lonely search.'

Minutes later Biddy kicked against a large meatbone, long-since stripped clean. 'Come on,' she said, 'let's get out of here. It's probably all that's left of the postman.'

Morrison returned to the hotel and found Biddy in the kitchen with Mrs Macleod. She sat on a stool eating a jam tart and watching the woman roll out pastry. The girl told her father about the fishing tackle, the white house on the clifftop, and the ghost dog that haunted the bay at night. He'd had a depressing day and it was only when Mrs Macleod added to his daughter's story that anything began to penetrate his brain.

'I'm sorry, I'm afraid you'll have to say that again.'

'Oh Daddy, you never *listen*!'

'The white house above Skerrymor Bay is supposedly for sale. I say supposedly because the old couple are being very choosy about their purchasers,' said Mrs Macleod.

'Why would I want to buy it?'

'Because,' explained Biddy patiently, 'once upon a time Mr Ferguson used to net salmon. Now the old man is past it and all his fishing tackle is just rotting away.'

'How do you know all this?'

'Cluny,' answered Mrs Macleod. 'And the child's quite right. He sold his catch locally and at the fish market in Glasgow but as he grew older, and when he lost the dog, it all seemed to become too much for him. Now the couple just bide their time until they can retire to Edinburgh and share her sister's flat.'

Later, as she climbed into bed, Biddy asked him, 'Shall we buy the house?'

'We'll certainly go and look at it.'

'Do you know how to net salmon?'

'I can learn.'

'Did I tell you the dog drowned in a gale when their boat hit Morrison's Rock?'

'No, you didn't.'

'Perhaps the reason he haunts the bay is because he's

waiting for Morrison to come back. Wouldn't that be ghoulish?'

'You're frightening me to death.'

'It's a thingumajig you get from above.'

'A sign?'

'Yes.'

'Maybe it is at that.' He felt a sudden surge of hope. Things needed to get better and he could well use a break. Perhaps this was it. As he tucked her in he promised, 'I'll find the solicitor in the morning and we'll go and see the house together.'

'Good,' said Biddy.

'I wonder what Mrs Macleod meant when she said they were very choosy about their purchasers?'

'They'll like us,' his daughter answered him sleepily. 'We're the best.'

They arrived at the house just before lunchtime armed with an appointment to view from the solicitor. The Fergusons welcomed them warmly enough and, rather than regarding them with suspicion, seemed if anything distinctly nervous. The fisherman was a short man, bent and withered by a lifetime of wind and salt water. His wife was even smaller and followed him wherever he went repeating all he said like an echo.

'All the fixtures and fittings go with the house,' said Ferguson.

'Fixtures and fitting,' repeated his wife.

'And the carpets and the linoleum, they all go with the house as well.'

'Carpets and linoleum,' verified Mrs Ferguson.

The house was old and shabby, but spotlessly clean. There was nothing that a screwdriver, paintbrush, and a few rolls of wallpaper couldn't put right, although one or two of the features were unique to say the least. The four of them were still standing in the tiny hall when the fisherman said, 'I'll show you the bathroom. It's under the stairs.'

'Under the stairs,' was spoken by Mrs Ferguson and Morrison simultaneously, the first in confirmation, the second in surprise.

'Are you sure?' asked Biddy.

Ferguson opened the door to reveal a miniature bathroom contained within the confines of narrow walls and sloping ceiling. A hip bath at the near end and, behind, a toilet where the ceiling neared the floor and on which only the seated position was practicable.

'Show them the kitchen,' Mrs Ferguson urged her husband in a stage whisper.

The kitchen was a good-sized room with a woodburning stove on one wall which served to heat the water and cook their meals. Mrs Ferguson took up the commentary in her own domain. 'Now here's the wee hook where the children used to hang their coats; I put a table here where you may set down your messages when you come in through the back door; and this cupboard on the wall is where Mr Ferguson keeps his dram.' It was all recited carefully as if the new owner was to memorise and continue the routine. 'They all go with the house,' she concluded triumphantly.

'Would you care to see the dining-room?' asked Ferguson.

'The dining-room,' the woman repeated so there'd be no mistake.

'I'd love to,' said Morrison.

Ferguson opened a door and they peered inside. The dining table itself had been pushed up against a wall because the room was occupied mainly by a large iron bedstead in which lay an extremely old man who was completely yellow. Biddy let out a slight cry of alarm and stood close to her father.

'My wife's dear father,' explained Ferguson. 'He's the reason I put the bathroom downstairs.'

'Does he go with the house as well?' whispered Biddy.

The dining-room led directly into the living room, separated only by wooden dividing doors which at present were folded back against the walls. 'We keep them open so the old man can see what's going on,' said Ferguson.

'Do they close?' Morrison asked the question casually and thoughtlessly, but instantly regretted it. The fisherman threw a nervous glance towards his wife.

'Oh aye, they close all right,' he said uneasily.

'They close all right,' she echoed. With visible premonitions of defeat the couple unfolded the hinged panels from the wall and pushed bolts into the ceiling until only the centre door remained. They looked at each other again.

Morrison said quickly, 'It's really perfectly all right. I –' He was too late. With a sudden display of desperate strength the two tiny old people gave the final panel so mighty a slam that the yellow man in bed leapt several inches in the air and a slate was heard to slide from the roof. Then the four of them watched the door slowly swing open again and Morrison refrained from asking any further questions.

Upstairs they saw the principal bedroom which enjoyed a stunning view looking directly out to sea. A more reasonably proportioned bathroom was beside it and the third door off the small landing was locked.

'Where is my bedroom?' asked Biddy.

Again the old couple exchanged worried glances.

'Are you sure you really want to see it?' Ferguson enquired.

'Want to see it,' echoed his wife.

'Yes, please,' Morrison replied.

Consumed with curiosity, and realising they were within moments of discovering whether or not they were suitable purchasers, Morrison and Biddy waited whilst, after a *sotto voce* conference, Mrs Ferguson produced a key. She bade them wait on the landing until she had 'made him ready' and Biddy felt a twinge of fear. Having seen the yellow geriatric downstairs she wondered who or what was about to be revealed. Ferguson eyed them carefully as his wife quickly let herself into the room and, from behind the closed door, the three of them heard muffled movements until, loud and clear, there came a blood-curdling snarl accompanied by a cry of pain. The old lady reappeared vainly attempting to staunch the flow of blood from her hand.

Thus they met the ghost of Skerrymor – a seven-year-old

collie who, far from drowning off Morrison's Rock, had swum ashore and refused to go anywhere near the sea ever since. As Biddy was to observe later this was not the result of canine intelligence because this particular dog was as thick as two planks. He'd been proud enough to stand at the dinghy's bow when times were good but after his cold douching, followed by a long and uncomfortable swim ashore through the pounding surf, he laid the entire blame at Ferguson's door and refused to leave the house. Occasionally the fisherman would insist on dragging the collie into the open air for exercise but he was of slight build, whereas his dog had grown large and immensely strong, and the instant the animal caught sight of breaking waves he shot back home pulling his master horizontally behind him. After nightfall the couple would heave him out of the back door until his panic-stricken howls obliged them to admit him again. The dog had no conception of his own strength and, despite their protestations of love, the frail Fergusons were quite unable to handle him – a situation they found humiliating. Even worse, pets were not permitted in their sister's flat so the Fergusons were forced to hang on in the house rather than have him put down.

Now the dog crouched menacingly by the window eyeing the intruders with growls and bared teeth. 'Sometimes he's all right,' Ferguson assured them feebly.

'It's just high spirits,' agreed his wife as, mournfully, she saw another potential sale disappear.

Suddenly Biddy called out, 'Come here, MacGregor.'

'His name is Sandy, dear,' said Ferguson.

'Sandy,' confirmed his wife. 'Not MacGregor, Sandy.'

'Sorry,' said Biddy. 'Come here, Sandy.' The dog growled viciously. 'Come on, Sandy, come to Biddy.' The ears were laid back and the growls became an open-throated snarl. Biddy changed her tactics and spoke loudly and sharply. 'MacGregor, come here at once you stupid animal!'

Taken by surprise at the change of tone the dog slowly shuffled across to the child. He sniffed carefully at the pointing finger before sitting down as her hand began to stroke his head.

'Careful, dear,' from Mrs Ferguson.

Biddy lay down on the floor, talking quietly to the dog in top-of-the-bus French. 'Eskersay voosavay le grand fear ou ettezvoo juste stupido? Jettador les chiens especialment collies comme voo. Ilnaypar possible voocudavey un fear de moi parceque jeswee une petite girl,' she whispered into his ear, 'et vous et me cudjouez ontranoos touslesjours.' Slowly he rolled on his back, paws in the air, for his chest to be rubbed. 'C'est muchbonner, maitnon nous canbee amis.' Now she looked up at the Fergusons. 'You know your problem? You've been calling him by the wrong name!'

The moment of truth arrived as Morrison enquired, 'What is the asking price of the property?'

'The dog is included in the fixtures and fittings,' insisted the Fergusons, speaking together.

'How much?'

Ferguson hesitated. 'Without the dog, £15,750. *With* him . . . just £15,000!'

'What about the leasing rights?'

'I own the fishings.'

Morrison drew a deep breath as he reached the crunch question. 'And the fishing tackle? And workboat?'

'I put five nets down on this station, as it spreads three miles to the west of Skerrymor and four to the east – seven miles in all.' The man spoke confidently now he was within his own expertise. 'There are seven bag nets and ten leaders though I'm afraid some need replacing. The posts are good, so are the ropes, and the fisherman anchors of course. The boat needs a good overhaul but she'll take you anywhere, no bother.'

'How much?' Morrison breathed again.

'Shall we say £17,000? Making £32,000 in all?'

Biddy rested her head against MacGregor's and grinned up at her father. He tried to smile back but failed – he didn't have £32,000 or anything like it.

CHAPTER TWO

SCOTTISH LAW relating to the catching of salmon dates back to the fourteenth century and is of Roman-Dutch origin born out of the overall Baltic Alliance agreements reached around that time. English and Scottish law are at variance with each other but this is only one among many instances where the two countries operate happily under differing sets of rules. Coastal fishing rights were owned originally by the Crown but, over the years and for a multitude of reasons, it disposed of certain areas which then became heritable rights as well as a completely separate estate not necessarily connected with the land adjoining it.

The Atlantic salmon is anadromous, meaning that it returns to spawn in fresh water after making most of its growth in the sea, and extraordinarily finds its way back to the very river from which it migrated as a juvenile. Spawning occurs from October to January in the reaches of the river where suitable clean gravel exists. The female fish will remain stationary while rapidly threshing her fins to create a current which forms a shallow bed in the gravel. There she lays her eggs and at once moves aside for the male to take her place and fertilise them. Then both fish work fins and tails to cover the eggs and the job is done. The ova hatch in the early spring and a few weeks later the fry emerge from the gravel. When they are a year old they become known as parr and to most people are indistinguishable from brown trout except for fingermarks along either side of their body almost as if they had been picked up by a human hand. They remain at this stage until the spring of their second year, sometimes longer, then suddenly they turn silver and the urge to travel is on them.

These smolts descend to the sea and many hundreds fail to survive their first hazard; in becoming accustomed to the salt waters of the river estuary they fall easy prey to cormorants, herons and gulls. The fortunate ones escape and disappear to feeding grounds which are not fully known but which may be as far away as Greenland if they spend two or more years at sea. Wherever they are the supply of krill must be plentiful because their growth rate is phenomenal. Those that return to spawn after only one winter are called grilse but others which are away for two or three years are known as salmon. However long it takes, the instinct to return to the waterplace of their birth eventually arrives and they commence the incredible swim home, without feeding on the way, putting in occasional forced bursts of speed to escape predators, and thereby forming the muscles which give their flesh its distinctive texture, flesh already tinted delicate pink by the crustaceous diet.

Once it makes a landfall the salmon follows the coast trying and rejecting river estuaries until it finds, some say through pheromonic extrudation, the unique balance of factors in the water causing it to recognise its own river.

It was from this final coastal run that Morrison proposed to make his living. At each net position he would stretch a leader net some forty-five fathoms seawards from the shore causing the salmon to follow it outwards until it was lured into the bag net head or trap; trap because the heads are so constructed that the opening to each chamber of netting seems to the fish to be less dangerous than the alternatives. The salmon, which has limited underwater vision, should therefore find its way into the head of the net and be confined within the enclosed space.

He would not be permitted to fish for the 168 days of the close season, generally speaking from September to February, nor again during the season from midday each Saturday to the following Monday at six o'clock in the morning. As if this were not enough the salmon, because they are not *au fait* with the laws (or perhaps after six

47

hundred years they'd figured it out) do not always favour fishermen with a run at the time when the nets are in position, so the law holds the balance, ensuring that enough fish survive to spawn and complete the age-old cycle on which its survival depends.

Morrison heaped a supply of fifty pence coins by the telephone and dialled a string of numbers. The phone was in the hall and he'd chosen a time to make the call as private as possible but he dreaded the passing of any fellow guest.

'Rustington 43262,' said his mother-in-law.

'Hello. It's David.'

'Oh David. How's Biddy?' Such were her priorities, thought Morrison.

'She's fine. Fit as a fiddle and happy as a sandboy.'

'She's getting enough to eat?'

'She never stops.'

'Hotel food isn't the same as home cooking.'

'This is better than *my* home cooking.'

'Is she there? May I talk to her?'

'Yes, of course. Hold on.' He handed the receiver to Biddy. 'If it starts to whistle push in another coin.'

'Hello Grandma.' He half listened to his daughter's end of the exchange, his stomach churning and resolve weakening as the crucial part of the conversation drew near. During the night it had seemed possible but now her brusque tones made the chance of agreement seem remote. Biddy said, 'I'd like to go now please because Daddy hasn't much money. Goodbye Grandma.'

She handed the receiver back to him and he cupped a hand over the mouthpiece. 'Could you scoot off into the lounge while I talk to Granny?' There was a nervousness about his face that caused her to feel uneasy. She left the hall but waited just the other side of the door where she could hear his end of the conversation.

'Hello.'

'What does she mean you haven't any money?'

'It could have been better worded. She meant loose change for the phone.'

'I see. How are you, David?' She'd thought of it at last.

48

'Very well indeed. Mending rapidly, the air is like a tonic.'

'Good.'

'Look, there is one thing. An opportunity has come up for me to buy a small salmon fishing business. I can't explain the detail on the telephone but I'll write and tell you all about it.'

'Where is it?'

'A place called Skerrymor Bay. You wouldn't believe how pretty it is, a small white house overlooking the seashore with all the equipment on the beach together with exclusive fishing right for seven miles.'

'Is it safe for Biddy?'

'Oh yes, perfectly. Apart from anything else <u>she</u>'s very intelligent about the sea. The thing is I need to borrow some money.'

'Who from? Not from us, surely?'

'Well, I had wondered . . .' It was even worse than he'd thought it could be. 'The turnover potential is enormous and, given a couple of good seasons, it would be a short-term loan.'

'How much do you need?'

'Twenty thousand pounds, actually.' The words were gulped out miserably.

'Good heavens, David. What do you think we are? You'd better have a word with Patrick.' It would have to be a quick word, there were only two fifty pence pieces left. However, he felt easier with his father-in-law.

'Hello, son. How're you doing?' The soft Irish burr was at least friendlier.

'Pretty good, thanks. Very good, actually. Look, there's this –'

'I know, I could hear what you were saying. The trouble is I'd need to sell investments.'

'Yes, I realise that.'

'It's an awful lot of money.'

'But very cheap for what they're offering. The house, workboat and the nets together with ice-making plant and all sorts of other things for thirty-two thousand pounds.'

'I'll have to think about it.'

'Of course.'

'I can't manage all of it, anyway.'

'I understand.' He heard a muttered conference at the other end.

'The wife says why not bring Biddy down here and we can all sit down and talk about it?'

'I think I understand that too.'

'I bet you do.' There was humour in the voice.

'If it's a condition we'll have to forget it.'

'Sleep on it, eh?'

'Fine. I'll wait to hear from you.'

In the lounge Biddy felt a wave of hurt. As first she thought it was because she'd overheard her father attempting to borrow money but then she realised it was the dismissive wave which preceded his conversation that had upset her. 'Why did you send me away?' she asked him.

'It was private,' he replied briefly.

'I thought we were in this together.'

'There are still some things.'

'I heard anyway.'

'How?'

'I listened!'

'Okay,' he said, carefully, 'we have to lay down a few ground rules. The heavy financial bit and all major decisions belong to my half of the partnership. Understood?'

'We always went to the bank if we needed money.'

'That was when I had an employer paying in at the other end.'

'Some people have heaps of money in their accounts. Maybe the bank will lend you some of theirs while they're not using it.'

'That's a slight over-simplification but the basic thinking is good.'

'We don't want to borrow money from Granny. If we do she'll sort of come with it.'

He smiled at her perceptiveness but it would have been

disloyal to leave the sentence hanging. 'Granny's all right,' he observed dutifully.

'Oh she's all right,' agreed Biddy. 'When she hugs you she smells of soap suds.'

He was entirely unoptimistic about hearing favourably from his in-laws so he decided instead to try the bank manager, an outside chance at best because his account had been transferred to the Glasgow branch only a few weeks earlier and the manager didn't know him from Adam.

Their drive began with a thirty-mile journey along a single-track road where neatly kept passing places were set so close together than one wondered whether it would not have been simpler to have constructed a wider road in the first place. Steep hills frowned forbiddingly on the narrow track, undergrowth surviving in a thin covering of soil with rocks showing through like hessian in a worn carpet.

They seemed to drive for so long that Morrison began to doubt his direction. He saw a figure walking towards him and stopped, lowering his window. 'Excuse me, are we heading towards the Stryne Ferry?'

'You are.' The man spoke with a German accent. 'You've a little way to go yet.'

'How far?'

'Three cattle grids. Turn right after the third one.'

'Thank you.' He let out the clutch and moved on. 'Wouldn't you know,' he said to Biddy as he raised the window, 'that I could be lost in the wilderness of the Scottish Highlands and manage to pick a German to ask the way?'

'Funny way they measure distances up here – by cattle grids.' She was right – the first one did not appear for six miles.

Behind them Sigmund Morhof looked after the disappearing car. So that was the stranger wanting to buy the Fergusons' business. Interesting.

They saved themselves a long run round the edge of the loch by using the Stryne Ferry which crossed the narrow neck where the rushing tide attempted to sweep the boat away on each of its crossings throughout the day. The

Stryne Ferry was the ugliest little vessel ever to earn an honest living plying between two concrete jetties less than a mile apart. The shapeless boat, whose hull was dressed overall in old car tyres, ferried four vehicles at a time on its flat deck. Two men operated this hardworking battered old boat and, despite the unrelenting dullness of their daily grind, remained constantly cheerful and somehow spread news of interesting arrivals and departures over a forty-mile radius without once leaving their posts. Large notices advised on life safety and signs warned that tickets must be retained until the end of the voyage. With a full load the small craft rocked perilously as it breasted the tide and great gouts of blue smoke spouted from the funnel as its worn engine took the strain.

They shared together the awesome magnificence of the scenery through Glencoe and Rannoch Moor where the vast plain rises up to the hills on either side in a perfect semi-circle. There was snow in plenty on the high ground and the sun shone from a clear blue sky flooding the flat ground in a brilliant light topped by dazzling peaks to their left and right. They ate their sandwiches by the Bridge of Orchy before continuing down to Loch Lomond whose breadth increased as they covered its seemingly endless length, until the main road twisted and turned through the trees of Dumbarton and the magic was over.

The bank was busy next morning but the manager saw him almost immediately. Biddy took the news badly that she was to remain outside during the interview, and they had a *sotto voce* argument among the milling customers at the very time Morrison needed a clear and relaxed mind. She could not possibly understand that no father relished the thought of his daughter watching him beg for a loan and, anyway, he intended to reveal the background to his decision to move north which included details he preferred her not to hear.

'But we're supposed to be partners,' she whispered angrily.

He sat her down firmly in a chair. 'I've neither the time nor the inclination to argue about it now. Later maybe but just at the moment your role in the partnership is to sit down and shut up.'

The interview did not begin well. 'Yes, yes, yes,' said the manager testily after Morrison had explained his scheme for the second time. 'The bank does participate in a number of ventures of this sort but my experience is that whilst you and I know that the salmon follow the coast until they meet your leader net and obediently become trapped, the trouble is no one seems to have told the fish.'

'That's always a good joke, of course,' replied Morrison stiffly, 'but the fact is the instincts of generation after generation for over a thousand years have told the fish. We simply take advantage of their habitual behaviour pattern.'

'Quite so.' The manager flashed a sudden smile. 'Your point is well taken. So the only question mark hovers over your own ability, your personal dedication and . . .' he coughed delicately and smiled across the desk,' forgive me, your health and strength.' Morrison looked up sharply. 'Oh yes. I know a bit about commercial fishing. Working a heavy boat alongside the cliffs in ten-foot waves requires strength and courage. I – ah – do not doubt the second quality for one moment, if I may say so.'

'You needn't doubt the first either. The illness is behind me and, besides, I shall engage a skipper for the first season.'

'Oh, *will* you?' The manager leaned back in his chair and appeared genuinely interested.

'Of course. I'll be the new owner, I trust I shall not also be a fool.'

'How would you see the arrangement working?'

'I need a crew of four, including myself, to visit five net positions twice daily. An experienced skipper needs one good man and a couple of willing students whom he can train into a team. I intend to hire a top-class skipper and I'll do my damnedest to be his 'good man' until I've learned enough to take the helm. Or, rather, the throttle.'

'The throttle?'

'When you're working near cliffs the throttle is more

important than the helm.'

'Ah, *is* it?' said the bank manager who knew that already. 'I can see you are not going into this – ah – lightly.'

There came a knock on the door and the head cashier came in hesitantly. Morrison was annoyed by the interruption coming at the very moment he seemed to be making headway. 'Excuse me, Mr Burnham, please forgive me for intruding but we seem to have just a spot of bother outside.'

'What is it?' asked the manager.

'It's your daughter, sir,' the cashier said to Morrison. 'I rather think she's trying to hold up the bank.'

They found Biddy sitting on the counter alongside a teller's window talking earnestly to each customer who arrived to conduct his business. Between the presentation of their cheque and being handed the cash the child was able to impart the nub of their problem and explain how her father was negotiating with the manager even as they talked. If a customer was paying into his account she was able to explain in greater detail.

'Young lady,' the manager called sternly. 'Will you come down from there at once!' Biddy obeyed and walked over to them meekly. 'Are you this gentleman's daughter?'

'Yes,' whispered Biddy.

'Then not only have you caused my customers considerable annoyance, you have also interrupted a conversation of the greatest importance.'

'I'm sorry.'

'Don't be sorry. Just don't *do* it.' The manager led the way back to his office, dismissing the head cashier with a brief wink. Biddy stood still in the middle of the bank until the man turned and summoned her imperiously. In the office he said to her, 'Now madam, I wonder if you would do us the courtesy of sitting down and shutting up.' He was unaware he had repeated word for word the instruction issued earlier by Morrison, who was somewhat put out by his daughter's instant, unquestioning obedience. The difference was that she wasn't frightened of him whereas she was terrified of the bank manager.

'I'm sorry about that,' he muttered awkwardly.

'Not at all. It enlivened a routine morning. Now then, about your loan. I'll need to go to head office on this one but I've got all the figures perfectly clear. I'll recommend that the bank comes in for a third of the proposed capital and first season running costs. Unhappily,' he smiled again, 'we'll take a first charge on the house, the boat, and *all* the equipment until the loan is repaid. But find yourself the balance, bank it here with us, pledge your own third, and we're in business. Subject, that is, to head office approval.'

'Will we get that?'

'I think so, when they hear what I have to say.' He turned to Biddy. 'Young lady, may I ask what it is you have in your hand?' She looked at him with wide, frightened eyes and slowly held up two pound notes and four fifty pence pieces. 'Where did you get that from?' She turned her head slightly and indicated the bank outside. 'Was it given to you by one of my staff, which would render it unarmed robbery, or by my customers which would render it – ah – remarkable?'

'From the customers, sir.'

'All I can say is, Mr Morrison, that provided your daughter is on our side our fortunes are as good as made.'

It was late in the evening before they arrived back at The Last Resort. A letter awaited them and the envelope was addressed in his father-in-law's hand. It had to be bad news, *she* would have written had it been good. Somewhere round the back of the hotel Biddy let loose the high spirits coiled tightly by the long car journey and he took the letter up to their room to read before unpacking the overnight bag.

Dear David, he read. *I won't prevaricate because I know you'll not want a couple of paragraphs of gush before getting down to the purpose of this letter. Martha and I have thought very hard about your proposal and naturally would like to help all we can. I must say investing into a fishing business is not quite our line of country, particularly at our age, but if the figures turn out the way you say they will we might see a small return before senility overtakes us.*

Morrison liked the old man's direct and easy style. The

next paragraph was in a different colour of ink. Either he'd paused briefly to refill the pen or, as became evident from the words, it was written several hours after the first. *The thing is Martha feels that such an atmosphere would be very bad for Bridget, fishing can be a dangerous business, not to say extremely odorous if you fail to dispose of the catch quickly! She thinks Bridget would be better off staying with us at least while you're getting it together. I think you'd be very wise to consider this carefully because we would not want our grand-daughter to turn into a* – the last three words were crossed out and replaced with – *lose touch with the good things in life.* 'Fishwife' was the word the old man balked at, thought Morrison. *Let us know what you think,* the letter finished, *and I'll arrange to make £5,000 available to start you off. Please give our love to Bridget and tell her the Pullmans' cat next door has had kittens and she can have one for herself when she comes to stay with us. Yours sincerely, Patrick.*

So it was clear enough. The loan was conditional on his giving up Biddy, for a time at least. He wondered what sort of a fight Patrick had put up on his behalf.

Morrison left the letter on the bed and went downstairs in search of notepaper. It occurred to him that the smart thing to do would be to write quickly and pretend the letters had crossed. The ruse would avoid open confrontation and he could tell them that the bank had responded so well that he no longer needed to bother them. With the bank's one-third added to his own capital he still needed to raise £9,000 but somehow he was confident that now he was so far advanced he could unearth a shareholder to pick up the balance. Anyway, it went without saying that Biddy was worth a sight more than five grand.

He'd heard her thunder up the stairs and when he returned to the bedroom she was reading the letter. 'What are you going to do?' she asked.

'Get a letter in the post as quickly as possible.'

He pushed aside the clutter on the dressing table and sat down to write. He heard Biddy fold the letter and push it back into the envelope. Seconds later a pair of arms slid round his shoulders from behind and he looked into the mirror to see his daughter's face pressed into his neck, her eyes brimming with tears.

'Tell them to get stuffed,' she muttered.

As Debbie stood on the escalator carrying her up from the Underground she found herself hemmed in by a group of men who occupied both sides of the moving staircase. She tried to excuse her way past them but they were too engaged in noisy conversation to notice her struggling with weekend case, handbag and umbrella. A strong gust of musky air blowing up from the tunnels beneath played havoc with her hair and she was powerless to do anything about it. Outside in the street, city rain fell dirtily on crowded pavements and her raised umbrella jostled against a thousand others as she walked the two blocks to her office.

She was a full two hours late for work but was beyond caring. She kept telling herself it was the height of absurdity to fly from Scotland in a private jet only to fight her way through wet milling throngs for the last few miles. Bruce Cornelius had offered his chauffeur-driven Rolls but he failed to realise she was a working girl who suffered already sufficient unspoken criticism from her colleagues.

The commissionaire outside the Parkinson-Small Group offices held the door for her. 'Good morning, miss,' he said, touching his cap. As the lift doors closed on her he added for the benefit of the receptionist, 'It's all right for some!' The receptionist grinned.

In the lift Debbie decided yet again that she would abandon the Scottish weekends. On Fridays the idea spelled romantic luxury tinged with excitement, but on Mondays it was sheer bloody murder. Besides, she'd been twice since meeting briefly the man with the shock of grey hair and interesting face but he'd never responded to her invitation and she hadn't seen him again.

There was a message in her typewriter. *Please telephone the chairman*. She dialled the internal number before removing her coat.

'Chairman's suite.' If only that woman knew how her plum-in-the-mouth voice annoyed people.

'It's Debbie.'

'Oh hello, Debbie,' the voice said with well-practised warmth. 'The chairman wanted to see you earlier but he has someone with him now. Did you have an enjoyable weekend?'

'Yes, thanks. Will you call me when he's free?'

'Why don't you just come up in twenty minutes?'

'Okay.'

In the ladies cloakroom she changed from boots into high heels, combed her hair, freshened her make-up, and felt a bit better. The flight had not improved her hangover but at least the shortage of sleep didn't show. In the secretary's office she helped herself to a cup of coffee from the cona and enjoyed the prim look of disapproval on the woman's face.

'He's free now, Debbie.'

'Thanks.'

Parkinson-Small's face was redder than usual and his small round body, seated in the high-back chair behind an enormous shiny desk, squirmed with indignation.

'Where've you been?'

'Scotland.'

That was another thing. The time was approaching when she'd really have to find a job somewhere else. Their relationship had been useful at first but now it was becoming a career hindrance. The fact that her position brought toleration rather than respect from those she worked alongside of was bad enough, but when he probed jealously into her every move their life together became impossible. Nowadays he revealed only occasionally the driving force which had powered him to the heights of success and, as pampered expense-account living dulled his wits, Debbie began to realise he was becoming increasingly no more than a figurehead.

'Is this to become a weekly event?' She shrugged slightly. 'Who did you go with this time?'

58

'Nobody.'

'I don't believe you.'

'Peter Turnbull was coming but he ducked out at the last minute.'

'Why?'

'I've no idea. Maybe he's bored with me. I'm certainly tired of him.'

'His father is chief executive of Town and Country Tours and I am a member of their board.' The observation seemed irrelevant to Debbie so she said nothing. Parkinson-Small glared at her with small angry eyes but after a moment he gave a grunt and handed her a file from his desk. He instructed the girl to take over the administrative responsibility of the annual Nottingham Conference, which included handling the delegate invitations, the hotel bookings, the conference facilities, and organising the accompanying social programme. It was something she did well and the preceding year's interchange of views between the Group's subsidiary companies had proved invaluable as well as enjoyable.

Before she left his office Parkinson-Small tried a mollifying smile. 'See you tonight?' he enquired.

'Not if it's to be an evening of rebuke,' she replied stiffly.

As the door closed behind her he stared at it thoughtfully. He must mastermind the next few months with supreme care if he was to prevent the girl tiring of her favoured position and seeking fresh challenges elsewhere. She had talent, there was no doubt of it, and although he resented her becoming part of the nefarious Cornelius entourage he believed her when she claimed that the so-called relationships were nothing more than newspaper fiction. The exchange of views in comfortable surroundings was sound business policy – what else was his own Nottingham Conference? Even so a spot of personal investigation might not go amiss, particularly if it was combined with pleasure. He pressed the button of his intercom.

'Yes Mr Parkinson-Small?'

'When is my first free weekend?'

·'Let me see – er –' He could hear her thumbing through the pages of his diary. 'The end of March unless you'd like me to change anything?'

'No, the end of March will suit me very well. Draw a line through from the Friday to Monday inclusive.'

'Certainly. Is there anything I should arrange?' There was a note of censure in her voice, loyalty fighting against disapproval.

'Not yet. I think I might go – ahem – fishing.' There was a silence so he added, 'In Scotland.'

In her own office Debbie read through the file. She knew any good secretary could make the necessary arrangements and felt patronised when she was singled out and entrusted with the task. Nevertheless she enjoyed the detail and found satisfaction from putting together the myriad ingredients for the three days without omission or error.

Annoyingly, her mind strayed back to the man who'd introduced himself as David Morrison. Never before had she chased after anybody, particularly someone met fleetingly in a country bar. Maybe she had been irritated by his failure to telephone, perhaps she was as spoiled as Peter Turnbull had accused during their last quarrel, but this man had a fresh-air feel about him, of adventure, of simplicity – all of which contrasted refreshingly to the circle in which she moved. She had established that he and his daughter were a one-parent family and he planned to buy a house above Skerrymor Bay. Nobody seemed to know how old he was . . .

. . . damn it, she only wanted to *see* him again. What the hell was wrong with that?

Once when a heavy frost brought shimmering brilliance to winter sunshine Cluny hurried towards The Last Resort. On cold days he had a habit of turning up in search of a simple well-paid task, a mug of tea, or a wee dram to hold body and soul together until opening time. Macleod was well used to delivering a brusque sentence or two calculated to send the surly vagrant on his way, but on this morning the man clearly had another quest in mind.

'Have you seen Miss Biddy?' he enquired at the back door.

'Of course I've seen her,' retorted Macleod. 'There's few of us not aware of her presence after seven o'clock in the morning.' An awareness grew that there was something different about the man standing before him.

'Could I have a word with her?'

'She's taking breakfast with her father.' Suddenly he knew what it was. He could see Cluny's head! In fact the old leather hat the man wore morning, noon, and so far as Macleod was aware, night, was being twisted between awkward hands. 'Are you suggesting I should interrupt them with the news that Cluny is waiting on the doorstep?'

The dour little Scotsman unconsciously returned the hat to his head and, as he tugged it firmly down, his belligerent personality reaffirmed itself. 'She'll be fashed if you don't,' he declared. 'When I'm back here tonight with my news of the day and she hears I was calling for her this morning, she'll no be speaking with you again.'

'What a profound relief that would be.' Nevertheless it was a rare occasion indeed when Cluny thought of anyone but himself and he regretted his sharp response. 'All right,' he said, 'just wait here a moment.'

Moments later Biddy charged into the kitchen, remnants of toast and marmalade adhering to her mouth. 'Bonjour monsewer,' she cried.

'We haven't time for all that, Miss Biddy. This is important.'

'What is it?'

'Come with me and I'll show you.'

'Right.'

Biddy stepped out of the door without hesitating and was at once ready to take to the hills with him, or whatever else he suggested.

He placed a hand on her shoulder. 'You'll need a coat and a stronger pair of shoes,' he advised. 'It's a tidy step and there's a nip in the air.'

'Right,' she repeated and disappeared inside. When she

61

reappeared a few moments later she wore an anorak and scarf, short boots, thick socks and gloves. 'My father wants to know where we're going.'

'I don't know,' Cluny replied. 'Tell him it's up to the deer we're going to follow.'

Biddy shouted back into the depths of the hotel. 'We're following a deer. Probably into the mountains or forests someplace.' With that scant information the old man and the girl went on their way.

Inside Morrison looked up at Macleod. 'Do you think the search party might want something a bit more precise?' he asked.

'You're no strict enough wi' that young lassie, if I may say so,' commented the landlord. 'You let her run all over you.'

'We have a satisfactory working arrangement.'

'I don't see many signs of it from where I stand.'

Morrison folded his napkin and rose to his feet. 'I'll tell you what,' he said easily, 'I'll refrain from making any observations about how you run your hotel if you will keep to yourself any thoughts on how I bring up my daughter.'

'There are the other guests to consider.' By way of reply Morrison looked round the deserted dining-room with exaggerated care. 'Oh well, there'll *be* other guests. We'll likely be crowded when the season's on us.'

Morrison grinned. 'Of course you will. Look, any trouble with my kid, just let me know. Okay?'

'Och, she's right enough,' said Macleod generously. 'Just a touch of high spirits every now and again, eh?' After Morrison had left the room he added to himself, 'Now and again. And again and again and again and again . . .'

Cluny took Biddy to the start of the foothills at a point where the river dropped steeply down a near-vertical rock-face before splashing its way into a deep gully. Above them bare trees awaited the spring and clouds scudded fast across the sky. The man sat down on a large flat stone sheltered from the wind and took out his pipe. 'We'll just bide here a wee while and wait.'

'What are we waiting for?' asked the girl.

'A roe deer. She'll appear up there, to the left of the thicket. Can you see?'

'Yes.'

Cluny explained that at break of dawn he'd been walking around the outskirts of the wood attending to his own business – he did not enlarge on its nature and Biddy felt it wiser not to enquire – when he came across the roe deer standing perfectly still in the middle of the path. It looked at him with large brown eyes before turning slowly and walking into the thicket. He knew at once that the animal wanted him to follow and when, instead, he'd hurried down the hill he'd looked round at the point where they were waiting and had seen the deer staring down after him. 'She wanted me to go with her then but I thought you might like to come along as well. Thought you might like to share the adventure,' he concluded grumpily as he filled his pipe.

'Thanks, Cluny.' She watched him tamp down the tobacco and light it with a match expertly shielded against the breeze. 'How will the deer know you've come back?'

'I told her. She'll keep a lookout.'

Biddy accepted his confidence unquestioningly. He had an air of assured authority born from a lifetime of experience when he was discussing nature, the sea, or the weather. She looked up towards the thicket, squinting against the bright sunshine, until an hour later she saw it. Somehow she'd missed its emergence from the bushes but now it stood quite still. 'Cluny,' she whispered.

He looked up quickly. 'Nice and steady now,' he warned, rising to his feet in a smooth unhurried movement. 'She has to understand we know what we're doing and she won't want to be rushed.'

'Do you reckon she's wanting help?'

'I'm sure of it.'

'It must be pretty serious for a doe to trust a human being.'

'That's why we mustn't let her down.'

They climbed towards the animal who watched their approach with a steady unblinking gaze. As soon as they were within earshot Cluny began talking to it in a quiet matter-of-fact way. Without turning his head or altering his tone he told Biddy to tuck in the end of her scarf to prevent it flapping and distracting the beast An instant later she found herself staring at an empty space where the deer had been. 'Where's she gone?'

'It's all right, I saw. You must never take your eyes off her for a moment. This is a big thing she's doing.'

'Sorry.'

They pressed on into the trees trying to walk quietly through the tangled undergrowth. Cluny pushed his way through steadily, sometimes holding a gap open for her to follow, never for a moment allowing his gaze to stray from the course they were following. Once she thought she saw the deer's head briefly and to their right but the man continued straight on. 'She's over there, Cluny.'

'I know where she is. She's only keeping an eye on us – this is the track she's been using the past few weeks.'

The deer flashed back into view again, more urgent now and they knew they were nearing the cause for her concern. Suddenly Biddy laid a hand on Cluny's arm and held up a warning finger.

'What is it?' he asked.

'Ssh! Listen!'

He strained to hear what her young ears had picked up first. A faint, whimpered moan of an animal in pain. They crept forward, pushing the shrubs aside, taking care to move quietly but assuredly in order to avoid giving the slightest impression of stalking. The deer was standing closer now, desperation submerging instinctive fear. They broke through into a tiny clearing, no larger than a cupboard, where in years past some forest labourer had dumped a heap of tangled barbed-wire, which had now become rusted but nonetheless sharp. Helplessly entangled in its midst was the fawn. Initial panic had caused it to thresh about in blind attempts to escape but the movement had served only to drive it deeper into the barbs. Now it lay motionless, a mass of blood oozing from torn flesh.

Cluny spoke quietly, but loud enough for both animals to hear and draw comfort from the calmness of his voice.

'This'll take a little thinking about, and we'll only make a bad situation worse if we move in without a plan.' Despite his caution the human voice caused the baby creature to attempt further movement and its mother moved closer. 'You'll see we canna reach the wee beast from here without treading on the wire,' continued Cluny, 'and that will hurt him more if it doesn't kill him altogether. So we'll need to cut our way to him.' He produced from his sporran a pair of wire cutters, which normally acted as a key to forbidden places. Biddy had learned early to hide her surprise by the items which emerged from the Scotsman's sporran – packed into the tiny space there seemed to be sufficient equipment to stock a workshop. Still talking he snipped at the wire having first tested that it was the free end which would spring clear. Biddy was shocked by the sight of the pathetic animal but drew strength from her older companion's calm authority. Gingerly she pulled aside the barbed strands as he cut them to make a path along which they advanced side by side. They worked quickly but it was a full half-hour before they reached the trapped fawn and by this time it was almost silent.

'I'm going to deal with the barbs one at a time and cut each clear three or four inches either side of where it's into him. That way we'll have shorter lengths to ease away. I'm going to leave the long length until last because that will hold him still while we work.'

'Right,' said Biddy.

It seemed ages before they could start removing the barbs themselves and this Cluny did with infinite care, his voice soothing, the hands gentle but firm. Biddy crouched by the fawn's head, stroking its neck, but the animal was near unconscious.

'Can we take it home? It'll die if we leave it here.'

'We need something soft to wrap him in.'

'My vest. It's soft as anything.'

'Good. Let's have it.' Without hesitation Biddy stood up, removed anorak, jumper and blouse, before pulling the vest over her head. 'It's a very small vest, but then you're not that much bigger than a fawn yourself,' observed

Cluny.

'I'll use the blouse as well.'

'Very good, but then slip back into your jumper and anorak. It's not a day for sunbathing.'

The animal struggled again when the last barb was clear but its movements were feeble. Biddy wrapped the beast in her clothes and, on a nod from Cluny, gently picked it up. At this the mother became extremely anxious. 'It's all right now,' said Cluny. 'We're taking your wee bairn to –' He turned to the girl. 'Where are we taking it? You'll not be popular at the hotel.'

'To the Fergusons,' declared Biddy firmly. 'I'll go in every day.'

The deer had not expected the fawn to be taken away and was greatly disturbed, following close behind as they descended the hill. Once Biddy looked up shyly at Cluny before screwing up her eyes and wrinkling up her face in a contortion of mock agony, to cry quietly, '*Eee-ow-ee*, the pain. The 'orrible *ex-croo-shiating* pain!' When she opened her eyes it was to see Cluny looking at her with a spark of affection.

Mr and Mrs Ferguson reacted quickly and positively, clearing a small compound and bringing in a bale of hay. Cluny and Biddy cleaned and disinfected the wounds whilst the mother deer ran back and forth nearby. They tried to cover two of the deepest cuts where the skin was particularly jagged but doubted the plastered lint would stay in position for long. The creature seemed to improve as they worked, whereupon the doe calmed down and stood nearer.

'There's not much more we can do here,' said Cluny. 'We'll bed her down for the rest of the day and leave the gate open for mother. I dare say they'll be gone by the morning.'

'I hope not,' said Biddy. She picked up her bloodied vest and blouse and surveyed them with sudden concern. 'They'll go raving mad when they see these.'

'I'll explain what happened,' he assured her.

She switched her gaze to him, a studied look as if seeing

him for the first time. It was very plain that together they added up to a fairly disreputable pair. 'Thanks,' she said smiling, 'but I don't think it'll help much.'

In for a penny, in for a pound, she threw the vest away and began to run back to the hotel. As she went she took off her anorak and put on the bloodsoaked blouse over the pullover. Several cars were parked in the small car park outside the kitchen and she sounded the hooter of one of them whilst simultaneously slamming shut the barn door with an echoing crash. Continuing to run she burst into the kitchen where she stood panting for breath. Mrs Macleod came hurrying into the room, saw Biddy, and screamed.

'Hello,' said Biddy.

'Are you all right?' cried Mrs Macleod.

'Yes, thank you.'

Panic turned into anger. 'That was a very wicked thing to do. You nearly gave me a heart attack.'

'Sorry.'

'Where have you been? What have you been doing, you bad girl?'

'Fighting,' said Biddy. 'You should have seen him before he was taken to hospital,' she called as she ran off to find Morrison.

That evening Mrs Macleod tackled Morrison after Biddy had gone to bed. 'I'll not say she's *bad* because she has one or two saving graces. But undoubtedly she is an extremely naughty child. I don't like to complain but sometimes things have to be said.'

Twice in one day was coming it a bit strong, thought Morrison, but he didn't argue as he had with Macleod because he had a respect for the landlord's wife. He listened as she continued. 'Whatever she'd been up to this morning I can't imagine but she told me a silly lie which, if I may say so, was downright rude. She needs a thoroughly good spanking.'

'Ah, well I can fill you in there. She'd helped Cluny rescue a fawn trapped in a tangle of barbed-wire. She carried it in her arms for over two miles.' He failed to prevent a note of pride entering his voice. 'Not bad for a kid

·of her age.'

Mrs Macleod sniffed. 'There's another thing. She mixes with that awful old man far too much. He's a bad influence.'

Morrison thought long and hard about the Macleods' comments on the way he was bringing up his daughter. It was quite true that he was no heavy-handed disciplinarian; on the other hand Biddy seemed to appreciate when she could run wild and when good behaviour was the order of the day. Oblige her to remain quiet over an extended period and it was as if a spring became tightly wound inside her; the moment pressure was relaxed there was neither rhyme nor reason in the sudden release of energy. He wasn't too strict about bedtime, finishing up her food, or washing behind her ears; preferring to concentrate on the more important things in life and allow the mundane to fall naturally into place. He reminded himself that those who were all too quick to criticise had not seen the remarkable maturity she had displayed during his illness, nor the occasionally perceptive comments she made in conversation. He felt she could be a genuine help in his salmon fishing enterprise and was confident she would tackle some of the shore jobs, such as weighing and packing the catch or cleaning and repairing the nets. Naturally there would be a few crises along the way and here was one of them. He climbed the stairs to have a few words with his daughter.

In their room Biddy stood in front of the mirror, wearing only her pyjama bottoms, examining herself critically. That morning, as she had pulled off her vest for the fawn, she thought she'd noticed something and now here it was confirmed. The faintest hint of two rounded swellings like buds making a first appearance in spring. She was not at all sure whether she was happy about it.

The door opened behind her and Morrison stood there. She turned, instinctively concealing herself behind crossed arms. He looked down at her quizzically. 'What are you doing?'

'Nothing. Couldn't you have knocked?'

He closed the door slowly. The crises were coming thick

and fast today and he hoped he was going to cope with this latest one. 'Yes, I dare say I could have. It's never been necessary before. Is it now?'

'There are private things that are my half of the partnership too.' She stood meek and unsure. Morrison collected her pyjama jacket from the bed and stood behind her holding it open for her to put on. Then he turned her round and stooped to do up the buttons.

'Sure there are,' he said carefully. 'We're all allowed certain secrets. But if the secrets become *worries* then they're best talked about. Just you and me, eh?' She made no reply. He lifted her into his arms and sat with her on his knees on the stool in front of the dressing-table mirror. He reached for a comb and tried to make sense of her tousled hair. 'Beginning to get a bust, are we?' he said casually.

'A bit.'

'That's just fine.'

'I'm not sure. It could be a nuisance.'

He smiled at her reflection in the mirror. 'Shall I tell you something? I came upstairs to talk about a couple of complaints I had today about your tomboy behaviour. People are saying I don't bring you up in the right way.' He tipped her head slightly to reach a tangled knot of hair. 'Now I'm here it strikes me the only place I fall down is that I forget all too often that you're a little girl. A very pretty little girl and, if Mummy was anything to go by, you're going to grow into a beautiful young woman.' He stopped combing as he saw an echo of Wendy looking at him from the mirror. 'I'll tell you something else. Whatever Mummy did, fishing, sailing, playing tennis, she always remained a beautiful woman. She was tremendously active and when she took part in any sport it wasn't like some girls, prissy and awkard, hell no. When Mummy cast a line she *cast* it, when she served a tennis ball it came over the net like a rocket, she could change a jib sail in a force five as well as any man, but when she came back to the cockpit, water running from her oilskins, she was a *woman*. Don't worry about growing up, Biddy, be proud of it.' He began combing her hair again and she looked a picture of

69

childhood.

'Was Mummy naughty when she was a little girl?'

'I'm not sure. I don't imagine Granny gave her many opportunities.' He stood up and carried her to bed. 'I can't get cross about some of your antics as long as at least once every day you remember to be a little girl.' He tucked her in gently before stooping to kiss her. 'We have to create a good impression around these parts so try not to ruin our reputations in one fell swoop.'

'All right.'

'Goodnight, darling.'

'Goodnight.' He turned out the bedside lamp and crossed to the door. Biddy looked at him silhouetted against the landing light. 'Don't worry about what anyone says, Morrison. I think you're bringing me up just fine.'

Halfway down the stairs he realised she'd called him Morrison instead of Daddy. It was probably because everyone else did. Actually, he thought he rather liked it. He passed Mrs Macleod in the hall and tried hard to look like a man who had recently delivered a thoroughly good spanking.

The deer with its fawn was still there the next morning. Nor did it leave the day after that, but on the third day Biddy arrived to find the compound deserted. 'I looked out of the bedroom window first thing,' Ferguson told her, 'but they must have left during the night.'

'Oh well,' said Biddy, 'I dare say they must have been quite grateful in their own way.'

CHAPTER THREE

SIGMUND MORHOF had arrived in Britain by parachute in November, 1944. He'd floated down on a pitch black night and seen flames engulf the bomber from which he'd leapt seconds earlier, before watching it circle slowly downwards in a ball of fire to explode on hitting the ground about eight miles away. He'd felt no emotion over its destruction, he'd never felt safe in the machine and at that particular moment he experienced only indescribable relief that he'd got out in one piece.

He was a tall, well-built young man with strong features. Carefully brought up and well educated by his father, a seafaring man, he'd spent his early life among boats where he learned the cunning of fine seamanship, arranging for wind and tide to do the heavy work for him, his eyes flashing with excitement when facing a new challenge and his face always creasing readily into laughter. At eighteen, when responding loyally to the call to arms, he volunteered naturally for the navy whereupon, with traditional efficiency, the German war machine had promptly drafted him into the air force. Following weeks of intensive training he'd been awarded his wings long before he himself felt fully confident he could make the aircraft do what he wanted. Nothing so ugly could possibly fly well.

He'd been taken to a prisoner of war camp overlooking a loch in Argyllshire where immediately he'd become unpopular with his brother officers by declaring that his experience of armed conflict thus far had involved six missions which had done nothing whatsoever for the German cause and further resistance as a prisoner of war struck him as being utterly fruitless. So, finding himself at odds with his companions, he'd sought satisfaction out of the working parties deputed each day to undertake local labour. He'd joined a farming group and at once discovered deep enjoyment from handling the soil, cultivating crops, and rearing livestock. The local farmer had been quick to recognise his talent and, such were the pressures then on desperately understaffed landowners, Sigmund was given increasing responsibility and freedom. He'd spent one complete afternoon working alongside the farmer's daughter and in those moments the war seemed a thousand miles away which, with the Allies approaching his Fatherland from two sides, indeed it was.

Back in camp the senior German officer had ordered him to take advantage of the trust he had earned by creating a situation whereby his working party could cause a major crop failure and thereby score a victory over the enemy. Sigmund had nearly laughed out loud at the puny plan outlined by his superior but by this time he'd realised he was more frightened of the Germans than of the British.

Thus, he could never sensibly explain the action he took when one evening he'd returned to the farm to pick up the camp transport and discovered a field of sprout seedlings had been misplanted deliberately in such a way as to cause them to wither and die by morning. He'd dived beneath the hedge and remained concealed until his compatriots had departed. When he'd emerged to begin the impossible task of replanting them single-handed, the farmer had spotted him at once and, with a tired sigh, had joined him. The two men had worked side by side until past nine in the evening at which time four military policemen arrived at the farm. Incredibly Sigmund had recruited their assistance before submitting to arrest and, by the light of jeep headlamps, he led his bizarre team until three o'clock when the job was completed.

The next day, after a severe reprimand from the camp commander, he was returned to his hut. That night his fellow officers conducted a mock trial, sentenced him, bound both hands behind his back and after lights out they crucified him by driving a garden fork through both feet and pinning him to the very ground he evidenced to prefer to the soil of his Fatherland. The British found him at dawn and rushed him to hospital more dead than alive.

During his slow recovery he had resolved to escape. As soon as he had learned to walk again, a function he was never to achieve perfectly, he'd left the prisoner of war camp for the last time in an army ambulance. When it had slowed up at some crossroads he'd rolled out of the back and lain motionless in the road until the vehicle disappeared round a bend. Then he'd limped to the farm where the family hid him until Germany finally capitulated.

There had been those who suggested that the British knew where he was all the time. *Of course* they knew! It was a local decision by the camp CO that in a war so nearly won it had become meaningless to punish him further. Besides, it was the only recorded incident of a man getting out of a prisoner of war camp in order to escape from his own side.

After an emotional reunion with his family Sigmund had returned to Scotland with their blessing in time for the downfall of Japan. He'd married the farmer's daughter and together they'd fished and farmed for a living until he'd recently retired with enough in the bank to see them through the remainder of their days in tolerable comfort.

Now he sat in the manager's office at Barclays Bank nervously fingering a letter. *Dear Mr Morhof, When next you are passing by the bank I wonder whether you would care to look in for a short chat? Yours sincerely, Felix Burnham*. Felix was an old friend but a bank manager nonetheless and Sigmund did not like banks, which was why he'd made a special journey – customers who live in Ardnamurchan are not given to 'passing by' their Glasgow bank very often.

'I have something which may interest you,' began the manager.

'Yes?' enquired Sigmund politely, concealing an absurd sense of relief that nothing had befallen his money held on deposit.

'A man came in to see me the other day. I have to make it clear,' the manager added with scrupulous caution, 'I know nothing whatsoever about him and references have yet to be taken up, but my first impressions are favourable. He was good enough to take me into his confidence and, when I heard what he had to say, my thoughts went to you.' The German inclined his head. 'He hopes to purchase a salmon station somewhere in your neck of the woods –'

'Is he English? With a young daughter?'

'Er – yes,' replied the manager, surprised. Then with feeling, 'Definitely he has a young daughter.'

'Then I know of him. In fact I guided him towards the Stryne Ferry one day last week.'

'He has recently suffered a succession of personal tragedies, including the loss of his wife, but now he plans to start life afresh. He's very green, of course, but he seems to be setting about things in the right kind of way.'

'So I'd heard.' Sigmund wondered when the manager would come to the point.

'My understanding is that if he is successful in purchasing the station together with the tied house and ancillary equipment, he would be in the market for an experienced man to skipper the workboat.'

'Ah.' The German shook his head doubtfully. 'If you're thinking of me, my activity has slowed down in recent years. That is if it hasn't stopped altogether.'

'I don't believe it. You've said often enough that retirement and boredom walk hand in hand. It would be for only one season.'

'Well, thank you. I might just go along and see him.'

'There's no commitment, you understand. I've not even mentioned your name.'

'Commitment? Surely all you're recommending is that I apply for a job?'

'It's no place of mine to make a recommendation, merely to effect an introduction. Let me give you his name.'

The manager made a pretence of shuffling through some papers.

'I know his name. It's David Morrison. He is staying with

his daughter at The Last Resort, and the property he wishes to purchase belongs to Mr and Mrs Ferguson at Skerrymor Bay.'

'Yes, that is correct in every detail,' said the manager smiling.

'Then tell me something I don't know.'

'I was about to. He – ah – needs some money to get started.'

'My God. You mean I crew for him –'

'Skipper for him,' the other man corrected.

'Train him at any rate. Now you suggest I invest in him as well.'

'I think I was most careful to point out it was no place of mine –'

'Indeed you were,' interrupted Sigmund. 'You bring together the ingredients but refuse to mix the cake.'

'Nicely put.'

'How much?'

'It would be for Mr Morrison to disclose the precise amounts.'

'How much for me?'

'I would estimate nine or ten thousand.'

'I don't have that kind of money.' Then, catching the bank manager's expression, added, 'Not to throw around at any rate.'

'It's up to you. My role ends with the introduction.'

'Your job begins and ends with knocking on doors and running away.' Sigmund rose to his feet. 'Thank you for thinking I might be interested,' he said formally before suddenly smiling broadly and holding out his hand. 'Next time anyone asks me for directions to the Stryne Ferry I'll ask there and then if they want to borrow ten thousand pounds. It might save me a bloody journey to Glasgow!'

The internal telephone buzzed quietly and Bruce Cornelius lifted the receiver. His secretary said, 'There's a Commander Campbell on line two. He's calling from Fort William and reversed the charges.'

The millionaire smiled at the gratuitous item of information. 'Put him through,' he said, picking up another phone. 'Good morning, Bob.'

'Aye, well, I thought I'd better give you a call.'

Such an opening line was invariably the prelude to gossip and the second line usually followed as 'There's something you ought to know.' He wasn't too keen on Robert Campbell. Although the retired naval commander had helped steer him in the right directions when first Cornelius decided to build the Scottish mansion, and since then had advised on setting up a number of cottage industries which had been useful in smoothing out some awkward corners, he found the man's continuing acquaintance cloying and his brusque pomposity irritatingly overbearing.

The deep fruity voice at the other end continued, 'There's something you ought to know.'

'Yes?'

'I can't remember if ever I mentioned this to you but there's an old chappie up here by name of Ferguson who owns the salmon fishing rights on a stretch of coast around Skerrymor Bay.'

Cornelius had a photographic memory for names and faces. 'You did mention it, Bob. I thought about buying but there were conditions.'

'Aye, well there's someone else sniffing around there now. An Englishman, David Morrison.'

Again the instant recall. 'I met him two or three weeks ago.'

'Oh you did?'

'When you forgot to get any drink in.' Cornelius could not resist the dig and was pleased that from then on some of the pomposity evaporated. 'So Mr Morrison is buying the Ferguson property?' he enquired.

'For a paltry thirty-two grand, so I hear.'

'Good luck to him.'

'Man, you're no leaving it at that? We're talking about a goldmine!'

Thus far Commander Campbell's goldmines had proved beneficial only as tax losses. 'What do you suggest I do?'

'Buy it! Top the offer before anyone signs anything.'

'Why?' the millionaire asked quietly.

'Because under Scottish law the moment the offer's confirmed in writing –'

'No, no. I know that, Bob. I mean why should I filch it from under Morrison's nose?'

'We're looking at a fortune if the business is run correctly.'

The conversation was entering familiar territory. The commander would recommend that Cornelius purchase the business and put in a Scotsman to run it, thereby enhancing his reputation further. He suspected too that somewhere along the line Bob Campbell gained also in glory and percentage. 'I'll think about it. Thanks for telling me.'

'Rumour has it that the Englishman is short of the asking price.'

'Thanks, Bob.' It was repeated more firmly.

'Aye, well, if there's anything I can do . . .'

'Thanks, Bob.' Cornelius hung up.

The Cornelius Scottish mansion was an inapposite edifice in monstrous poor taste and one which many would have liked to see razed to the ground were it not for the business the millionaire brought to the area. He was a man who had made his pile by his wits and increased it by his accountant's brilliant exploitation of holes in the tax laws. Whilst his bank balance grew his zest for life grew with it although, sadly, his discrimination remained with his beginnings. He spent weekends at the mansion expending energy with dynamic lustiness in company with stunningly beautiful, demonstrative free-loaders. It was a long way to travel but nowhere was too far to get away from Mrs Cornelius who, beyond developing a startling ability to spend his money, had made no attempt to join him in the social climb out of the humble start they'd made when he'd got her into trouble and her dad had insisted on marriage. For the most part she put up with his infidelity in return for his income, only now and then voicing her objections in arguments of spectacular vehemence, any one of which would pale into insignificance if ever she discovered, on his accountant's advice, he had put the property in her name. Bruce Cornelius was a man who loved to be loved and had cultivated a gentle politeness which seemed to work extremely well for him. However, it did not in any way diminish his ruthless love of acquisition and cutting out the English newcomer, trespassing in his patch, struck him as being rather a good idea.

He asked his secretary to get his girlfriend Debbie on the line. When she came on he asked, 'Darling, do you remember a man called David Morrison we met in the bar of The Last Resort?'

'Vaguely,' she lied.

'Didn't we ask him for a drink or something?'

'Yes. He never turned up, did he?'

'Ask him again would you?'

'Why?'

'I want to see his face when I tell him something.'

Morrison and Sigmund took to each other immediately. Their first meeting was easy and unaffected, the German endeavouring to form an opinion of the other's potential and the Englishman trying to satisfy himself on whether their personalities would blend into a working team. Neither made any reference to financial arrangements until well into the conversation and then it was Morrison who raised the subject. 'Perhaps I should tell you before we go much further that all this is a pipe-dream at the moment. I'm afraid I've not yet raised sufficient capital so a final decision will have to wait. I can add that I'm so nearly there that I don't intend to let go now.'

Sigmund smiled sympathetically and the two men continued to talk for a further half-hour without Morrison being aware that it had become a question and answer session, with him the one being questioned. When there came a pause in the talk it occurred to the younger man at last that it was he who had just been interviewed. He watched as Sigmund moved to stare out of the window with

78

studied unconcern.

'Would you think it an idea if we went over your projected figures together? Who knows, I might be able to offer one or two pointers.'

In that moment Morrison knew fate had dealt him a good hand and, through the good offices of a strange bank manager, he was on the brink of forming a partnership. He was unaware, of course, that even as they spoke Bruce Cornelius was instructing his solicitor.

The two men completed their preliminary work by lunchtime with Sigmund promising to look into the hotel again the next morning in order to put forward a positive proposition. The German appreciated that Morrison had followed the drift of his questioning and drawn his own conclusions, but he had never before made a decision of this kind without discussing it with his wife and he had no intention of breaking the habit now.

They moved from the residents' lounge into the bar where they found Biddy seated at a table and talking to a man who looked as if he needed rescuing. Morrison crossed at once and was introduced to Mr Peregrine.

'Is my daughter being a nuisance?'

'Not at all. Quite the reverse, in fact. She has a thirst for information that is most refreshing.'

'It's also insatiable when you get to know her better. May I buy you a drink?'

The man studied the remaining contents of a half-pint glass. 'No, this will do me nicely thank you.'

Morrison bought drinks for himself and Sigmund before they sat down with Biddy and the stranger. Mr Peregrine turned out to be a consultant for a nature conservancy organisation with especial interest in endangered species. He was a smallish man whose balding head was made the more distinctive by two symmetrically placed tufts of grey hair sticking our horizontally from above each ear. He wore rimless glasses over faded blue eyes and an expression of meek vagueness which, however, frequently broke into a ready laugh. He explained that he was in the area to talk with the Forestry Commission who were about to commence a massive new ground clearance scheme on land bordering the river.

'Indeed, the very river that passes through this property,' he said.

'And what in particular are you hoping to preserve?' asked Sigmund.

'Dead trees,' smiled Mr Peregrine. Then, having enjoyed his little joke, he enlarged on the reply. 'To be more precise the otter holts they conceal.'

'Is the otter an endangered species?' Morrison enquired with surprise.

'In England, very much so. In Scotland, not yet.'

'What is the problem?'

'To be frank we have yet to identify the precise cause of a quite bewildering crash in population. They have resisted the wrath of man since the Middle Ages when countrymen took a dislike to sharing such delicacies as eels with the friendly otter, and furthermore found a ready market among glovemakers for their pelts. They survived the otter spear, trapping nets, and specially trained otter hounds, until suddenly some twenty years ago they began to vanish. The disappearance is total in some regions, like the Midlands and industrial parts of the south.'

Biddy said, 'Mr Peregrine fastens radio transmitters to their backs.'

'They are quite small,' the man explained, 'and the harness drops off automatically after a few weeks. Until we know how they live we cannot be sure why they're vanishing – they are secretive beasts.'

'You think the Forestry Commission could inflict further losses?' enquired Sigmund.

'Not at all. They are normally most co-operative. You see, your average otter likes a ten-mile stretch of luxuriant waterway with two miles or so of bankside thickets. It's possible that intensive farming, the replacement of water-adjacent oaks, ashes, and sycamores with willows and alders to prevent bank erosion, drainage schemes, and industrial requirements have all combined to bring about extinction. Our concern now is to establish secure havens wherever we possibly can.'

Sigmund Morhof took his leave and after lunch Biddy went off with Mr Peregrine who seemed happy to continue his lecture into her willing ear. During the afternoon Morrison requested Mrs Macleod's permission to borrow an iron and ironing board.

'You might as well let me do it for you,' she said. 'These jobs don't sit well on a man.'

'They sit just fine when he's on a tight budget.'

'I make no charge for your use of the washing machine and soap powder, so I might as well throw in my own service for good measure.'

'You're very kind. I'll remember these weeks when the fruits of the sea have made me rich.'

'And when will that be?' Mrs Macleod asked as she set to work on his shirts.

'Soon, I think. I have a feeling in my bones.'

'Good. I'll miss Biddy but a hotel is no place for a child all the time.'

'You're wonderfully patient with her. I know what a handful she can be,' Morrison said politely.

'Och well. She'll be away to school in a week or so.'

He was silent and, turning from the ironing board, she saw him standing stock still, a shadow of total astonishment on his face.

'Yes, I imagine she will,' he replied uncertainly.

'You're not telling me you've made no arrangements yet?'

Morrison's stomach felt as if an express lift had stopped suddenly. The truth was he hadn't given a thought to Biddy's schooling since arriving in Scotland and, needless to say, his daughter had not seen fit to raise the subject herself. 'There's been so much to do,' he admitted lamely.

'There's some things more important than others,' Mrs Macleod commented. 'You'll be having the educational authorities down on your head.'

'You're absolutely right, of course, and I'm grateful you mentioned it. Tell me, what sort of schooling is available?'

'It depends on what you want.'

'A normal education. I gather it's very good in Scotland.'

'It's good in the universities right enough but I wouldn't know what to say for the rest of it,' she declared. 'Some of these posh schools are so old fashioned they can only turn out army officers, ministers, and Members of Parliament.'

'Even so, I want Biddy to attend a private school.'

'Are you telling me that? What happened to the tight budget?'

'I'll work my socks off. My parents afforded it for me and I'll do the same for Biddy. Besides, I wouldn't want her to go away – she must live at home.'

'Is that for your sake or the bairn's?'

'For both of us, I like to think. She responds to people, you see. Okay, so she must have the groundwork in basic subjects, but she learns more about things of direct concern to her from people like Cluny, yourself, and even Mr Peregrine.' She folded a shirt and picked up one of Biddy's vests as he continued. 'I don't imagine she'll ever become one of the world's great scholars but – ' He paused, and looked thoughtfully out of the window for several moments before going on. 'Where I used to work they were obsessed with examination results. If it had been me handing out managerial posts and facing half-a-dozen candidates all waving their university diplomas, whilst a seventh showed me *photographs of something he'd done*, I know whom I'd choose.'

'That's because you're a practical man yourself.'

'Maybe.'

'Was it a son you wanted when your wife was expecting?' she asked with surprising directness.

'I'm very happy with what I've got, Mrs Macleod,' he answered briefly in a tone that discouraged further questioning.

She placed a pair of his pants on the board, surveyed them briefly, and decided they weren't worth ironing. 'You'd best go and see Miss Mahoney, the headmistress at Park Lodge.'

'Miss Mahoney? Wasn't she in the dining-room on the night we arrived?'

'That's right. The lass with her was one of the teachers. Now if Biddy goes into Caroline Kelso's class you'll find none better.'

'Well, thank you, Mrs Macleod. I might just do that.'

The Reverend and Mrs Kelso could not help but wonder when first Janet Mahoney had tried so hard to convince them that their daughter Caroline was an exceptional pupil of rare brilliance. The headmistress of Park Lodge School had paid several visits to the manse during the girl's final term in ever increasing efforts to persuade them to allow her a further academic year of advanced tuition. 'Anything less would be to squander a precious gift,' Miss Mahoney argued in her low, husky voice, 'because such a talent is given by God and He doesn't bestow these things lightly.'

Mrs Kelso had always considered Caroline to be a very normal child, perhaps quieter than most in keeping with her father's calling, but nothing out of the ordinary. The minister had been flattered, he made no bones about it, but what worried him was a distinct feeling of uneasiness when he was in the presence of Janet Mahoney. No one could doubt her ability or her dedication but always he had found it impossible to dispel stirrings of disquiet when the woman discussed their daughter. The two of them had brought up Caroline with strict regard for doing the right thing and keeping faith with her conscience. Because their own horizons were somewhat limited, they embraced a fail-safe system whereby they decided anything they didn't fully understand was almost certainly wrong. Caroline had never been taught to laugh, a full-throated guffaw being considered rather coarse, and the wideset grey eyes beneath her severely brushed fair hair were invariably serious. She grew tall and slim, always simply dressed, like a girl who had become a maiden-aunt before her time.

The thing was that the headmistress's suggestion had made such a mess of their plans. The minister had been offered a larger church near Loch Lomond and there was no doubt in his mind that in worldly terms this represented a considerable promotion. Both he and Mrs Kelso had regarded themselves as fortunate indeed that the move coincided with the end of Caroline's schooling and here was Janet Mahoney throwing a spanner in the works and sowing the seeds of a guilt complex.

Caroline herself had seemed really not to mind. Beyond expressing a desire to take up teaching as a profession she had been contented to leave the decision to her parents. After a particularly passionate plea using words which, they discovered years later and all too late, were lifted straight out of *The Corn is Green* the two good people had accepted Janet Mahoney's proposal that Caroline took up residence in the school with her, and later would teach a junior class as soon as she was qualified to do so.

For several years Caroline had been happy at Park Lodge and when she visited her mother and father in the new vicarage reported favourably on the generosity of Miss Mahoney who had personally helped over costs and allowances for a necessary spell at a teachers' college. Young men did not look in her direction very often and when they did she caught the sharper edge of the headmistress's tongue. Once the woman and the young girl holidayed together in a hotel in Majorca but the week was blemished by some remarkable and rather frightening behaviour by Janet Mahoney after too much sangria at dinner, although Caroline had found herself more embarrassed by the non-stop self-recriminations and apologies which continued throughout the following day.

If her parents were puzzled by the unfulfilled promise of academic achievement they had never commented on it and, by the time Caroline had earned sufficient qualifications to take junior classes, she had discovered two things. Firstly, she was heavily indebted to her head-mistress both morally and financially and, secondly, she had never previously experienced anything more worth-while doing than teaching young children. She lived with Janet Mahoney in the flat over the school and, in addition to her school duties, worked willingly as secretary, cook and companion until these additional responsibilities fused into the daily routine and Caroline became virtually a prisoner. The headmistress was not ungenerous and during the holidays they travelled extensively, the older woman guarding her protégé with a jealous possessiveness which, for a long time, Caroline's sheltered upbringing made her fail to notice.

Now the Easter holiday was being fully taken up by a burst of energetic interior decoration as Janet insisted on rejuvenating Park Lodge from top to bottom and Caroline was helping without either woman questioning for one moment whether or not she wanted to.

In their hotel bedroom Biddy sat up in bed, freshly bathed, hair combed, and pretty. 'You don't have to bother about school on my account,' she assured Morrison.

'Whose account do you reckon it's on then?'

'There's heaps to do if we're moving into the white house. You can't manage without me.' Clear green eyes sparkled up from freckled face.

'That's true enough, but I'll have to manage as best I can and you pitch in at weekends.'

'You don't seem to understand, Morrison. I'm trying to tell you that school's a *waste of life*. Stuck indoors with all that learning stuff when you can be outside *doing* things.'

'I agree with you. Listen, right deep down inside I actually agree with you, but this thing is bigger than both of us and we have to go through with it.'

'Oh, you can get me out of it,' she pleaded. 'You can do almost anything. Write a note, tell them you're ill. *I'll* write and explain you need me beside you morning, noon, and night.'

'You won't write to anybody.'

'Why not?'

'To start with you can't spell.' He settled her back into the pillow and pulled the sheet up. 'Here's what we do. You and I will go and see this Miss Mahoney and then have a family conference on our plan of campaign.'

'You always win family conferences.'

'Don't you believe it.'

'You'll win this one anyway,' she predicted mournfully.

'I mean, you're really *into* this school thing, aren't you?'

'I think it's a bit important. Not to mention it also being the law.'

'So why don't I go to school next term and not bother seeing people now?'

'We go together, Biddy.' The discussion was ended.

'Suddenly this became the worst day of my life,' Biddy muttered.

Morrison was still smiling as he walked down the stairs having tucked in his daughter for the night. When he reached the hall he realised he didn't really know where he was going. It was the same every evening; the hours between kissing Biddy goodnight and retiring himself were devoid of anything to do. It was the time he missed Wendy most of all. A burst of laughter came from the bar and he headed in that direction.

The usual crowd were in there. Cluny glaring into his beer with the sullen surliness which characterised his attitude towards life, four old men who sat on a bench in a row and watched the comings and goings without ever exchanging a word, and a group by the bar listening to the latest summary of world opinion from Macleod. Morrison hesitated, wondering whether he wanted to stay.

'Hello.' The girl's voice came from behind him and, turning, he saw Debbie looking up at him from a corner table.

'Hi.' He was pleased to see her, and said so. She was dressed for the cold, expensively and simply, and sat alone with a martini. They shook hands. 'Would you like another of those?'

'Not for the moment, thanks.'

'Are you alone?' She nodded. 'I'll get myself a Scotch and join you if I may.'

She watched him standing at the bar, creased trousers, pullover, grey hair over young face. His easy-going casualness was uncontrived and she liked the natural way he leaned, listening with the others to Macleod's story whilst waiting for his drink. He was unlike anyone she'd ever met. She couldn't resist smiling when she saw him join in the

laugh that followed the landlord's anecdote even though he
could not possibly have picked up the gist of his tale. He sat
down in the chair opposite and toasted her with his glass.

'Cheers,' she responded, raising her own.

'Are you here for the weekend?'

'Yes.'

'Not out of drink, I hope?'

She smiled politely. 'As a matter of fact I looked in to see
you.'

'Oh? That's nice.' Then, seeing her feel for words he
added quickly, 'You must have thought me awfully rude
last time. The thing was we'd just arrived and Biddy was a
bundle of energy that weekend.'

'It didn't matter a bit.' Nevertheless she was pleased he'd
made the apology. 'This time I bring greetings from Bruce
and his personal invitation to the house.'

'He's the man you were with?' She nodded. 'Well, that's
very kind. Er, may I ask, why would he want to see me?'

'I don't know.' He saw her frown slightly. 'At least, I
think maybe I do. Look, have you eaten?'

'Yes. Biddy and I have a cross between high tea and low
dinner before she goes to bed.'

'I haven't.'

'Doesn't your host feed you?'

'I skipped out to talk to you.'

'This grows more mysterious by the minute.' He drained
his glass and stood up. 'Right, I'll drink coffee and watch
you. Not here, though, we'll do better at that little pizza
place in the village. How will that suit?'

'You don't mind being dragged out at short notice?'

'It's the most exciting thing that's happened all day.'
Excusing himself briefly he ran upstairs and looked in on
Biddy. Fresh air and exercise had worked their magic and
the child was already sound asleep. Mr Peregrine was in the
dining-room eating a solitary meal but Morrison preferred
to take his young companion elsewhere.

When he returned to the bar she saw he had put on an
anorak with a bright woollen scarf carelessly thrown round
his neck. As they left the bar conversation ceased

momentarily and the four old men on the bench exchanged significant glances.

'Your car or my banger?' he asked outside.

'Why not walk?' she suggested.

'Splendid.'

They strode together through the cold night air and she told him a little about herself. In return he gave her the broad headlines about his own recent past, keeping it short and matter-of-fact.

'What about before that?' she asked.

'You mean my family, upbringing, and all that stuff?'

'Yes.'

It was good to talk to an adult, intelligent being again. Biddy was pretty good for her age but it was fairly juvenile conversation. Debbie was undeniably attractive and Morrison was flattered by her interest.

'I had a rather unspectacular childhood,' he admitted. 'My parents split up when I was twelve and I was dispatched to a somewhat gloomy public school where classwork was centred on the academic and "the game was the thing" on the playing fields. Holidays were turn and turn about with Mum or Dad and, frankly, I looked forward to termtime. By the time I reached the fifth form my father had shoved off to Australia and Mum remarried. Two holidays with them proved too great a strain for all of us so when I left school I got myself apprenticed to an engineering firm and lived in digs.'

'Do you ever see any of them now?'

'Not really. I never heard a peep out of Dad and Mum and I live different lives. I think she was genuinely upset for me when Wendy died and, indeed, they offered to help with Biddy. Then the in-laws stepped in with their own special brand of religious bigotry, not to mention their often-voiced opinion that my side of the family was not out of the top drawer, so Biddy and I pressed on together.'

'What a sad story.'

'Worse things happen. I've got the greatest kid you ever met and some not bad memories on the whole.'

Debbie smiled at his honest assessment. When they

reached the little café she studied his face while he persuaded the owner to cook a snack and rustle up a bottle of wine. She saw a strong personality with a hint of stubborn determination. Most of her acquaintances were flaccid spoon-fed ornaments of society who gave forth with well-turned ambitious phrases even while they were drifting downstream with the tide. She noticed too that not once had he delivered one of those lines of wet sophisticated flattery towards her, if she was to gain his admiration it was clear she'd have to work for it.

He'd decided to eat a second meal and as the owner headed towards the kitchen he looked directly at her over the table.

'Well?'

'It's not really a mystery.'

'Don't disappoint me.'

Debbie's expression grew more serious as, for the first time, she doubted the wisdom of telling tales out of school. 'May I ask a question first? I think you're interested in a property at Skerrymor Bay?'

'Yes.' His smile was replaced by a narrowing of the eyes.

'So is Bruce Cornelius,' she said shortly and watched the blood drain from his face. 'Look,' she continued gently, 'I don't know why I'm doing this and it's probably best you don't ask too many questions.' She told him about the monosyllabic telephone call and what she'd further deduced during the flight from London. 'I know that man. If he has a weakness it is wanting something for no better reason than someone else has got it.'

'A weakness I assume he can afford to indulge.'

'Oh, Bruce can afford anything. And does when the mood is on him.'

'Christ.' Morrison rested both elbows on the table and rubbed at his jaw with both hands. He felt the anger whelling up inside him. His tiredness and the recent illness combined to prevent his controlling it and, stupidly, he knew he was about to over-react.

'Nothing is signed,' Debbie said, trying to backpedal. 'I gather his solicitors think there's some hang up.'

'It won't be anything his kind of money can't overcome,' he said grimly.

'Truthfully I meant only to pass on his invitation. Then when I saw you –' She shrugged.

'Thanks,' he muttered.

'It'll be the end of my visits here if he finds out.'

'What goes on in that house anyway?' he enquired irrelevantly.

'Not a lot.'

'You've got yourselves one hell of a reputation.'

'It's all in the mind. Bruce likes to have friends around him, that's all. Come and see for yourself.'

'Like hell!' She watched the anger suffuse his face. 'I don't know why you came looking for me, Miss Debbie Whatever-your-name-is, and I don't want to appear rude. Your rich friend might be able to gazump my living but I'm damned if he'll see my face when I hear about it.' She was shocked by the power of his bitterness. 'Only you had that pleasure!'

'I thought I might be able to help.'

'Help? Help who? I presume your next ploy would be to find out how much I was paying so your boyfriend wouldn't be unneccesarily out of pocket?'

'That's not fair!' Now she was angry. 'Did I say one word about – ' She stopped as she saw him rise to his feet.

'I'm sorry you gambled your weekend orgies to warn me because there's not much I can do about it.' He slapped a five pound note on the table. 'I hope that covers the cost of your supper.'

He had cooled down in every sense of the word by the time he reached The Last Resort and sat by the bar window awaiting the girl's return to collect her car. When he saw her enter the car park he walked out of the door.

'I'm sorry about that,' he said. 'It was nice of you to tell me.' Debbie made no reply. She simply opened the car door, got in, and drove off.

Morrison couldn't blame her. He went back indoors and climbed the stairs to his bedroom. In the bar the four men on the bench exchanged a second significant look.

He was still awake when it struck half past two. He remembered how Wendy had weaned him away from the periodic loss of self-control which had punctuated his youth but, he mused as he turned over in bed for the hundredth time, it had returned in full force that evening. Debbie had shown only kindness and he had demolished it in a couple of cruel sentences. He could see the expression in her eyes, first surprise then a hardening into anger which ended any hope of using her good offices to persuade Cornelius to back off from purchasing the Fergusons' property.

He turned over yet again. Why should he be reduced to pleading? Because Cornelius had money and Morrison didn't, that's why . . . He was falling now, rolling over and over glimpsing occasionally the ground rushing closer..The impact never arrived because the room was filled with smoke and Cornelius was behind the wardrobe. He crept towards him but suddenly the man reached out, his arms three feet longer than he remembered them, and grabbed him by the shoulders. He screamed out in fear . . .'

'Come on, Morrison, wake up!' Biddy shook him into wakefulness.

'Okay. Thanks.'

'What was it this time?'

'Nothing. A mess.'

'You must've woken up the hotel.' Then, 'Are you all right?'

'Yes.'

'Only you're not laughing. You usually laugh your head off!'

'Not a great deal to laugh about.'

'What's wrong, Morrison?'

He shook his head to clear it. 'Nothing, darling. I'll tell you in the morning. Don't worry.'

Impulsively she eased back the bedclothes and slid in beside him, her arms came round and she held him tightly. '*You're* worried, I can tell.'

'Things don't always run smoothly. It wouldn't be so much fun if they did.'

'It's not fair if you're worried. You try too hard to

deserve that.'

'Thanks, darling, that was nice.'

'I think you're terrific.'

'Go to sleep. I'll fill you in tomorrow.'

'I can always give up going to school, if that'll help.'

'Shut up.'

'I bet that's what your nightmare was about.' Seconds later she was asleep and he released himself gently from her grasp. He turned over just once more, then he slept as well.

When he told her next morning Biddy seemed more concerned about his seeing Debbie again than she was about the news. 'Old Ferguson will never sell to anyone else,' she declared dismissively.

'That's good to hear but what makes you so sure?'

'MacGregor.'

It was true he hadn't taken MacGregor into account the previous night but he couldn't believe it would make much difference. 'Oh darling, for eight thousand pounds he'd have the dog put down.'

Biddy's face paled but she made no direct reply. He marvelled again at his lack of tact but it was too late to pull back the sentence. After a moment she said curtly, 'Why don't we go and find out immediately after breakfast?'

The fisherman was chopping firewood outside his back door when they arrived. Morrison decided to take the bull by the horns and pretend ignorance about any other offer. 'I had a good meeting yesterday,' he ventured, 'and I think I might have some good news for you by the end of the week.'

He looked for signs of hesitation in Ferguson's face but the old fellow replied calmly enough, 'Well, I'm glad to hear that, Mr Morrison.'

Later, Morrison's curiosity overcame his good sense. 'Did you – er – receive any other offers, by the way?'

'Aye, there was one but I'd already given you my word.' He gathered up some sticks and rose to his feet. 'And we're all gentlemen around these parts,' he said with dignity.

Sigmund Morhof agreed to a partnership and things began to move rapidly. They drew up a draft agreement,

Morrison confirmed purchase with the Fergusons, and Sigmund briefed a firm of solicitors to act on their behalf.

The old fisherman and his wife moved out one Thursday in February and by lunchtime the evidence of their forty years habitation of the white house had been removed. The little yellow man was taken away in an ambulance and, watching quietly from the boathouse, Morrison and Biddy saw Mr and Mrs Ferguson stand in their front doorway and hold hands as they looked back into their home for the last time. The moment came to say goodbye to MacGregor and as the frail old lady stooped down the collie put both paws on her shoulders knocking her flat to the ground, where he licked her face in fond farewell until her husband fastened the lead and began to walk him towards the boathouse.

Inside he said to Morrison with quiet dignity, 'I pray the house will give you the same happiness it has to Marjorie and me over forty years.'

'Thank you.' The fisherman glanced at the rusted remnants of his life's work, gave the boat a light pat, and walked out stiffly, his back straight and head high. Biddy sat on the ground hugging MacGregor and when she and her father looked at each other there were tears in their eyes.

They went into the house and Morrison was shocked to see how dilapidated the place appeared now its faults were no longer concealed by furniture. 'Hello house,' called Biddy, 'we're going to make you young again.' She looked round at Morrison who nodded his agreement.

'Let's start by lighting a fire in every room and scrubbing the place from top to bottom.'

He was disheartened by his lack of stamina. There were so many battles to be fought and won yet he felt drained from scrubbing a floor. He could hear Biddy working away upstairs and it sounded like there was plenty of water swilling about. Suddenly a drop landed on the back of his head and he looked up to see a rapidly expanding damp patch on the ceiling. 'What the hell are you doing?' he shouted before racing upstairs.

She was sluicing water from a bucket on to the bedroom

93

floor and sweeping it around violently with a broom. 'I've poured in bags of disinfectant,' she assured him, 'and I'm going to slosh all their germs downstairs and out of the front door.'

'Why bother?' he yelled at her. 'It's pouring through the ceiling already.'

'Uh-huh! Too much water?' she asked needlessly.

'If you can't think don't help.' He pushed her out of the way crossly and snatched a floorcloth to repair the damage. 'Silly idiot,' he muttered.

It was the first time he had shouted at her from unreasonable bad temper. Biddy was well used to the peremptory tones of a father correcting a daughter for bad behaviour or whatever but she had not previously incurred his wrath at a time when, in fact, she was doing her best to help. Later she would become accustomed to this facet of his nature, which was more of a release of frustration than genuine anger, and remain as unscathed as water off a duck's back, but on that Thursday surprise caused her to take the unjustified rebuke badly. She left the room and later he saw her outside the house, both hands in the pockets of her jeans, wandering disconsolately towards the boathouse. MacGregor followed behind her. 'Great,' Morrison thought to himself. 'Here I am, weak as a kitten and I just sacked my helper.' For the next three days she disappeared on long explorations with Cluny and her conversations with him were brief and strained but he was too busy to notice either her absences or silences.

Pickfords delivered their own furniture on the Saturday and by the Sunday they were installed comfortably enough, the lounge and dining suites, G-plan bookcases and modern hi-fi looking incongruous in the white house.

He decided he would have the close season with nothing to do but decorate and the best plan was to camp until then and concentrate on catching fish. Cluny had again taken Biddy off on some secret assignation but Sigmund was coming over at midday so Morrison decided to impress him by laying a mooring for the workboat. He was no stranger to the task having encountered if often enough when he and

Wendy sailed together but he was at once taken aback by the bulk and size of professional fishing tackle and considerably dismayed by its sheer weight.

He found a CQR anchor in the boatshed and shackled to it a longish length of chain. To the other end of the chain he shackled a wire cable which had loops back-spliced into each end. Finally he tied a terylene warp to the larger upper loop, which would fit over the workboat's samson post when it was moored, and attached it to an orange-coloured buoy. This preparatory work took longer than he thought but by 11.30 he was ready to row it out in the dinghy and drop the mooring into place. He studied the chart on which Ferguson had drawn the precise position of the Skerrymor Bay station base net and selected a point for the workboat where there would be no danger of fouling. In order to avoid any mistake, and because he was anxious to demonstrate meticulous efficiency to the German, he took a handbearing compass to plot the exact position on cross-bearings.

He was appalled by the combined weight of the anchor, chain, and cable when he laid it in the stern of the dinghy. He placed them in reverse order, the buoy with its rope first, then the wire, on top of this the chain, and finally the anchor with one fluke over the transom fairlead ready for him to let it go, whereupon it would pull the rest of the mooring into the water as it sank to the bottom.

He was about to launch the dinghy when something made him look up towards the cliffs. On a distant promontory four old men had appeared and had seated themselves on a bench to watch him. One of them had a pair of binoculars which were passed around so that each could take turns to a close-up view. Before pushing the dinghy into the surf he gave them a wave to which they did not respond but simply settled themselves more comfortably. One of them lit his pipe.

The dinghy took a fair amount of water inboard from a couple of waves breaking before he was afloat beyond the surf and, suddenly, he wished Biddy was there to give him a hand. He jumped aboard and began sculling rapidly into deeper water. The backwash from the rocks caused a steep chop as waves bounced against each other and Morrison found it delicate going with only two or three inches of freeboard showing, but he rowed to the approximate position. He reached down to pick up the handbearing compass but by the time he was ready to take a reading the boat had drifted several yards to windward. He paddled back but this time the tide spun it clean round even whilst he held the instrument at arm's length.

The old men on the bench appeared to be enjoying themselves.

He decided to abandon the compass bearing and rely on guesswork. He made a show of taking a couple of readings for the benefit of his audience before easing himself from the thwart and moving aft to the heaped-up mooring. The dinghy's bow came clear of the water and he was at once in danger of plunging beneath the surface. He sat down hastily to reconsider his tactics. Keeping a careful eye on the waterline, he found he could fingertip the end of the anchor. He tried lifting it up but by the time he had sufficient hold to heave it over the stern he found he had drifted nearly a quarter of a mile.

He rowed back to the mooring position but continued to row for another two minutes until he was beyond it. Then very carefully he lay backwards until the weight of his body was well forward in the dinghy. Using his long legs he manipulated the anchor and chain until it was balanced on the transom. By this time he was lying quite flat and, peering over the side to check his drift, he saw he was practically over the spot.

The old men on the cliff seemed to be having an excited argument over whose turn it was for the binoculars.

Morrison counted up to ten and shot his feet forward with all his strength. The anchor, chain, cable and buoy tumbled overboard whereupon the stern, so suddenly relieved of their weight, rose vertically in celebration and the entire dinghy disappeared bow first beneath the waves. He broke surface spluttering and gasping, mercifully clung to the now upturned dinghy, prevented an oar from escaping and began to kick for the shore. After what seemed an eternity a pair of strong arms grabbed his shoulders and hauled him through the breakers.

'I see you've laid the mooring,' commented Sigmund. 'It's not *quite* in the right place but we can always move it later.'

Morrison rubbed the salt water from his eyes and looked up at the cliff to where four old men were walking away, well satisfied with the morning's performance.

CHAPTER FOUR

MOST HISTORIANS will insist on crediting John Knox with
laying the plan of the Scottish educational system although
it was Catholic priests who, before the Reformation, had
founded the fifteenth-century universities of St Andrews,
Aberdeen, and Glasgow. The Knox vision of a school in
every parish met with understandable indifference among
the upper classes – after all, who would want to spend
money plundered from the Catholics to educate people
who were more easily controlled in an uneducated
condition? However, with the establishment of the Church
of Scotland in 1696 his plan began to be realised and, with
poverty offering the stimulus to inventive effort, the
foundations were laid for the finest education system in the
world. Scotland was the perfect example of a country which
could offer employment to, and use the talents of, its
educated sons and it was a cruel irony that an unduly high
proportion of notable scholars packed their suitcases on the
day they were handed their degree and sought foreign fields
to exploit their knowledge. Between 1900 and 1920 more
than a million Scots emigrated.

Thirty-five years later Morrison and Biddy bucked the
trend by emigrating from England to Scotland. As they
paused outside the three-storey converted house that had
become Park Lodge, Morrison could not help but doubt
they would discover within personification of the system
which gave rise to the enviable boast.

He had made Biddy wear her old school uniform for their
first visit to the school that weekend. The girl had objected
strongly but when she had descended the stairs in freshly

pressed skirt and blouse, brushed blazer and hat, she'd looked very pretty. It was weeks since she'd looked anything but a tomboy and Morrison was startled by several indefinable reminders of Wendy.

'That's better,' he'd said. 'You look like a little girl again.'

'You've put a suit on,' she'd observed. 'Are we trying to impress someone?'

'First appearances are important.'

'Do you reckon the headmistress is agonising over what she's going to wear for *us*?'

A distant shouted 'In here' was the response to his tug on the bell pull and they stepped through the open front door to follow further calls until they found Miss Mahoney standing on top of a stepladder painting a classroom ceiling. She wore a pair of men's check trousers, rollneck jersey, a scarf over her head, and liberal daubs of white emulsion.

'Forgive us for not answering the door, Caroline and I have got *a tempo* going,' she excused herself in a hearty voice. 'Anway, welcome to the seat of all learning,' she continued, thrusting a paintbrush towards him then, laughing, exchanging it for a hand that was only marginally less covered.

He shook it gingerly. 'You've taken on a massive job in here,' he murmured.

'Not just in here. The entire school. It's like the Forth Bridge – Caroline and I no sooner finish than the wretched kids mess it up again. You remember Miss Kelso, of course?'

'Yes indeed. How do you do?'

The teacher gave him a polite smile and turned to Biddy. 'If your father decides to send you to Park Lodge you'll come into my class – would you like to see where we work?'

'Yes.' Biddy was suddenly subdued.

'In fact I'll show you everywhere if you like and you can give us marks for interior decoration.'

'Yes.'

The headmistress interjected, 'Yes, *Miss Kelso*. We're

very strict about that sort of thing.' She resumed slapping paint on the ceiling. 'You take a look round as well, Mr Morrison. Then we can have a talk.'

'Thank you – Miss Mahoney.' She looked at him sharply but the pause was unintentional.

Morrison responded instantly to the bright gaiety of the rooms, remembering the dusty gloom of the public school he'd attended. Walls and woodwork were coated generously in bold, cheerful colours, desks and tables had been sandpapered and varnished. He liked the formica-covered worktops, the spotless lampshades and patterned curtains, even pictures on the walls as well as the occasional vase of flowers.

'I think learning should be fun,' Miss Kelso was saying. 'You can't have fun in drab surroundings.'

Biddy was warming to the schoolteacher who treated her like an adult and looked directly at her when she spoke. 'My best subject is Nature Study,' she confided.

'Really? I don't imagine you saw a great deal of nature in the centre of a town. How was it your best subject?'

'Mr Collins made it interesting. He told us stories about the animals.'

'Good for him. What was your worst subject?'

'Most of the rest.'

Morrison watched them as they talked, the teacher tilting her head to concentrate fully on what the child was saying. Miss Kelso was the sort of person one passed in the street without a second glance. She did nothing to draw attention to herself, her clothes were neat enough but made no attempt to exploit her tall, slim figure, her fair hair, pale complexion, and grey eyes. She wore little make-up and it was as if her life had provided her with nothing that was worth dressing up for.

Soon Biddy was speaking with confidence and suddenly the teacher laughed. She was attractive when she laughed and Morrison thought probably she would be more attractive still if anyone had ever taken time to pay her a compliment.

The following Sunday, Biddy took MacGregor and went

off with Cluny to the spot near Macleod's land where the team from the Forestry Commission were preparing the vast, newly acquired acreage for tree planting. A large yellow, mud-bespattered JCB earth-moving machine was grubbing out hedgerows near the river which later would be replaced by a strong wire fence. Cluny was fascinated by the power of this mechanical monster and by the skill of its driver. He confessed to Biddy that he had stood for hours at a time, ignoring cold frosts and drenching downpours, watching the bucket dig great scoops from the ground, lay them neatly to one side, before inverting to form a crude rake which smoothed the soil and even bestowed a final pat before moving forward to take the next bite. Cluny had shown Biddy so many wondrous facets of nature that now she was amused that he could stand for so long in rapt admiration of a machine. At one point the driver switched off the motor and shared with his audience the warming contents of his flask. For ten minutes Cluny sat at the lifeless controls, making engine noises, whilst Biddy perched behind watching MacGregor hunt for rabbits.

She returned to the white house in time for a scratch lunch and afterwards expressed herself ready to work. Sigmund was keen to launch the workboat with as little delay as possible prior to laying the nets. These were badly in need of repair and he wondered if the girl was up to the task.

Although Biddy had regarded Sigmund's entrance into the scene with some suspicion she had taken to him in a matter of hours. She could see how he deferred to her father on certain matters whilst taking charge of anything where his skill and experience could be of benefit. She found herself obeying his orders unquestioningly, he was easy to learn from and he gave her exciting tasks to perform. Both he and Morrison treated her as an equal and she impressed them in return by determinedly seeing a job through even when she had grown tired of it. 'The thing about Biddy,' commented Sigmund, 'is that she may grumble like hell about something I give her to do, but she'll never do it badly like other kids of her age.'

He showed her how to hoist the nets on a series of tall posts let into the ground in a field behind the boatshed. Each post had a block at its head and Sigmund leaned a ladder up and climbed to thread a length of strong cord through the sheave. After he had completed two he saw Biddy shinning up the vertical post with the end of the cord between her teeth. 'That old ladder is too heavy for me,' she observed as she slid to the ground with the cord safely through the pulley. Together they threaded the remaining blocks before securing the ends of the upper edge of the long nets. By pulling on each cord in turn they were able to raise the nets up the posts a few feet at a time and carry out the necessary repairs along their length.

He taught her how to use the netting needle, a small wooden bodkin incorporating a length of twine, and she watched his hands become a blur as a hole disappeared in seconds before he snipped the twine with a small sharp knife.

'Hey,' she cried, 'could we have an action replay on that?'

He smiled and repeated the action more slowly. 'Look, I am only tying a succession of mesh knots which preserves the net effect and replaces the section which has been holed.'

Biddy took the netting needle and copied his action. Her first knot took three minutes and she surveyed the length of net stretching away across the field. 'This is going to take *forever*,' she commented.

'You'll become quicker with practice.'

'When does the season end?'

'August.'

'You'll catch more salmon by tickling their tummies than waiting for me.'

He left her to struggle with bodkin and twine in order to assist Morrison in the formidable task of launching the thirty-foot clinker-built workboat. 'It'll take ten men to shift it an inch,' Morrison said.

'Instead there are just two of us,' replied Sigmund, 'and labour is expensive.' He turned and pointed out to sea.

102

'With any luck you will find a ring let into the outermost rock on the very tip of the headland there. Take the dinghy and shackle a heavy block to the ring, pass the end of the wire cable through, and row back to shore with the end as I let it out. Okay?'

'Fine. Then what?'

'I'll fetch my Land-Rover, hook one end of the cable to the towbar and the other to the boats samson post, then drive towards Fort William!'

'Whilst simultaneously pulling the boat towards Skye,' laughed Morrison.

'We'll put down wooden rollers so she still has a bottom when she reaches the sea.'

'Sounds easy enough.'

Sigmund smiled to himself – it was far from easy. He walked back to the netting posts to help Biddy whilst at the same time keeping a weather eye on his boss.

He heard MacGregor barking before he reached her. The dog was frantic, running back and forth between the girl and the boatshed, obviously distressed.

'What's the trouble?' he called to her.

'I've no idea. He just went mad.'

'Something's worrying him.' They watched the dog for a few moments before he said, 'I know what it is. He's remembering!'

'You mean he doesn't want us to re-open the business?'

'All this equipment is a load of bad news to him. It reminds him of what happened before.'

'Cluny told me the dog used to go out in the dinghy with old Ferguson.'

'Yes, until they both came within an ace of losing their lives. He'll never go to sea again – and he doesn't want you and your father to go either.'

'You're just going to have to get used to the idea, Sunny Jim,' Biddy told MacGregor. Then she stooped and called to him quietly but firmly. *'Viens-tu à Biddy, mon brave. Les jours mauvaise sont finis.'* MacGregor stopped barking and looked at the girl, ears raised enquiringly. *'Il fait nécessaire pour nous nous faire un vivant, et nous assiste, bien?'* She cuddled the collie and he began to whimper into her ear, as if explaining the dangers.

Morrison began well enough. He selected a sturdy block from the selection in a corner of the boatshed. He tried to spin the pulley wheel only to find it was seized solid but a few squirts of penetrating oil and a couple of sharp blows with the hammer freed it before he coated the whole thing generously with grease. The wire cable was a different matter. To start with it had a life of its own and years of lying coiled had caused it to become adamant about assuming any other shape. Moreover, age and usage had parted some of the strands and sharp ends waited ready to gouge deep into careless hands. He manhandled the uncompromising bundle to the beach and painfully laid out sufficient length to stretch as far as the rock ring. The return half would be Sigmund's problem, he thought grimly. He took a turn round the thwart of the dinghy and then heaped the remainder in any old how so that it would pay out over the transom as he rowed. For the second time that day he heaved the dinghy into the surf but his self-confidence suffered a jolt when out of the corner of his eye he saw that the four old men had returned to their seat on the promontory. They seemed to have a peculiar ability to foretell disaster.

The row to the headland was no more than sixty feet but it was a hard pull. Several times the cable kinked and caught so that he had to kick it clear, causing the dinghy to rock perilously. At last he reached the rock ring. He'd judged the length nicely and only about two fathoms remained in the boat. He shipped oars and leaned over to grasp the ring. At that moment a wave lifted him up and he found himself clutching at slippery rock instead. The next second the wave dropped him again, wrenching his hands away, and dousing him with a generous dollop of icy water. Sailing men hate working close to shore, normally preferring plenty of water beneath the keel, and Morrison found the seemingly simple task of threading the sheave tantalisingly difficult under these circumstances. He decided to pass the dinghy's painter through the ring in case

104

of accident and then, by pulling his way along the rock, tautened it so that the bow and stern were held steady. Then he took hold of the ring and block before freeing the cable from the thwart. Each wave caused his arm to feel it was being wrenched from its socket whilst simultaneously smothering him with water but, gritting his teeth, he clung on and concentrated on passing the end through the block. As it appeared through the opposite side he felt a surge of triumph and quickly grasped its end with both hands. He gave a tug which timed perfectly with a receding wave causing the dinghy to drop so suddenly that he pulled himself clean out and into the sea. He hung on to the cable for dear life and only when he surfaced did he let go with one hand and grab the painter. Climbing into a dinghy is difficult at the best of times; near rocks and clutching a wire cable it's well-nigh impossible. By the time he'd scrambled in over the side Morrison was cold and exhausted. He made fast the end and looked towards the shore where he saw Sigmund and Biddy watching him. Could they be laughing? Surely not, he thought. The silly idiots! Anger made him row with all his might and he surfed the dingy on to the beach atop a wave before jumping out and handing the German his end of the cable with stiff dignity. 'I believe you wanted this!'

'Very well done,' praised Sigmund.

'You might have noticed I became a trifle damp,' he replied sarcastically.

'But you brought back the cable, the dinghy, and yourself. That kind of determination is the very essence of a good fisherman.'

'Terrific, Morrison,' said Biddy. 'You just don't know how to give up, do you?'

'Let's have some tea while I dry out.' He led the way to the house. On an impulse he turned round to view the distant promontory. This time the four old men returned his wave. It was the least they could do; after all, the last thing they'd expected was a matinée.

After tea a full hour was spent with shovel and spade clearing the shingle into a roughly even track sloping away from the boathouse to the water's edge. Then Sigmund and Morrison laid lengths of branches across the track to encourage the workboat to roll down, whilst at the same time rigging a preventer, a thick rope to check it from running out of control.

It was an enormously strong, monstrously heavy, flat-bottomed craft. Beneath the keel, and running from bow to stern, was a tunnel which housed the propeller. This enabled it to be used in close proximity to the nets without risk of their fouling the screw. Everything about the boat was thick. It needed to be because, at times, there could be four men leaning over the side hauling in a net filled with salmon – anything less sturdy would roll over and founder.

When the track was ready and the rollers in position Sigmund attached the end of Morrison's hawser-wire to a ringbolt beneath the hull. The other end was fastened to the towing bar of the Land-Rover and the younger man took the wheel with his eyes glued to the driving mirror to obey instantly hand signals from the other. Biddy left the nets for a few minutes and climbed up beside him. Inch by inch they edged forward, using fourwheel drive and clutch to exert a steady pull. The workboat emerged proudly from the boat-shed, faced the sea and, as Sigmund ran back and forth replacing the rollers, took to the water for the first time in several years. Then he launched the dinghy and climbed aboard with the painter.

As soon as it was afloat Morrison and Biddy ran from the Land-Rover, removed the hawser from the ringbolt, and climbed aboard to join Sigmund. Morrison took the helm, the skipper started the engine, and Biddy went forward with the boathook. Ten minutes later the workboat was safely moored and shipshape. They rowed ashore and their first day's work was ended.

'Very neatly done,' observed Sigmund. 'You notice, we have no audience for our successes.'

'No, they only turn up to watch the disasters.'

'True. They have a sixth-sense for these things.'

A thought occurred to Morrison. 'Of course, we could have used the workboat to lay the mooring.' Sigmund threw him an apologetic grin and Morrison could have kicked himself. '*Hell!*' he said.

After Sigmund had left for the day Morrison turned his thoughts towards preparing an evening meal for Biddy and himself. Cooking was almost the last straw after so many hours of sheer physical labour and he decided to take a short rest before starting. As he sat down in his armchair he felt decidedly weird.

'Morrison,' she was crying faintly. Then louder, 'Morrison, *please*.' He wrenched his eyes open and realised it was pitch dark. A log fire blazed in the grate and by its light he saw the wide, worried eyes of his daughter. 'Morrison, wake up.'

He attempted to shake away his lightheadedness. 'Sorry, I must have dropped off.'

'Dropped off? You passed out! Do you know what time it is?'

He looked at his watch – 8.45. He'd been unconscious for three hours. 'Damn, I'm sorry. I must have overtired myself. Give me a second to get it together.'

'I've been yelling at you for ages.'

'Well okay, I'm awake now.' He spoke sharply, suddenly irritated. 'I'll cook us something to eat in a minute.'

'I've done it,' she said in a choked voice. 'Somebody has to work around this place.' Then she was on her knees with her head in his lap crying tears of relief. 'Oh Morrison, I wish you wouldn't *do* that! You scared me.'

He was instantly apologetic. 'Hey listen, I'm all right,' he said gently as he stroked her head. 'I was tired, that's all. I haven't worked a day like that since I can't remember when.'

'Lighting fires and cooking meals at the end of it just isn't on.'

'No, it isn't,' he agreed. He could see an urgent need for a further demand on his dwindling resources. 'We need someone to look after the house for us during the season.'

'We need Mummy, that's what we need,' she mumbled into his lap.

'Don't say that, Biddy. Don't ever say that again.'

She looked up at him, face streaked with tears. 'But we *do*! I'm not saying anything about anything, and I don't mean it the way you think.'

'It's you and me together, darling.'

'I know, and most times that suits me fine. But when you go like this on me I'm *frightened*.'

He nodded. 'I'm sorry,' he said again. 'Look, we can get a housekeeper and pay her. Like we pay Sigmund.'

She was silent for a little while as she considered the thought of a housekeeper. Then she stood up as if marginally satisfied at least. He smiled up at her. 'What did you get us to eat?'

'I cooked a "Biddy's Boomerang".'

'Oh God!' 'Biddy's Boomerang' was so-named because it came back on you in the middle of the night. The concoction evolved from their sailing days when Wendy cooked in one saucepan on a single calor gas burner. A chicken portion for each person, onions, rice, sausages, a small can of peas, another of tomatoes, sultanas and herbs. Biddy tended to add other odds and ends from the fridge before allowing the whole lot to simmer for over an hour.

However Morrison was hungry and it tasted good. Whilst he was eating he saw her hands. Her fingers were raw and bloodstained. 'Biddy, what on earth have you done to your hands?'

Her eyes went heavenwards. ' "What have I done to my hands?" he asks. I've mended five miles of bloody fishing net, that's that I've done to my hands.'

He rose from his chair, moved round the table, and lifted her clean into his arms. 'You are the most terrific daughter any man could be blessed with.'

'I love you, Morrison.'

'And I love you too, darling.'

Biddy attended Park Lodge after half term and almost immediately began to cause trouble – not in the classroom where she cultivated considerable respect for Miss Kelso, but outside.

The boys from Downham came out of school fifteen minutes after the girls but, because they were situated nearer to the village, some girls – the walkers and stragglers – joined with them for the last half-mile. The fifth formers were already of an age when they dared not admit failure to find a boy they could 'walk out with' and each day there were several assignations outside the gates of Downham.

Biddy was too actively involved with life for thoughts of boyfriends to enter her head so her meeting with Andrew was pure chance.

'Hello.' She looked round as he caught up with her.

'Hello.'

He fell into step beside her. 'What's your name?'

'Have we met?' she asked suspiciously.

'No. That's why I'm asking your name, stupid. Mine's Andrew Campbell if that makes it any easier.'

'I'm Bridget Morrison.'

'Bridget's not much of a name. It's not as good as Andrew.'

'You don't meet a lot of girls called Andrew. Anyway, people call me Biddy.'

'Biddy's better than Bridget. Actually, it's even better than Andrew. Can you throw stones?' he asked with startling irrelevance.

'I don't throw them very often.'

'I throw stones terribly well. I bet you I can hit that greenhouse from here.' It was a disused greenhouse where the shattered panes indicated it had regularly been a target. 'Do you bet I can't?'

'No.'

'I say, you're awfully dull.'

'I'll bet you can't throw a pane of glass from the greenhouse as far as the road.'

'I'll bet you I can.'

'Let's go and explore it.' They left the road and walked across the fields to the greenhouse.

'You see,' explained Biddy, 'the weight of a stone in relation to its size allows it to travel through the air further than a sheet of glass which is much lighter.'

'I know all that,' countered Andrew, 'but a flat piece of glass has an aerodynamic quality which sort of allows it to fly.'

'Only if it's spinning,' she observed.

'Yeah. And when you throw a stone you can give it a final flick with your finger which you can't with a bit of glass; not without your finger coming off, that is.'

'Throw it backhand,' advised Biddy. 'That way you'll get the spin, the aerodynamic qualities, and the distance.'

Anxious to show off Andrew picked up the first piece of glass he found and threw it unskilfully towards the road. It fell far short, covering less than half the field. 'Wind's against us,' he declared.

'That was useless,' scorned Biddy. She found a triangular shape about the size of a dinner plate, brought it across her body, and then stretched her arm and opened her shoulders in a sudden movement. The glass sailed high through the air and landed only a few feet from the road. Sensing the danger of a serious loss of face, Andrew removed his jacket and set about the business in earnest. He landed his pane fair and square in the middle of the road at his fourth try whereas it took Biddy six attempts before scoring a direct hit. Then they both became more proficient and were able to shatter their glass on the tarmac with practically every throw. After twenty minutes of lobbing they heard the distant sound of a car approaching and moved quickly inside the wrecked greenhouse to hide themselves from view beneath the staging. The car drove past and if it suffered a puncture the fact was not made apparent immediately.

'You throw quite well for a girl,' he conceded. 'What else can you do?'

'Practically anything.'

'What's that mean? Sewing, and cooking, and things like that?'

'No, it means fishing, exploring, sailing, and things like that.'

'Do you kiss?'

'No.'

110

'I do.'

'Not with me you don't.'

'Want to bet?'

'If you do it'll only be the once.' The words were issued as a warning but, unfortunately, Andrew read them as an invitation. His arm went round her shoulder in a sudden, vice-like grip, and three seconds later his right eye was beginning to close from a stinging, swift upper-cut, his left eye was blackening from a swinging left-cross and, as he covered the pain with both hands, an expertly swung, book-laden satchel caught him full in the sightless face and bloodied his nose.

Biddy hadn't reached the road before a second car rounded the bend, but this time the driver spotted the river of broken glass and pulled up quickly. A large bearded man climbed out of the driver's seat.

'Have you seen this?' he demanded of Biddy as she drew near.

'Not yet. I was just coming to look at it.'

'Who do you think put it here?'

The girl gave a quick look towards the greenhouse but was not surprised to see that no help could be expected from that quarter. 'I did,' she said to the man, 'I threw it all the way from that greenhouse, isn't that a long way?'

'You *threw* it?' he thundered, glaring down upon her and causing her composure to dispel like air from a pricked balloon. 'That must be the most stupid thing I've ever heard in my life.' Looking at the roadway Biddy had to agree with him. 'What's your name?' he wanted to know.

'Bridget Morrison.'

'Oh, so you're Bridget Morrison, are you?' He glared at her with flashing black eyes. 'Well, Bridget Morrison, now we'll see how clever you are at sweeping the road clean again.'

'I don't have a broom.'

'That, young lady, is your problem.' He pulled open his car door and began to squeeze himself inside. 'I'll be passing by here in thirty minutes and if I find one sliver of glass lying in the road then I'm round to see your father

111

quick as a wink. Understood?'

After the sound of his engine had died away Bridget cupped her hands around her mouth and shouted towards the greenhouse.

'You were a fat lot of help,' she called out.

'There was nothing I could do,' came the faint reply. 'That was my father!'

The first week of March blustered its way through the Highlands with torrential rainfall and galeforce winds which penetrated the stoutest of clothes bringing damp chill to the depths of man and beast. Scotland is not a country where one can await the passing of inclement weather before tackling tasks of the day and, whilst Morrison raced against time to lay his nets before the season was too far advanced, in the countryside behind Skerrymor Bay the local inhabitants could be seen attempting to continue their lives as usual.

Near Macleod's land the team from the Forestry Commission made progress, working now in a sea of cloying mud. Cluny continued his vigil of admiration accompanied occasionally by an unwilling Biddy.

'It's a stupid game,' she declared watching him handle the lifeless controls after the driver had departed. 'I mean, if you could start the engine that *would* be something.'

'Dinna be so daft,' Cluny rebuked her, his verbal engine effects suiting him fine.

'This isn't any fun at all,' said the girl as she jumped down from the machine and began to walk home.

On one such afternoon Mrs Burgess let herself into the tiny terraced house which was one of eight shapeless grey dwellings angled meaninglessly across one corner of a patch of wasteground outside the village. The house was in the middle and a stone was set in the wall immediately below the eaves on which was carved the year '1880'. Two years earlier the neighbours had thrown a small party to observe the centenary but none of the guests knew quite what they were celebrating, who had built the horrid houses originally, or why.

As she closed the front door she could hear the television in the front parlour. Her husband sat glaring balefully at the screen from the first transmission for schools to the closing-down epilogue, seldom looking up or acknowledging her presence in any way. It had taken two decades of married life before she realised that Burgess neither saw nor cared whether the brasses shone, the floors were polished, or the windows cleaned. He had thumped into the house each evening to change from clothes which stank of fish into others which smelt of whisky before thumping out again to stand alongside his mates as together they drank towards the moment when the day's toil in the fish-gutting room was obliterated from the memory. After the second stroke his world became confined to the square footage before the television set and Mrs Burgess left him to it and escaped into the fresh air for as long as she dared.

Now she peered in at him but he made no response so she moved on to the kitchen where she set about clearing the dinner things and preparing his tea. Plates and dishes were stacked in the stone sink, the fire had died down and the water was lukewarm even after she'd allowed it to run. The place was a mess; Mrs Burgess knew it and was ashamed. When the company had insisted on early retirement it was his mates, those who had stood with him in long rows, gutting, packing, and despatching the night's catch, who had clubbed together to buy him the small black and white television set. From that day forth she only saw the back of his head unless she squeezed in between him and the fireplace. It was then she despaired and ceased to clean the rooms beyond, preferring to clean the homes of others instead, people whose lives quickly assumed a more important role in her scheme of things than anything which took place in her own house.

She gave him his tea on a tray and he ate it without moving his eyes from the screen, except once when the fork missed his mouth and he stabbed the side of his upper lip. There was a quiz show on and Mrs Burgess envied the teams their carefree humour. She sat slightly behind him, eating her own meal, watching and wondering. Her life lay elsewhere and one day Mr Burgess would have another stroke and she would be released from the marriage vows which had brought nothing but misery.

She allowed the thought to linger and, as it gathered strength, she decided to count the money in the tin. It was concealed behind the hot-water cylinder in the airing cupboard; she knew to a pound how much was hidden in there, but she thought she'd count it anyway.

In the boathouse they worked through the daylight hours and into the evenings by electric light. It was a race against time because officially the new season was already upon them although thus far there had been no reports of salmon being caught along the coast in any quantity.

Morrison was glad to be fully occupied and found the painful thoughts of his recent past submerged totally by the weight of work.

Every piece of equipment needed attention; some were rusted, others seized solid, certain parts had rotted and needed replacing. Where a repair lay within their own skill or ingenuity he felt they were moving forward but in the case of the ice-making plant they were reliant on suppliers delivering specialised items for out of date models and the delay involved was especially frustrating.

Sigmund pitched in wholeheartedly and during the preparatory period there developed an understanding between the two men which laid the foundations of good teamwork. The day approached when they were ready to lay down nets on at least two stations and commence fishing in earnest. It was time to recruit a boatcrew. The skipper unhesitatingly recommended Buzby and Bobo whom he had trained originally when they were still university students and he assured Morrison they were the best he'd worked with. He was surprised and delighted when they responded favourably by return post to his invitation to join them for the season.

Buzby and Bobo arrived at six o'clock on a Sunday

114

evening and Sigmund was to join them all for dinner to celebrate the inauguration of the full crew. Biddy was at first quite awe-struck by their appearance.

'My word, but they're big,' she muttered as Bobo swung off the train carrying a knapsack, canvas holdall and suitcase, followed by Buzby so nicknamed, presumably, because his entire body was thickly covered with curly blond hair, who approached down the platform with a battered suitcase and six brown paper parcels. 'But I mean, they're *big*,' repeated Biddy.

'How will we get them and all that lot in the car?' queried Morrison.

'They'll have to put the grand piano on the roof rack.'

Then the two were on them, overwhelming Morrison and Biddy with broad smiles and mighty handshakes.

'Mr Morrison? I'm Buzby. Hi!'

'And I'm Bobo.' Biddy noted that Bobo was the one with the blue shirt, there was little else to distinguish her and absolutely nothing to identify her as a girl.

Morrison led the way to the car. 'Jump in and pack your stuff all round you any-old-how,' he advised. Buzby heaved the two suitcases on to the roof rack which buckled under their weight, Biddy sat in the front engulfed by parcels, and the newcomers sat beside each other in the back, the girl still wearing the knapsack, with the holdall on their knees.

'Are we staying in the caravan like before?' enquired Bobo.

'Yes, if that's all right with you.'

'You bet it is,' replied the big girl with a giantsize coquettish look at Buzby.

At dinner Biddy watched them dispose of cold lamb and pickle with a mountain of spaghetti and then polish off an apple pie baked in their largest tin. 'Are you two mercenaries married yet?' enquired Sigmund during the meal.

'Can't afford to marry,' replied Buzby. 'Can't even afford to see each other very often.'

'Your invitation came right out of the blue. An absolute godsend,' agreed Bobo.

'I'd just failed to get a road repair job,' said Buzby.

'You? Working on the roads?' exclaimed Morrison. 'With your education, that's ridiculous.'

'Tell me where else, Mr Morrison. I didn't work at all for twelve months after I graduated.'

'Forget all that,' advised Bobo. 'We're here now and we're going to land you so many salmon, Mr Morrison . . .'

For the rest of the evening the conversation was to do with fishing, boat-handling, net-changing, packing and marketing.

'Do you have a good factor in Glasgow?' The question was put to Morrison but Sigmund replied.

'The best,' he assured them. He'd introduced Morrison to Bob MacPherson the previous week and they'd agreed to despatch their catch each day for him to sell on their behalf in the market. The factor is the most crucial link in the chain between fisherman and customer. The selling operation of so perishable a commodity is one where time is of the essence and the entire business side is conducted on a basis of mutual trust, there is no other way. He is usually a man of enormous experience whose advice is sought and taken. MacPherson had greeted Morrison with an element of reserve but his doubt arose only from human problems when dealing with someone new to the game; anyway it was swept aside when he knew that Sigmund was involved, which gave Morrison a complete season to establish a reputation of his own.

'How many nets, Mr Morrison?' queried Bobo.

'Two immediately, but five eventually. We've had a mountain of work to do on the gear.'

Sigmund added, 'It's largely due to Biddy that we're ready to start so soon.' Four pairs of eyes gazed at the girl and she squirmed in slight embarrassment, then squirmed again from annoyance that she'd squirmed the first time. 'And we lay the first net at eight in the morning,' Sigmund finished with an enquiring glance at his host.

Morrison nodded. 'Fine. We'd best get a good night's rest.'

In his bedroom he turned out the light before getting into

116

bed and spent a few minutes looking out of the window. There was a crescent moon and he could see the workboat riding comfortably in the bay. The sea was quiet and the forecast good so, with a degree of luck, they should get through Day One without too many dramas. He was about to turn away from the window when his attention was drawn to the caravan. It was nearly a quarter of a mile away but from where he stood he could see it rocking violently. He grinned to himself. 'At least Buzby knows she's a girl even if she doesn't look like one,' he thought. Then, idly wondering whether the caravan could withstand such a beating right through until September, he climbed into bed and was asleep almost at once.

Sigmund had spent hours studying the Admiralty chart and making his own soundings before deciding to alter slightly the line of the long leading net which would guide the salmon into the bag. This had meant setting a new ringbolt into the rock and this task had been given to Morrison.

'Shall I take a sledgehammer and bang in the spike?' he'd asked.

'You could,' Sigmund had replied. After a pause, he'd continued, 'but the ring would almost certainly come out again the moment it had to cope with a heavy strain. On the other hand, you could drill a hole, drop in the spike, and pack it with pieces of wood. After a couple of tides the wood will swell and hold anything you care to name for a hundred years.' He smiled to soften the correction. 'I told you, Morrison, always allow the sea to do your work for you!'

Sigmund had set a pair of leading marks, one practically on the shore and a second some hundred yards inland, which precisely represented the direction the net would take. He was anxious that as the salmon breasted the tide it would meet the leader net head-on and, by keeping the two posts in line, he could place the net precisely as he'd drawn it on the chart.

Now he meticulously made ready some one hundred and fifty fathoms of synthetic rope, tying coloured ribbons at the precise points where the 'leader', the 'bridle', and the 'fish court' would later be fixed. Then came thirty fathoms of heavy chain, and finally a one-hundredweight fisherman anchor. Once marked they loaded the enormous heap in the stern of the workboat, making a firm tie to the sternpost wherever there was a coloured ribbon, and preparing it in reverse order so that the anchor buoy went aboard first and the shore ringbolt shackle last.

Then they were ready to lay this marker rope. Sigmund suggested that Morrison should do nothing except watch their first attempt and Biddy, to her disgust, was peremptorily ordered to remain ashore. The skipper stood amidships by the engine throttle, Bobo took the helm, and Buzby stood by her as they conned the craft nearer and nearer to the rocks of the cliff. Bobo kept her eyes glued on Sigmund as he gave instructions and, with the workboat rising and falling on the waves, Buzby chose his moment to step swiftly on to the slippery rock, grasping for a handhold and clinging on to the end of the rope at the same time. He clipped the shackle to the ringbolt and leapt back on board, all very neatly considering it was his first attempt for nearly a year. Now Sigmund slowly took the boat out without removing his eyes from the leading marks and calling for tiller adjustments as they went. The rope paid out astern and when the first coloured ribbon appeared out of the heap, the boat was held temporarily by the tie. The rope came taut as the forward motion of the boat took effect and rose clear of the water. He waited until he was perfectly satisfied they were exactly on station before ordering Buzby to cut the tie. They proceeded thus until only the anchor and anchor buoy remained on the transom, the engine straining against the tremendous weight of chain curving away behind the boat to the marker rope now stretched taut as a violin string. 'Let go,' he called, and Buzby cut the final tie. The anchor splashed overboard and the first part of the task was completed.

The seaward end of the anchor wire would be affixed to a bridle which, effectively, split the rope into four lengths. Two would be used to hold the head of the bag net whilst the other two became spares for the weekly task of net changing. They brought the workboat inshore again and took aboard the lighter but bulky nets themselves, together with four poles which would hold the bag open and taut. Now they ran two cleeks from the shore to the bridle and from then on they were able to maintain their exact position by running the marker rope through thole pins in the gunwale. They tied the bag net to the bridle and began to pull themselves shorewards along the marker rope whilst the net paid out over the stern until they could make a tie to the up-tide cleek. Then, obeying Sigmund's philosophy, they allowed the tide to drift them onto the cleek on the other angle and made fast there. Working to instructions Morrison released the marker rope and began coiling it inboard whilst the others heaved the workboat shorewards, paying out the leader net as they went. Buzby repeated his death-defying leap to secure the end to the ringbolt before unhitching the marker rope. The net was in position and it remained only to steam back to the head and push the poles down to get the whole works fishing.

Watching Sigmund make a final adjustment to the 'junk' which would take up any slack as tidal conditions altered, Morrison wondered whether he would be able to make such superb seamanship appear so effortless. He called out, 'What about some beer and sandwiches before moving up the coast and setting net number two?' Everyone agreed.

Early the following morning the four of them paid the first of what would be twice-daily visits to the nets in order to bring ashore the catch. There was one grilse swimming around in the Skerrymor Bay bag net and absolutely nothing whatsoever in the second. Naturally they were disappointed but Morrison surprised himself by experiencing a twinge of excitement that they had caught *anything*. It was a start and, if nothing else, it showed that the thing was going to work. Aloud he commented, 'From here on the business can only build.'

When the new owner stepped ashore carrying his prize Biddy asked, 'Is this what you've been referring to as the fruits of the sea?'

'This is it.'

'Well, congratulations,' she said sarcastically. 'I'm standing ready with the scales, the boxes, the ice, the addressed labels, and what do I get? One lousy fish.'

He laughed and threw an arm round her shoulder. 'I'll have you know this is a very fine fish. It's our first fish.'

Sigmund said, 'Look at it this way, we wouldn't want the salmon to be running when we have down only two nets.'

'Okay,' said Morrison, 'so here's what we do today. All hands on the tackle – you're in on this, Biddy. Come hell or high water we lay a net a day for five to be in action by Friday.'

'How do you want us to work?' enquired Sigmund.

'You and Buzby on anchors, chains, bridles and poles. Bobo and Biddy on warps and nets.'

The crew nodded and began immediately to set to. Biddy stood by her father and asked quietly, 'Morrison, have you noticed anything about our seagoing skipper?'

'No, what?'

'He always dresses the part; whatever he's doing he has to be properly dressed for it.' Morrison looked across and saw the German heading towards his car and noted the blue serge trousers, short boots, dazzling white pullover and cap. He held his pipe firmly in his mouth with his right hand and this completed the effect.

'You're right, aren't you,' he mused. 'He was wearing the full continental businessman's suit, complete with waistcoat, spats, and buttonhole when we discussed the partnership.'

'Now you just altered his job what's the betting he comes round the back of his car in a crisp set of dungarees?'

A couple of minutes later Sigmund emerged wearing exactly that. Morrison and Biddy giggled at each other before she saw he was carrying a bottle of whisky and five glasses. 'It is a custom,' he explained, 'to welcome the first grilse with a dram of neat whisky. We must drink to a good season.'

The next day three nets bagged a total of seven salmon

120

and grilse, the Thursday saw four nets bag four, Friday's five nets brought in only three, but on Saturday there were no less than eleven, bringing the grand total for their first week to twenty-five.

In Glasgow the factor obtained a good price due to the season having just begun, but Skerrymor Fisheries ended their first five days' trading having incurred a loss. The returns would need to be of a very different order if they were to meet running costs but at this early stage Morrison was far from dissatisfied. They were in business, he was running his own affairs, and there was a cash flow of sorts. He'd shown an enterprise that was going to pay off and he felt good. He could pinpoint precisely the moment his confidence had returned in full flood; it had been the night when Biddy had awakened him from his nightmare, hugged him tightly, and whispered, 'I think you're terrific.'

A mile or so away Alistair Macleod was giving The Last Resort a head-to-toe springclean. Towards the end of the month he anticipated the first thin trickle of tourists to arrive and catch the start of the new warmer weather. His brochure boasted *Private fishing in the hotel's own grounds* and, because the advance reservations were well down on the previous year, he had taken the unusual step of inserting an advertisement in the columns of the *Sunday Times*.

He worked amidst a sea of tools because he believed in dealing with each room *thoroughly*. That is to say, he had alongside him the vacuum cleaner, broom, mop, hammer, nails, screwdriver and screws, paintbrush and tins, wallpaper and paste. He intermingled the tasks of cleaning and polishing with slapping up a length of wallpaper here and touching up the paintwork there. By the time he finished a room it seemed not to know what had hit it, but it was *clean*.

It was a time of year when he was able to provide the awful Cluny with any number of dull jobs, mostly of a fairly unpleasant nature down in the darker depths of the old house, but just when he needed him there'd been neither sight nor sound of the man. Macleod was working in the back bedroom and pondering on his surprising absence in a week where sorely needed pounds were available when he became aware of the distant sound of the telephone ringing in their private sitting-room downstairs. He allowed it to continue in the hope that Mrs Macleod would deal with the caller but, suddenly fearful the ringing would cease, he dropped his cleaning and hurried to answer it himself.

'The Last Resort,' he announced breathlessly into the receiver.

'Good morning.' It was a woman's voice, businesslike and formal. 'Would you put me through to Reception?'

'You are through to Reception. This is Alistair Macleod speaking.'

'Good. I would like to reserve a single room with private bathroom for Mr Parkinson-Small from 27th March to 4th April.'

'We can manage the room right enough but I'm afraid the hotel doesn't rise to private bathrooms.'

'Oh.' It was uttered with a calculated note of surprise.

'There's a wee handbasin in each room; normally it suits perfectly well.'

'Would you hold on a moment.' He heard a subdued exchange at the other end before the woman came back on the line. 'That will be all right as long as the room is one of your best.'

'We'll make him very comfortable, I promise you that. Mr Small, did you say?'

'Mr Parkinson-Small,' she corrected. Then she added carefully, 'Mr Parkinson-Small is chairman of the Parkinson-Small Group of Companies and you might be interested to learn that he is also a director on the Board of City and County Tours Limited.'

Macleod was not one to betray sudden excitement and simply commented calmly, 'We'll look forward to making him welcome.'

'Very good. I'll send off a confirmatory letter today.'

On replacing the receiver the hotelier permitted himself a moment of anticipatory relish. It was well known that the big tour companies regularly selected hotels during the

122

off-season and a pleasant stay in the right atmosphere could often lead to heavy bookings. If this chap was a chairman in his own right as well as being a member of the board of City and County undoubtedly he was extremely influential.

Macleod looked down at the telephone. 'That could well be the most important call I receive this year,' he told the instrument before writing Parkinson-Small's name in the hotel register against the best bedroom on the first floor.

He pulled on gumboots and heavy mackintosh and ventured out of the back door of The Last Resort to inspect the hotel's principal amenity. Following the heavy rains the river should be in full flood and the keen anglers who surely would follow his first important guest would be tempted towards several locations where the rushing torrent held forth promise of good sport. He trudged to the most favoured spot, his boots squelching through the dank undergrowth. When he reached the steep bank he was surprised to note the water was nothing like as high as he'd expected; moreover, to his considerable consternation, the level appeared to be falling by the minute.

He stood transfixed, staring in horror at the declining river, and beginning to feel it could only be a judgement upon him for the minor indiscretions of a lifetime.

By midday the riverbed was dry and Macleod's brochure was in breach of the Trades Descriptions Act.

CHAPTER FIVE

COMMANDER CAMPBELL looked into the bar of The Last Resort at lunchtime. He could count on the fingers of one hand the number of occasions on which he took his midday drink in a public bar but he needed to have a word with Alistair Macleod.

Campbell was a large man whose face was covered by a moustache and bear beneath a thick mass of jet black hair which grew low down on his forehead. Penetrating the foliage were a pair of alert eyes as piercingly black as his hair. He had spent twelve years in submarines, although Biddy was heard to query how ever he squeezed into one and how it remained upright after he had done so, but now he was posted to a shore job and when off duty could be observed wearing black trousers and white rollneck pullover tending his garden with controlled energy whilst simultaneously carrying on a conversation with his wife through the open kitchen window.

'The entire rosebed is in the wrong place, d'you see? The idiot who put it here never bothered to check his aspect.'

'Check his what?' came Mrs Campbell's voice from within.

'Look where the sun is shining from, you daft ha'porth.' By next morning the rosebed would be seen fully planted up in front of a south-facing stone wall and there would be some who suspected the commander had picked the whole thing up and carried it across the garden in the middle of the night.

He was a man who liked to be a part of the community. He welcomed any opportunity to play a role in the affairs of the village, always provided it was a *leading* role of course. He offered his views on the occasional scandal, put his weight behind charitable causes ensuring at the same time that his own money remained safely in the bank, and he acted as the community ambassador where the millionaire Bruce Cornelius was concerned. Not only had he introduced one or two potential cottage industries to him but the introduction had earned him a commission on those occasions Cornelius agreed to back the venture.

He considered Macleod to be a useful ally, mainly because he occupied a position where one could be abreast of local gossip. There were things going on in the village and it was just possible that a man behind the bar could have heard a whisper from some careless mouth.

Today, however, Macleod seemed positively distrait. Usually he listened attentively when Campbell had something to say but now his eyes were glazed and he kept muttering some damn-fool thing about someone making off with his river.

'You can't take a river away, man. Not a *river*!'

'I tell you it's gone. There's no a drop o' water to be seen.'

'Why don't you get that man of yours to walk upstream until he finds where the trouble lies?'

'Because he's disappeared as well, that's why. I'll go myself as soon as we close – I only discovered it just before I had to open up in here.'

'Well I'm telling you there's one or two matters need attending to. That Morrison child filling the road up wi' broken glass was only the start of it. The same day our Andrew was beaten up by a gang of hooligans.'

This got through to Macleod. 'Beaten up?'

'The boy came home covered in blood, both eyes blackened and one o' them closing fast. He said there were three of them, two held his arms behind his back while the big fella set about him.'

'I wonder if they know anything about my river.'

It was useless talking to Macleod in his present mood so Commander Campbell took his problem out of the bar. He

125

resolved to call on the Morrison girl – it was just possible she'd seen something.

At about the same time another conversation was taking place between Janet Mahoney and Caroline Kelso in Park Lodge School. The headmistress did not mince words.

'She's spoiled rotten and needs bringing down a peg or two.'

Although Biddy was more at home up to her waist in water clearing a snagged warp than seated behind a classroom desk wrestling with mathematics, she had made a reasonable effort in her own way. She liked Miss Kelso, who had a great gift for transforming the dull into something more interesting, but six hours of daily confinement within an educational environment succeeded mainly in coiling tight her internal spring of energy and in the playground she was as badly behaved a child as anyone could remember.

The headmistress went on, 'Bridget Morrison is invariably at the bottom of any trouble and if things don't improve we'll have to make an example of her.'

'I disagree that Biddy is spoiled,' the teacher argued quietly. 'When you consider all she's been through, and is still experiencing come to that, you cannot say in all honesty that her father has spoiled her.' She smiled slightly. 'One-parent families on a limited income don't throw up many opportunities frankly.'

'You don't need money to spoil a daughter,' snapped Miss Mahoney.

'Too much independence, maybe,' reasoned Caroline Kelso. 'Freedom to express opinions in adult company, undue attention given to her wishes, praise lavished on her achievements . . . all these things . . .'

'You have described perfectly my experience of a spoiled child,' interrupted Miss Mahoney warningly.

'Maybe I have.' Caroline was undeterred. 'On the credit side she does practically a day's work before coming to school in the morning, and another when she gets home. She looks after her father like a girl several years older, she holds no fear of anything whatsoever, and when she

126

chooses to display it Biddy has the most enchanting personality I've ever come across.'

'There speaks the voice of experience, I suppose?'

The younger girl flushed. 'I think I know Biddy.'

'Her name is Bridget Morrison,' cried Miss Mahoney angrily as a flash of jealousy glowed in her eyes. 'How often have I spoken to you about allowing personal relationships to develop in your work?'

'I'm sorry, Janet.'

A bell rang and feet were heard scampering down corridors to classrooms. Janet Mahoney folded her napkin and rose from the lunch table.

'What do you advise me to do about her?' asked Caroline.

'Nothing. I will send for Mr Morrison myself. I shall make it clear to him that whilst his daughter is in our care we shall see to it that she abides by my standards of behaviour and conforms to my rules.'

'Is this not something I could handle? The girl is in my class.' It was said without defiance but the headmistress turned on her quite viciously.

'This is my school, Caroline, although you enjoy special privileges. Kindly remember you are only a teacher here.'

'Very well, Janet.'

At the same time as Janet Mahoney and Caroline Kelso were returning to their classrooms Mrs Burgess was walking towards the white house. She had been working for Mr Morrison barely one week but already a pleasant routine had developed. On those days when the rain held off for long enough to do the washing in the morning she liked to return to tackle the ironing in the afternoon.

She was a large lady whose ample bosom and massive bottom dominated her comings and goings. She cleaned the house with tremendous energy, leaving furniture and ornaments spotlessly clean and usually dented.

When breaks appeared in the scudding clouds and the sun shone in fits and starts, punctuating the rainfall with brilliant flashes of incandescent beauty, she would appear in the back door and sniff the air to establish whether there was sufficient drouth to hang the clothes out to dry. Being unwilling to waste a sinkful of soapy water she brought her own washing with her and, with a gusting wind blowing from the south-west, her directoire knickers ballooned out like a spinnaker and whizzed round the clothes hoist with Morrison's and Biddy's smaller garments chasing after them in fruitless pursuit.

She disapproved of her new employer's careless upbringing of his daughter. She'd wondered about him when first they'd met outside the church; indeed, she'd observed to her friends that it was the duty of clean living, decent men to maintain standards and here in the white house she could see they were being allowed to slip. Had she been blessed with a child things would have been different and her thoughts prompted a wistful smile when she contemplated that had she married a man like Mr Morrison instead of her own wreck of a husband life would bear no comparison with her present lot. Before she knew him well enough to speak freely their talks progressed uncertainly during his brief visits to the kitchen, with Mrs Burgess probing for an opening whilst he watched her banging down the electric iron with such force that he wondered how long the ironing board could survive the punishment.

Biddy was a handful, there was no questioning that. Critical as she was of Morrison's lack of discipline she had to feel sorry for him when, on the Friday, their halting conversation was interrupted by a hammering on the front door.

'Do you want me to see who it is?' she offered.

'No it's all right. I'll go.'

He hurried through the narrow hall but by the time he opened the door the caller had gone. Almost immediately there came the sound of urgent knocking on the back door. He returned to the kitchen to find Mrs Burgess had let in Alistair Macleod.

'Ah, you're in!' The hotelier appeared dishevelled and upset.

'Good afternoon.'

'Have to see you. Need a good talk. No point in mincing words.' Macleod's words were uttered in a series of short bursts.

'Well, sit down and have a cup of tea.'

'No time. No time.'

'Is anything wrong?'

Mrs Burgess paused in her ironing, sensing a strong hint of drama.

'Wrong?' spluttered Macleod. 'You stand there and ask if anything's wrong. Don't you know? Haven't you heard?'

'I'm afraid I haven't.'

'Your daughter, sir!'

Morrison's heart sank. 'What's she done?'

'Dried out my river, sir!'

'Dried out your river?'

'Dried out my river. And by the same token, dried out the reason tourists come to my hotel, and dried up my living.'

'I don't understand.'

'Am I not speaking plainly? Do you not understand English? Your daughter has –'

'Yes, I can hear what you're saying, but that doesn't mean I understand it. Your river is a mile long, forty feet wide and two feet deep. How can my daughter have –'

'Diverted it, sir!'

'Diverted it?'

'I would be grateful if you would not repeat everything I say.'

'But, dammit, I don't understand.'

'It's action we need, laddie, not comprehension. Come to that I've never understood *anything* your little girl does. She's a menace to mankind.'

Morrison lost his temper and shouted back. 'Biddy is ten years old. How the hell could she divert a river?'

'By driving a bulldozer!'

'But Biddy can't drive a bulldozer.'

'THAT'S WHY SHE'S DIVERTED MY RIVER!' the hotelier explained at the top of his voice.

When the two men reached the site Morrison saw that for

once Macleod had not exaggerated. To his dismay the riverbed was practically bone dry and scarcely a trickle of water ventured its way down the old course. 'Who says Biddy did this?'

'Cluny told me. Thirst overcame desire for concealment.'

'That makes it gospel, does it?'

Macleod shrugged irritably. 'I'll not go into the why's and wherefore's of it now. What are you going to do about it, that's what I want to know.'

'Me?'

'You're an engineer, aren't you? You told me you were a very good engineer.'

'Look, Macleod. I'm starting a new *career*. We're setting down the nets now. I haven't got time –'

'Would you want to see your daughter in trouble? Very serious trouble?' the man demanded stubbornly.

'Are you threatening me?'

'I am.'

'I don't believe my daughter was responsible.'

'She *says* she was responsible.'

'She does?' Uncertainty was in Morrison's voice.

'The lassie admits it.'

'Well –' Morrison stared at the riverbed, lost for words. 'I just don't believe it,' he repeated without much confidence.

Morrison found her among the netting poles, slight figure in faded patched jeans and Muppet T-shirt, small face concentrating beneath the unruly tangle of red hair. 'I want a word with you.'

She looked round at his face. 'Uh-huh!' she said.

'Come on, what's the explanation? What happened?'

'You're not going to believe this –' she began.

'I'm sure I won't, so skip the phoney story and come straight to the truth.'

'You're cross, aren't you?' she observed.

'Of course I'm cross. If you want to know I'm very angry. What happened?'

'Well, I was driving this great big –'

'Biddy!' he interrupted with exasperation. 'You could

never reach the pedals of a bulldozer. Who do you think you're kidding?'

She turned away from him and stared stubbornly at a hole in the net before reaching up to repair it. 'If they thought Cluny was driving he'd be in the most awful trouble.'

'Ah. So that's it.'

'He might even be sent to prison. Cluny says Mr Macleod would sew him up.'

'Sue him, not sew him up,' corrected Morrison. Then he added with honesty, 'Well it comes to much the same thing, I dare say.'

'He hasn't any money.'

'He can join the club,' mumbled her father.

'They'd send him away.'

'So you cooked up this cock-and-bull story between you?'

'Sort of.'

'I'm surprised at Cluny allowing you to take the rap. Unless, of course,' he said sternly, 'you talked him into it in the first place.' She concentrated on the repair. 'Did you?'

'Sort of.'

'Did you or didn't you?'

'I might have *suggested* he climbed in and started it up. I mean, he might have got the idea from something I said.'

'Why, what did you say?'

'I said, "Why don't you climb in and start it up?" ' She turned back to him to share the memory of the monster suddenly going berserk and digging a great gouge out of the bank, allowing the river to discover a new, easier course than the one it had followed for centuries and cascade joyfully along the ditch left by the scooped-out hedgerow to rejoin the original route just beyond Macleod's land. 'You should have seen it, Morrison. It was like a movie when the water flooded out.'

'I wish I could begin to fathom out what goes on in your mind. Does it ever occur to you that I'm trying to earn us a living here?'

Biddy's face showed sudden hurt surprise and, by way of

answer, she tugged angrily on the netpole cord. He looked down the length of suspended net and realised she had repaired it entirely by herself. 'We're ready to go on the Ferrick station now.'

He sighed. 'Okay. I'm sorry I said that but the fact remains either I have to pay for the breached river bank to be replaced or I mend it myself. As we don't have any money it doesn't leave a wide choice.'

'Can't they shove the soil back with a bulldozer?'

'Have you *seen* it?' She nodded and there was no need for him to say any more. 'That old devil Macleod is blackmailing us, thanks to your knight in shining armour routine.'

'I'm sorry, Morrison.'

The telephone was ringing in the house and he strode away to answer it. The girl followed more slowly and, as her face came round the door of the room, she realised she was in even deeper trouble.

'Yes, she's here. What's the trouble, Commander?' His eyes rested square on her while he listened. 'Glass? What glass?'

She ran into the room. 'He's broken our agreement – I swept up every speck!'

He waved her quiet and she plonked herself crossly into a chair. '*How* many?' The distorted sound of Campbell's voice continued for several seconds. 'Hang on, I'll ask her.' He placed a hand over the mouthpiece. 'When you were walking home from school yesterday did you come across a – er – "gang of fifth form louts"?'

'No.'

'Do you know anyone called Andrew?'

'Yes.'

'This is his father. When he arrived home last night his left eye was closed, his right eye black, and a nosebleed had ruined his shirt. He says he was set on by three older boys, two pinned his arms to his side while the third hit him.' Then as the receiver squawked, 'What was that, Commander?' At last the faintest hint of a smile. 'He says that even so his boy put up a terrific fight.'

132

The brief pause had given Biddy a moment to think. 'Maybe I might have seen something.'

'What?'

'A fight behind the old greenhouse. It was a long way off.'

'Could you recognise any of the boys?'

'No.'

He spoke into the telephone again and she watched his face as he completed the conversation. He knew she had lied. After he'd hung up he crossed the room slowly and sat down opposite her. His look spoke volumes so, without further prompting, Biddy told him about the incident. When she came to the bit about hitting Andrew her father interrupted.

'You did *what*?' Suddenly his voice was dangerously low, the most ominous she'd ever heard it, but Biddy was too upset by this time and threw caution to the winds.

'I said I hit him, Morrison. What'd you expect me to do, let him rape me?'

The explosion came. 'That wasn't funny. Don't let me hear that kind of talk come from you now or ever.' He'd never been so angry. 'What sort of little hooligan are you turning into?'

She felt tears well up behind her eyes and a sob expand in her chest. 'He's older than I am, for God's sake, and *miles* bigger. I didn't like what he was doing and –' The sob burst and speech became difficult. 'I thought you'd be proud of me.'

'Proud of you? Why would I be proud of a kid who gets involved in street fights?' He saw her stare across at him like someone who'd just been betrayed by her only friend. 'You're going to apologise to that boy,' he concluded.

She didn't reply but sat punchdrunk from frustrated indignation about his attitude towards the beastly Andrew. She vowed to get even. To get even with them all. With the old commander who broke his promise about the broken glass, his bullying son, and most of all with her unjust parent.

*   *   *

Debbie finished giving the chairman a progress report on the Nottingham Conference arrangements and sat back comfortably in the chair, crossing her legs. She liked him in this mood, genial, relaxed, and good-humoured. Parkinson-Small looked at her across the vast expanse of his polished desk and thought what a pretty girl she was.

'I'm visiting one of your weekend holiday haunts on Thursday,' he confided.

'So I heard. Except I thought it was Friday.'

'I find I can sneak away earlier. Who told you anyway?'

'Your toffee-nosed secretary.' Then she added calmly, 'It's all right, your secret is safe with me.'

He grinned sheepishly. 'A man needs to get away on his own. Angling is a solo sport.'

'That's a pity. I was thinking of coming with you.'

He leaned forward quickly. 'Would you? I mean, that would be different.' It was a long time since she had been so friendly towards him.

'There's a man up there I want to see.'

He failed to hide his disappointment. 'Bruce Cornelius?'

'No. Someone else.'

At least she was coming with him. 'I'll ask my – er – toffee-nosed secretary to call the hotel and fix a sleeper for Thursday night.'

'Okay.'

Back in her office Debbie wondered if she was being wise. She thought about the brief note she'd penned to David Morrison.

> *Dear David,*
>
> *Telling tales out of school was ill-advised and perhaps your response was understandable. I'm genuinely glad it came right for you in the end.*
>
> *Sorry I 'swep' off in a huff and thanks for the pizza. I'll let you have the change from the bill if ever we meet again.*
> *Sincerely,*
> *Debbie.*

134

There had been no reply. Still, it would be nice to see how he was getting on. She'd enjoyed his company so much until the outburst.

In The Last Resort, Macleod took Morrison into his private sitting-room and closed the door.

'To be frank, I never imagined for one minute your girl had driven the vehicle herself.' Then a warning finger, 'Although if you ever quote me I'll deny I said that. Anyway, I'm right sure she had a hand in the matter if only by thinking it all up. So you –' now the raised finger became horizontal, pointing towards Morrison, 'are going to bring back my river for me.'

'I can't, Mr Macleod,' protested Morrison. 'I've a living to earn.'

'I just lost mine,' the hotelier argued. 'I tell you this, laddie. If you don't help me I promise you'll never pull a fish out of the sea.' Morrison was on the verge of asking how he could possibly enforce such a threat but before he could do so the man went on softly. 'On the other hand, if you do, I'll undertake to buy the largest salmon of your catch every single day of the season.'

'Well –' Morrison shook his head doubtfully.

'Come on, man. We only have a week before my first reservation. And this chap's *important*.'

'We could try diverting the river back.' It was said with little confidence.

'You'll never do it. Come and see for yourself.'

Again Macleod's words proved to be only too true. The gap gouged out by the JCB had been made wider and deeper by the force of water, an increased flow resultant on the rain, and had dug itself into the new course. Repairing the gash would be no mean task and certainly beyond the ability of a few amateurs wielding spades. Morrison stared down thoughtfully into the enormous chasm of a dried-out pool before the two men walked alongside the river until it rejoined the original course tantalisingly close to, but just beyond, the hotelier's land.

135

'We'll have to talk to the Forestry Commission,' advised Morrison.

'They'll ask questions.'

'They're going to do that anyway. The point is, they're the only people with equipment that's up to the job. Even then its going to be one hell of a problem with the river in flood.'

'They'll take forever, man. I mean, they'd doubtless move quick enough if it was their fault but, as things are, they'll want to establish responsibility and all the rest of it.' They returned to the hotel property and Morrison was looking down into a second deep pool that was practically on the boundary. 'We've less than a week,' Macleod reminded him for the umpteenth time.

'There's water in this one,' observed Morrison. 'The pool above was dry.'

'We're fairly close to the sea here; there's a backwash on the spring tide.'

'How deep is it?'

'Very deep. Twenty feet or maybe more in the centre.'

'It's almost a miniature loch.' Morrison was gauging the width of the pool which, including its now dried-out rocky shores, must have been some sixty feet across.

'You have an idea?' Macleod asked. Then, as a statement, 'You have an idea. I can see it in your face.'

'It's rather wildcat, I'm afraid, and it probably won't work.'

'Come on, man,' cried the other excitedly, 'out with it.'

Morrison wasn't ready to commit himself. 'Could you run me into the village?'

Macleod was one who could appreciate those moments when action speaks louder than words. He clapped his hands together and hurriedly led the way to his car.

In the village, Morrison asked Macleod to pull up outside the fire station. The doors were closed and locked but the two men peered in through the windows at the gleaming red monster within.

'You're mad,' said Macleod.

'Not that one,' replied Morrison. 'I mean the old one parked round the back.' They walked around the side of the building and found the battered old vehicle, so recently replaced by a modern appliance, unceremoniously abandoned in a small yard.

'It'll no work; they'll never allow us.' He watched the younger man walk slowly round the old fire engine, taking in every detail, before turning back to the hotelier with mischievously excited eyes.

'Mr Macleod, I'm going to provide you with the only circulating salmon river in the world!'

Morrison's plan was as desperate as Macleod's concern. He'd resolved to hack away the downstream lip of the upper pool and replace it with a crude dam. Then, using the fire engine and taking advantage of the tidal backwash, refill it to the brim so that water could be released whenever the river effect was required.

'How long would it give us?' demanded Macleod.

'Maybe an hour, probably less.'

'But we could keep the engine pumping so it flowed continuously.'

'Hardly,' warned Morrison. 'River flow is measured in Cusecs – that is, cubic feet per second. Fire engines pump gallons per minute. But we could keep filling up the pool provided – er – you could keep your guest . . .' He hesitated as he sought for the word '. . . distracted.'

It took three whole days of the precious week for Macleod to persuade the local fire chief to let him hire the appliance for a month or so prior to necessary repairs being carried out on the ruptured river bank. He pitched in with every argument he knew, including modest bribery, but in the end the good man acquiesced for no better reason than the sheer pleasure of watching a few Sassenach holiday-makers attempting to fish a river where the water was going round and round. On the Thursday several locals saw them driving it up the hill towards The Last Resort and one or two of the brighter sparks worked out the reason. It was not long before everyone in the village had been told of Morrison's mad scheme but, tourism being an important factor in the community's income, not one word was breathed; after all, pulling the wool over the eyes of English visitors was part of the sport.

They parked the fire engine on a small plateau where it was hidden by the steep rockface of the waterfall and where its noise would be blocked by the stone cliff as well as the sound of falling water. They ran a pair of feeder hoses to the deep pool, concealing them without much difficulty in the undergrowth. 'Sink the intakes deep,' advised Morrison, 'there'll be a tremendous suction when we start up.'

They ran hoses up to the dried-out pool where Morrison's homemade lock-gates appeared strong if not picturesque. 'We must have more hose,' he declared. 'It's not pressure we want, but quantity.'

'I'll see what I can do,' said Macleod, hurrying away. Morrison decided that he liked the fellow. The landlord was so obviously a scoundrel, his chicanery so transparent, that it was fun to become a part of his opportunism. He opened fully the nozzles of the hoses they'd laid and returned to the plateau. He was not the least surprised when the engine fired immediately and the pump ran sweetly and smoothly – firemen are as proud of their machinery as ships' engineers. He ran fast uphill to the outlets where the water was gushing out satisfactorily but it was at once apparent that to fill the pool would take a minimum of twenty-four hours.

When Macleod returned the two men gazed disconsolately at the water flow, a pathetic dribble when compared with the rush required to achieve realism. 'Maybe I'd be wiser to just come clean with him,' muttered the hotelier.

'Like hell,' replied Morrison. 'Listen, when you launch out on a life of crime you have to learn faith in your fellow blackguards. Come on, let's lay the other hosepipes.'

As they worked Macleod said, 'I saw the Forestry boys whilst I was in the village. They've agreed to repair the breach.'

'When?'

'A couple of weeks, maybe three, no more. So you see,'

138

the hotelier went on as if it made everything all right, 'we'll only be pulling the con for a wee while.'

'When does this guest of yours arrive?'

'I told you. Saturday afternoon.'

'We might as well keep this thing pumping then, and fill the upper pool.'

The older man had a thought but hesitated before voicing it. 'Er, Morrison, those fish you're letting me have . . .'

'Yes?'

'You couldna keep some of them alive, could you?'

In the kitchen of the white house Biddy tucked into bread and jam watching Mrs Burgess slam the iron down on a shirt-tail and press a path towards the collar, shattering three buttons in the process. The housekeeper glanced at her and tried again to find a point of contact with the independent, self-willed child.

'Have you made any nice friends at school?'

'Not a lot.'

'You surprise me. I know several very well brought up children who attend Park Lodge.'

'So we run around the playground throwing a ball to each other. That doesn't make us friends.'

'You are a funny little girl.' Biddy squirmed under the patronising description. 'Who do you talk to when you want to *talk*?' Mrs Burgess gave the last word special emphasis to indicate she was referring to *private things*.

'I talk to Morrison.'

'Who, dear?'

'Morrison. He's my father!' The woman's a fool, thought Biddy.

'I've never heard of a child referring to her father by his surname.'

'Well now you just did,' but Biddy contrived to smother her reply under a massive mouthful of bread, rendering it indecipherable.

'I mean serious talk,' continued Mrs Burgess, '*personal*

139

talk. Sometimes a little girl prefers another woman.' The invitation was pathetically obvious.

'Morrison does just fine, thank you.'

'What about Miss Kelso, do you talk to her?'

'Only when she asks a question, and then it's kept pretty brief because mostly I don't know the answer.'

'I didn't mean schoolwork talk.'

'What's all this with *talking*? Why do I have to *talk* to people. What do we *talk* about?'

'Never mind, dear,' Mrs Burgess sighed dispiritedly, 'you'll find out when you're older.' She ran her iron violently up the front of Morrison's pants inflicting lasting damage. 'Sometimes I think you're not entirely a normal child. You're very grown up, which is a good thing in some ways I'm the first to admit, but you should never forget you're only young once. "Little girls are sugar and spice and all things nice," ' she purred poetically.

Oh God, spare me this, thought Biddy.

'Little girls should enjoy dressing up in pretty party clothes, playing with their dollies and learning how to sew and cook.'

'May I go now? I've finished tea.'

'Very well, dear, but heed what I've said.'

'Oh I will,' agreed Biddy generously. 'Although, I've got to tell you, it doesn't sound quite my scene.'

She ran out of the room but after a few seconds the door opened slowly and she came in again, her expression thoughtful. 'What sort of dressing up? she asked.

'Pardon, dear?'

'These girls who dress up. What do they wear?'

'Oh, well, when I was a toty wee thing everyone wanted us to look like Shirley Temple. She was a child film star in those days and she used to wear such pretty clothes. Party dresses, little boots and white socks, a ribbon in her hair . . . you know dear, you could look like her if you tried.'

Biddy flashed the housekeeper a smile of such devastating charm that the woman's heart melted. 'Thank you, Mrs Burgess. You've just given me an idea.'

*   *   *

Parkinson-Small left his London office at 12.30 on the Thursday to keep a lunch appointment with his solicitor. He arranged to meet Debbie at her flat that evening but during the afternoon he planned to visit Lillywhites of Piccadilly to 'get himself correctly kitted out'. First he set about the business of eating a good lunch, food and drink were matters to be taken seriously, and it was well after three before his chauffeur picked him up from the restaurant and dropped him outside the famous London store.

Parkinson-Small was as good a customer as he was a bad angler. Inexpert in assessing the technical merits of various accessories he settled instead for anything that was brightly coloured or gleamed with shiny varnish. A patient salesman spent an hour with him watching him try on green trousers and orange waistcoat which under a face reddened by exertion gave him the appearance of a squashed traffic light. Finally the salesman was rewarded by the sight of the tubby little man departing with plus-fours, check shirt, yellow tie, suede jacket, woollen socks, long waterproof leggings, several sets of flies, new rod and reel, gaff net, wicker lunch basket, and a very fine fisherman's hat. Parkinson-Small was nothing if not enthusiastic and stepped out into Piccadilly actually wearing his purchases. His chauffeur by that time was completing his twenty-eighth circuit of the block but drove clean past his employer, believing him to be an Easter edition of the Michelin tyre man.

When Macleod telephoned Morrison there was a positive note of panic in his voice. 'They're here,' he announced.

'Who's here?'

'My guests.'

'You said tomorrow afternoon,' objected Morrison without noticing the other man had slipped into the plural.

'I canna help that, they're here *now*.'

'Look, I'm terribly tied up here, Macleod,' pleaded Morrison.

'You canna let me down at this stage, man.' His voice was pitched several tones higher. 'This boy's a financial wizard in the City of London. Probably a useless fisherman but influential enough to keep my rooms filled until October!'

'Where is he now?'

'In the dining-room.'

'Can you keep him there?'

'I reckon it's the only place I *can* keep him. I'll dig out the special cognac.'

'Give me an hour. Whatever you do keep him inside the hotel.'

'Aye, I'll do my best.' Then he added, 'Though I'll no guarantee to hold the girl –' but Morrison had already rung off.

Before Morrison could rush out of the house the telephone rang a second time.

'Can't get to the bottom of this bullyboy affair.' It was Commander Campbell. 'Something fishy going on.'

'Look, not now, Commander. Can't we let sleeping dogs lie?'

'Dogs left alone don't lie, they rush around shagging the arse off each other. Must get it sorted out once and for all.' The commander was not a believer in pronouns.

'What do you want to do about it?'

'What about a spot of tea on Sunday? Bring your girl over.'

'I don't want any third degree stuff, she's had enough.'

'No, no. Thought not in my mind, assure you of that. Besides, might have been unjust – did a good job sweeping up that glass.'

'Okay, Sunday's fine but I must fly now.' He replaced the receiver and hurtled out of the house, shouting as he ran, 'Biddy, come with me. I need you.'

The girl joined him without question and within fifteen minutes they were on the banks of the dried out riverbed. By this time there was nobody within a twelve mile radius who had not heard about the circulating salmon river and, on an impulse, the local fire officer had called the second, brand new, fire engine to the scene. 'In for a penny, in for a pound,' he told Morrison. 'With both appliances running we might give you another quarter of an hour's flow.' Biddy looked around with interest; it seemed the fireman had been followed by half the village.

'Morrison, what the hell are we up to?'

'Don't swear, darling.'

He emerged carefully from the bushes and looked towards the distant hotel. Almost immediately he caught a desperate wave from the dining-room window and did his best to mime that both engines were about to start pumping and there would be some noise. Macleod seemed to understand but was clearly trying to warn him about something. Morrison couldn't figure out what the man meant but obviously there was no time to waste. He hurried back to the firemen and just missed seeing Debbie emerge from the hotel.

As he rounded the rockface the noise from the appliances sounded deafening but, incredibly, seemed to be deflected away from the pool itself. The tide was on the ebb and, with hundred of gallons being sucked out every minute, he was worried by the speed at which the level was falling. He hurried Biddy upstream to the homemade lock-gate.

'Who on earth built this?' she enquired.

'I did.'

Biddy made a rapid amendment to her tone. 'Good, isn't it!'

'Now listen. If you shin up that tree you can just see the lower pool. When I wave don't waste a second. Run for this sledgehammer and swipe out the wooden block. The entire gate will fall away so whatever you do, don't fall with it.'

'Okay.'

Morrison returned to the lower pool and practically bumped into Debbie.

'Hello,' she said.

'Hi. What are you doing here?'

'Weekending. What's up, is there a fire or something?'

'No, nothing serious. You wouldn't believe me if I told you.' He was glad to see her; the adrenalin was flowing fast and he was delighted she would see the fun.

Debbie said, 'I'm so pleased I ran into you. I wanted to –'

He stopped and took both her hands into his. 'So did I.' He smiled down at her. 'Let's forget that evening and start again, eh?'

By way of reply she stood on tiptoe and kissed him lightly on the lips. Biddy, perched unsteadily in a distant tree, saw the kiss and decided the scene needed breaking up. She climbed down and crossed to the sledgehammer.

Debbie took his arm and they walked towards the pool. 'Did you get my letter?'

'What letter?'

'I guess that answers my question.'

'What did it say?'

'It sort of apologised.'

Behind him the fire engine revved up its engine. 'Look, I'm a bit tied up here. Can I call you?'

'Sure.' She walked with him as he moved across to conceal evidence of the appliance having been by the pool. 'The letter also congratulated you on beating Bruce over the Ferguson property.'

'I have the inbuilt Highland sense of right and wrong to thank for that.'

'I'm glad anyway.' She looked again at the crowd and the two fire engines. 'What's going on here?'

He was filled recklessly with the spirit of dare-devilry. 'You catch us redhanded in a moment of subterfuge. There is some important buffer in the hotel who has arrived to fish a salmon river and it is important to Mr Macleod that he does just that.' He worked as he talked.

'But everyone comes here to do that.'

'Not directors of travel agencies. Now if you look carefully at *our* salmon river you will observe a rather important ingredient is missing.'

'There isn't any water,' she exclaimed in surprise.

'Ah-ha! You are not just a pretty face!'

'Well, *tell* him for God's sake.'

'There's no need. "Morrison & Macleod – miracles to order." ' The words died in his throat as there appeared through the overhanging shrubs a trickle of water which

144

grew instantly into a great flood. 'Christ, she's started it up!' he exclaimed.

'Good God,' she said, staring at the rushing stream. 'What a cheap fraud!' He looked at her in surprise. 'You've joined with Mr Macleod in one of his nasty confidence tricks,' she accused.

'To be perfectly honest we're trying to create a salmon river for one of the hotel's most valued guests.'

'You mean the old boy in the dining-room?'

'Yes. Do you know him?'

'He's my father.'

Parkinson-Small considered Macleod to be a jolly good chap. Not only had the fellow laid on a splendid lunch with a couple of powerful Martinis and a dashed drinkable wine, but here he was entertaining him with a rare recital on the bagpipes while he savoured a cognac. The only trouble was that everything in the room was becoming a trifle blurred.

'Don't wish to appear ungrateful and all that, but an hour of the pipes is a touch heady when you're not used to it.'

'Just one more lament – a little thing I wrote myself.'

'If you don't mind, my dear chap. Feel I must have a breath of fresh air. Can't wait to try the water, to be frank.'

'Ah.' Macleod glanced out of the window. He could see the new fire engine reversing slowly out of sight and suddenly someone waved to him. He gave a definite start and looked again – it was Debbie. He turned to Parkinson-Small. 'Very good. I'll take you down myself.' His guest stood up unsteadily. Dressed in his incongruous fishing attire he looked like a refugee from a carnival float.

When the two men emerged from the hotel, Macleod was surprised to see some thirty local sightseers disporting themselves with carefully acted casualness along the banks of his private river. Several had brought their rods with them and were giving so burlesque a performance of enthusiastic amateur anglers that he wondered whether their presence would be a help or a hindrance. The important guest who waddled at his side looked like someone out of a Christmas pantomime but his heart sank when he saw Morrison talking to Debbie. The awful truth would emerge and his charade would be exposed.

Determined to play out his role to the bitter end he led Parkinson-Small to the water's edge.

Morrison had done a fine job, he was the first to admit it. The river gurgled and chattered its way over the stones just as briskly as if it were the real thing. The faint roar of the concealed pump was practically drowned by the waterfall. As Parkinson-Small made his appearance he drew a faint round of respectful applause which, Macleod thought, was overdoing it.

Now he was actually here some of Parkinson-Small's confidence deserted him. As a matter of fact he wasn't feeling exactly on top of things. He was aware of smiling faces, rushing water, the sound of wind, and the swirl of the current as he stepped out to make his first cast. Just an hour or so, he thought, time enough to get down to the real thing on Monday.

After only five minutes he felt a tug on his line. A tremendous sense of excitement coursed through his veins; a catch on his first outing would be something, especially in front of all these nice people. The pull was steady and he tried to control a rising panic that he should lose the fish.

'I've got something here,' he called.

Macleod was by his side in an instant, realising with alarm that what his guest could feel on his line was the suction from the powerful pump. 'Play it carefully, man,' he advised with an anxious glance towards Morrison. Parkinson-Small reeled in but the tug lessened as he drew away from the submerged outlet valve. 'Let her swim awhile,' tried Macleod. The little man took a step forward and the pull increased so rapidly that he slipped causing his brand-new Lillywhite hat to fall into the water. He reached for it at once but to his inebriated eye it seemed to make three quick circles and disappear down a whirlpool.

He was sorry to lose his hat but Parkinson-Small had true red sporting blood in him and, at this moment, playing his fish was the first priority. Nevertheless he did not pretend anything other than surprised delight when ten minutes later he saw his hat floating downstream towards him.

146

Unfortunately once more he wasn't quick enough and he watched it stop just out of reach, whizz round three times, and disappear again.

At the same moment his line jerked. The rod came alive in his grasp. This was it! A strong fish, a real fighter, but now he felt capable of landing it. Slowly, slowly, backwards. Wind in a few turns. The salmon was weakening. He was patient, cool and collected, only his bristling moustache betraying his determination to impress the crowd who by this time were on their feet.

Macleod was aware of a voice speaking quietly just behind him. 'It's all right, Mr Macleod,' said Debbie, 'you're secret is safe with me.' He looked round with an expression of profound relief which changed into doubt as the girl added, 'For the time being at any rate.'

At that moment Parkinson-Small lifted his rod to the vertical and his catch broke surface.

He'd caught his hat. It looked a bit mangled but it was definitely his hat.

To Morrison's horror the river's flow ceased as instantly as it had begun, and far sooner than he'd anticipated. The lower pool emptied like a bath until Parkinson-Small, still holding his rod at a forty-five degree angle, was standing in a puddle of water that lapped around his ankles. The assembled villagers gave him a generous round of applause.

As soon as lunch was finished the next day Biddy disappeared into her bedroom to prepare herself for a social event and, bearing in mind Mrs Burgess's advice about little girls being sugar and spice and all things nice, she delved into the back of her wardrobe in search of something suitable to wear.

An hour later she descended the stairs and Morrison could scarcely believe his eyes. She wore a party frock made for her by Wendy for some school play long since past. It fell straight from the yoke, with puff sleeves and a flower-basket appliquéd on the front of the skirt. She had put on small buckskin boots over white socks and she'd tied a blue ribbon bow in her hair.

Whilst they walked the distance to the Campbells' house this scrubbed-faced picture of innocence developed a lisp and suddenly forgot how to pronounce her 'r's'.

Morrison, who had twice awoken in the small hours worrying into his ill-tempered treatment of his daughter earlier in the week, decided against enquiring into the girl's motives behind the charade; there was some devious plan afoot and he felt the less he knew about it the better.

'Hello, you two,' the commander called as they came through the garden gate and approached the house. 'How are you, Morrison? Good week with the nets?'

'Excellent, thank you.'

'Good.' The black eyes swung down on to Biddy. 'Now then, young lady, let's you and I make a fresh start, eh?'

'Yeth pleathe, Mithter Campbell.'

He couldn't recall the lisp but the first meeting had been brief and he'd been considerably annoyed. 'It's Bridget isn't it?' he confirmed as he shook the tiny hand and looked into her green eyes with their childlike naivety. 'Andrew,' he bellowed into the house.

His son emerged unwillingly, avoiding his father's gaze and looking nervously at Biddy. 'You haven't met my son, have you? Andrew, shake hands with Bridget.'

'Hello, Andwew.' The green eyes turned to him without recognition.

'He had an unfortunate encounter with three bullying louts who'll know which side their bread's buttered if I catch up with them,' the commander continued. 'Two of the wretches pinned his arms and the third set about him.'

'So you were telling me,' murmured Morrison.

'What a wotten twick,' added Biddy.

They met Mrs Campbell and the five drank tea and ate cucumber sandwiches, Biddy and Andrew sitting quietly whilst the grown-ups talked about naval philosophies and salmon fishing expertise.

'Salmon eh?' he barked at Morrison at one point. 'I'm uncommonly partial to a slice of smoked salmon washed

148

down with a glass of chilled Chablis. Do you smoke it yourself?' A pent-up premature chuckle forecast the joke in its wake. 'Or are you trying to give it up?' whereupon a torrential outburst of laughter thundered around the room crashing against the polite smiles which greeted it. 'D'you want me to fix an order?'

'A regular order certainly wouldn't go amiss.'

'A nice drop of fresh salmon never came to any harm. Leave it to me, they might be chopping the defence budget to shreds but I'm damn sure the officers' mess can run to a weekly feed on your salmon.'

'Thank you very much.'

Campbell waved a hand, brushing away gratitude. 'My dear fellow, I admire a man with spirit, d'you see? Take the troubles you've encountered; did you give way beneath the burden? Did your spirit desert you? No sir, it did not! Dammit, you came to the Scottish coast and set up your own business. Damned laudable!' Then the commander went on to talk about his son, a fourteen-year-old of whom he was immensely proud. From his description the boy sounded something of a terror but Morrison smiled at the big man's loud enthusiasm and interjected complimentary phrases whenever there was a pause. It was clear he had stumbled across a man of influence and this was a commodity both his new business and his public relations could well use.

Every now and then the commander looked across at Biddy, clearly trying to reconcile the child in his living room with the tousled tomboy he'd met on the roadway. 'Why don't you take Biddy upstairs and show her your train set,' he suggested to Andrew.

'Would you like to?' the boy asked.

'Where ith it?' she enquired.

'In my bedroom.'

'You want me to go to hith bedroom?' The eyes came round to her father, a wicked glint in them, small hand balling into a fist out of sight of all but him. The grown-ups laughed at her innocent question and sat back comfortably after the children had left the room.

149

As soon as they were alone Andrew turned to the girl. 'What's with the lisp?' he asked, only to find his manliness suffered a nasty jolt as the sugar and spice child hung her head. 'I'm thowwey I thtwuck you in the fathe, Andwew,' she said contritely.

'Hey, steady, not so loud.'

'Okay, Buster, hear this.' Her voice developed a sudden rough edge as she allowed herself to release the feelings of injustice she'd kept bottled up over several days. 'You and me are going to do a deal, right? I'll keep quiet about the non-existing bullyboys if you tell your dad you were with me when we threw the glass.'

'I can't.'

'Morrison said I was to apologise to you and I'll do it in front of your dad if you don't agree.'

'He'll kill me.'

'And Morrison will suggest a stone-throwing contest on the beach.' The voice reverted – 'And I can't thwow thtoneth for thauthageth!'

The Campbells were greatly impressed by Morrison and utterly enchanted with his daughter. As they all bid each other farewell she managed to grind her heel into the boy's foot, simultaneously whispering sweetly, 'Don't forget.'

On the way home Morrison asked, 'How are you going to remember to continue that burlesque performance on every occasion we meet the Campbells in future?'

'It won't be necessary,' she replied confidently.

Biddy was right. That evening Andrew faced his father and, with pale face and faltering voice, he made a clean breast of the greenhouse affair and went on to own up that there had been no fifth form louts. This last was beyond the agreement with Biddy but it was the only means he could think of to ever establish credibility in front of the girl. In any event it was the first time in his life he'd told the full truth to the commander and, to his absolute amazement, he found an understanding he never knew existed. When he came to the bit about Biddy landing an upper-cut and a left-cross the older man let forth a deep chuckle, and, reaching out an arm, drew his son to him. They had never before shared a confidence and the feeling was good.

Morrison prayed he had seen an end to the interruptions and distractions in order that he might concentrate his undivided attention to the business of catching fish. Unhappily the dreadful week was still to reach its conclusion. Although the farcical affair of Macleod's river and the necessary tea-party with the Campbells had both taken place over the weekend and, thus far, he had not let down his crew, it couldn't be denied he'd made a pretty bad start. He looked down at the girl walking beside him.

'We'll put all that behind us, eh?'

'Yes.'

'Let's pretend this weekend never happened.'

'Does that include your dinner with the Debbie woman last night?' she enquired.

He grinned at her protective and suspicious face. 'You don't have to worry about her. When her father had caught his own hat after it had bobbed down the river twice he sort of sussed out he was being made a fool of. He wasn't too pleased. I doubt we'll be seeing Miss Debbie again.'

'And I don't suppose we're Mr Macleod's best friends either.'

'You suppose right.'

'What with my bulldozer and your circulating river we're not doing too good are we.'

'Doing too *well*,' he corrected.

'Yeah. We're not doing that either.'

'Never mind. Tomorrow morning we make a fresh start.'

The white house came into view. There was a small car parked outside.

'Uh-huh!' said Biddy.

'Whose is the car?'

'I'm just going upstairs to change my clothes.'

She ran off. Inside the house he found his visitor being entertained after their own fashion by Buzby and Bobo.

'How nice to see you,' he said as he shook hands.

'Forgive me for calling unannounced,' apologised Caroline Kelso. 'I wondered if we could have a quiet word.

It's about Biddy!'

The teacher left again sixty minutes or so later and, the subject of their conversation having failed to appear downstairs, Morrison climbed up to her bedroom. Biddy lay in bed fast asleep, her clothes strewn about the room, and MacGregor lying protectively on the eiderdown. It was barely seven-thirty and he pondered whether to awaken the girl and take up the matter without further ado – he doubted she was really asleep anyway. Then he thought maybe she'd had enough for one week, he was jolly sure he had. He gathered together the discarded clothes, putting some in the wardrobe, others in drawers, and the remainder he put aside for washing. Her anorak lay bundled in a corner of the room and when he picked it up something rustled in the pocket. He unzipped the opening and pulled it out.

It was Debbie's letter.

CHAPTER SIX

MARCH TURNED into April and the days grew longer. The winds lessened, the sun increased in strength, and the cold lost its bitterness. Currents caused by heavy rains and melting snow affected the tidal streams in firths and lochs, and in long narrow lochs like that which lay near to Skerrymor Bay, where the drainage area was small, the outgoing tidal stream greatly increased in duration and rate.

It's possible that the abnormal conditions somehow affected the salmon run, fishermen will always find a reason for everything, but the simple truth was that that year the catches continued to remain negligible for an unduly long time. They were worrying days for Morrison. The crew had to be paid, transport costs met, fuel purchased, together with countless overheads, quite apart from repayments on the bank loan. The paltry returns fell far short of the weekly outgoings. They had been successful in bringing into play all the nets as well as ancillary equipment and each station was visited twice daily. In bed at night he fell into an immediate sleep of exhaustion to awaken in the small hours and suffer a procession of misgivings until dawn brought a second spell of unrefreshing slumber. His nightmares paid regular visits and Biddy always shook him out of them, but then they didn't laugh together as they'd used to.

The first half of the month was made significant by the occurrence, in different places, of three spectacular arguments. In one way or another each was to affect the future life of Morrison and Biddy.

The first of these took place in the London house of Bruce Cornelius and his wife.

'You're never going up to that Scottish hell-hole this weekend, are you?' she demanded.

'Why not?' It was his regular response to the familiar cue.

' 'Cos I'm going to left here on my tod, that's why,' she retorted. 'I wouldn't say no to being took out myself once in a while.'

'You got took out – ' He remembered his better education and started again. 'I took you out Tuesday and Wednesday.'

'Yer, great,' she agreed sarcastically. 'Stuck at a top table between two dreary businessmen whose small talk run out after they agreed about the weather. What d'you get up to, anyway?'

'Where?'

'You know where. Your lah-di-bloody-dah Scottish mansion.'

'I gotta lotta business up there.'

'That's not what I heard.' She poured coffee from an expensive percolator into a bone china cup, slopped in cream from a solid silver jug, and spooned in brown sugar until the liquid slopped into the saucer. He turned his head away, he couldn't bear her clumsy habits. 'I think I might come wiv yer,' she mused.

'You'd be bored outta your skull,' he warned nervously. 'We don't even get to talk about the weather.'

'What happened about that fishery place you was after?'

'I never got it, did I? Someone else beat me to it, didn't he?'

'What did you want it for?'

' 'Cos he wanted it.'

'Who's "he"?'

'Just somebody.'

'You never give over, do you?'

'Not if I can help it.'

'You're materialistic, d'you know that?' It was the longest word she knew. 'Too materia-bloody-listic by far.'

'Yeah, well, somebody has to keep up with your spending habits.'

She pointed a warning bone-china cup at his face. 'You can keep that right out of it,' she shouted. 'You going up north wiv yer fancy bits o' skirt is one thing but making snide comments about my spending is something else. Oh yes, I know what goes on in that Highland hidy-hole 'n one of these days I'm comin' up to catch you at it.'

The confrontation might not have been blessed with style but at least both parties managed to put their point across. The second argument took place in Yorkshire and was of a quieter, more insidious, nature. On this occasion neither protagonist ever voiced their precise meaning.

'There'll be some who have not been to Mass this morning,' Martha said to Patrick as they left the Catholic church.

'I dare say,' sighed her husband, knowing to a word all that was to follow.

'Despite his marriage vows,' she continued bitterly whilst simultaneously flashing a society smile at a neighbour. 'They promise that offspring of the union will be brought up in the Catholic faith, but there are those who are all the same as the rest.'

'He's going through a difficult time.'

'And doubtless missing the good influence of a daughter who knew where her duties lay, God rest her.'

'In fairness,' he said slowly, 'they had begun to lapse long before the Lord took her from us.'

'You'll not say that in my hearing,' cried Martha angrily. 'You're a fine one to find fault, I will say!'

'I wasn't –'

'You'll not deny he stood before the priest and made a solemn vow about following the preachings of the Church.'

'Yes, yes. I know all that. But we're not in any position to cast aspersions until we see for ourselves how he's bringing her up.'

'I'll not be gagged. Nor will I be seen in that Godforsaken place.'

'Then you can keep your opinions to yourself.'

'Don't you dare speak to me like that. If you were half a man you'd have had the courts on to him by this time and brought our grand-daughter safely to where she belongs.'

They walked the rest of the way home in silence.

The third argument took place outside the boathouse in Skerrymor Bay.

'What did Miss Kelso want?' sobbed Biddy.

'Well it wasn't to give you the Victor Ludorum!' He glared down at the child. 'Will you tell me what it is gets *into* you? And why everyone I meet complains about your behaviour?'

'I don't know. Maybe 'cos I hate school and the school hates me.'

'Nonsense.'

'You don't understand, Morrison. I was getting on well at Saint Elizabeth's before I had to leave.'

'Your last report was the worst I ever saw.'

'Yes, but they understood me there. Here I'm just a foreigner.'

'Miss Kelso knows your good points as well as your bad ones, and was fair about them both.'

'She I hate most of all.'

He was surprised. 'Why?'

'I just do.'

The teacher had stayed for nearly an hour, speaking earnestly, eyes grave beneath severely set fair hair. 'Bridget is the most interesting pupil I've ever taught. Incredibly intelligent for her age, a quick alert mind, and a simply tremendous imagination.' She creased her forehead in unspoken apology for what was to follow. 'It's this last which so often proves her undoing. She dreams up outrageous pranks and her leadership causes other girls to follow. She can be extremely wicked.'

'Oh Lord,' he'd groaned.

'No, wait. It's not all bad!' She'd sat forward in her chair, a hand moving instinctively towards his before being checked. 'Every now and then I find myself tuned to her wavelength; it was an accident first time but now I search for it whenever I can. It would be so wrong to crush that spirit by misguided punishment.' She'd spoken with deep sincerity and there'd been a pause as her grey eyes met his. 'Which is why I'm being disloyal to the headmistress and calling to see you unbeknown.'

'I appreciate that.'

'Janet and I don't always see things the same way, and I know she intends to talk to you herself about Biddy. When she does I want you to know there are two sides to every argument.'

And here was Biddy declaring a dislike for the only friend she seemed to have at Park Lodge. He remembered wishing Miss Kelso would smile just once and regretted the serious subject matter which kept her face so concerned.

Biddy said, 'Maybe you'd see things clearer if you realised I'm going through a difficult age!'

They were bad days.

The coastline on either side of Skerrymor Bay was bordered by steep cliffs whilst a range of high hills in the hinterland ran roughly parallel with the coast. In winter onshore winds whose direction was slightly inclined to the coastline were deflected to blow directly down the Sound of Sleat and, where this narrowed at a point only a few miles from the bay, there was often a big increase in speed. With the coming of spring a few days of settled weather brought local peculiarities due to the topography. The sea breeze blew instead towards the land and became quite strong during the afternoon but dropped to a flat calm around sunset. In the night a gentler land breeze took over until morning. One day the sun shone continuously and for eight hours warmed the land by several degrees. Through the night the land gave up its heat to the night wind and this relatively warm air flowed over a colder sea until the dew-point and sea temperature converged, resulting in thick fog.

When Morrison looked out of his bedroom window the workboat was lost to view and, within half an hour, he was rowing Buzby and Bobo through the quiet of a dead calm. Now they leaned over the side of the sturdy workboat and

157

together stuck their fingers through the holes of the bag net. They met with a sheer weight never previously encountered and, drawing deep breaths of thrilling anticipation, the three began to heave it in at the same time as Morrison and Buzby shifted their grasp and moved towards Bobo in the centre to force the netted salmon into a more confined space. Then with a final gut-wrenching haul they brought the catch inboard and, without allowing themselves even a few seconds' breather, faced a frantic five minutes stunning the threshing, gasping, mass of fish.

Generally speaking the atmospheric conditions that result in fog are not good for net fishing so the crew considered their hauling in a bag net teeming with fine quality salmon to be nothing short of a well-deserved miracle. Morrison could not remember experiencing a deeper sense of satisfaction which was only slightly marred by considerable physical exhaustion. They brought the workboat inshore and he called to Biddy to telephone Mr MacPherson in Glasgow to tip him off and also to ask Sigmund to meet them at the second station where his added strength was needed.

MacPherson said, 'Tell your father I know already and we're all standing by. Reports have been coming in from all round the coast. There'll be a drop in the price, that's inevitable, but even so I think we'll make him a happy man.'

'I'll tell him, Mr MacPherson.'

'Aye. And Biddy, when you box them be sure to pack the fish tummy side up.'

'Tummy side up, right,' repeated the girl in agreement. 'Er, why is that, Mr MacPherson?'

'Because they look better and they eat better, that's why.'

For day after day the four-man crew performed the strength-sapping task five times in the morning and five times more in the early evening. In addition they completely changed one net each day in order to maintain a regular rotation of cleaning and repair. By close time on the first Saturday following the start of the run they had run out of boxes, out of ice, and out of strength. Morrison, particularly, was grey from exhaustion.

'Are you okay?' Sigmund enquired anxiously.

'Sure. Glad to see the weekend though.'

'When did you last see the doctor?'

'There's nothing wrong with me MacPherson's cheque can't cure.'

'You could leave the three of us to handle a few trips while you stay ashore and supervise despatch,' suggested the German.

'Go through all I've been through only to miss the fun?'

'Don't overdo it, my friend, there are too many people depending on you.'

The following Tuesday the team netted and marketed seventy fine fish which was to stand as a record for the season. By coincidence that day saw the arrival of MacPherson's cheque for the previous week and Skerrymor Fisheries were able to make the first meaningful repayment against the bank loan. In that moment Morrison knew without question he was going to succeed.

Mr Peregrine's London office was of modest proportions to say the least. He did not object to the cramped 'cupboard' allotted to him because he preferred to be out in the field anyway. He disliked paperwork intensely and the small tufts of grey hair above each ear stuck out horizontally as a result of both hands scratching his head to encourage the brain within. The Scottish Report worried him. Not so much the accident which had caused the temporary diversion of a river, no lasting damage had occurred, but the brief paragraph referring to poaching. Although it was too early in the year to expect activity of any size, reports of movement inside specialised nesting areas were disturbing. His discomfort was made the more so by a letter in the same post drawing the society's attention to illegal bird trading in the public bar of an East End public house.

It was something that needed looking into.

*   *   *

He heard a click as the receiver was lifted. '426,' her voice announced.

'Miss Kelso?'

'Yes'

'It's David Morrison.'

'Oh hello.' Her voice warmed in recognition and, strangely, he felt a tingle of pleasure.

'I promised to get in touch so that we could compare notes about Biddy.'

'Yes. When would you like to do that?'

'Well, as a matter of fact, I don't have a great deal to report. Not much that's good, at any rate. You heard about the greenhouse saga?'

'No.'

'Oh. Well, we could discuss that, I suppose. Has there been any word from Miss Mahoney?'

Her voice hesitated. 'There has been a certain development in that direction,' she said carefully.

'She hasn't called me yet.'

'No, I know. I think I can explain why, but not on the telephone.'

'Okay. Then we ought to meet. Shall I come to the school?'

'That wouldn't be a terribly good idea.'

'Where then? I wonder, would you care to come here to lunch one day?'

'I'd love to.' She sounded genuinely pleased.

'That would be marvellous. Could you manage Saturday? About midday?'

'I'll look forward to it.'

Buzby and Bobo had asked if they could borrow the car that weekend and take a tent to Glencoe. Their energy seemed boundless. Biddy planned to spend the day with Cluny and, for no reason he could define clearly, he didn't mention the appointment with her schoolteacher.

He was outside the house when the car arrived and he walked down the drive to meet her. She wore a dusky pink pleated skirt and flowered chiffon blouse with soft frills around her neck. Her fair hair was set less severely than previously and as she straightened up from stepping out of the car she touched it lightly as if to check a new style.

'Am I late?' she enquired.

'Slightly, but well worth waiting for. You look awfully nice.'

'Thank you.' She smiled with her eyes as well as her mouth and walked beside him to the house, standing only an inch or so shorter than he.

'Drink?'

'Please.'

'What would you like?'

'Something long and cold.'

'Right.' He poured Cinzano Bianco into a crystal tumbler, topped it up with lemonade, added several cubes of ice and a twist of lemon. She crossed to the window to take in the view.

'You can see Skye very clearly.'

'When you can see Skye clearly it means it's going to rain, and when you can't, it *is* raining.' He repeated the old joke to relax the strangeness between them and she laughed politely.

'I hear you're doing terribly well.'

'These past weeks haven't been bad at all.'

'Congratulations. It was a courageous bid.'

'I have a wonderful crew. Me, I'm still learning.'

'Do you ever hear from Old Ferguson?'

'Once only. A formal acknowledgement of various papers.'

'A strange man. He used to take me out in the workboat when I was a little girl.'

He handed her the drink. 'It's still the same boat. I'll take you out in it again if you'd care to come.' Then he added with a grin, 'Now you're a big girl.'

'We'll see.' She sat gracefully into a cane chair from which she could continue looking out across the Sound. 'To be absolutely honest I'm not terribly keen on being afloat. I'm easily frightened.'

'It's only sensible to have a healthy respect for the sea.'

'Healthy respect is one thing. Arrant fear is something

161

else. I say, this is the most delicious drink I've ever tasted,' she said, changing the subject.

They persevered with idle inconsequential chat for a full half-hour, contented to allow the main subject of their meeting to take its place in the natural progress of conversation. He liked the tall, quiet girl sitting in his living-room, and through the exploration of a variety of topics he discovered a dry and occasionally devastating wit and a warm laugh when something he said appealed to her sense of humour. Neither made any conscious effort to flatter the other but gradually the exchanges became easier as chords were touched and responded to.

'Are you hungry?'

'Starving.'

'Good. I love to share a meal with a hungry girl.'

'What are you giving me to eat?'

'You'll never guess!'

'Not fresh salmon?'

'Don't you like it?' he asked in sudden anxiety.

'Like it? I adore it. Listen, fresh salmon might be bread and butter to you but it's sheer luxury to the rest of us.'

He opened a chilled bottle of Sancerre; they began with a small Ogen melon before the salmon mayonnaise and crisp salad, followed by cheese, biscuits and coffee. After lunch they decided to walk the clifftops for a couple of hours. Morrison had been prepared to hunt out a pair of Wendy's boots but the girl quickly stopped him, saying she carried shoes and wellingtons for all contingencies in the boot of her car.

An hour later they walked comfortably side by side, the afternoon sun warm on their faces, a gentle breeze zephyring in from the sea, the waves breaking gently a hundred feet below them. As he'd locked the front door she'd said with mock formality, 'You keep a good table, Mr Morrison.'

'Please call me David.'

'Fine. As you know, I'm Caroline.'

'May I call you Carrie?'

'If you want to. Why?'

'It's my favourite name.' Now, as they took the narrow lane that would bring them back to the house by a different, inland route, at last he raised the question of Biddy. 'Why haven't I received the dreaded call from the headmistress?' he asked.

She drew a deep breath and slowed the pace slightly. She was immensely relieved that more than three hours had elapsed without his raising the subject – had he done so earlier she knew she would have been less forthcoming with her answer. 'Because,' she said, 'Janet Mahoney and I have had a terrible argument.'

'Not about my daughter, surely?'

'No. Although it's perfectly true to say that Biddy was the catalyst, and Janet would think that in seeing you she would be scoring points off me rather than genuinely pursuing Biddy's interests. Whatever her failings,' she added, 'Janet is scrupulously fair where the children are concerned.' But less fair with her sycophantic servant, she thought as she recalled the tumultuous rage her threat to resign had provoked. Shouted accusations which became personal as well as professional. At first Caroline had been shocked, then she knew she had to escape from the woman's clutches.

'Bear with me if parts of this are fairly incoherent. To start with I ought to give you the last sentence first to prevent you worrying needlessly about your daughter. Biddy is a simply marvellous kid with more personality in her little finger than the rest of my class put together. With that level of devotion towards you, that level of all-devouring interest in everything natural taught her by yourself, Sigmund, and even Cluny, and that level of sheer energy, it's scarcely surprising if the whole thing blows up from time to time. Sitting behind a school desk must be purgatory on earth for that child and, frankly, I need to be convinced about exactly how much good a formal schooling does to a mind like hers.'

'Or harm? Is that what you're saying?'

'No, I'm not.' She shook her head positively. 'All I'm saying is that while we persist with *this* type of education for

163

that type of pupil then we have no right to get up-tight when it backfires on us.' She gave a tight smile. 'It is on that point that Janet and I disagree so fundamentally.'

'What is your alternative?'

She glanced at the side of his face. 'I suppose it's no secret that Biddy considers herself to be an absolute dummy at maths?'

'Three end of term reports since primary school have brainwashed us into believing it.'

'Right. Then let me tell you something. I went out and bought her a book on coastal navigation, and an Admiralty chart. She and I sat down together, and d'you know what we did? We plonked you in the middle of the Sound of Sleat in a sailing boat doing six knots with a three-knot current driving you sideways but reducing its strength as the tide fell, and threatening to change direction after slack water. We had to give you a course to steer for Skerrymor Bay and, of course, that meant we had to know exactly where you were and how long the journey would take.' Her eyes were excited now and her voice enthusiastic. 'Suddenly Biddy realised what mathematics is all about and that moment of discovery was my most satisfying experience in six years of teaching.'

'Did I make it home all right?' he enquired.

'I reckon you could take her out there and give her a practical test. She might not get her sums right first time but the point is she understands *why* she's doing them. Better yet, she *enjoys* it!'

Now Morrison looked at the teacher with open admiration. 'You are exactly the type of person Biddy responds to and needs. I'm no academic, God knows, but I agree with your approach.'

This time she didn't respond to the warmth of his words. 'Well, that's it,' she said, 'you'd better hear the rest. I'm leaving Park Lodge at the end of term and probably leaving the district altogether shortly afterwards. I have to break free, David, before it's too late. I think the argument over Biddy opened my eyes to what's happening to me.'

Back in the white house he made a pot of tea and they

drank it together before she insisted on helping him clear away the lunch.

'I'm genuinely sorry you'll be leaving the school,' he said as they worked side by side in the kitchen. 'I value your advice about Biddy but I think I'll let the problem look after itself for a week or two because, strangely enough, I'm more concerned about you just at the moment. I feel extremely guilty if our arrival on the scene has upset the *status quo*.'

'Please don't regard it like that. How could you possibly assume any responsibility? Anyway,' she went on, 'it's probably a good thing. The day had to come eventually.'

'Do you really consider it necessary to leave the district altogether?'

'Yes. Besides, I think I want to go. It's all too easy to fall into the trap of believing that life begins and ends in Skerrymor Bay.'

'Where will you go?'

'Look,' she said firmly, 'I intended to talk about myself in so far as it related to Biddy's education. I've already said far more than I should.' She smiled her warm smile. 'You are particularly easy to talk to. But the rest is plain boring and we'd do better to change the subject.'

He was washing up the lunch plates and she stood near him with the wiping-up towel. He turned and faced her. 'I don't think you're boring at all,' he said.

The back door burst open and Biddy came in, breathless and ready to dive headlong into an excited account of her day. She saw the schoolmistress taking the plate from her father, a domestic moment of unaffected naturalness. The young girl stopped dead in her tracks as she experienced another of those emotional lurches as hitherto dormant instincts belonging exclusively to the female of the species warned her to defend her territory for the second time. Debbie had never posed much of a challenge with her obvious prettiness and transparent shallowness, but this one was far more dangerous. This one was calm, serene, assured, and *older*. This one could wreck everything.

*　　　*　　　*

Biddy lay stock still, not daring to move the binoculars from her eyes. She didn't stir for a full five minutes, the sun hot on the back of her head, the eyepieces steaming up, an ant crawling up her leg. Ten feet away Cluny sat in the shade of a tree, leaning against the trunk and sucking on an empty pipe. He marvelled at the determination written in every muscle of the girl's slight figure. It was she who had spotted it out of the corner of her eye, then just once again as she turned her head. Cluny, instinctively, advised her to keep walking and they carried on, without varying their pace, until they'd rounded a hillock whereupon they'd doubled back to the spot, crawling flat on their stomachs.

At last she whispered, 'Yes. There it is again!' A telltale glint for a fraction of a second but long enough to pinpoint the position. Now, through the glasses, she could see the man. He'd been within her field of vision all the time but only when he raised his own pair of binoculars was she able to distinguish him from the undergrowth concealing him.

She heard a soft rustle and Cluny was up alongside her. He took the glasses, resting his elbows to steady them. 'The big pine tree, taller than all the others,' Biddy directed.

'Got it.'

'Move down to its base then slowly look left about two hundred yards until you hit a patch of broom.'

He obeyed until the brilliant splash of yellow came into view. 'Got it.'

'He's at the top end, half hidden by the shrubs.'

'I canna see him.'

'You will. I waited ages.'

He preferred to trust her young eyes and, instead, shifted his attention upwards and to the left. The magnified image revealed a narrow track winding upwards. 'I've found his car,' he muttered after a while. 'It's red, I can't tell the make.'

'He'll have left the road at Pintarroch Point,' she surmised, 'and bumped along the forest track until he was out of sight.'

'Aye,' agreed Cluny. 'Concealed from the road but not from here.'

166

'He wouldn't expect anyone to overlook him from this side.'

'He's right. Only idiots like us climb up scrub covered rock faces!'

She threw him a grin. Then, 'Can you see what he's looking at?'

'Not yet, but I can guess.'

Again it was the girl who spotted them first. A pair of golden eagles, soaring and gliding in majestic flight, wing-tips splayed out and upturned. She watched them as they dived to hunt the forest and fields, skimming low with strong, controlled wingbeats. Their flight prompted Cluny to jerk his binoculars back to the broom and now he saw the man, whose attention had been similarly attracted.

'Listen,' he said. 'He's got black hair, thin on top, a small moustache. I think his face is sort of blotchy red but maybe he's hot like I am.'

'Fat or thin? Short or tall?'

'I canna tell, he's sitting down. Thick-set I think. Beer-belly. Young, perhaps twenty-five or thirty.'

The eagles soared back into view, climbing almost vertically for several hundred feet, before gliding lazily downwards in immense circles. Biddy grabbed the glasses and followed the last few seconds of the flight before the magnificent birds wing-braked and came to rest together. 'I've pinpointed the nest,' she said triumphantly. She swung her glasses back to the man. 'So has he,' she added soberly. She continued to stare intently through the binoculars. 'I don't like you,' she muttered to herself, 'with your big fat tummy and greedy eyes.'

Many species of British birds have found themselves in a situation of declining population due partially to their naturally slow rate of reproduction but more particularly to the unwelcome attention paid by various interested parties in their eggs and chicks. Over-enthusiastic, impatient bird-watchers cause nests to be abandoned, photographers failing to follow an agreed code of practice frighten nesting pairs from their security; but the professional illegal bird trader has caused far and away the more serious loss.

Worse, the rarer the breed the more active his attention until the eggs and chicks of endangered breeds become as marketable as gold nuggets. Sometimes operating in gangs the thieves are as skilled in their crime as the protectionists in their conservation and the introduction of laws coupled with severe penalties serve only to make the prize more attractive.

The telephone rang in the white house and Morrison picked up the receiver. 'Hello.'

It was Macleod. 'I've got your daughter here, Mr Morrison.'

His heart sank. 'Oh God, what's she done *now*?'

'Done? Like as not she's done us all a power of good, laddie,' barked the hotelier. 'What's the matter with you, do you no have faith in your own kinfolk?'

'What's up, anyway?'

'Can you get over here? Your wee bairn has spotted a poacher and we're planning a council of war.'

They were gathered in the bar of The Last Resort. The doors were closed and the drinkers were invitees of Macleod. Mrs Macleod was serving toasted snacks to their guests.

'We have to move fast.'

'Tonight?' urged Commander Campbell.

'We'll be needing a measure of official support,' advised Mrs Macleod, with a look towards the local police force whose head was deep inside his tankard. 'You can be sure there's more than one and we don't want to lose them,' she went on.

'Question is,' posed the commander, 'is there anything there for them to steal?' His eyes turned to Biddy. 'Did you see any eggs?'

'I'm sorry, sir, we were almost a mile away.'

'No,' declared Cluny positively. 'The birds were hunting together. But it'll no be long.'

Macleod, who had assumed leadership, made up his mind. 'Right. We'll have to catch them red-handed so best we keep watch as well.'

'Surely,' protested Morrison, 'they must have their eyes

168

on nests all over the place. Shouldn't we find who owns the car?'

'Done that,' said the police force.

'Can we follow it?'

'Done that,' the policeman repeated, holding out his tankard for a refill. 'The trouble is as soon as you've both covered a couple of miles along the mountain road the police car sticks out like a sore thumb.' He belched quietly as if to emphasise his point.

'Right,' said Macleod again. 'Campbell, you've made sure our party is above board with the authorities. Donald,' he said to the policeman, 'we want a couple of your boys in at the kill. I'll lay on a round the clock watch with a tally-ho code and we'll catch the wee buggers with their spoils as they return to the car.'

'But by that time they'll have done the damage,' cried Biddy.

'That's right,' agreed Cluny, 'and they'll only be fined five hundred pounds at most so they'll be back in action within a fortnight.'

'No they'll not,' Macleod assured him quietly. 'Sure we have to obtain positive evidence, and five hundred pounds might be the maximum fine. But by the time we've finished with them they'll no be in action again this side of Hogmanay.'

The force made a round of the pubs that evening and, with the evidence of the car together with Cluny's description, identified the man Biddy had discovered and was able to report that the gang numbered four. Three of them struck him as being fairly small fry but one, certainly, was looking for an important capture with its proportionately high reward.

It never grows completely dark in northern Scotland during the three weeks on either side of midsummer's night, and half-an-hour before midnight Campbell thought he could still detect the faintest touch of pink from below the horizon when he relieved Cluny from his spell of watch-keeping. Alistair Macleod was a great one for taking overall control and organising things, he mused, although if one was to take rank into account it should have been himself the others turned to. As things were, Cluny and the Morrison child had gone straight to the hotel and he'd been brought into the picture at too late a stage. He decided he must have a word with someone about that because, he thought as he rolled on to his back and gazed up at the stars, his retirement was becoming imminent at which time he fully intended to assume a leading role in the local community. Looking back on his naval career he valued the companionship but regretted the insularity of submarine life. During his seagoing years he had been king of his tiny floating empire but how narrow were his philosophies and how ignorant he'd become of events at home.

He awoke with a start just as the sun was tipping the hills to the east and splashing daubs of red across the higher peaks. He shot up in panic and directed his glasses towards the eagles' nest, fumbling fingers fighting for focus. Nothing. His guilt would remain undiscovered. Asleep on duty! God, what wouldn't he have done to any unfortunate sailor under his command in similar circumstances? But wait, there *was* something . . . a movement. He massaged his eyes and peered again. Now he saw it clearly; a rope swinging from a lower branch. Above and behind, the red car parked several hundred yards from the road. He felt a rush of adrenalin, brought about more from fear of admitting his failure than from fear of making a citizen's arrest. He reached for the ex-WD 'walkie-talkie', pressed the transmit button, and whispered, 'This is Gold Bird, this is Gold Bird. We have visitors in possession. Tally-ho!' He began to crawl towards his own car, keeping flat to the ground, when to his horror the receiver suddenly blasted into life with the distorted sound of Macleod's voice. 'Gold Bird, this is Control. Well done, laddie! We're on our way and we'll run the buggers to ground in no time!' He must have left the volume control full up because his ears rang from the sheer noise of Macleod's excited shout which now echoed around the hills. Campbell turned and, lifting himself, craned his head to peer back at the tree. Three men stood by the hanging rope and a fourth man was climbing down it. All of them stared in his direction!

Even at this distance it was obvious they'd seen him. He was about to abandon all pretence at concealment and make a dash for his car in a last attempt to head them off at the crossroads when he saw something else, causing the blood to freeze in his veins. The stocky figure of Cluny was striding down the hill behind the poachers. Cluny, who was used to sleeping rough, had maintained his own personal vigil and now, in the wake of Campbell's failure, was about to attempt to arrest them single-handed.

He could see the sturdy little Scotsman had spotted the poachers, and he suffered a wave of impotent helplessness as he watched the four men turn together and see Cluny. He stood transfixed for two seconds before springing into action – action which was to prove a full half-hour too late. 'A complete shambles,' muttered Campbell as he ran, stumbling, to his car. 'An utter complete bloody shambles.'

Morrison climbed out of bed the moment he heard the telephone but even so Biddy reached it before him. 'Right,' he heard her say briefly before hanging up. 'They're there,' she announced, 'we're to go up at once.'

'Not you, darling.'

'You're joking!' She ran up to her room to pull on jeans and jersey over pyjamas. 'They're my prisoners – I spotted them, remember?'

Argument was useless and timewasting so he dressed as hurriedly as she and together they ran for the Morris. Within ten minutes he was changing gear for the climb up to Pintarroch Point and looking anxiously into his rear view mirror. 'I can't see any sign of the others. If it's just you, me and Campbell taking them on I hope they're only little chaps.'

'You could lick anybody.'

'Your faith in me is touching but right now an Aborigine midget could take me five rounds.'

They continued to climb for a further five minutes before reaching the crossroads. Morrison slowed out of habit, which was fortunate because out of nowhere a red car came screaming down the hill and shaved past, missing them by inches.

'That was them,' shouted Biddy. 'Turn round, Morrison.'

He used the crossroads to make a three-point turn and had just angled the car whereby all four exits were blocked when Campbell roared in from the far side of the valley and screeched to a standstill.

'Have you seen them?' the commander yelled.

'Down the hill,' shouted Morrison. 'I'm just turning.'

'No, leave them to me,' ordered the commander. 'You go to the nest – I think Cluny's in trouble.' Without question Morrison threw the gear into reverse allowing the other man passage. 'Utter complete bloody shambles,' they heard him shouting as he accelerated down the hill.

'What do you think has happened to Cluny?'

'No idea,' he replied briefly, 'except it sounds like things have gone wrong. Where's this nest?'

'Hell,' said Biddy, 'I don't know from this angle.'

'Campbell was right, it *is* a shambles.' He drove on for a couple of minutes. 'This is impossible – I've no idea what to look for.'

'Some sort of track leading off to the left. Then it must be a steep climb down on foot.' He slowed to a near crawl, searching the undergrowth for a sign of recent car tracks.

A sudden shout from Biddy. 'The eagles!' He saw them immediately. 'They're excited,' she declared, 'yesterday they were majestic.'

'Down here,' he muttered and swung the wheel hard left. His eyes were good, he'd spotted tyre skids on the road as if a car in a hurry had gunned up over-fast. Two hundred yards along the rough track they came to a dead end. Biddy leapt out, calling as she touched the ground.

'Cluny!'

There was no reply. 'Steady now,' Morrison warned. 'Take it easy – we won't be any use to him if we bust an ankle.' It was slow going and a good fifteen minutes passed before they found the rope. Two minutes later Morrison came across flattened undergrowth along the edge of a near-vertical rock face and, anchoring himself firmly with hands and feet, leaned far out and looked down. It was then he saw Cluny. The little Scotsman was lying on a natural shelf some fifteen feet below. He was quite still and one leg was impossibly doubled up beneath him.

'I'll go down,' volunteered Biddy.

'Wait,' he ordered firmly. 'We'll get the rope and I'll lower you.' It was a matter of moments to put a bowline on the girl and despite her neglible weight he took a cautionary turn around a tree. She stepped unhesitatingly over the edge whilst Morrison kept the line taut, letting it out as she climbed down. The trouble was that she disappeared from view at once and he had no idea how she was doing.

'Morrison,' came her voice.

'Yes?'

'There's nothing to cling on to here and I've five feet to go. I'm going to kick myself out – each time I shout let me down a foot at a time. Now!' He visualised her swinging out into space and he paid out twelve inches of rope. They repeated the manoeuvre four times more until he heard, 'Okay, I'm there.'

She crouched down beside Cluny, secure in the knowledge that her father had firm hold of the rope. 'Don't attempt to move him,' she heard him shout warningly.

Cluny was barely conscious and in terrible pain. His face was bruised and bloodied and she guessed he'd taken a beating before being pushed over the edge of the rock face.

'Morrison.'

'Yes?'

'He's badly hurt. I think his leg is broken. It's a mountain rescue job.'

His voice came back immediately. 'I'll pull you up again and we'll go for help.'

'No, I'll wait down here with Cluny.'

'You're sure? I might be an hour.'

'Yes, I'll be fine. Only make it quicker than that for Cluny's sake.'

Three minutes later Biddy and the Scotsman were alone. She took the old man in her arms and whispered in his ear, '*Eee-ow-ee*, the pain! The 'orrible *ex-croo-shiating* pain!'

He climbed through waves of pain to attempt a tortured smile. Her voice was music to his ears. He'd thought he was dead.

The entire operation, as Commander Campbell had rightly observed, turned out to be an utter shambles. Macleod had run out of petrol a hundred yards from the hotel and had to wait until nine o'clock for the filling station to open, the policeman involved was officially off-duty until lunchtime seeing as he'd worked several nights on the trot, and the rest when the crunch came had decided a comfortable bed held more attractions than chasing after birds' eggs. Campbell's car wasn't up to the chase and the thieves drove off into the dawn carrying their spoils with them.

Now, however, the situation had changed dramatically. The single push which had toppled Cluny over the side of a rock-face had instantly altered the crime from illegal trading to one of attempted manslaughter. The incredibly professional mountain rescue team had arrived not in an hour but within twenty-five minutes. Morrison and Biddy were impressed by the efficiency with which they rigged and lowered a stretcher, strapped the old man to it, and lifted him comfortably to the top. By mid-morning he was in hospital, the leg set, and voicing his first complaint about the bedside service, and by lunchtime he had described to the police how he had attempted to apprehend the culprits and admitted to putting up a pitifully poor showing in the short scuffle that resulted.

'The man was mad,' declared Campbell. 'Plucky, I'll grant you, but to tackle four desperate poachers single-handed, and at his age, when he must have known I had things under control was nothing short of stupid bravado.'

Biddy said nothing, allowing the bar-room conversation to wash over her head whilst she struggled to make sense out of certain timings. She and Morrison had seen the red car speeding away seconds before Campbell had reached the crossroads. When they reached the nest it was clear the men had been disturbed but not until *after* they'd taken the eggs. How had the delay arisen? It struck her that Cluny must have entered the fray in the absence of any action from elsewhere.

She discussed it later with Morrison. 'It seems to me,' he remarked, 'that the Campbell family experience some difficulty in sticking rigidly to the truth.'

At first Cluny's outdoor life seemed to have set him up for a rapid recovery but then there developed a touch of pleurisy which prevented his discharge from hospital. The Saturday fortnight was Biddy's eleventh birthday and, fishing or no fishing, Morrison resolved it would be a special occasion. 'Let's you and me go to Edinburgh,' he suggested, 'we'll buy you some new clothes, do a spot of sightseeing, take in a theatre and stay the night in a hotel.'

'Wow, Morrison, can we afford all that?'

'Of course we can. For you we can afford the best.'

'Okay.'

'It's ages since we did anything like that.'

'We *never* did anything like that,' she corrected.

The nets were providing a good income. Although the catches had fallen considerably from the numbers taken during what Morrison referred to as 'the bountiful fortnight', he was marketing more than he'd originally estimated and the prices were holding up very well indeed. Of course the profits from six months had to be spread over the second unproductive half of the year, and during that summer he had no idea how he was going to turn an honest penny during the winter. However, for the time being he was contented with his lot and feeling fitter than he had felt in months.

His high spirits were undiminished even when Sigmund said, 'I have something to show you.' They walked to his Land-Rover and he opened a basket.

'A salmon,' exclaimed Morrison.

'Caught by a line in the upper reaches of Pulcready. Look closely.'

Morrison took note of his serious tone and studied the fish. At once he spotted the fungus growth. 'It's diseased.'

'Yes. Ulcerative dermal necrosis. It's a killer, David, and

175

there's no cure.'

'What is it?'

'They think it's caused by a virus; the fish become ulcerated and infected with fungus. The disease appears to run in cycles, rather like myxomatosis in rabbits. You're looking at very bad news, last time we all lost our shirts.'

'Why, will the fish *we* catch be infected?'

'No, but the reduced numbers spawning in the next cycle will mean fewer survivors for us to catch. Once the disease is present in a river the numbers are drastically reduced.'

'If it's incurable there's nothing I can do, and worrying won't help.' Morrison didn't mean to sound dismissive but life was good and for once he was free of care.

Sigmund smiled. 'That's what everyone says. Poor "Salar the Salmon" is fighting more interruptions to his life-cycle than he can cope with. I was in the harbour last week when the fishing fleet came in. One skipper had four boxes of salmon each with a layer of white fish on top for concealment.'

'Drift netting?'

The man nodded. 'It's illegal in Scotland. They use a nylon net which is immensely strong and practically invisible. The fish that get away are mostly too badly injured to reach their breeding grounds.'

'Yes, we've found one or two of those in our own nets.'

'Then there is a new threat off the coast of Greenland. Since they discovered the Atlantic feeding grounds they're using long lines and nets to devastating effect. They're pulling up 1,200 tonnes a year. Our method of earning a livelihood is simple and delightfully old fashioned, man versus beast with elementary tools of the trade, but I wonder how much longer we can survive in the fight against massive commercialisation?'

'Come on, Siggy. I'm too busy surviving my first season!'

The German put the fish back into his basket and snapped the lid shut with an air of disappointment. As he climbed into the driving seat he made a last try. 'There are associations and trusts. We need voices if we are to be heard.'

'Heard by whom?'

'Parliament. It's our only hope. EEC quotas, a common conservation policy for the whole of the British Isles, the banning of drift netting, the tagging of salmon, and official licensing of all dealers.'

'You want me to add my voice?'

'Soon it will be one of direct experience.'

'I'll think about it.'

Morrison closed the door on him and Sigmund wound down the window. Morrison made a mental note to tell Biddy the German was wearing tweed plus-fours, jacket, waistcoat with a gold watch-chain, and a monocle. This was obviously the correct outfit for country gentry to express political concern about river fishing. Sigmund gave a slightly cynical smile as he switched on the ignition. 'The trouble is that by the time the fishing MPs get up here the grilse are running, they get good sport, and think we're doing no more than cry wolf.'

Morrison watched him drive away. 'There's another way,' he thought, 'start a fish farm. That way the smolts never make it to the Atlantic at all.' He returned to the house, putting such thoughts to the back of his mind for later consideration.

It would have been better if he'd forgotten them altogether.

CHAPTER SEVEN

THE DOCTOR lived in an ugly house on the outskirts of the village. The patch of front garden dividing the surgery door from the pavement had never experienced the tending care of fork or spade, and access to the weed-smothered path was through a wrought-iron gate which clung to its post by a single hinge. Twice daily, patients could be seen lifting it bodily off the ground on entering and leaving because no one had the heart to complain to the good doctor that when they were feeling under the weather fighting their way past this obstruction was almost the last straw.

He was protected from malingerers by a tartar of a receptionist and it was necessary to undergo a verbal cross-examination with her before she unwillingly pointed towards one of the upright chairs in the waiting room, by which time everyone present was aware of the intimate details of each newcomer's sickness.

The ability of the man was unaffected by the locale, however, and Morrison had found him to be marvellously sensitive to his slow recovery to full health.

'Well, Mr Morrison, how are we feeling nowadays? Still tired out, are we?'

'Exhausted, but managing.'

'Aye, but it gets you down, doesn't it? That's the thing about tuberculosis – it comes on within a week like a dose of bad 'flu and takes maybe a couple of years to go away again.' He examined the latest set of X-rays and pointed towards the offending area for his patient to see. 'But you're doing a grand job of beating it away, there's no questioning that.'

'I've been feeling much fitter these past few weeks. I

have a hunch it's something to do with the size of the catches!'

'Mind over matter – one of the best cures I know until the truth catches up with you and demands rest, isn't that true?'

Morrison nodded. 'When I sleep it's more like passing out. I've frightened my daughter more than once.'

'It's something you need to watch. It can come at you so suddenly if you push yourself too far.' He snapped out the light of the X-ray display and turned to face him. 'But you're doing well, your mental security is doing a lot for you whilst fresh air and time is looking after the rest. I'll tell you what we're going to do – we're going to cut out the tablets altogether and see what happens.'

'That's marvellous news, I can't tell you!'

'Aye, well we'll not get too cocky until we've tried it a week or two. Give me a ring and keep me in touch twice a week, eh?'

'Fine.'

Morrison left the doctor, his morale uplifted and his step lighter. He looked back on the days he'd had to take fourteen tablets a day, different colours, shapes, and sizes. To come out the other side and see the back of them was a landmark in his life.

When he arrived home he walked past the telephone twice before picking it up and dialling her number. It was difficult to believe a man of his age could feel so stupidly hesitant but he feared polite rebuff.

'426.'

'It's David Morrison.'

'Hello, David.' He was cheered by the warmth of her greeting.

'It would be wrong to pretend I was phoning about Biddy. I'm calling because I'd like to see you again.'

'I'm very flattered.'

'You mentioned about joining us in the workboat one day.'

'Correction. *You* mentioned a ride in the workboat and, because we'd only just met, I made polite non-committal noises.'

179

'Obviously you'd rather not.'

'There are other things I'd prefer.' The laughter in her voice disappeared as she added seriously, 'I'd love to invite you over here and cook a meal for you, but it's not my home and, anyway, you'd hate the atmosphere.'

'I think I would rather,' he agreed. 'Are you alone now?'

'Yes, it's all right.' *It's all right*, he repeated to himself, as if their assignation must be kept secret.'

'Why not come and have dinner with us? Tomorrow. Come straight from school and give Biddy a lift.'

'This is becoming very one-sided. How do I return your hospitality?'

'I'll think of a way,' he promised. 'I'll still be working the nets when you get here but Mrs Burgess can give you some tea and Biddy will look after you.'

'That will be lovely. I'll see you tomorrow.'

The following evening it was past six before the workboat returned to the bay and as they approached the beach Morrison saw Carrie walking down from the house. Sigmund conned the bows right into the slight surf and Buzby jumped ashore to take the boxes and gear handed down by Morrison and Bobo.

'Where's Biddy?' Morrison called out.

'She went up to her room. Homework.'

'Homework?' he exclaimed. 'Usually that's not looked at until after stern words at bedtime.'

'I must be a good influence.' She watched them off-load the evening catch, then she exchanged polite words with Sigmund before accompanying Morrison back to the house. Buzby and Bobo put the workboat on the mooring and the skipper drove home.

'Darling,' he called up to Biddy as they came through the back door.

'Coming.' The girl crashed downstairs and into the kitchen. 'How many?'

'Nine. Nothing here and nothing in Ferrick. They're all a good size though.'

'I'll go and deal with them.' Biddy turned to the door without a glance at the schoolteacher.

'Biddy, you left Carrie all by herself,' he said accusingly.

His daughter didn't even turn round. 'I always call her Miss Kelso,' she said and was gone.

He felt her hand on his arm. 'Leave it, David,' she said before he could call Biddy back. 'It's all right, really.'

'She was damn rude,' he said angrily.

'Don't be cross. She has to make her point and nobody's told her about subtlety.'

'What is her point?'

'Oh, be fair. This is her house and I'm intruding. I think she might feel I constitute a threat.'

'Okay, I'll go along with that. Let me apologise on her behalf and I'll deal with it later.'

'You could let time take care of it. Biddy and I mostly get on well.'

'We'll see.' It was brief and unintentionally peremptory but as it was an area in which Carrie was particularly anxious not to interfere, she changed the subject.

'Tell me what usually happens now. So that I can fit in.'

He relaxed again and closed the back door. 'What usually happens now is that I go upstairs and shower off the smell of fish, and then I cook dinner. Mrs Burgess has prepared the vegetables, look,' he lifted the lids from three saucepans containing peeled potatoes, parsnips, and beans, 'and this afternoon I made the biggest trifle you ever saw. Until you have witnessed the appetites of Buzby and Bobo you haven't experienced the ninth wonder of the world.' He opened the refrigerator to reveal a massive glass bowl and at the same time took out a leg of lamb. 'If you want to help you could stick this in the oven – regulo 6.'

'Fine. The sooner it's in the sooner we eat.'

'We've laid the dining-room table tonight – in your honour. Buzby and Bobo are even changing into their best clothes – whatever that means.'

She looked at him, a touch uncertain. 'I brought a dress too. I wasn't sure and – well, you said come straight from school.'

This time he was cross with himself. 'You've been working all day as well and I'm just as stupid as Biddy!

181

Listen, there's bags of hot water, I'll shower quickly, then the bathroom is all yours and you can use my room to change.'

A little later they stood together in the bedroom. 'It's rather masculine, I'm afraid. I do my best but I lack finesse.'

Her eyes went to a framed photograph on the bedside table. 'Is this a picture of your wife?'

'Yes. That's Wendy.'

'May I see?' He nodded and she held up the photograph and studied the face. 'She was beautiful,' she said softly.

'Yes.' He moved and stood beside her.

She asked, 'How did it happen?'

'Cancer.'

'Poor girl. Poor you, too.'

'She suffered but, mercifully, fairly briefly. Mine took a bit longer.'

Carrie turned her head to see his profile as he continued to look at the picture. 'And now? Are you over it now?'

'Sometimes yes, sometimes no.' He gently took the photograph from her and replaced it by the bed. 'But I'm definitely over it as far as this evening is concerned.' He smiled at her, warm, frank, welcoming. 'Help yourself to anything you want.'

The dinner party turned out to be a magnificent success. Buzby and Bobo were in splendid form, joking constantly at their own expense and accepting the teasing of the others in fine good humour. Biddy forgot her initial feeling of hostility and gained several laughs with her surprisingly adult wit. Morrison had cleverly seated his daughter opposite him and, as hostess, she was carefully attentive to their guests. Carrie sat on his left and he recalled to himself how accurate had been his first assessment of her in the school when he'd noticed how attractive she became when she smiled, and surmised how much more attractive she would be if people complimented her. Now, enjoying the appreciation of the dinner party, she sparkled with totally relaxed gaiety; the new hairstyle softly framing her face, unconsciously neat in her movements, she became more than attractive – she became beautiful. At one time or another everyone around the table had experienced sad disillusionment but that evening, for three or four precious hours, there was only laughter.

By midnight the candles were blown out, the dishes stacked for the attention of Mrs Burgess next day, Biddy was in bed, and Buzby and Bobo had retired to their caravan. Morrison walked Carrie slowly to her car. They chatted easily and, after she'd tossed her holdall into the back seat, she turned and kissed him lightly.

'Thank you for a lovely evening, I didn't want it to stop.'

'There'll be others.'

Behind them the caravan began to rock rhythmically, gently at first but with ever increasing violence. She giggled. 'Whatever's happening to Tristan and Isolde?'

'The wine seems to have gone to their heads.'

'I hope the caravan can stand up to it.'

He took her hand and, looking down at it, held it between his own. 'I'm taking Biddy to Edinburgh in two weeks. It's her birthday.' Now he raised his eyes to hers. 'Would you come and help us buy her some new clothes?'

'Will she mind?'

'To be honest I'm not entirely sure.' Then more firmly, 'But Biddy will have to get used to the idea of me having my own friends. Come to that, so will Janet Mahoney. I don't see why you and I should have to bother keeping secrets from either of them.'

'You're absolutely right and standing here with your caravan being shaken off its axles I don't think I can argue with you.'

'We're leaving crack of dawn on the Saturday, staying the night, and coming home the next evening.'

'I'd love to come, David.'

'That's marvellous.'

She eased herself gracefully into her car. 'Did you know the Royal Ballet is in Edinburgh? *Swan Lake, Pineapple Poll*, . . . ' She smiled up at him and added cheekily, 'Just thought I'd mention it!'

'We'll see. I am to ballet what you are to workboats!'

She laughed and drove home. Morrison gave a final wave as she bumped down the rough track leading to the road and turned towards his house. It was a rare evening with the faintest zephyr of a breeze blowing warmly from the south. Behind him the caravan reached a climax of violent swaying before suddenly becoming still. Morrison grinned to himself but wondered nevertheless why, on such a night, he had allowed Carrie to slip away. The telephone was ringing and he quickened his pace, wondering who could be calling at such a late hour.

'Hello?'

'Can you come round? He wants to see you. Now!' Commander Campbell's voice was slurred.

'It's past midnight, Commander.'

'No time like the present.'

'Can you tell me what it's about?'

The voice at the other end became close and muffled as a hand was cupped over the mouthpiece. 'He's a multi-millionaire who's interested in you, that's what it's about!'

'Won't he still be interested in the morning?'

'Och, man, what happened to yer ambition?' the voice demanded testily.

Morrison thought quickly. Probably aided by the wine he'd consumed he felt carefree enough to accept the crazy invitation. Anyway, he had a score to settle with Bruce Cornelius quite apart from his natural curiosity as to what his parties were really like.

'Okay. I'll be there in ten minutes – it'd better be worth it!'

'Do you know how to get here?'

'Yes.' He hung up and checked quickly that Biddy was all right. The girl was sound asleep and MacGregor gave him a quiet growl. He wondered about waking Buzby in the caravan to let him know he was going out but decided their being near at hand was security enough.

Morrison approached the mansion up the mile-long drive winding past massive rhododendron shrubs and among trees which had stood through at least a generation. Formal gardens surrounded the building itself where professional

184

landscapers had endeavoured to earn an honest fee by creating tasteful formations whilst suffering the considerable handicap of their customer's wishes. Floodlit statues overlooked their work, unlikely cascades and fountains were illuminated by underwater lamps in blues, greens and yellows, and Mr Cornelius clearly had a weakness for gnomes who carried lanterns and peered out into the night with ugly immobility. He parked his car where the drive bordered a wide terrace and lights blazed from sliding glass doors the size of a double garage. He walked past a young couple playing table tennis on a covered patio and beyond he could see other guests enjoying an indoor swimming pool. He was not sure what he had expected to see but it all looked perfectly harmless.

Debbie opened the door to him. She wore a strapless evening gown of emerald green, her skin was gorgeously tanned, hair piled high on her head showing to perfection the delicate bone structure of face and shoulders. They had barely time to exchange greetings before Bruce Cornelius hurried along the hall, arm outstretched, and wearing a wide welcoming smile. 'Hey, it's *good to see you*,' he exclaimed, grasping Morrison's hand. 'Fancy allowing us to drag you out at this hour.' His deep, quiet, almost shy voice was instantly disarming.

'The commander suggested it was urgent.'

'Between you and me our friend Campbell's had a drop too much but it's true enough I have been wanting to chat you up on a coupla things.' He led the way into an enormously proportioned living room with fitted white Indian carpet, leather chairs, and furnishings in steel and glass. A buffet table ran the length of one wall laden with deliciously prepared food but the guests had mainly eaten and some now watched a soft-porn movie on the video. Campbell sat staring glassily at a young girl's legs but rose when Cornelius called him and the three men went into a room, equally large and almost identically furnished, with the exception of one wall covered from floor to ceiling with books which, although brand-new, were almost certainly purchased by the yard. Debbie brought him a large whisky in a cut glass tumbler on a small silver tray with a decanter and syphon. As she floated out Cornelius said, 'All my guests come from down south – they fly up with me in my plane. I prefer that to messing about with the locals – gets the place a bad name.'

Morrison said nothing. There was nothing he could think of to say.

'I'll tell you what was on my mind, Mr Morrison.' Cornelius smiled charmingly. 'I hope you're going to think it was worth getting up in the middle of the night for.'

Campbell had sunk heavily into a deep armchair and was lighting a cigar. His host quietly fetched an ashtray and placed it on a small occasional table by his side.

'I been looking into this salmon fishing business. Now, you could write a book on what I don't know about it so you mustn't take exception if I get a couple or three things arse about.' Morrison nodded. 'It seems to me that we're falling behind the times in the way we set about catching them. I mean, what I always say is you can't stop progress, and when you look at what's going on all round you what you're doing down in Skerrymor Bay is the equivalent of fishing off the end of a pier with a piece o' string and a bent nail.' Cornelius raised a defensive hand even though Morrison had not stirred. 'I'm not talking out of turn, am I?' he asked anxiously.

'Not a bit. As a matter of fact my bent nail has been doing rather well lately.'

'You've taken offence, I can see it. He's taken offence,' he said accusingly to the commander.

'No, he hasn't. He's too smart for that.'

'I'm not smart, but I haven't taken offence either,' Morrison assured them. 'Please go on.'

'I know how well you're doing and I've heard all about how you set the business up. You done a tremendous job. That's why I was so keen for us to have a meet.' Cornelius had sat down but now he stood up again as if he felt more comfortable on his feet. 'Let me ask you a question, David.' An enquiring look, 'Can I call you David?'

'Please do.'

186

'Let me ask you one question, David. What happens from September to February?'

'I paint the house, rebuild the sheds, install new equipment, refurbish the gear.'

'But do you make any money?'

'Not a lot.'

'And yet people still eat. They still buy fish. They'd still fancy a drop of fresh salmon if you could give it to them.'

'Are you going to tell me about fish farming?'

The commander interjected, 'I told you he was smart.'

'Let me say three things about fish farming, then I'll finish,' said Cornelius. 'One, the farms supply a commodity at a time of year when it's not readily available. Two, they provide work in an area where work is scarce. And three, they get a subsidy from the Highland and Islands Development Board. Oh, and there's a fourth thing,' he went on with a wide grin, 'they save the grilse a helluva long swim to find its dinner.'

'It is, of course, that swim which does a great deal towards giving the flesh its particular texture and the krill it finds off Greenland also provides the distinctive pink coloration which at the fish farms has to be put in with a dye.'

'All right, David, I agree with you. So now let me tell you something about the customers who *buy* the salmon,' said Cornelius who, typically, had forgotten his promise about finishing. 'Your average salmon is paid for by an *expense account*. Did you know that, David? It's paid for by one business executive wanting to impress another business executive, and by the time they've roughed up their palates with Martini and talked their deals between mouthfuls, they're not going to *notice* the texture or give a stuff about where the colour comes from.'

'Is that a reason for selling poor-quality fish?'

'Oh, you've got to have your proper salmon for your discerning customer, of course you have. But if your expense accounts, who couldn't tell salmon from mackerel, want to play about showing off to each other then let's you and me make a bob out of it. Besides, it can't be that bad

187

elseways the H. and I.D.B. wouldn't have nothing to do with it, would they?'

Morrison felt scarcely qualified to evaluate whether the Board would or wouldn't, so instead he asked, 'What is your idea, Bruce?'

'I got it in mind to set up a fish farm at the head of Loch Stryne. I think it's going to be the thing of the future and it'll provide a bit of work for a few bodies. Mind you, what I know about it wouldn't fill the back of a stamp,' he ended modestly. Considering he hadn't stopped talking for fifteen minutes Morrison guessed he was more knowledgeable than he cared to admit. He found Bruce Cornelius enormously likeable and entirely different from the image which preceded him. He seemed to have surrounded himself with the ingredients of high living but then allowed it all to happen without becoming too personally involved. Perhaps he yearned to have friends – self-made multi-millionaires often do, Morrison thought.

'Where do I fit into it?' he enquired.

Cornelius held out his arms as if handing the question back to him.

'You tell me, David.' He glanced at the commander who had fallen asleep, his cigar extinguished and resting on his chest in a small heap of ash. 'Campbell here says you're one who gets things done and, if he'd managed to stay awake, I'm sure he'd repeat in front of you everything he said to me. The thing is, I get the *ideas*, see what I mean? Then I need someone to make them work for me.'

'Is that what you want me to do?'

'I'm inviting you to think about it and then come and see me when you're ready. Set up some enquiries, find out what it's all about, what the rules and regulations are, how much it'd cost, estimated turnover – you know the score more than I do. I think we'd work well together.'

'That's extraordinarily generous of you. I'll take up your offer to think about it.'

'That's what I'm saying, isn't it, David? Look, I'm going to do this, know what I mean? When I make up my mind I usually go through with things. The point is whether you want in or out – and that's up to you.'

'Fine. I'll come back to you in a week or so.'

'There's no hurry. Give me a call whenever you're ready to talk.'

The business concluded Cornelius relaxed and proved himself a brilliant raconteur. After a while they returned to the main room where everyone had gathered to watch the end of the pornographic movie. Their host smiled his way past and led Morrison on to the terrace. As they skirted the buffet table Morrison pointed a finger at a large fresh salmon.

'Atlantic run or battery raised?' he enquired with a grin.

'What do you think, David? You and me can raise 'em and we can sell 'em. That don't mean we have to eat 'em.'

Cornelius showed him several rooms in the house. He did so with shy pride and no hint of boastfulness. 'I put it all in the wife's name,' he said. 'The accountants said it would be better and she didn't argue. She's never even been here – God knows what would happen if she ever turned up.' God knows indeed, thought Morrison. 'That reminds me,' Cornelius went on. 'I got a yacht on a mooring outside Mallaig, I haven't been on it since I can't remember when and people say it's in a helluva mess. I suppose you couldn't take a look at it for me?'

'I dare say. What d'you want me to do?'

'Whatever's necessary. Let me have a bill when it's done. She had a refit at the start of the season but there'll be a load of weed growing on her bottom. Have her took out of the water and anti-fouled 'n' everything. Know what I mean? Here, why don't you take her round to your Skerrymor Bay and sail her regularly? She's a beautiful thirty-foot sloop and beautiful things should never be left to lie idle.'

'Well, I'll go and have a look anyway.'

They had returned to the library. The commander was still dead asleep and Cornelius promised to say goodbye for him in the morning. 'You don't want to stay the night?' he asked. 'Debbie would like it.'

'No thanks. I have a young daughter at home.'

'You're a lucky man, David. D'you know that?'

189

Her voice enquired mildly, 'Who says Debbie would like it?' She stood framed in the doorway, cool, sophisticated, stunningly beautiful.

'Would you believe anyone could put their foot in it as often as I do?' enquired the millionaire, apparently unabashed. 'Give the man another drink, darling, for Gawd's sake.' He passed her in the doorway. 'I'd better go see what my layabout house guests are doing.'

'The movie's finished,' said Debbie.

'Did the boy get the girl in the end?'

'Several times.' He laughed and left. Debbie came into the room, closing the door behind her, and glancing distastefully at Campbell. 'The navy appears to have sunk without trace,' she said. 'Will you have one for the road?'

'I think I've had enough.'

'I'd like one. Keep me company.'

He smiled. 'Of course.' She poured two strong whiskies, splashed in soda, and carried his to him, standing close. 'Cheers,' she said, looking up at him with cool eyes.

They touched glasses and drank. 'Are we still on speaking terms?' he enquired.

'Whyever not?'

'My last vision of you was a back striding indignantly towards the hotel.'

She crossed to the french windows and pulled open the curtains. 'My father and I had come to Scotland together, I think in an effort to know each other better. You slightly confused the issue. Then, when I thought about it, what you and Macleod did was rather a compliment in its way. You worked so hard just to impress him.'

'That's true enough.'

'Anyway, my anger was shortlived.'

'I'm glad to hear it.' He sounded pompous which had not been his intention. She looked at him quizzically.

'You're very formal.'

'I'm sorry, I don't mean to be. It's just that we don't know each other very well and our last two meetings came unstuck.'

'Then let's make sure this one sticks.'

In the armchair Campbell began to snore. His face, collapsed in slumber, was not a pretty sight and in a brisk movement Debbie opened the french windows and stepped out on to the terrace. Morrison had no option but to follow and a moment later they stood beside each other in the cool night air.

'Have you seen the Cornelius Folly?' she enquired.

'No.'

'I'll show you.' She moved slowly down a flight of steps on to a close-cut lawn. He walked by her side, the night air was without chill and a crescent moon hung low over the distant sea casting a brilliant patch of silver towards the land. 'Isn't that the most ridiculously theatrical view?' she said. 'Millionaires can lay this sort of thing on, you know.'

'Why do you come here?' he asked, suddenly serious.

She glanced at him. 'I need notice of that question. To wait for something to turn up, I suppose.'

'And has it?'

'Not yet and, to be frank, I've grown a trifle bored with waiting.'

'You don't strike me as the kind of girl who'd sit around waiting for something to happen.'

'Why not?'

'Because you are so obviously capable, self-possessed, and unbelievably beautiful.'

She laughed huskily and took his arm. 'Why, thank you, Mr Morrison,' she teased, 'this meeting is beginning to stick already.' Then she too spoke more seriously. 'David,' said she, choosing her words carefully, 'listen to what Bruce has to say – I think he wants to make up for –' she hesitated slightly, '– the last time.'

'He hasn't put you up to this?'

She stiffened immediately. 'That's why I was cautious in my choice of words. No, David, he hasn't mentioned it beyond admitting a grudging admiration for the way you beat him to the draw at Skerrymor Bay. He likes strong men.'

Morrison recalled that the only reason he won the first encounter was because old Ferguson possessed a unique loyalty towards upright behaviour, but he decided to keep it to himself. Instead he relaxed and squeezed her arm in his. 'Thanks for telling me.'

'And if I can manage not to sound like a brazen hussy, I want you to know I like strong men as well.' He was spared the need to reply because they had arrived at a pyramid-shaped stonebuilt summerhouse overlooking a natural pool. There was an arched recess which housed deep seats covered in soft white leather. 'And here we have,' she announced, 'the Cornelius Folly. So named because of what takes place within than for any other reason.'

'It's – er – quite something.'

'Come and sit down.' They sank deep into the seating and she reached out to press a switch on the side wall whereupon the entire structure began to revolve slowly until they were facing the view. 'Crazy, huh?' She leaned back and placed both hands behind her head. 'The other switch reveals a bar if you feel the need,' she invited.

'No thanks.' When a girl as beautiful as Debbie makes a pass at a completely unattached man who has wined and dined well, there would have to be something wrong with him if he turned down the opportunity. So, without enquiring further, Morrison kissed her. Her lips were soft and moist against his and her arms came round his neck. He was at once transported to a new plane of sheer physical pleasure and when her mouth opened to allow a quick darting tongue to play upon his own, his entire body was flooded with a rush of adrenalin.

It was a long time before either of them spoke a word. Then he observed quietly, 'I thought you said not a lot happens at these parties!'

She gave a small shake of the head, not wishing to talk, her mouth still seeking further satisfaction. Her hand expertly undid a button and slipped inside his shirt. It was all extremely enjoyable and he was surprised by the speed at which things then began to progress. His eyes opened briefly and he caught her looking at him even as they kissed. In that instant it all went wrong. It was a look of calculating enquiry as to whether they were about to share

192

physical excitement without love. Despite the expensive surroundings the act itself seemed a cheap devaluation of miraculous occasions with Wendy. Roused as he was he broke away, kissed her gently on the forehead, and did up his shirt.

'The man was right, David,' she said. 'Debbie would like it.'

Morrison laughed aloud as he drove home. Six months ago he'd been out of work whereas tonight, in the space of an hour, he'd been offered a job, a yacht, and a girl. He'd have taken her too if it hadn't been for that look.

The first Saturday in July brought a heatwave to the whole of the British Isles.

The populace reacted in their customary way. Many took to their cars in search of pastures where the sun's rays could be enjoyed the most, only to spend the greater part of the day fuming in the concentrated oven-heat of traffic jams. On beaches and promenades the fine spell brought a jettisoning of winter gear rather than any display of summer clothes, where men sported plimsolls, rolled up trousers, discarded jackets and wore open neck shirts, whilst women carried their cardigans instead of wearing them, suspicious that the afternoon might see the return of a sudden cold snap. At the airports sunseekers were already dressed in shorts and gaily coloured shirts, casting worried looks over their shoulders as they boarded the plane, fearful that their investment might be proved unnecessary. At home people watered their still-wet gardens, played tennis in the parks and cricket on the greens, in the pubs they carried their warm beers to dusty tables in sweltering car parks, and while the sweat poured from forty million bodies a single television weatherman promised that the day would 'continue rather warm'.

In their house in Yorkshire, Patrick and his wife drank their morning coffee seated on the veranda. He watched her fingering the single sheet of notepaper and thought again how much he disliked the expression of critical distaste she wore almost constantly on her face these days. She passed the note to him, holding it between finger and thumb as if it were contaminated, before returning her spectacles to their case and snapping it shut.

'He hasn't exactly spread himself,' was her comment.

He had to admit that his son-in-law's letter was brief but at least the hurried jottings contained encouraging news. Biddy was as fit as a fiddle, she was doing better at school under a superb form mistress, they were going to the ballet in Edinburgh for her birthday, the catches were still excellent in quantity and quality although it was mainly the grilse running during this part of the season, and the bank loan was significantly reduced.

'Not a word about bringing our grandchild to visit us,' she observed with a sniff of derision.

'Hardly while he's trying to make a go of the fishing,' Patrick said gently. 'There is an open invitation for us to visit them.'

'It's too far. What would happen to the garden here?'

'Relate our garden to David's business and you begin to appreciate his problem.'

'Don't point out the obvious, Patrick.' She took the letter back and recovered her spectacles. 'Does he mean they're *all* going to Edinburgh, the form mistress as well?'

'He doesn't say that.'

'I don't understand what's going on up there, I really don't. I'll worry myself to the grave thinking about how he's bringing up Wendy's child.'

Patrick felt no such concern. He recalled the years of lyrical happiness a quarter of a century since when his daughter was Biddy's age and they were still in Ireland. Although socially ambitious his wife had yet to become devoured by aspiration towards position and possessions, and Patrick had enjoyed unfettered freedom to live his life to the full. One minute he was away in Dublin raising the wind, the next he was making the rafters ring with his friends at home, and through those paradisiacal days he watched Wendy grow up and he was a proud man. It was he who instilled her love for the open air, her keen pleasure in physical prowess, and all the time she became more be-witchingly beautiful than he'd dreamed possible. He'd fought his wife's disapproval of young David when first he caught their Wendy's eye because by then they'd moved to England and the years of turning a pretty penny became two decades of drawing a salary, and some of the fun departed from him. He wept when their daughter died but if there was one fight still to be fought it was to preserve that part of himself that had been inherited by Biddy.

'Let the garden go hang,' he said with sudden energy, 'why don't we join them in Scotland and share their adventure for a while?'

'There's no room for us and from all accounts it's a squalid little house.'

'Living rough were the best years of my life. You might as well know that the spark left us the day we feared getting our hands dirty.'

'Is that a criticism, Patrick?'

'No. It's regret, that's all.'

He rose from his chair and went out to mow the lawn. She'd never heard him speak so sharply to anyone, let alone her, and she was hurt by his words. Had their years of struggling to better themselves meant nothing to him?

That night in bed she said, 'We could try a week or so in Scotland if that's what you want.'

There was a pause before he stirred in the bed alongside her and said, 'You'd be too intolerant of their short-comings.'

'I don't mind hardship as long as it's *clean*.'

'Do you mean clean, or polished?' he asked. 'David said he'll not be able to give the place even a lick of paint before October.'

'Don't you go on at me any longer, Patrick. If you don't appreciate our style of living it's too late to regret it now. I've said I'll come so let that be the end of it.'

'I'll write to them in a day or two,' said Patrick, and went to sleep.

On the Sunday the temperature had climbed into the eighties and heat rebounded off concrete and brick as Mr

Peregrine stepped off the bus and paused on the pavement in order to consult his London road map. He was a stranger to the East End and, indeed, totally unfamiliar with the task he had in hand. Neither was it one he relished, but when the office received yet another telephoned complaint he felt it part of his duty as head of the section to conduct a personal investigation. One or two of his colleagues had volunteered noisily, almost eager to become involved in something which held out promise of a good scrap, and had worn ill-concealed smiles when their senior took it upon himself to answer the call. Mr Peregrine was not built for rough stuff and felt no anticipatory coursing of blood through his veins this Sunday morning; rather he experienced a sickening dread and wondered whatever he would do if anyone knocked off his glasses.

He found the name of the street he was looking for and began to walk. He took a firm grip on himself, insisting that there was no danger whatsoever in today's operation. He had to do nothing more than buy a drink in a public house and take careful note of all that went on. He hoped they had been misinformed and that nothing illegal would be taking place but the moment he entered the pub it was clear to him that the complaints were well founded.

The bar was packed to suffocation and the smell of steaming bodies offended his nostrils, but as he forced his way through the jostling throng Mr Peregrine was able to count at least fifteen cages whose owners were actively engaged in illegal bird trading. There were cages everywhere, on tables, on the bar, on fruit machines, and on shelves along the walls. He saw canaries, goldfinches, linnets, redpolls, a magpie and a kestrel. He bought himself a drink and this enabled him to lean against the bar and observe the scene more leisurely, whilst disguising his interest with the upturned glass. There was no sign of any bird having been ringed in accordance with legislation under the 1954 Protection of Birds Act and there was before his eyes ample evidence to justify a raid. He allowed ten minutes to pass before finishing his beer and leaving the pub. On his way out he asked a man with a cage containing about a dozen goldfinches how much they were and was assured they would cost him no more than £1.50 each. He had already seen money exchanging hands several times and had established this was the going rate; the only reason Mr Peregrine had stopped to talk to the man was because something about his appearance struck a chord in his memory. His black hair was going thin on top, his face was a blotchy red, he had a small moustache and he'd answered Mr Peregrine's enquiry in a thick Glaswegian accent.

He walked round to the local police station where the senior officer agreed to provide two plainclothes officers for a raid the following Sunday providing a warrant could be arranged in the meanwhile. This was sworn in court on the Tuesday and his colleagues responded enthusiastically to his call to action five days later.

The heatwave continued, bringing joy to a few and a shortening of temper to many, when Mr Peregrine, uncomfortable in his role as raid leader, briefed his men. He requested that they make their separate ways to the pub, spend half-an-hour establishing the culprits and move in on a pre-arranged signal from himself. His heart was in his mouth when he entered the bar. This time he observed some twenty-five dealers and the customers were jammed hotly shoulder to shoulder, leaving little room to manoeuvre. He could see the plainclothes men mopping their brows a comfortable six inches above the heads of those around them and out of the corner of his eye he saw his colleagues flexing their arms, impatient to enter the fray. Suddenly he found himself alongside his Glaswegian dealer from the previous week and, blinking nervously behind his spectacles, Mr Peregrine gave the signal and addressed the man.

'I have reason to believe you are – ' It was as far as he got. A round clout caught him on the side of the face causing his glasses to spin to the floor. Totally unable to see, Mr Peregrine sank to his knees, feeling helplessly for the spectacles, and listening to the shouts and scuffles surrounding him. Someone trod on his hand, then he was knocked flat to the ground, whereupon countless customers ran all over him as they made for the door, one stood directly on his cheek and his mouth was filled with dust and the taste of blood.

Three minutes later it was all over and the noise diminished to odd shouts coming from the pavement outside. His hand made contact with his spectacles, one lens was missing and the other cracked, but he put them on and the pub came back into focus. The bar was totally deserted; the birds, the illegal traders, the cages and customers, had all disappeared. He staggered to his feet and shakily made his way to the door. Outside the plainclothes officers, supported now by three uniformed constables, were ushering a small group of men with their caged birds into a police van, but the large majority of culprits had mingled successfully with the crowd of spectators and melted away. Mr Peregrine heard the flight call of a single goldfinch and through his cracked lens saw the lone flyer find its own way to freedom as it disappeared over the rooftops.

Abject about his failure he stood still as one of the officers approached him. 'There was only one really nasty customer in the place and he was the one you picked on to make your citizen's arrest. You'd have done better to leave him to us.'

'I'm sorry,' apologised Mr Peregrine. 'I made the most dreadful mess of the whole thing.'

'Not at all, sir,' the officer said. 'Thanks to the way you distracted him we were able to pounce. I have a feeling that one might have a slightly more serious charge to face.' Mr Peregrine saw his blotchy-faced, black-haired dealer being led to the van. 'It's funny isn't it,' the plainclothes man continued, 'the *trouble* people will take over a few wild birds.'

'Yes, it is,' agreed Mr Peregrine.

'I'll tell you what, sir. I think I'd like to buy you a drink.'

That same evening, some five hundred miles away, Janet Mahoney watched Caroline Kelso pour the coffee in silence. They had not engaged in meaningful conversation since their argument and the headmistress was beginning to fear the relationship was beyond retrieval. She felt bound to admire the change in her former pupil; it was as if she had come alive of a sudden and Janet was too honest not to admit that it could only be herself who had prevented it from happening earlier.

'We'll still be friends?' she said right out of the blue.

The younger woman looked at her over the coffee pot. 'Of course we will, Janet,' she replied steadily.

'It would be too stupid for us to go through all that we have, and end up as enemies.'

Carrie added cream to the cup and dropped in a lump of sugar before passing it across the table. 'I don't regret anything I have ever done.'

'You don't think I've caused your life to be wasted?'

'Not one bit.'

'Then how do we find ourselves in this present *impasse*?'

'Because you will not accept that I have a life of my own outside the school.'

'Oh him!' Despite herself Janet allowed a note of scorn to colour her voice. 'The father of a child in your class. You really ought to know better.'

'Please let us not go over it all again, Janet, I really couldn't bear it.'

'It's him you changed your hairstyle for, isn't it? And bought all the new clothes.'

Carrie took a slow sip of coffee to avoid replying in anger. When she spoke her voice was steady. 'Yes it is,' she admitted, 'but when I referred to my life outside the school I was thinking, in fact, of something else.'

The teacher was not prepared to be more forthcoming, not least because it would mean confessing there had been little response to her applications for a job down south and absolutely none that was favourable. With only a matter of days to go before the end of summer term she was discovering a paucity of opportunities for advancement, and the large majority of posts for which she was qualified existed in schools not dissimilar to Park Lodge. Added to which (and this was something she certainly did not wish her headmistress to suspect) her feelings for David were causing her some concern. She was past the age of young infatuation and was acutely aware that her admiration for the man, and the warm contentment she found in his company, caused her to long for his calls. All in all it was not the best time to contemplate leaving Skerrymor Bay, not when she was falling in love.

'You can't stay here, you know.' It was if Janet had read her thoughts.

'I know. You made that clear last time we talked.' On that occasion the threat had been screamed across the room from a woman intent on wounding. Then had followed the tearful retraction and pathetic pleading. Tonight the head-mistress sounded more in control of herself.

'Where will you go?'

'I haven't decided.'

'It's not that I want to turn you out.'

'How long may I stay?'

'I'll need to find a replacement teacher.'

'Does the bedroom go with the job?'

'That was crude and unnecessary.'

'It was intended as a practical question. I wondered if I had until the end of the summer holiday.

Janet was beginning to become tearful and Carrie desperately wanted to avoid a scene.

'I never sacked you,' declared the headmistress in a strangled voice. 'Remember that.'

'You imposed intolerable conditions.'

'Which I withdrew.'

'In words only, the thought remains.' Carrie gave a deep sigh. 'Look, Janet, let's not argue any more. Tell me when you want my room and I'll clear out.'

The mouth was quivering and the hands were clasped as the older woman teetered on the verge of histrionics. 'We'll always be friends, Janet, nothing can change that. Never-theless the time has come when we go our separate ways.'

The hysteria erupted. 'If you leave me now don't expect to come back. There'll be nothing for you here and I never want to see you again.'

'Very well, Janet. I'll leave at the end of term.'

'You can clear out tonight as far as I'm concerned,' the

headmistress shouted through gasping sobs.

'Don't you think that's rather dramatic? People would ask questions and I'm sure neither of us want them to hear the answers.'

'All right then. It's only days away.'

Carrie nodded slowly, put down her cup, and made to leave the sitting-room. By the door she turned and looked at the other woman with a sad smile. 'It seems we've ended up as enemies after all,' she commented.

The birthday was as much a failure as the dinner party had been a success.

Biddy sat in the circle seat and wondered when she had ever felt so utterly bored. There was this poofter man and leggy girl prancing about the stage accompanied by music that went *on and on*, nobody said anything, and God knows what the story was about. The only grain of comfort was that she sensed that Morrison was equally bored and only Caroline was actually *enjoying* it.

They'd arrived in Edinburgh shortly before lunch and bought her dresses in a hurry. 'Choose anything you like,' her father had invited but every time she reached for something that caught her eye both of them shook their heads disapprovingly. Caroline became 'ever so sensible', Morrison looked at his watch, and Biddy agreed to everything they said just to get it over. She would shove the dresses into the back of her wardrobe and absolutely never wear them.

She felt Morrison's hand take hers so she returned his squeeze and grinned up at him. Morrison was all right and this whole fiasco was costing him a fortune. It would have been magical had it been just the two of them. Maybe she'd wear the beastly dresses once or twice to avoid upsetting him.

They'd checked into the hotel and been given adjoining rooms. She was to share one with Caroline whilst Morrison had the other to himself. Biddy unlocked the communicating door in order that she might enjoy wandering in and out like at home.

As for the sightseeing . . .! Who cared about Arthur on his silly seat? Princes Street was long and the castle was *forever*. She'd spotted a poster advertising showjumping but by then it was too late to go. She imagined the stage in front of her covered with fences, gates, and hedges with the poofters and girls running round and jumping off against the clock.

She felt tired. They'd taken up the leader nets first thing for the Saturday close and it'd been a long, long day with still her birthday dinner to come. There was to be cake, she'd overheard Morrison ordering it. She must remember not to fill up on the main course and, above all, she must try and stay awake.

God, would this bloody ballet never end?

At 2.30 she emerged slowly from the depths of a dead sleep. Morrison was crying out in the next room, the moans increasing characteristically to his frightened yell as the familiar nightmare took hold. For a moment she forgot where she was and felt for the bedside lamp on the wrong side. She forced herself awake. Then she heard the sound of the communicating door open.

She remembered Caroline and almost immediately heard her voice in the next room. 'David. David, wake up! It's only a nightmare!' She must have been shaking him because he always gave a scream when he was shaken, which died suddenly at the moment he woke up. 'David, it's me. Are you all right?'

Then he was laughing. Relief bringing with it the infectious laughter Biddy loved so much. 'What was it about?' she heard the dragon ask. 'I can't remember!' Then she heard them both laughing. Like with Mummy, like with her. Usually she climbed into bed for him to cuddle her warm. So, doubtless, would Carrie. Soon the bedroom was silent again.

Biddy turned her face into the pillow. Hot tears, choking jealousy, sheer misery.

When Carrie woke up next morning the bed beside her was empty. There was no sign of Biddy. She thought she must be in the bathroom and waited for her to come out. She could hear no sound of running water. Perhaps she was with her father . . .

She left it for ten minutes before sitting up suddenly in bed. Had the child heard her get up in the middle of the night and go into the next room?

She knocked on the communicating door, opened it, and looked in at Morrison still asleep.

'David. Wake up. Biddy's gone!'

As soon as he had overcome an initial wave of panic Morrison worked out his daughter's probable objective and a few telephone calls confirmed his accuracy. The hotel porter's desk informed him she'd passed through the lobby at about a quarter to seven, the station booking office remembered a young girl enquiring the route to Mallaig and buying a ticket. It wasn't an easy journey and she must have blown every penny of her birthday money, but he held few worries on this score – Biddy was sensible and would make it back to Skerrymor Bay without difficulty. He phoned Sigmund and asked him to meet the train, then he tried to rid from his mind unbidden pictures of hazards that could befall an eleven-year-old travelling alone.

He was shaken to the core and deeply upset by her motive for running away. Angry too that she should cause both him and Carrie so much worry on a precious weekend's relaxation. How many times had he told her that problems could be *talked* about? Then he realised that on this occasion the problem was himself, so there was nobody left for her to talk to.

Carrie did her best but there was little she could say and for the most part she sensibly remained silent. Their drive home was strained and unhappy. Worse news was waiting for them when Sigmund hurried out of the white house as soon as he heard the car. His concern was all too obvious.

Biddy hadn't been on the train.

Carrie put the kettle on to make a cup of tea whilst, with an air of desperation, the men surmised on the child's whereabouts for the umpteenth time. She went through what must have been her thought process and cursed

203

herself yet again for her own thoughtlessness. The smart thing would have been to wake Biddy when she'd heard David calling out in his sleep; but she hadn't, so that was that. The girl had tried her best but failed to conceal her disappointment at the way the birthday had turned out and in the middle of the night she had drawn her own inevitable conclusions. Now she must have gone in search of somebody on whom she could unload her private fears and. . . . Suddenly Carrie knew exactly where Biddy was. She put down the cups and hurried into the living room.

'The train stops at Fort William. Telephone the hospital there.'

The two men looked up. 'Why?' asked Morrison.

'That's where Cluny is.'

He didn't see her when she entered the ward, he was lying back in the pillows gazing up at nothing, his face thinner and older, and Biddy thought the little Scotsman looked worse instead of better.

'Hello.' His eyes came round, brightening only a little when he saw who it was. 'How are you?' she asked.

'Bit of a cough. They say it's gone down on my chest.'

'When did you come in?'

'Yesterday. The day before. I can't remember.' There was a pause before he raised a hand slightly. 'Have you come all this way just to see me?'

'That's all right. I'm used to visiting hospitals.'

They sat silent again, this time for longer. Then she realised the old man was watching her.

'You'd best tell me about it,' he said at last.

'How did you know?'

'Something's wrong. It's written all over your face.'

She pulled her chair nearer to the bed and allowed her story to pour out. She told him everything from the first time the teacher came to lunch through to the disastrous birthday with its loathsome ending. 'Morrison and I were going to do this fishing thing together,' she finished, 'but every time I get back to the house there's someone else in

204

it. What with Sigmund, Mrs Burgess, Buzby, Bobo, and now Caroline – he doesn't seem to need me any more.'

Cluny closed his eyes for a moment before seeming to make a supreme effort. 'I never heard such poppycock in all my life,' he declared, a new strength in his voice. 'You come here and spill your selfish mean-mindedness over a sick man. I never knew the like.'

'I'm sorry, Cluny, I –' Her eyes brimmed with shocked tears at the sudden desertion of her friend, but there was no letting up.

'Now listen to me, you!' The old man struggled to raise himself on the pillow before pointing a crooked finger at her. 'Your dad has done his purgatory right down here on earth and when he comes to the Golden Gate, Saint Peter is going to wave him through. "You go straight in, Mr Morrison, because you already lost your good steady job and your beautiful wife and that's punishment enough." Right now the only thing he's got that makes life worth living is *you*! O' course he could've gone and drawn the national assistance and had everyone feel sorry for him, but that wasn't good enough for Mr Morrison with him wanting his wee bairn to grow up proud of her dad. So he comes up here, fits in with all of us who've lived rough all our lives and shows a few people what love is all about. 'Cos love is about getting soaked in icy water, handling gut-heavy nets, pulling in leaping slippery fish, 'n' not givin' up when you pull in no fish at all. And I'll tell you why he does it; he does it for the love of a red-headed green-eyed tomboy who he loves to the depths of his soul.'

The tears were coursing down her face. 'What about Caroline?' she sobbed.

His voice softened. 'You'll no deny him that? You're no so greedy as to take it all for yerself?' His hand felt for hers. 'Biddy, things will never be the same as when yer mam was alive – there's nothin' he can do to bring those days back, but he can try all he knows to make something like it! Most of all he needs the love of a grown woman who can make his life complete in a way you never can, and you'll not be complicating matters with your jealousy, d'you hear? Now get you away and start helping the man, 'cos while we're wastin' time bletherin' here the only thing left in Mr Morrison's life has run away!'

She looked at him for several moments. Then she nodded, wiped her eyes with the back of a hand, and stood up.

'And Biddy . . .' His voice had become a whisper.

'Yes?'

'Come 'n' see me tomorrow.'

'Okay.'

When she'd gone he lay back exhausted. He looked very ill.

Carrie saw Biddy run down the hospital steps and head across the car park towards the bus stop. She prayed that David's instant and generous decision would be proved right. 'You thought of it,' he'd said, 'you bring her home!'

She lowered the car window. 'Biddy,' she called.

The child stopped and looked across, before crossing slowly to the car. Carrie climbed out and waited, stooping slightly as she drew near. Without altering her pace Biddy moved straight into her arms, hugging her tightly and burying her face into her shoulder. Carrie felt tears, wet against her neck.

'Is Cluny all right?'

'He's okay,' came the muffled reply. 'Well enough for the old fool to give me the ticking off of a lifetime.'

Good for Cluny, thought Carrie, gently stroking the girl's tousled hair.

The voice in her neck added, 'He looked so old without his hat on.'

CHAPTER EIGHT

THREE DAYS later in the hospital ward at Fort William, Biddy sat beside Cluny's bed watching his face with steady unblinking intentness for a faint glimmer of hope. The old man hadn't stirred for hours and neither had the girl moved. Pleurisy and pneumonia had caught hold and this time the wee dour Scotsman wasn't going to win the fight. It was outside visiting hours but the ward sister allowed the child to remain; in a long career of nursing she'd never come across such simple, single-minded devotion.

Just before six o'clock Cluny's eyes flickered open briefly, and took in Biddy without apparent recognition before closing again. His breath came in short, faint, rasps, his lungs hardly moving. Then slowly, so slowly, his sunken face contorted into the caricature of a clown and his lips began to move. Biddy quickly leaned forward, her face close to his, to pick up his whisper. '*Eee-ow-ee*, the pain. The 'orrible *ex-croo-shiating* pain!'

They were his last words, and the last thing Cluny was aware of were Biddy's arms encircling him and holding him tight. It was a good feeling, one he hadn't experienced often in his life.

The sister was by the bed in an instant. She and a nurse gently moved the girl to one side and did all they could to revive the patient. Biddy knew her friend was dead and by the time she left the ward they were pulling a screen round his bed.

Carrie waited in the car park. Having allowed Biddy to miss afternoon school she had driven to the hospital immediately the last period was ended. She was there ready for the moment the child would need her and, if nothing else, she was helping David by allowing him to work without worry.

She looked towards the main entrance and there appeared at the top of the steps the slight figure of her charge. Carrie placed a hand over her mouth, smothering a fleeting smile, as soon as she saw the incongruous absurdity of the child's appearance. Biddy was wearing a funny hat. An instant later amusement changed to sadness as the teacher realised at once it was Cluny's hat, the battered, shapeless affair that had seen him through a score of winters and summers and accompanied him on countless poaching excursions. It was too large for Biddy, resting on her ears and practically down to her eyebrows. Her pinched white face and enormous green eyes, a deeper shade than normal, told the rest of the story.

Carrie leaned across to open the passenger door and Biddy climbed in, staring fixedly straight ahead. A couple of young probationers passed the car and made a light-hearted comment followed by a careless laugh, but the girl ignored it and Carrie pulled the door closed. She drove off without a word and they travelled in silence until they reached the outskirts of the town.

'He just died.'

'I know. I'm so sorry.'

'Can we have tea now?'

'Here or at home?'

'Here.'

It was easier said than done and Carrie wondered whether she should turn the car and head back towards the town centre. Then she spotted a shack-like café and pulled in. As they got out of the car she asked, 'Are you wearing the hat to tea?'

'Yes,' said Biddy.

Carrie drank a cup of strong tea while the girl went through a plate of sausages, eggs and chips, bread and butter, and a glass of milk. Halfway home she stopped the car just in time for her to leap out and bring the whole lot up again. The teacher wiped the clammy face with a freshener

208

tissue, laid her on the back seat, and stuck the hat back on her head. When she arrived at the white house Biddy was fast asleep and Morrison gently carried her up to bed.

Carrie was in the kitchen when he came downstairs again. 'Is she all right?'

'Fine. She woke up as I put her to bed, now she's lying there contemplating the ceiling. What are you doing?' he added.

'I don't know, really. Trying to surmise what you're all having for dinner – see if there is anything I can do.'

'You've done so much already.' He placed both hands on her shoulders and turned her round to face him. 'You're becoming a very special person, d'you know that?'

'Your little daughter is worth every bit of trouble, I promise you.'

'You must be bushed. Sit down, I'll make you a cuppa.'

'I'd sooner have a wee dram.'

'Done.'

While he fixed the drink she told him about the hospital and Biddy's appearance wearing the terrible hat. Most people have to suffer a number of emotional shocks to the system during their lifetime but Biddy seemed to be notching up more than her fair share even before she had reached her teens. Just as she would embark on some escapade of tomfoolery to counter a long period of inactivity, Carrie wondered whether the hat was a symbol of reaction to the death of her friend.

Morrison shook his head. 'I don't think so. My guess is that the reaction is still to come. The hat is – well, the hat is a typical Biddy. She'll probably wear it all her life!'

'I might sew in a crafty band,' promised Carrie, 'so at least she can see where she's going.'

The meal that evening was to be a straightforward mountain of spaghetti bolognese and she accepted his invitation to help him and the crew despatch it. Whilst she fried onions before throwing in the mince she told him of her conversation with Janet Mahoney.

'Where will you live?' he enquired with a hint of anxiety.

'I'll go to my parents at Loch Lomond until I have time

to think.'

'Loch Lomond? That's the other side of the world!' Suddenly he heard himself speaking words that came directly from his heart, bypassing the brain on their way to his mouth. 'You can't run to your parents, that's going backwards. Stay here with us where it's all happening!' Carrie turned from the stove in surprise. 'What you see here isn't enough to keep me satisfied for the rest of my life. This is just a start. I intend to build something which can look after all of us.'

He went on to describe his meeting with Bruce Cornelius, and Carrie leaned against the sink listening to and revelling in his youthful enthusiasm. The meeting with the millionaire had rekindled fires of ambition so nearly extinguished by circumstances. 'I don't envy him the life-style because, strangely enough, all that self-made success seems to have brought him a terrible loneliness. The important thing is, he's made enough money to pick and choose his challenges, and I'm to be involved in one of them. Everything is a stepping-stone to something else, don't you see, Carrie? If you go scooting off to Loch Lomond you're going to miss something tremendously exciting.' She stood quite still, her pulse quickened by the heady intoxication of his image building. 'Stay here,' he repeated persuasively.

'Where's here? In this house?'

'Yes.'

'I *couldn't*!'

'Why not?'

'What would people say?'

'The hell with what people say. You haven't any place to go so move in with us, it's as simple as that.'

'I wish it was as simple as that.' She cursed the protective upbringing which prevented her from handling the present situation with a degree of sophistication. 'I haven't been taught to think quite so directly.'

'Come and live with us. *Then marry me!*'

Her heart was beating and she felt helplessly inadequate. Surely grown women don't behave like heroines in romantic novels, she thought. His words hung in the air until the silence was broken by Biddy's voice.

'That's got to be the *wildest* proposal anyone ever made.' She stood in the doorway, hair tousled, pyjamas twisted. 'And don't say I was listening because nobody could help hearing.'

'Go back to bed, Biddy,' Morrison said. Then he added, 'Miss Kelso has to leave Park Lodge and I'm trying to persuade her to stay here with us.'

'Please come, Miss Kelso, just so's I can get a night's rest.'

Carrie was looking directly at Morrison.

'Are you serious? Yes, I can see you are. David I'll – I'll have to think about it. I mean, if I move in, where would I sleep?' Biddy turned her head enquiringly, and with studied interest, towards her father.

'There's all sorts of things can be arranged.' The child nodded sagely. 'We can turn the dining-room into a bedroom, meanwhile we'll put up a bed in Biddy's room.'

'Morrison, would it help if you told her you love her?'

'*Biddy, go to bed!*'

The green eyes came round to Carrie who repeated more quietly, 'Go to bed. I'll come up and see you later.'

'Thanks for always being outside the hospital.'

'That's all right.'

'I'd have missed you like anything if you hadn't been there.'

When Biddy had gone Morrison said, 'She's right, you know, I do love you.'

'I love you too, David, but I'd want us to be quite, quite certain.'

'Shall we try it together?'

'I'd like that.'

They moved to each other and kissed long and gently. The back door burst open and Buzby came in. 'It's starting to rain . . . oh, sorry!' he said and went out again.

That night a cold front moved in from the north, tumbling the high pressure system forever southward, across the channel and into France, until it had returned to

211

its regular home in the Mediterranean. In Skerrymor Bay the postman drove his van through pouring rain to deliver just one letter to the white house.

It was from Patrick.

During the night Morrison had pondered on his reckless vision of the future where his words, spoken out of involuntary impulsiveness in an effort to prevent Carrie leaving, were totally characteristic of his youth when he had been forever willing to flash out with an answer, his mouth speaking before his mind had thought.

Why did he want her to come and live with him? The answer was straightforward enough; she was wonderful company, extremely attractive, she got on well with Biddy, and although she did not share his love of sporting endeavour her mental prowess exceeded his and her conversation was stimulating. Above all, she appreciated him. Her admiration was a considerable incentive because Morrison had always performed better in front of an audience.

Why had he asked her to marry him? He was less sure about that and he slightly regretted his tongue running away with him. He was surprised by his sudden prudence, it was not a quality he'd shown as a younger man. Carrie had agreed to move in and time would look after the rest.

Now, within twelve hours of the decision being reached, came the letter from his father-in-law accepting his long-standing invitation to spend a few days at the white house. He had warned them often enough that it would be a case of camping until the passage of time held out sufficient opportunity for redecoration but he seriously doubted they would be expecting to walk into some kind of kibbutz which included cohabitation in both the caravan and house. He could visualise their abject horror at the thought of their grand-daugher being raised in such surroundings.

Perhaps the time had come for a cool assessment of just what kind of job he was making of preparing his daughter to face the world with elegance and style. For a start he went into her bedroom, and was at once appalled. The standing rule was that Biddy made her own bed in the morning and Mrs Burgess gave the room a thorough clean once a week, but he could not recall the last time he had checked on whether the routine was being followed. Her bed was unmade, in fact MacGregor was lying in the middle of it, and it was clear the housekeeper had long since abandoned the unequal battle of putting away sufficient of her flung-down belongings to provide a clear space that could be cleaned. Her clothes were everywhere, drawers and cupboards were left open, posters, pictures, and a rosette for some success in a junior riding competition were fastened to the wall with nails. One end of the curtain rail had broken from its support and was sagging into the room. The thing which most took him aback was that he'd sat on the bed only the previous night, combing Biddy's hair, and *hadn't noticed*. He stepped across the landing into his own bedroom. In all honesty he could not claim it appeared to be that much better: his jacket and trousers were on the back of a chair, the bed was more covered up than made, yesterday's shirt was screwed up in a corner.

Morrison went over the whole house becoming slowly overwhelmed by depression at the sign of neglect which lay everywhere. For months his eyes had looked but had not seen. What he saw now made utter nonsense of his flamboyant speech in the kitchen: what must Carrie have thought? Any promise the future held out was nullified by the Godawful mess that lay in the present. He might have caught some fish, and paid off a few debts, but only at the expense of totally ignoring fundamental living standards.

The thought of his mother-in-law's face when she saw the house was too awful to contemplate and it was in-conceivable that she and Patrick could sleep in it. As for Carrie, who'd actually been into every room, he shuddered at his brashness in suggesting she might care to move in. He dialled the number of The Last Resort.

'Alistair,' he asked when Macleod answered, 'would you have a double room available for a few nights from Saturday week?'

'You know I haven't, laddie,' the landlord replied. 'July and August are the only months I'm full.'

213

'It's very important.'

'It doesn't make any difference. Believe me, if I had floorspace for another bed I'd be using it. You'll find everyone's the same.'

'Okay.'

'Who's it for anyway?'

'The in-laws are coming to stay.'

'What's wrong with your place?'

'Just about everything, I'm afraid. I've been looking round and I appear to be living in a hovel.'

'Och, away. Fill 'em up wi' whisky, they'll no notice the wallpaper.'

'Alistair, there *isn't* any wallpaper.'

This was greeted with a rich laugh. 'Away now, I'm busy.' The line went dead. Morrison went upstairs again. Something was going to have to be done. He looked into the bedrooms once more and mild panic took possession of him. The truth was he just didn't know where to begin.

Below him he heard the back door crash open as Mrs Burgess arrived to cause further devastation in her pursuit of cleanliness. He thundered downstairs and burst into the kitchen.

'Mrs Burgess, have you seen this house? I mean, have you *seen* it?'

She looked up, startled by his tone of voice. 'What do you mean, Mr Morrison?'

'It's a slum, a shanty, a hovel.'

'Are you suggesting it's dirty?' He missed the dangerous edge to her voice.

'No, it's not actually dirty. It's untidy. No, untidy isn't a strong enough word. It's a mess!'

'Well I'm sure I'll not be taking the blame for that, Mr Morrison. If you find a speck of dirt in the house then you can hold me responsible, but for all its other sins you must look to yourself.'

'Yes, all right. It's just that I've been looking round –'

'You and your toty wee thing need a servant girl to trail in your wake, picking up all the things you throw down. I've barely enough time to clean up after you, do your washing and ironing and prepare the vegetables.'

'That's the trouble with all of us – there aren't enough hours in the day.'

'Then you shouldn't be wasting time laying blame where it isn't due, if I may say so.'

'Mrs Burgess, you've made your point and I apologise.' Why the hell am I *apologising*? he thought. 'I have some guests arriving on Saturday week and something has to be done about this place.'

'Well there's no use looking to me for anything more. Mr Burgess has been taken bad again and my hands are full.'

'Very well,' Morrison snapped to end the futile conversation. After a few moments her words sank in and politeness prompted him to say, 'I'm sorry about your husband. I hope it's nothing serious.'

'I dare say he'll pull through. He always has before.' There was bitterness in her voice and he decided against pursuing that tack any further.

'Did you know that Cluny died yesterday?'

She hadn't heard. Now she really was shocked. 'That would be the result of those villains pushing him over the cliff.'

'It was pneumonia, actually, but you're right in that the broken leg could have brought it on.'

'Miss Biddy will be that upset.'

'She is. I suspect there's some real grief still to come out, but at the moment she's being very good. She went to school this morning.'

'The last day of term.'

'Is it? Is it really?'

Mrs Burgess gave him one of her exasperated looks; there would be no easy absolution for his sin of criticising her work. 'Mr Morrison, do you know *anything* about what goes on in that school?'

At least here was a shaft he could catch and throw back. 'Quite a bit actually,' he admitted smugly.

He forced his concern about the state of the house to the back of his mind for the time being and concentrated on cleaning up the boxing and despatch room from the morning's catch, making more ice to be ready for the evening, and entering the log. Sigmund was aboard the workboat servicing the engine, Bobo had gone to the station and Buzby was putting together a mooring for the Cornelius yacht, having made up his mind, on Morrison's behalf, that its presence would lift the tone of the bay.

By early evening the rain had cleared and a shaft of sun found a break in the clouds to provide a spectacular rainbow which gave way, as the skies cleared, to a glorious sunset. They were still working the nets when Carrie and Biddy returned to the house.

School had broken up at lunchtime but the two of them had spent the afternoon shopping. This time it was the kind of shopping Biddy adored, visiting first a do-it-yourself shop in Fort William where they chose wallpaper and paints, brushes, sandpaper, and ancillary equipment including a collapsible pasting table, all of which they heaped into the back of Carrie's car. Afterwards they'd gone to find curtain material, a bedcover, and several reels of cotton. On an impulse they'd purchased brightly coloured matching dungarees and check shirts before, finally, Carrie called into her room at the school to pick up a couple of packed suitcases and her sewing machine.

'This is goodbye, then,' Biddy had overheard the head-mistress say in a tight voice.

Carrie had replied, 'I shall be coming in on Sunday to fetch the rest of my things. I want to thank you for everything you've done.' It was polite, strained, and formal.

In the car she'd given a deep sigh before starting the engine. 'Do you know what it feels like to be free?' she asked Biddy.

'I think so.'

'No you don't. You have to be confined to the point of suffocation before you can appreciate freedom.' Then she'd tossed her head, grinned at Biddy, and accelerated away with a screech of tyres.

By the time Morrison jumped ashore the two girls were dressed in their cheerful workclothes and were unloading the car. Biddy had topped her outfit with Cluny's hat and, when she joined Carrie, she was struggling towards the house with a gallon can of emulsion.

'I'm on holiday!' Carrie announced.

'You're out of work!' he grinned.

'Uh-huh,' she corrected, shaking her head. 'In September I'm out of work, today I'm on holiday.' There was a new confidence about her.

His eyes went to the pile of decorating materials. 'It's telepathy!' he exclaimed. He told her of his morning tour and resultant depression and she smiled happily as she listened. 'I sat in Biddy's room wondering where on earth to begin,' he finished.

She too had thought long and hard through the small hours and deplored her own timidity. David Morrison was a strong man and, despite his words, she knew she had yet to win his love. 'Oh you!' she chided. 'You know your trouble. You're either "up" or "down", there's no middle course.'

'Do you know what to do with all that lot?'

'Listen, you've got an interior decorator here. It's what I was doing when first we met, remember?'

He gazed at her in wonderment. 'I can scarcely believe it's the same girl.' Her fair hair glowed in the evening light, her eyes shared her laughter but became suddenly soft and questioning as he studied her face. ' "Divinely tall and most divinely fair," ' he quoted gently.

She rested both arms on his shoulders, entwining her fingers around the back of his neck. 'Tonight,' she whispered, 'I'm going to cook a meal for your army, then I'm going to sleep with you, and tomorrow I'm going to set about our home from top to bottom.' She slowly pulled his head to her until their lips met in a long kiss.

Buzby came round the corner of the boathouse. 'I finished laying the mooring . . . Oh, sorry,' he said and disappeared again. Biddy and MacGregor paused on the threshold of the front door and looked steadily at her father with the schoolteacher. 'I suppose we're just going to have to try to get used to this,' she muttered to the dog.

But she didn't like it. She didn't like it one bit. She was

only persevering with it because of what Cluny had said to her.

Carrie fitted effortlessly into the household routine, neatly side-stepping any embarrassments her presence could have caused. Whilst she gently took over responsibility in the kitchen, re-arranging it to her liking, instinctively she avoided unwitting trespass into areas where Morrison's custom and practice prevailed. She studied the house carefully, taking in the incongruity of apartment furnishings in the traditional setting, and decided how in time she could bring her own influence to bear. She guessed that most of the rooms were arranged as repeats from his former home. Indeed, it seemed to her that Wendy's presence could be found in every nook and cranny. She felt no resentment; there was no hurry, but she felt sure she could not respond to his impulsive proposal of marriage until the memories of his first wife were less close to the surface.

This was why Carrie had decided to tackle Biddy's room first and on the Monday, when Morrison returned to the house from the tour of his nets, he found them hard at work in his daughter's bedroom, Biddy up a stepladder taking down fittings with a screwdriver and Carrie on hands and knees sandpapering the wainscoting. The furniture had been dragged out on to the landing and into his bedroom. Outside, the rain, which had begun to fall again at dawn, beat a tattoo on the window panes and could be heard cascading down the drainpipe.

'Hi,' he said. 'Did I lose my first assistant?'

'Look at it this way,' advised Biddy, 'you might have lost an assistant but you gained a comedy act.' So saying she jumped off the steps whilst Carrie scrambled to her feet and, side by side in their matching outfits, they performed for him a newly learned soft shoe shuffle. Carrie so tall, Biddy so short and wearing Cluny's hat, the pair looked ridiculously funny and his infectious laughter at their antics prompted them all to giggle happily for a minute or so before resuming work.

Downstairs he discovered a monosyllabic Mrs Burgess wearing a carefully arranged look of shocked disapproval. 'I see you didn't waste time finding someone to clear up after you,' she commented provocatively, but Morrison was not to be drawn and ignored her taunt. She clearly regarded the schoolteacher as a fallen woman and would have said so given the slightest encouragement. Morrison was painfully aware that he would encounter all manner of reaction during the coming weeks until the village became used to the idea but, whatever views were expressed by the locals, they wouldn't hold a candle to those which would be voiced by his mother-in-law when she appeared on the scene.

He had intended to tell Carrie about the impending visit but after her kiss by the car, and the promise which accompanied it, all else seemed irrelevant. He was clear in his mind that the concern of his in-laws began and ended with the welfare of their grand-daughter, and it must be obvious to the most jaundiced eye that Biddy would be better cared for within something approaching a family atmosphere. A step-mother was better than no mother at all – particularly one who without conscious thought elected to give top priority to redecorating the child's bedroom.

By evening the 'comedy act' had emulsioned the ceiling, prepared the walls for lining paper, and given the woodwork a first undercoat. Sufficient furniture for the night was pushed back into the room and Carrie sank exhausted into a warm bath while Biddy preferred a dip in the sea despite the rain. Morrison kept a careful eye on her from the lounge window and noticed that MacGregor, who hated anyone entering the water, maintained anxious watch from the shore.

The dinner had been cleared away, Biddy was asleep, and the caravan was rocking gently, before Morrison and Carrie were able to talk to each other alone. Wearing a simple dress she sat relaxed in the lamp-light when he handed her the letter from Patrick.

219

'Damn!' she said after she'd read it.

'I could put them off.'

'No, why should you?' There was a slight pause. 'Would you prefer me not to be here?'

'No I wouldn't.' His firmness belied further discussion. She nodded, contented. There was no need for him to explain his thought process of the morning, she seemed to understand without words being spoken.

'I'll have our room done by the time they arrive,' she said. 'It's probably best we put them there.'

'You go in with Biddy and I'll take the day-bed down here,' he suggested. It was a satisfactory compromise. These were church-going people with their own sense of values, and there was little point in offending their code more than necessary.

'Very well,' she agreed. The only thing is, she thought ruefully, they'll almost certainly sleep in the newly decorated room before we do!

The next morning, after the catch had been boxed and despatched, Sigmund took Morrison to one side.

'I've been hearing things,' he began.

'Dammit, you know. You've met her!' responded Morrison, jumping to conclusions.

The German smiled briefly. 'No, no, not about Caroline. I'm delighted for you both.' His face grew serious again. 'I was referring to Bruce Cornelius.'

'How did you hear about that?'

'This is a small town with small talk. Is it true?'

'Nothing's settled. We talked briefly, and in the middle of the night. I'm to go back to him again when I've completed some preliminary work.'

'May I make it clear to you that, if what I hear is correct, I disapprove most strongly?'

'All right, Sigmund. Let's hear exactly what it is you have heard.'

'That Bruce Cornelius is to put up the money for you to start a fish farm.'

The skipper was clearly upset and Morrison realised immediately that here was something he must handle carefully. 'It's obvious that your informant is Commander Campbell who, as I recall, slept through the entire conversation and cannot be looked upon as a reliable source.'

'I agree with you there.' The eyes regarded him steadily. 'It would have been nice had you told me yourself.'

'I had every intention of doing so. I really did,' Morrison declared emphatically. 'Honestly, Sigmund, there's been so much on my mind and my feet have scarcely touched the ground.'

'I'm sure.' The German did not shift his gaze. 'Then why don't we talk about it now?'

Morrison felt completely wrong-footed by the direction the conversation was taking. He'd wanted to discuss the matter with Sigmund, to seek his opinion which he valued, but not to seek his permission which he didn't need.

'Bruce Cornelius has asked me to investigate the ins-and-outs of a fish farm. When I report back to him we're going to decide where we go next.'

'I see.'

Morrison strived to get back on even terms. 'We're talking about a winter job and, if I may say so, the close season is outside our terms of reference. Whatever I do is no affair of yours.' He tried a conciliatory smile to soften the words, but it failed.

'One,' said Sigmund, numbering the points off on his fingers, 'it is a dilution of your interests; two, to say it is a winter job is nonsensical – what do you imagine happens in the summer? Three, it *is* my affair to the tune of £10,000.'

'It goes without saying you will be consulted and rowed into anything I do in recognition of your investment.'

'Ah, well, that is the point you see. I don't want any part of it. I hate the whole concept.'

'Does that imply I'm to have no part of it either?'

'David, why are we talking like this? It's you and me, eh?'

The two men strolled towards the beach. 'You started all this when you showed me the diseased salmon and told me about the drift netting,' Morrison accused.

'I did so in the expectation you would add your voice to those of the rest of us in the protection of our interests. I did not think for one moment you would fly off in a different direction altogether.'

'I haven't flown off anywhere yet.'

'Why has Buzby laid a new mooring in the bay?'

'I've agreed to look after his boat for him. What's that got to do with it?'

'Look after his boat!' Sigmund gave an expressive shrug. 'Cornelius already pays a boatman in Mallaig to do that. I think he has lent it to you – as part of the softening up process.'

'Sigmund,' said Morrison with extreme care, 'let me promise you this. There is no way I will ever let you down over the £10,000 either financially or morally; there is no way I will ever forget all that you've done and are still doing; and there is no way I won't branch out into fish farming if I want to.'

'Good,' said the German. 'It's better that we know where we stand.'

Morrison was upset by the argument with his partner but, at the same time, he was determined not to be deflected from his course. The dormant furnaces of ambition had been re-fired and, with the added incentive of a new admirer, prepared to applaud his progress, he planned a climb to the pinnacle of success.

When Siggy returned during the late afternoon the two men worked the nets together, for all the world as if the morning's exchange had never occurred. Over the following fortnight there were to be so many incidents competing to distract him from sensing discord, and blinding him to reality, that he was to forget altogether their discussion.

Which was a pity. It had been the only early-warning he was to receive that all was not as it should be. From there on Morrison became as a small boat being tugged silently and unknowingly by an unrelenting current towards the rapids.

Throughout the remainder of the week the 'comedy act' carried on decorating and the outdoor team continued hauling in fish until, as they de-rigged the leader nets for the weekend close, Morrison reckoned they'd earned their relaxation.

In Biddy's room the transformation was complete. Carrie had tremendous flair and her touches had produced a girl's bedroom which was at once practical as well as feminine. Their only disagreement had been over the question of whether MacGregor should continue to sleep upstairs and this argument had been won by the Collie himself. At bedtime Carrie led him to his basket in the kitchen and he lay there dutifully, giving every pretence of settling for sleep, until the house was silent. Then he crept silently up to the bedroom where, surprisingly, he found Biddy's door ajar. The only thing was, the old dog had grown a little deaf with age and whilst he imagined he was running the gauntlet soundlessly Morrison and Carrie were giggling helplessly as they listened to him crash upstairs like a troop of guardsmen.

On the Saturday a blue sky was punctuated by drifts of broken summer cumulus and a fresh breeze rippled the waves with a million sparkling reflections. Buzby was all for bringing round the Cornelius yacht whereas Carrie was anxious to buy materials for decorating the principal bedroom.

'We can do both,' declared Morrison confidently. 'We'll motor round the headland and have her on the mooring by midday.'

Carrie was very nearly taken in but, looking out over the Sound and feeling the wind on her cheek, she knew that the moment Morrison felt the trembling deck beneath his feet he'd be gone for the day. 'You go and sail,' she said. 'I'll join you on board for tea.'

Any doubt he might have had was dispelled by Bobo electing to join the shopping expedition whereupon all five heaped into Carrie's car and she drove them to Mallaig. Morrison, Buzby and Biddy waved goodbye as Carrie and Bobo doubled back along the same road for the run into

223

Fort William.

Morrison's heart gave an exultant leap as he picked out *Sea Dancer* among the yacht moorings. She was a custom built sloop in white fibreglass and teak laid deck, based on a design looking like a cross between a Folkboat and a Nicholson 30. She had the most graceful lines with long overhangs and, apart from some oil around the waterline, was in nothing like the condition described by Bruce Cornelius. She snubbed restlessly against her mooring and Biddy sensed her father's keen anticipation to put to sea in what promised to be perfect sailing weather.

The boatman had received instructions from the millionaire and handed over the keys, albeit somewhat unwillingly, before ferrying them out in the harbour tender.

Once aboard, Morrison unlocked and slid back the hatch, lifted out the boards, and descended the companionway for a thorough tour of inspection. He was not surprised to find the boat was equipped comprehensively and he quickly came across a small flotation jacket which he slipped on Biddy. Whilst tying the waistband he warned sternly, 'Remember the golden rule; one hand for the boat, one hand for yourself. If I once catch you running around without holding on it's down below for the rest of the trip. Right?'

'Right.'

Starboard of the companionway was a chart table with, above it, barometer, chronometer, and echo sounder, whilst to port was a superbly equipped galley with sink, calor gas stove, and small refrigerator. The saloon appeared remarkably spacious with standing headroom for most of its length and comfortably fitted out. Through a bulkhead was a toilet and hanging space forward of which was a tiny two-berth cabin which had access to the foredeck through a hatch. A complete suit of sailbags was stowed here, mainsail, working jib, storm jib, genoa and spinnaker, and up in the bows was the chain locker in which the anchor chain was stowed when the vessel was under way.

The cockpit took up nearly half the boat although, aft,

the counter was unusually long. The diesel engine and heavy batteries were set below it amidships together with fuel and water storage tanks. All the sailing gear was of fine quality, stainless steel pulpit, winches, cleats, fairleads and shrouds, and a tall aluminium mast.

Morrison spent a full hour familiarising himself with the boat, testing the engine, checking the rigging, finding the appropriate Admiralty chart, before he rove the jib sheets. By this time Biddy was growing bored and anxious to start sailing. She was soon to discover that her father became an entirely different man when he was afloat. Even while his unquestionable ability brought with it a sense of complete security he seemed to become long on detailed perfection and short on temper. Long periods of ecstatic enjoyment were punctuated by squalls of angry shouting; when the boat was sailing full and bye he was the loveliest man in the world, a restless leech brought sharp rebuke to whoever was sail handling, and a clumsy gybe made him hell on earth. The more she sailed with him in the weeks that followed so would his outbursts become as water off a duck's back, but at first it was extremely alarming.

'Which sails?' enquired Buzby from the forecabin.

'We'll bend on the main and the genny.' Whilst these were removed from their bags and handed up to deck Morrison ran up a triangular burgee to the masthead. The two men guided the mainsail luff into a track in the mast and shackled the genoa to the forestay. After that they shackled on the halliards and were ready to hoist away. Seconds later the vessel shook with the maddened violence of wildly flapping sails. The sound was deafening and Biddy, crouching low in the cockpit, found the untamed power frightening. The sails continued to beat frantically as Morrison rigged a boom downhaul and Buzby made ready to release the mooring. Then her father was at the tiller, shouting for Buzby to 'let go' the steel loop around the samson post and 'back the genny' until the mainsail filled. There was a splash and she felt the boat drifting astern. In a flash Morrison was close by her, pulling in the jib sheet to the rattle of a winch, moving quickly back to the tiller still holding the free end until Buzby could come aft and make it off to a cleat.

Suddenly there was glorious silence. The sails filled, the boat surged forward heeling majestically to the breeze, bows shouldering aside the water in a smother of foam. *Sea Dancer* came wondrously alive and Biddy experienced for the first time the deep thrill which accompanies the moment a sailing boat enters its own sphere and becomes as one with the wind. Her father sat on the weather side, eyes forever on the move as he picked his way past the moorings towards the open water beyond. 'Come over beside me,' he called, and a second later she sat close to him, feeling the first flicks of spray, instinctively bracing herself as the boat heeled harder on its windward course. Buzby joined them and, seeing her legs dangling, pulled out an empty five-gallon water-carrier which he placed on the cockpit sole in order that she had something to push against. Then he produced a couple of cans of beer from his ditty-bag. 'Want anything?' he asked her. She shook her head. Being with Morrison on a thirty-foot sloop in a Force Four breeze was as much as she could cope with for the time being.

They beat to windward for over ninety minutes and when they were right out in the Sound the wind freshened and backed slightly. *Sea Dancer* revelled in the conditions and Biddy watched the water rushing past the leeward side with only inches of freeboard showing. For half an hour she'd had her hand over Morrison's on the tiller while he explained how a boat will sail 'against the wind' and made her observe the angle of the masthead burgee and how the clews of the sails were 'asleep' indicating that they were drawing perfectly. Then he allowed her to take the helm on her own.

At first she was nervous, remembering how he'd shouted at Buzby for steering carelessly when he'd taken it earlier. The tiller vibrated in her grasp, sometimes moving lightly but during a gust becoming so heavy she was nearly pulled from her seat. She dared not remove her eyes from the burgee which had remained rock steady when Morrison was steering but now pointed all over the place.

'Take it back a second,' she asked. He did so and she ran below to fetch a cushion which she placed where she'd been sitting in order to kneel on it. It seemed to her the additional height would give her greater control. 'Now let's have a *go* at this thing,' she muttered and took the tiller from him.

It goes without saying that a novice helmsman makes all manner of mistakes, usually by responding too late and then over-correcting. However, an experienced sailor can judge within minutes whether the sailing *instinct* is present in a pupil – if it's not no amount of theory will compensate and the newcomer might as well try to steer a train.

Morrison watched his daughter struggling with the tiller and felt an enormous glow of pride. The steering was all over the place, but she was aware whenever it went wrong and slowly her corrections became less frantic. The tiny figure, face concentrating under Cluny's hat, was actually sailing a thirty-foot boat. It was a moment he would never forget.

After twenty minutes he took back the helm. 'We'll do ten minutes on the starboard tack by which time the tide will be changing and we'll be set for a four-mile run into Skerrymor Bay.' He saw Buzby reach for the opposite jib sheet and then lean across to show Biddy how to flick her sheet clear of the winch as the bows came through the eye of the wind. 'Ready about,' called Morrison. 'Lee ho!'

He pushed the helm hard over and moved across to the other side of the cockpit. By the time he got there it had all gone wrong. Biddy flicked her sheet clear but then *didn't let go*. For a moment she was attempting to hold the entire weight of the wind-filled sail in her hands and as the terylene rope was pulled through her grasp she felt a searing, burning pain which was worse than any she'd experienced. 'Let it fly, Biddy,' he yelled, whereupon she'd let go and the figure-of-eight knot in its tail caught her a stinging blow on the side of her face. 'Sheet in, Buzby, what's the matter with you?' shouted Morrison. The sail was beating with a sound like thunderclaps but Buzby was unable to winch in his sheet. 'You've got it round the winch the wrong way, you bloody idiot!'

When at last they were sailing on the new tack Morrison said, 'That was the most ham-fisted manoeuvre I've ever witnessed.'

Biddy looked down at her raw hands where blisters were already beginning to form. '*Eee-ow-ee*, the pain,' she cried 'the 'orrible, *ex-croo* . . .'

Suddenly she was weeping. Deep racking sobs that surprised her with their intensity until she realised they had nothing to do with the pain in her hands. Morrison said to Buzby, 'Take over!' Then she was in his arms, his voice whispering, 'It's all right, my darling, I know. I *know*.'

He carried her below, wrapped her in a rug, and laid her down on the saloon bunk. After a while he returned up top and brought *Sea Dancer* round for the run home. With the wind astern the sound dropped until only the water rushing by could be heard. Buzby wasn't a good enough helmsman to trust on this more difficult point of sailing, so Biddy was left to sob her heart out all alone in the cabin until they picked up the buoy in Skerrymor Bay.

Janet Mahoney hesitated outside the manse at Loch Lomond. It would have been better had she abandoned her mission and turned round then and there, but by that time she had journeyed a very long way and it was this, as much as anything else, that decided her to go through with it.

'Miss Mahoney,' exclaimed Mrs Kelso when she opened the door. 'Well, this is a surprise.'

'I should have written,' the headmistress apologised.

'Come in, come in!'

Within minutes they were seated with the Reverend Kelso drinking coffee and fast running out of small talk. The purpose of the visit could be delayed no longer and Janet Mahoney drew a deep breath and stumbled into the opening sentences of her saga. 'There is something I think you ought to know . . .' she began.

After a little while Mrs Kelso was looking at her with an expression of hurt surprise but her husband listened attentively to the very end, his face expressionless. Janet Mahoney's story was basically one of a blossoming young schoolteacher who had misguidedly fallen in love with the father of one of her pupils, and had thrown up her career to go off and live with him in sin. As she talked Kelso detected an overtone of personal emotion in the apparently dispassionate report and correctly surmised that there was more to the talk than he was hearing. He had wondered so often why it was he felt uncomfortable in her presence and, with the passing of years, a suspicion had been born deep in his mind. In no way could the minister be regarded as a man of the world but, with the increasing freedoms of television and the press, not to mention the more liberal viewpoints of the Church itself, even he had become aware of relationships which once upon a time were shrouded in secrecy.

At last she was finished. The Reverend Kelso leaned forward and knocked out his pipe in an ash-tray. 'Tell me, Miss Mahoney,' he enquired mildly, 'why have you come here to tell us these things?'

'I felt it was my duty,' she replied self-righteously.

'Your duty,' he repeated as he held the pipe at arm's length to survey the empty bowl before pushing it back into his pocket. 'When somebody presses the button that will blow up the entire world it will be done out of a misplaced sense of duty.'

'I – I don't understand.'

'Was it also your duty to – er – ' he hesitated slightly, ' – misguide my wife and myself about your original intentions regarding our daughter?'

'At no time did I do any such thing! I believed then, and believe now, that Caroline has a great potential as a teacher.'

'Quite so. However, with the aid of hindsight, I am tempted to wonder if there was not another motive. A more personal one.' The minister could feel his wife's horrified gaze transfer to him. These were thoughts which had dogged him in the depth of night and had never until now been spoken aloud.

'I have put personal money into her future. I paid for much of her training.'

'I remember,' agreed the minister, 'and pray do not imagine we were not considerably impressed by the gesture.' Then he added quietly, 'But that does not answer my question about motive.'

'I didn't come here to be insulted.'

'Ah. With that statement I know we are both aware of what we're talking about.' The headmistress sat in haughty silence. 'What do you suggest we do?' asked Kelso.

There was another long pause before Janet Mahoney said with a change of tone, 'Talk to her. Make her come back.'

'Caroline is twenty-seven,' he pointed out.

Mrs Kelso decided to speak up. She'd been badly jolted by the news, and severely shaken by her husband's observation, but there was nothing slow about her reaction. 'Throughout his life, Miss Mahoney, my husband has reserved his anger for the Devil and his work. I'm not sure we do not have a servant of Lucifer in this very room. That you should consider us so stupid as to be totally ignorant of unnatural behaviour is bad enough, but to come here with lies and deceit is beyond belief. Your wicked so-called sense of duty has done no good whatsoever. It has brought us only distress.'

'We had a friendship once that was warm and beautiful.' All the force had deserted Janet Mahoney and she stared at the floor, a stupid, pathetic figure. 'There was never anything more.'

By mutual consent the minister and his wife rose to their feet at the same time and Janet Mahoney was ushered politely from their house. Her confused excuses and apologies echoed hollowly in the hallway before the front door was closed on her. Only then did the couple turn to each other.

'What will we do?' she asked.

'I think we must go and see Caroline,' he replied. 'There will be two sides to the story and I will prefer to hear our daughter's version. Remember this, only death is final.

230

Until then wrongs can be put right and, after all, we want only that Caroline should be happy.'

'That headmistress, she is a bad woman!' declared Mrs Kelso.

'I thought you spoke to her most sharply. You were very forthright.'

'You never said anything,' she exclaimed defensively.

'Why should I? I agreed with every word.' As they walked back into his study he placed an arm around her. 'Besides, had you not spoken when you did, I think I was about to hit her!'

Sigmund having made it clear he wanted no part of the projected fish farming scheme, Morrison was at something of a loss as to where he should start his investigation. There was a certain amount of official literature available, and this he read, but what he needed was personal contact with someone who could advise on all the wrinkles. He decided to go and see Bob MacPherson in Glasgow; the factor knew the fishing world from pole to pole and had been a tower of strength throughout their first season.

He asked the German to look after things for a day at the Skerrymor Bay end and set off for the city at first light. MacPherson was clear of the market by lunchtime and the plan was for Morrison to take him to lunch. In the circumstances, having established by telephone the subject matter of their business together, he had troubled to contact a colleague more closely associated with fish farming than himself and at one o'clock the three men sat down together.

They were still talking at four o'clock but by then Morrison had made copious notes and was immensely grateful to his new friends for the generosity they had shown him both in their advice and time. Naturally the two men would each expect his business to come their way if his enterprise got off the ground but no hard and fast conditions were made at this early stage. He resolved to write his report for Bruce Cornelius during the week and deliver it by the weekend before his in-laws arrived. It would be an impressive and comprehensive paper and would have a good feel to it.

He arrived home a few minutes before midnight and Carrie was waiting for him. It was good to walk through his front door and find her there, he'd looked forward to the moment throughout the journey and now it had arrived he experienced a deeply satisfying sense of normality. There was a short note from Siggy setting out the day's catch and the prices paid in the market – he was unaware, of course, that Morrison already had the information – and soon he was giving Carrie an account of his meeting.

She felt better as she listened to him talking. He had been too full of his own news to notice how strained she looked and, anyway, a part of the strain had evaporated with the warmth of his greeting. She watched his face, the eyes tired from the hours of driving but shining with enthusiasm nevertheless. He was telling her everything because he wanted to share it with her, it would be but a short time before she became an inseparable part of his life, and her reaction to his story was as important to him as food and drink. Realising this, she smiled appreciatively and tried to concentrate on the next few sentences to make up for the number she'd permitted to be drowned by her thoughts. She loved him. She was quite sure of it now. He needed her and she needed him. She would go through with the visit of Biddy's grandparents, and wait until the salmon season was ended, but after that she hoped the question mark would be lifted from their relationship.

There was silence and she was aware suddenly that he had asked a question and awaited an answer. 'I'm sorry, darling, what did you say?'

'Have you heard a word I've said?'

'Yes. Yes, of course I have. I think it's wonderful.'

'I asked what sort of day you'd had.' She looked directly at him, wondering whether to tell him or save it until a night's rest had put the awfulness into perspective. He made the decision for her. 'Come on, tell me. Something's wrong, isn't it?'

'I went shopping today.' She tried to keep her voice

232

matter-of-fact. 'At first it felt weird but then it became rather dreadful.'

'What became dreadful, Carrie?' He had a sense of foreboding and thought he knew what she was going to say.

'I have lived in this village for twenty-seven years so when I walked into the High Street it took me a full ten minutes before I realised people I have known all my life were crossing the road in order to avoid me. I couldn't believe it at first, and when I did I put it to the test by wishing terribly bright "good mornings" to all and sundry. Some responded briefly, others just nodded, a few totally ignored me.' Her eyes were bright with tears and he moved quickly on to the settee beside her and drew her to him until her head rested against his shoulder. 'I actually forced Nancy Drummond to stop and talk to me by hanging on to the pram but the moment I released it she scuttled off like a startled rabbit.'

'I never imagined these things happened in 1983.'

'Our village isn't in 1983 yet. It was Mrs Lindsay in the grocers who crowned it all, she never was one for mincing her words. She said it was as well Janet Mahoney got rid of me because she for one wouldn't want her little girl taught the evil ways of a kept woman.' Morrison sighed, for the moment words escaped him. Carrie finished, 'It appears my erstwhile headmistress has been putting it abroad that she dismissed me *because* I came to live with you.'

'The woman's a liar.'

'People tend to believe liars, their stories usually sound more convincing.'

There was a pause during which he absorbed her bad tidings. Then he said, 'Look at me.' Carrie leaned forward and turned her head to him. His eyes were serious. 'I love you, Carrie, and there's no reason why we shouldn't marry straight away. It's not normally my style to be irresolute – maybe I just wasn't ready for someone like you.'

Her expression matched his as she reached for his hand. 'You're not free of Wendy yet, I can feel myself being compared still.' She squeezed his fingers to prevent a hasty denial. 'Listen, I don't *mind*, darling, not yet. I would never expect you to forget her – how could I with her personality imbued in Biddy? But that doesn't mean I want her remembered constantly. I'll know when you look at me and see only Carrie. Then I'll marry you.'

He looked at her for several moments. Then he nodded slowly. 'Okay. So we have some choices open to us. We can ignore village reaction to our sin and plough on regardless, which is a nice thought but difficult for me and utterly impossible for you; or we can move away and set up shop somewhere else, which would be running away; or we can set about putting our own house in order and hope that by being ourselves we'll win back your lifelong friends and acquaintances.'

'Your place is here for the time being and I'm sticking by you.'

.On their way upstairs they surprised MacGregor who, under the impression that at one o'clock everyone must surely have retired, was creeping up to Biddy's bedroom. He attempted a burlesque performance of a dog who had awoken to find himself sleepwalking and headed downstairs again. Ten minutes later all was dark when he tried again. This time he made it and, settling himself silently at the foot of Biddy's bed, he gave a deep sigh of satisfaction.

All was right with his world.

They took Mr Burgess directly into Intensive Care. His eyes flickered open, dulled by the drugs, and he saw they'd given him a television set. It had a tiny screen with a picture of a green line that danced up and down regularly in time with his heartbeat. He watched it with customary intentness and even saw the moment it became an undeviating straight line. The programme must have finished because it faded out, television set and all.

When Mrs Burgess heard the news she went to the airing cupboard and pulled out a biscuit tin. She had never lied to her husband and didn't consider that keeping silent about his disability pension constituted a lie. The firm had sent for her and actually apologised that it was only £5 a

234

week and would terminate at his death. That had been nearly ten years ago and it was best he never knew – he'd have only spent it on drink.

After she'd counted the notes twice she went to her handbag and took out £5. Adding it to the contents of the tin brought the total to £2,500.

CHAPTER NINE

HALFWAY up Edinburgh's Mount stands the impressive nineteenth-century Assembly Hall in the courtyard of which presides a statue of John Knox wearing a dour Scottish scowl and raising his hand in dogmatic argument. To this hall each year come churchmen of most creeds to attend sessions of the Church's General Assembly. These good people debate on a wide-ranging list of subjects from theological disputation to Sabbath observance, from the waning influence of the Church to its attitude towards the use of contraceptives. Occasionally the exchanges take place at some considerable volume as fiery-tongued ministers from the Highlands thunder forth their narrow-minded viewpoints, rooted immovably in four centuries of dogma, and invariably outvote Lowland realists with their more liberal, modern minds. Nevertheless, the Church's heart pumps strongly in this pseudo-Gothic building and the theory is that the burden of their talks will circulate through the arteries and veins of churches, chapels and pulpits until the message reaches the farthermost limbs of its flock.

In practice the circulation of the Word is of poor order, coming up against obstructions or dead ends, sometimes discovering that here and there a limb has become completely severed from the main body of the Church. More often the message finds itself mixed up among a variety of subjects, and advice given locally would astound those at the source of the recommendations. One year the Assembly debated separately the questions of keeping the Sabbath holy and birth control, and the story goes that a young Highlander, married late one Saturday, asked his minister if it would be proper to consummate the union in view of the fact that the Sabbath was only minutes away. He was assured that consummation would be in order just so long as he didn't enjoy it. The end result is that the large majority of decent, clean-living souls base their beliefs on a mixture of upbringing and sporadic religious instruction, with its attendant dangers of illogicality. Once in a while such people have been known to join the ranks of partisan witch hunts.

One such instance was the treatment by her friends of Caroline Kelso.

The simple truth was that an older woman, with unnatural tendencies, had persuaded this young girl to live with her for seven years. Admittedly the tendencies were kept under firm control and on the rare occasions they manifested themselves the young girl instinctively parried them. Indeed for most of the time she was unaware of their meaning. Thus the relationship was akin to a girl with a maiden aunt, the latter jealously guarding a treasured companionship, the former trapped by the conditions surrounding her stay. The fact remained, however, that these two women cohabited year-in, year-out, and the village saw nothing strange in that fact, and allowed them to teach their children. The girl grew into a young woman and when at last her natural urges caused her to break free and live with a man, who had no unnatural tendencies whatsoever, at once the wrath of the village fell upon them. She became as a scarlet woman and an unhealthy influence on their young. In an age when permissiveness has reached a point where even the most liberal minded pause to ponder on the uninhibited behaviour of the young, it was incredible that there existed still a last stronghold of middle-age pietism where sanctimonious recrimination could be unleashed upon the relatively innocent victim.

It was to give Carrie the worst seven days of her life.

It had begun well enough when at the end of an interminable telephone conversation with his mother-in-law, during which Morrison had resigned himself to meeting

237

them off a train in Glasgow, Patrick had obviously snatched the receiver from his wife and said, 'Ignore her, son, we'll come by car. You're too busy to traipse all over Scotland meeting a couple of folks off a train. I'll get my map out and we'll be with you in time for tea on Saturday.' Although the drive from Glasgow would have provided ample opportunity to forewarn them about Carrie, Morrison was mightily relieved not to make the journey twice in one week.

Saturday arrived, a fine morning but with a gusting north-westerly threatening rain later. Morrison saw Biddy look longingly at *Sea Dancer* but sailing that day was positively out. So she telephoned Andrew Campbell and offered to show him the spot from where she and Cluny had first spotted the bird thieves. Morrison warned, 'Back in time for tea. All right?' She nodded. 'And I mean *in time*; that is, washed, changed, and ready for Granny.' The girl shrugged into her anorak, stuck on Cluny's hat, and ran off to meet Andrew. Buzby and Bobo were to have a make-do-and-mend day on nets and tackle, leaving Morrison free to help Carrie prepare for their guests.

Much to Carrie's relief he elected to get in the shopping, or messages as she called it, but beyond encountering a few sidelong glances there were no difficulties. In one shop he suspected the assistant was about to make him miss his turn so he moved quietly and stood looking directly down on her, whereupon the glint in his eyes caused the woman to change her mind. In any event it seemed as if local indignation was centred more on Carrie than himself, although nobody went out of their way to greet him.

The white house looked clean and welcoming. The two bedrooms shone invitingly whilst elsewhere polished furniture, fresh flowers, and carefully placed ornaments combined in an attempt to disguise lack of decoration. Buzby and Bobo had cheerfully agreed to eat in the caravan although they improved on the plan by deciding to cook themselves a special meal aboard *Sea Dancer*. Morrison wondered if a thirty-foot sloop could rock as much as a caravan. They were all working busily when, at three o'clock, into this hive of industry, Patrick's elderly Rover arrived.

Morrison hurried over to them. 'Hello. Welcome!'

'Wonderful journey,' enthused his father-in-law, 'we enjoyed every mile.'

'Whatever time did you leave?' asked Morrison, knowing the Irishman was a great one for making an early start.

'Yesterday. Stopped off overnight.' He climbed out of the car and added quietly, 'Even *she* was impressed. I'll swear I detected a softening of the features when we drove across the Great Glen.' Morrison grinned and moved round the car.

'Hello, Mother,' he said opening the door.

'Good afternoon, David. Where's Biddy?'

'As a matter of fact she's not back yet. You're a bit earlier than we expected.'

'You surely don't allow her to go out alone?'

'Oh, she's okay. She went up in the hills with a boy-friend.' He collected Black Mark number one for that nugget of information. He'd forgotten the careful path that must be trodden when conversing with his mother-in-law. Her expression snapped shut causing Morrison at once to lose his nerve over the more important news he had to impart. So he walked her to the nets where Buzby and Bobo were working and, whilst they talked briefly, he hurried back to his father-in-law who was lifting three heavy suitcases from the boot.

'She's packed enough to last us a month at least,' he observed.

'Patrick, I need your help,' Morrison said, endeavouring to remove undue urgency from his voice.

'You've got it, son.'

'You'll be meeting a Caroline Kelso in a minute. She's staying in the house until we can get married. I know it's a shock but can you prevent Mother going into orbit?'

'Personally I'm very glad for you and, no, I can't prevent Mother going into orbit.' Morrison should have known better than to ask. 'But I'll do my best,' promised Patrick.

'Take those inside, we'll follow on behind.'

Morrison picked up the two largest cases and hurried ahead, put them in their bedroom, and was down at the front door by the time they reached it. The deed was done and had it been a period movie his mother-in-law would have now been reaching for her smelling salts but, as she passed him, she recovered sufficiently to flash, 'What a fine thing to be told the moment we walk in the house!' He showed them into the living room where, seconds later, Carrie joined them.

Her entrance was quite breathtaking. Not just her appearance, she wore a bright apron over a cotton dress; but the force of her personality. She was at once cordial, warm, sensible, and capable. Her handshake was firm when she was introduced to his mother-in-law. 'How nice to meet you – you're exactly as Biddy described you;' and it was soft when she met Patrick. 'You've caught me preparing dinner, I hope you like steak and kidney pie.' It was his favourite dish, a fact she already knew. Then to both of them, 'Let me show you your room. You might like to freshen up after your drive while I make some tea.' The couple obediently followed her upstairs and Morrison brought up the rear with the third case. After Carrie had closed the door on them they paused on the landing, finger on the lips, like children.

'Well!' they heard her voice of disgust from inside.

'Nice girl!' came Patrick's reply.

'Living together!'

'His actual words were "staying in the house".'

A snort. 'Fine example for our grand-daughter. Don't you care about your grand-daughter?'

'Nice room this.'

'It's clean anyway.'

Carrie smiled at Morrison. She reckoned she'd got the old man sewn up in the opening round. As they crept downstairs Biddy arrived home with Andrew. If she hadn't actually forgotten her grandparents were arriving it was immediately apparent that something had occurred which was of greater importance. She cradled a bundle of feathers which turned out to be not one but two starlings – one quite dead. Carrie saw at once why Biddy had carried them home – the two birds were joined together Siamese-twin style at a joint in the leg. The girl had placed them on the floor while she cleared the kitchen table and the live bird was pathetically dragging its dead brother and flapping its wings in hopeless efforts to escape.

'What are you going to do?' asked Carrie.

'Emergency operation,' declared Biddy. 'Andrew here will assist.'

'You can't do it now, darling,' said Morrison, 'Granny and Grandpa are here.'

'This is a matter of life and death, Morrison.'

This was absolutely pure Biddy. She had her own list of priorities and even if all things were equal her grandma would not have ranked spectacularly high on it. Carrie threw him an 'if you can't fight 'em, join 'em' look and pitched in to make ready the operating table.

At the moment Patrick and his wife entered the kitchen the two adults and the children were stooping over the table, the surgeon wielding an extremely sharp kitchen knife whilst her assistant held down the patient.

'We're going to have to do this without anaesthetic,' muttered the surgeon.

'The shock will kill it,' ventured Morrison.

Carrie said, 'If we do nothing it's definitely going to die; if we try, it *might* live.'

By the door the old woman held out both arms and called, 'Biddy! Come to Granny, darling.'

'I'll be right with you as soon as I finish this.' She looked at Carrie and indicated the knife. 'Is this sterilised?'

'I dipped it in a kettle of boiling water.'

'Right. Here's what I'm going to do. I'm going to amputate the dead bird's leg half-an-inch above the joint.'

'Will the pain transmit to the live bird?' asked Andrew.

'We'll find out in a second.'

Patrick and his wife edged forward to peer down on the birds at the moment the surgeon made the single incision. Morrison removed the dead brother, Andrew handed over cotton wool and a bottle of TCP, Carrie took the knife out of harm's way. The surgeon disinfected the wound and gently picked up the terrified patient.

In fact the starling seemed all right. It was Granny who fainted clean away.

The next morning Patrick wanted a full tour of the fishing station and Morrison enjoyed showing him everything. Biddy also took her grandma round more briefly but the woman seemed less interested in their work than in prying into details of how she and her father lived. Later the lure of *Sea Dancer* was too tempting to resist and Morrison offered to take them for a short sail using, this time, Bobo as crew. His mother-in-law declined, pointedly observing that she intended to attend morning service even if no-one else saw fit to do so.

'I'll come with you,' Carrie promised quietly.

'I think it highly unlikely we are of the same faith,' came the stiff reply.

'There is a Catholic church. It's a fair drive and you'll not find it if I don't run you there.'

'Hm.' The older lady was taken aback by the gesture but could not bring herself to express gratitude.

In fact Carrie was relieved to be handed an excuse for avoiding the local service. She wasn't sure she could take the sight of Janet Mahoney raising her deep voice to heaven with every pretence of sincerity, and she still nursed hurt shock from the previous day when Mrs Macleod had stared directly at her without a flicker of expression.

However, she was not to be spared further humiliation. On their way home through the village her companion insisted they stop outside the small newsagent so that she might buy an *Observer*. When they emerged from the shop she all but bumped into Mrs Burgess who, despite her recent bereavement, appeared to be wearing a new hat.

The housekeeper nodded briefly and said without preamble, 'Oh there you are. I was hoping to see you in the kirk this morning. I was wanting you to tell Mr Morrison I'll not be coming round to the house any more.'

'But, Mrs Burgess, *why*?'

242

'Let's just say I'd prefer not to, and let it rest at that.'
'Very well.'

Mrs Burgess would have done well to leave it there but she was unable to resist the temptation of imparting the item of news which lifted her from the ranks of cleaners and elevated her to an equal footing with her betters. 'Tell him I'd have been away all September, anyway. I'm going on a cruise!' Carrie watched Mrs Burgess cross to a group of people, her face carrying an appropriate expression of grief which was in contrast to the triumphant flash her eyes had shown seconds earlier. One woman laid a sympathetic hand on the housekeeper's arm and Carrie shook her head in wonderment at such hypocrisy.

Morrison brought *Sea Dancer* into the bay and neatly on to her mooring. Patrick had revelled in every moment of the sail and shared his son-in-law's joy at the sight of Biddy taking the helm. As they rowed ashore Morrison was surprised to see Sigmund waiting for him by the boathouse. He introduced Patrick and they made polite conversation for a moment before the German turned to him.

'Could we have a word?' He looked strained and worried.

'Sure.'

Bobo went to the caravan and Biddy walked her grandfather to the house. Sigmund came directly to the point.

'Did you see Bob MacPherson when you were in Glasgow last Wednesday?'

'Yes I did.'

A small nod. 'He told me of your discussion.'

'There was nothing secret about it.' Nevertheless, Morrison wondered why the factor had spoken to Sigmund.

'Secret enough, though, for you to have said nothing to me.'

'I told you, Sigmund, that I have every intention of taking the fish farm idea to the next stage.'

The German sighed and pushed both hands deep into his pockets. 'You and me, we seem to work to different standards. We are partners, no? We have both invested time and money into this.' He waved a hand at the equipment all around them.

'Yes, but I said before –'

'Please listen to me,' Sigmund interrupted. 'I warned you when last we discussed the matter, but it seems you have no conception of how strongly I feel.'

'You made it clear enough that you want no part of it.'

'Correct. Also I want no part of anyone connected with it.'

'Oh.' Morrison felt as if an icy douche of water had hit the pit of his stomach.

'If you insist on persevering with this enterprise,' Sigmund went on, 'then I want out altogether.'

'I see. Well, you're quite right, I misconceived your depth of feeling. I might add, I don't understand it either.'

'If I explained you would only disagree, and we would argue needlessly. The point is I am bitterly opposed to the principle of raising salmon in fish farms and have reached a position whereby I can afford my prejudices.'

Morrison took a couple of thoughtful paces and then looked all round the boathouse. 'This isn't going to be enough, Sigmund. I'm not even sure it isn't a dead end. I think you know I'm not a greedy man, but I'm ambitious. Also, let's face it, life is shortly to become more expensive for me.'

'There are other things than raising salmon in captivity.'

'Agreed. But it's not every day a great opportunity is handed out on a plate.'

'I see.'

Morrison made a gesture of impatience. '*Someone's* going to do it. If it's not me he'll find someone else. I'd be mad to throw up a chance like this.'

'All right, David.' The German licked his lips, his only indication of discomfiture. 'I would like my £10,000 back, plus my share of the season's income.'

Morrison's stomach took a second jolt. 'Immediately?'

'Yes please.'

'That would be a very serious setback for me.'

'I know.'

Siggy turned and left the boathouse. Morrison followed

slowly and leaned against the door watching him climb into his car and drive away. He felt numb with shock but, he thought grimly, if Sigmund Morhof thought he could beat him so easily he'd better learn he was dealing with sterner stuff.

A voice beside him said, 'Well, you certainly blew that one!' Biddy was seated on an upturned crate.

'Were you listening again?'

'Every word.'

'One of these days I'm going to beat the hell out of you. Listening in on private conversations is disgusting.'

'Has the dragon got £10,000?'

'The dragon – ?' But the perpetuation of the nickname was softened by a note of affection. 'I don't think so. Besides, I'm supposed to be the breadwinner.'

'What'll we do now Sigmund's gone?'

'Carry on without him.'

'But he was a friend. Can we do all this without friends?'

'If we have to.'

Her hand came into his. It was a rough little hand, the hardened skin scratched and blistered from her outdoor life. 'Once upon a time I thought it was going to be just you and me together, but it was awful hard work, Morrison. And cold! Back in February it was *freezing*. Sigmund, and Buzby, and Bobo . . . and Cluny . . . they made it seem warmer.'

'Buzby and Bobo will be leaving as soon as the season finishes.'

'I wish they weren't. I wish you hadn't let Sigmund go.'

'One thing you have to learn about me. I can stand anything except criticism.'

'Where the hell will we find £10,000?'

'Don't swear. I'll find it.'

'I wish Cluny hadn't gone. I even wish Mrs Burgess hadn't gone.' Then in a very small voice, 'And most of all I wish Mummy hadn't gone.'

He felt the numbness return and knew he had to tread carefully. 'I do too, darling, but she has, and we can't be forever looking over our shoulder spending time in vain regrets.' He looked down at the small hand in his. 'And Caroline Kelso, she isn't instead of Mummy, she's to do with the future, she's part of the life that's opening up ahead of us.'

'I shan't call her "Mummy".' A fact rather than a threat.

'There's no need. Just let things come together in their own time.'

'You wouldn't go away too? I don't want ever to wake and find you gone.'

He shifted his gaze to her freckled face. 'I don't go under that easy.'

'And you wouldn't take her away without me?'

'Never.'

'Maybe she won't turn out too bad.' They went indoors to lunch.

Afterwards he telephoned Bruce Cornelius. The millionaire answered the phone personally and Morrison announced himself.

'Hello, David. How's it going?'

'Fine. I've written a report for you.'

'I hate reading, David. Come and tell me about it.'

'Fine. When?

'Now. This afternoon. Everybody's here, we're having a lot of fun.'

'The thing is, we've got guests.'

'Bring them along. Hey, they tell me you found yourself a beautiful bird, you clever so-'n-so.'

'Where on earth did you hear?'

'My spies. I'd love to meet her. Bring her to tea. Bring 'em all to tea, and you and me can go in the study and talk, eh?'

'Well, that's very kind. Oh – er – Bruce, if your guests are running a videotape would you censor it?'

'Say no more. I know what you mean. I got a lovely nature programme here which shows a couple of giraffes having it off with each other – it's all right when it's animals. It's educational!'

'Yes. Great,' Morrison agreed doubtfully.

'Is this wise, we ask ourselves?' asked Carrie when he

told her of the invitation.

'Why not?'

'Rumour has it he keeps a house of ill-repute.'

'I wouldn't go as far as that. He flies in house-guests for the weekend – they seemed very nice when I was there.'

'Be it on your head – they're your in-laws.'

'Besides, he's a millionaire. She's mad about millionaires.'

'So am I.'

Within five minutes his telephone rang and he recognised the familiar voice of Commander Campbell. Obviously he was with Cornelius and had been told of Morrison's visit.

'Bruce tells me you've prepared a report.'

'That's right.'

'You didna' tell me!'

Not another, thought Morrison. Why does everyone expect to be *told* everything? Aloud he asked, 'What's the trouble, Commander?'

'I assume you've no forgotten it was I who made the introduction?'

'I remember perfectly.'

'Very well then.' There was a pause as if the man was expecting Morrison to say something. When he didn't his voice came again, uncertain, 'Hello?'

'Yes I'm here. I'm afraid I don't know what you're talking about.'

As on the previous occasion it sounded as if a large hand was cupping the mouthpiece as the commander's voice became close and muffled. 'What are you offering, man?'

At last the light dawned. 'You want to be paid for introducing me to Mr Cornelius!'

'Is there anything strange about that? I could have recommended any number of people, but I chose you.'

'I was extremely grateful.'

'Good. Now let's see the colour of your gratitude.'

'How much?'

'Ten per cent of any business you do with him.'

'You're raving mad!'

'What are you offering then?'

247

This is the weirdest town I ever lived in, thought Morrison. 'I'm not actually offering anything but if you insist, and if Mr Cornelius and I reach agreement, I might part up with half of one per cent.'

'I'll accept that,' said Campbell and rang off.

Debbie opened the door to them, provocatively allowing her eyes to light up when she saw Morrison. She coolly surveyed Carrie then stepped aside allowing them to pass. He had never seen his mother-in-law so effusive and when she met the millionaire she became positively gushing. 'What a lovely home and how nice that you're able to relax at weekends. Are these your daughters?' Morrison heard her ask as she was shown into the living room. Patrick winked and followed them in.

'Have you seen that girl before?' whispered Carrie.

'Debbie? Yes, she's always here. She fancies me rotten!'

'Imagine me locked away in that school all my life and *this* going on not six miles away,' she muttered.

Commander Campbell and his wife met the in-laws and minutes later the four were in deep conversation, helping themselves to tea and cake from a trolley which was replenished constantly by one of the girls. Patrick noted his wife was more impressed by this side of their son-in-law's new life than anything else she'd seen thus far. She became extravagantly supportive in his enterprise and overplayed the role of benevolent mother-in-law to sickening effect. She cooed happily in what she fondly imagined to be high society and Patrick thought it best she continue to live with her illusion. He himself warmed instantly to Bruce Cornelius, who was his type of man, and contrived to be invited to sit on the business discussion that was to follow later. Biddy settled herself in front of the television and a young actor took Carrie off to play table tennis.

In the study Cornelius took the report from Morrison but laid it on the arm of his chair, preferring to let the younger man speak. He liked what he heard and was impressed by the thoroughness with which the homework had been done. People were inclined to be taken in by the millionaire's anxious shyness and forgot that a razor sharp shrewdness lay behind the mild exterior. His assessment of Morrison was perceptively accurate when he judged him to be ambitious, hardworking, and willing to tread on a few corns on his way to success, including, Cornelius surmised without rancour, his own. He was glad he had found himself a girlfriend because here was a man who enjoyed playing to the gallery, and would work the better if praised – and better work brought higher returns.

He was on the verge of giving a verbal go-ahead before handing the deal over to his lawyers to thrash out detail when Morrison announced his condition. Cornelius had been expecting Morrison to play hard to get but his audacity took him somewhat by surprise.

'Bruce, there is one thing, and you should hear it before we go any further.' Patrick admired his son-in-law because most men would have grasped with both hands anything Cornelius was prepared to offer. 'I don't consider Skerrymor Bay to be a bent nail operation and I think it crucial that we continue to market salmon caught at the very moment it's at its peak of condition; that is, after its Atlantic run but before its journey up river. So I would plan to continue my own business, placing it on a day-to-day basis in the hands of the two people who presently crew for me. I would want you to buy into it to the tune of £10,000.'

The German, Morhof, must have ditched him, decided Cornelius. 'What terms?' he enquired.

'Three ways until the bank's paid off, then sixty-forty in my favour.'

The millionaire thought, yes the German's definitely left him – probably because of me. Aloud he said, 'I'll have my boys look at it. Okay?'

'I want your agreement in principle now.'

'You have it.' Now Cornelius leaned back, his decision made. 'All right, David, we'll . . .'

At this precise moment the door to the study burst open and Debbie shouted in, 'Rolls-Royce, brown, coming up the drive.' The effect of her announcement was devastating. There were shouts outside and the millionaire shot to his feet. 'Lock the doors. Lock all the bloody doors!'

He rushed to the french windows leading to the lawn and slammed home the bolts. His panic would have been comical had it come at a less vital time.

'What's the trouble?' Morrison called.

'It's my wife, that's the trouble,' yelled Cornelius. He was running out of the room

'What difference will locking the doors make?' asked Morrison running with him.

'It'll stop her coming bloody in, won't it!' replied the millionaire.

In the drawing-room with its gigantic windows leading out on to the patio Morrison saw the startled faces of his mother-in-law and other guests while Cornelius bolted and locked the entrance. The young men had run to lock other doors in the house, while their free-loading young ladies huddled nervously by the fireplace.

The Rolls pulled up outside, and an expensively dressed middle-aged lady with brilliant blue hair and angry red face took one look over the exterior before approaching the front door. Cornelius crept down the hall on hands and knees and knelt on the doormat.

'Go away,' he shouted when he heard her try the door.

'Let me in,' came the reply.

'What are you doing here?'

'It's my house. You gave it to me.'

'Go away,' he ordered again.

'You've got girls in there, haven't you? Stinking tarts!'

Morrison's mother-in-law said to Campbell, 'They're his *daughters*!'

'Like hell they are.'

'Are you going to open this door?' shouted Mrs Cornelius.

'No, I'm not,' answered her husband.

There came a pause before he heard her footsteps retreating. In the drawing-room they saw the woman round the corner of the house and return to the car.

'She's going,' said Debbie breathlessly.

They watched the chauffeur open the rear door but Mrs Cornelius ignored him and climbed into the driving seat.

As the car began to move Cornelius ran back from the hall. 'No, she's not bloody going! She's bloody coming in!'

'Look out,' shouted Morrison.

The guests hurled themselves out of the way as, two seconds later, the gleaming brown Rolls-Royce smashed through the sliding windows with an ear-splitting shatter of glass and came to rest in the middle of the drawing-room. Mrs Cornelius climbed slowly out of the car.

'Now then – ' she began ominously. There was a faint rustle as Morrison's mother-in-law fainted clean away and Commander Campbell caught her as she fell. Then, realising he'd just lost Morrison's commission, he decided he might as well let her drop to the floor.

'They experienced considerable difficulty in manoeuvring her into the car but the old lady seemed fit enough by the time they returned to the white house, and in remarkably good voice.

'Such goings-on!' she raged as soon as she heard Patrick reached the seclusion of their bedroom. 'I've never been so shocked and upset.'

'I thought it was the funniest thing I've ever seen.'

'What's to become of Biddy? What's to become of our grand-daughter?'

'What do you suggest?'

'We must rescue her from a society where normal decent morals count for nothing. David never amounted to a great deal in my opinion however much you defend him, but now he's sunk to the depths of dissipation. We have to think of the child.'

'I think you'll find it difficult.' Patrick told her about the morning sail before going on to describe their son-in-law's creditable performance in front of Bruce Cornelius before it was interrupted by the catastrophic entrance of the millionaire's wife.

'That he should take us to that hell-hole. That he should take Biddy! What he does with that tart downstairs is his own affair but –'

'I'll not have that,' her husband interrupted sharply. 'It's my understanding she's a daughter of the manse and we've no cause to think ill of her.'

'She's sleeping with David!' cried Martha angrily.

'To be precise, David is roughing it downstairs on the daybed.'

'And the daughter of the manse, as you're pleased to call her, walked into a Catholic church this morning as bold as you like.'

'Out of kindness to you,' he corrected firmly. 'Besides, maybe she's sensible enough to worship the Lord in her own way and not be tied down by convention.'

'You're blind, Patrick. She was cut dead in the village this morning, the cleaner has left, there's goings-on at night in that caravan out there, and the whole place smells of fish.'

'So it does. And it smells of hard work, of courage, of love and contentment. My God, it smells good!'

Morrison never heard from Bruce Cornelius again. He telephoned his London office time after time but a secretary told him that he was in conference, away at meetings, or out of the country. Eventually he heard the Scottish property was up for sale.

Patrick was out of bed at crack of dawn on the Monday. He was experiencing a rebirth of energy here in Scotland and when Biddy had suggested he join them in the workboat he had accepted like a shot. Their task would be to re-set the leader nets following the weekend close, something the crew performed with the extreme proficiency of practice.

Neither Buzby nor Bobo made any comment on the absence of Siggy. If they'd heard anything they certainly weren't saying. It took two dinghy trips to ferry everyone aboard and then they prepared the Skerrymor Bay leader without delay. Patrick watched Morrison take the engine while Bobo positioned herself by the huge tiller. Biddy went forward as bowman and appreciating her slight figure could scarcely cope with the weight Patrick joined her to assist as directed. He made an easy return to his origins and found himself wondering wistfully why he had ever deserted the fresh wind and rain for the life of an office executive. His quest to ensure that a part of himself still lived within his grand-daughter was more than fulfilled and he admired the way Morrison encouraged her to exploit the limits of her young ability whilst simultaneously watching her every movement, ready to leap in at the first sign of difficulty. Now grandfather and grand-daughter worked the foredeck together and Patrick felt good.

They reversed to the foot of the cliffs for Buzby to make fast the leader to the 'land end' and remove the spare rope which had replaced it over the weekend. The foredeck made a bungle of the second leader and drew a sharp rebuke from the skipper. Biddy corrected the fault and remained unmoved by the exasperated shout. Minutes later, by the cliff, Buzby called for reverse engine and Patrick saw Morrison push the gear *forward* instead of backwards, then hastily put it right. 'I see our skipper can make mistakes too, but no one shouts at him,' he commented easily.

'No, Grandpa. He has to fill the propeller tunnel with water before the blades can bite. That's the trouble with Morrison, he never makes mistakes!'

They motored round the headland in the chill morning air and the two chatted easily, young and old together. The years melted away. Patrick relived the magical moments with his Wendy and here was this girl re-echoing exactly her mother's youth. He glanced back to where Morrison stood amidships, tall, confident, capable. The Irishman felt a warm affection for the man; he had no criticism whatsoever about the life his grand-daughter was leading. If anything he envied it.

In the white house Carrie's morning was going less well. She gave Morrison's mother-in-law breakfast in bed, mainly to provide uninterrupted time to tackle the housework in Mrs Burgess's absence. Her work was interrupted by the telephone ringing. It was an anonymous caller who wished to pour scorn on her shameless behaviour. She listened aghast at the vitriolic accusations before the breathy voice began to recite a string of filth, calling her a fornicating nymphomaniac, and she realised she was experiencing her first obscene telephone call. She said loudly, 'This is the operator, what number are you calling?' and the man rang off.

She was shocked and very shaken. She tried to dismiss the call for the pathetic sickness it was but the awful words uttered so close to her ear had been very frightening. She forced herself to put the incident to the back of her mind and continued cleaning the house until she could talk to David.

Her guest came downstairs demanding morning coffee. 'Do you have a newspaper?' she asked imperiously.

'Not delivered. I'll bring one in later for you.'

'I couldn't live without the *Daily Telegraph*.'

Carrie found herself being cross-examined about her parents, her childhood, her position at the school, and even the books she enjoyed reading. All her answers met with a disapproving sniff so she tried to chat about some of her travels, sight-seeing, as well as her visits to the theatre and ballet. She made no impression and saw she was addressing an immovable mind. The woman followed her about the house, making no attempt to help, but continuing to fire her critical questions, as if gathering evidence of unsuitability to be used at a later date.

My God, Carrie thought to herself, the only time this woman is quiet is when she faints.

As if answering a prayer the doorbell rang. When she opened it a police car was parked outside and the Force stood in the porch.

'Good morning, Donald.'

'Morning, Miss Kelso.'

'Have you time for some coffee?'

The Force shuffled awkwardly. 'Well, as a matter of fact I'm here in the line of duty really, miss.'

'What can I do for you?'

The Force coughed, pulled out a notebook, and adopted his official tone. 'Is this the residence of Miss Bridget Morrison?'

Carrie heard a sharp intake of breath from behind her.

'Come on, Donald, you know perfectly well it is.'

The Force looked over his notebook. 'I have to ask like that, Miss Kelso,' he explained. 'It's official procedure as laid down in the handbook.'

'Go on then.'

'Is she at home?'

'No, she's out in the workboat with her father.'

'Ah. Then I will just step inside, Miss Kelso, and await her return.'

'What's she done?'

'We have reason to believe she can help us with our enquiries into a case of manslaughter.'

It could have been better worded. What the Force meant to say was they wondered if Biddy might attend an identity parade but, as it was, his announcement was followed by a dull thud in the hall behind as the mother-in-law began another period of silence.

Over in The Last Resort Alistair Macleod was becoming angry. With a hotel filled to bursting with tourists his days were occupied in tending their needs, and at this time of the year he was inclined to grow out of touch with happenings in the village. However it was still possible to detect a Scottish voice in the bar as local customers made themselves heard amid the clamour of Sassenach holiday-makers. It was one of these voices that had put the hotelier into the picture about some extraordinary behaviour on the part of his compatriots.

Now, in their private sitting-room, here was his wife admitting that, not only did she know about it, she was part of the 'Kelso Boycott'.

'Will you explain to me what she's supposed to have done, for heaven's sake?' he asked.

'You know full well. Haven't I just been telling you?'

'You've told me the lass has moved in with David Morrison.'

'Well, that's it, you old fool. They're in the same house, living in sin.'

'For God's sake, is that all?'

'It's enough to earn eternal damnation, Alistair Macleod, and don't you forget it.'

'And are we so pure we can stand on the sidelines and pass judgement? Are our souls so clean we can afford to pass them by in the street and no say a word?'

'We can let them know how we feel.'

'And how do we feel about the young couple in number seven? Are we talking to them?'

'They're different. They're English.'

'They're *paying*, that's how they're different. We take their money and turn a blind eye, that's what we do. You're a hypocrite, woman, d'you know that?'

'You'll not dare stand there and call me a hypocrite to my face.'

'I'll dare call you a whole lot of other things if I hear any more of this nonsense. Good God, woman, I've known that lass since she was a wee bairn. I know her to be a good person, God-fearing, and honest, which is more than I can say for that Janet Mahoney.'

'Who's passing judgement now, pray?'

'Aye, well, that woman's always struck me as being a bit strange, with that bass voice and men's trousers.'

'*Alistair!*'

'And what about David Morrison – what's he going to think of us all?'

'Och, *him!*'

'Aye, him. Him that's been a good enough friend to us, you know full well he has. Doesn't he set aside his best salmon each day, without the marks o' his net on its body so we can stick a hook down its throat and claim we caught it in our river? And didn't he drop everything to help us when the river dried up?'

'Neither of those affairs were anything of my doing.'

Macleod held a bony finger directly under her nose. 'But you *knew* about them and that makes you accessory to the fact. And you don't deny my claims to have caught the fish, so that makes you a liar too. Why don't you boycott me, and refuse to speak a word to me? Because I'd *welcome* it, that's why you don't do it!'

'I don't want to hear any more of this.'

'You'll no move from that spot till I'm done.' He glared at her. 'David Morrison rescued old Cluny from over the cliff edge; David Morrison opened up Ferguson's fishing business again and is making a go of it; and there's talk that David Morrison will start a fish farm in Loch Stryne to provide work for a few people, *so I'm no going to have Morrison think we're a bunch o' peasants!'*

Patrick and his wife decided they must return to their Yorkshire home no later than Thursday and elected to depart after lunch on the Wednesday. So on Tuesday evening Carrie invited Buzby and Bobo to join them for a farewell dinner. She had never experienced anyone more difficult to entertain than David's mother-in-law and anyway, during the season, it was virtually impossible to bring guests in line with the household routine dictated by the fishing. She got on much better with the husband, who showed an affinity for their work and took part in it comfortably. He had chatted to her as well, but the difference was that his questions seemed couched to elicit the good rather than the bad.

In a week when the housekeeper had left, there was trouble with the business, obscene phone calls and a village boycott, Carrie prayed that it might soon be over. The roast was in the oven and Biddy was with her in the kitchen helping prepare a large fruit salad. Through the wall they could hear Grandma sounding forth about the wickedness of allowing a young child to participate in a police identity parade and Buzby's quieter reasoned argument why it should happen. Extraordinarily, but not untypically, he was more successful in getting through to the woman than was Morrison.

Carrie asked. 'Do you mind doing this thing?'

'I want to do it,' Biddy replied briefly.

'After it's over I reckon there's not much more that can go wrong this week.'

257

They both heard the doorbell ring and, a moment later, the sound of Morrison opening the door. A man's voice said, 'This is the most unforgivable intrusion at this late hour, but our car broke down on the way here.'

Carrie went slightly pale and lifted both hands to her cheeks. 'Oh no!'

'You mean there *is* something else?' asked Biddy. Carrie nodded.

In the hall Morrison enquired, 'What can I do for you?'

The Reverend Kelso cast a look towards Mrs Kelso as if seeking assurance they were in the right place. 'I – er, that is – we believe our daughter Caroline – er – lives here . . .'

It flashed across Morrison's mind that dropping to the floor in a dead faint was a useful ruse, as practised by his mother-in-law, because it blanked out the awkward moments in life. However he managed to force a pretence of heartiness into his voice. 'Well, come in!' He stood aside as the minister and his wife squeezed past still apologising for the inconvenience of their timing. Carrie and Biddy appeared from the kitchen.

'Mother! Father! What on earth are you doing here?'

'I think you just took the words right out of their mouths,' Biddy whispered unwisely.

'We wanted to see you, my dear,' her father explained awkwardly.

'We've been hearing things,' added Mrs Kelso, as if that made everything clear.

'We really are most dreadfully –'

'Father dear, please stop apologising. Have you driven from Loch Lomond?'

'We pushed it most of the way,' Mrs Kelso said feelingly.

'We can easily find a hotel,' her husband assured them. Considering his was supposedly a rescue mission to save his daughter from a life of sin he showed a certain lack of backbone.

'You won't find a hotel with a bed in it tonight,' his daughter advised briskly.

'You'll have to stay with us,' added Morrison firmly. 'And we can't talk out here, come in and meet the others.'

258

He opened the living-room door where Buzby and Patrick rose to welcome the newcomers.

'Have you eaten?' asked Carrie.

'Well – ' began Kelso.

'No, they haven't,' Biddy finished for him.

'That's good,' said Buzby, 'we're just about to begin.'

'Oh dear – !'

As so often happens when the totally unexpected befalls the evening turned out to be a tremendous success. Patrick quickly made the Kelsos feel at ease with his considerable Irish charm and his wife despatched a procession of bright smiles in their direction – next to millionaires and bank managers, ministers of the cloth were well up the social ladder. Morrison made sure the wine flowed freely, Carrie pushed a card table on to the end of the dining table and laid two extra places, the roast beef was carved more thinly, and Biddy divided the potatoes and sprouts with a painful display of mental arithmetic.

But it was Buzby and Bobo who made the party. They shared a tremendous knack for instinctively rising to the occasion and saying the outrageous without once over-stepping the mark. The moment came when they even dared broach the subject of Carrie's boycott and she was momentarily alarmed, but Bobo's burlesque performance of a self-righteous citizen cutting dead a victim in a narrow street was hilarious. It was topped, however, by Buzby giving an impression of an obscene telephone call which, whilst never using one word of bad language, never-theless gave devastating caricatures of both caller and recipient.

Each of the three men reacted differently to the Buzby and Bobo dinner table performance. Morrison realised that here were two good friends putting their own perspective on a serious situation and succeeding in defusing an explosive atmosphere. The Reverend Kelso watched his daughter, hungry for comfort and then relaxing in the warmth of friendly humour. He had not realised Caroline was so beautiful a woman, with poise and confidence, grey eyes suddenly coming alive with laughter, her features softening with love when once Morrison sprang to her defence over some trivial matter. As for Patrick, he watched his grand-daughter Biddy playing an unassuming role, no attempt to enter the adult arena, attentive to her grandma seated beside her, and looking as pretty as a picture. Once she winked at him across the table and he wished the brief holiday was not due to end next day. His eyes went to his wife – the conversation seemed to pass over her head for much of the time but she kept an eye on the Reverend Kelso and laughed when he did. Patrick wondered where he had gone wrong in his marriage – probably when first he provided his wife with a taste of the good life.

Morrison and Carrie left their guests over coffee and put the last clean pair of sheets on the twin beds in Biddy's room. The Kelsos would sleep in there, whilst Carrie took the daybed downstairs, and Morrison and Biddy rowed out to sleep aboard *Sea Dancer*.

MacGregor accompanied Morrison and Biddy down to the beach. He ran back and forth in great agitation as they pulled the dinghy towards the surf. Seeing them row away from him he let forth a mighty howl and entered the water to swim after them. They returned to lift him inboard and, uncertain at first but gaining confidence, the dog took up his old position in the bows. It was the first time he had been to sea since Ferguson's accident. In the cabin of *Sea Dancer* Biddy and Morrison climbed into sleeping bags and turned out the light. Then, and only then, did MacGregor stand in the middle of the cabin and shake every drop of water from his fur with great thoroughness.

In the white house Patrick heard his wife stir in bed beside him. 'What on earth's happening in the caravan over there?' she asked.

'Nothing you'd remember,' he replied and settled for sleep.

Downstairs, Carrie realised she'd never got round to discussing the very thing her parents had travelled to see her about.

She talked with them next morning. They both assisted

with the mountain of washing up whilst the workboat was out at the nets and the awful mother-in-law was packing her cases. Carrie told them everything, it was the only way. Her father could see that she did not need rescuing. Her level-headed good sense exceeded his own. How well she had grown up and, when Caroline declared that she loved David dearly and would bring him to visit them when things had quietened, the minister felt justified in repeating to his wife the maxim that there was seldom a wrong that could not be put right.

Patrick had a thick head when he sat for the last time with Biddy in the bows of the workboat; it was the first hangover in as many years as he could remember and he almost welcomed it like an old friend. Buzby and Bobo were fairly quiet too but Morrison permitted none of them to lessen their efficiency.

There was a cormorant beneath the roof of the Ferrick station net. The bird must have dived beneath the surface in pursuit of food to find itself trapped under water. Violent flapping allowed its head to lift the net sufficiently to gasp in air but it was growing weaker and was half-drowned by the time they arrived. Biddy insisted on rescuing it and ignored her father's fuming at the delay. The bird managed to summon up sufficient energy to bite a chunk out of Patrick's hand before swimming clear of the boat but the only acknowledgement to come from amidships was, 'Serve you right!'

After lunch they watched the Reverend and Mrs Kelso drive away in a cloud of apology and blue smoke. Then Patrick made their farewells and climbed into the Rover. They hadn't rounded the first bend before his wife said, 'Well! It's straight to your solicitor and a court order to lift that poor child out of . . . out of . . . that *harem*!'

'I don't think we'll succeed,' said Patrick mildly. 'I don't think we'll even try!' They didn't speak again until Carlisle.

Carrie stood between Morrison and Biddy as they waved goodbye. 'Phew!' she said. 'What a week!'

'That has to be the understatement of the decade,' he said.

In five days they'd lost their partner, their millionaire, and their housekeeper. Morrison's dream of a fish farm lay shattered, and they desperately needed to find £10,000 if their existing livelihood was to be saved. The Force required Biddy to re-open old sores in search of the man who caused Cluny's death, and the village wasn't speaking to Carrie.

'One thing about Granny,' said Biddy, 'she never was a lucky charm.'

CHAPTER TEN

METEOROLOGICALLY SPEAKING August is a mean month in the Western Isles. Holiday-makers persist in the belief that it is a period of high summer against all the evidence of statistics from climatic tables compiled over fifty years of observations. Cloud cover for the four weeks match only those of winter and, so far as the rain they drop is concerned, October to December *and August* are shown as the wettest months with June emerging as the driest. Notwithstanding, the tourist continues to choose August for his summer holiday and, word of mouth sounding louder than official records, his memory of Scotland is coupled with bad weather.

Thus it was raining on the morning the police car arrived at the white house to take Biddy to the identity parade. The driver willingly accepted Morrison and Carrie as additional passengers but, as they drove out of the village towards the main road, he betrayed suspicious surprise when his mirror showed two more cars fall in behind him. Alistair Macleod and Commander Campbell could ill-afford the time but both men were determined that the key figure in the disastrous illegal bird trading affair should be well supported. Biddy sat in the back seat beside her father, serious and very nervous. Some would dismiss an identity parade as being a straightforward matter but for an eleven-year-old the responsibility was enormous. She wore Cluny's hat low over her eyes and ears, nothing would have persuaded her otherwise and Morrison wisely hadn't tried.

At the main police station they were greeted by a

detective-inspector who, if he was taken aback by his witness looking like a shrunken Don Camillo, didn't show it and personally thanked the child for her co-operation as if she was an adult. He explained her duties clearly and simply before taking her off to face the ordeal. As soon as they'd gone Campbell gestured silently and the other two followed him down a corridor to a strictly out of bounds window from which they could watch proceedings in the yard below. Eight similar-looking men stood in a line and immediately Morrison heard an intake of breath.

'He's there!' whispered Macleod.

'Who's there?'

'The wee bugger who didna pay his bill at Hogmanay!'

'Which one?'

'Wait. I've a feeling your girl will point him out for us.'

Morrison watched Biddy walk down the line alone. So small, so fragile, so serious. She reached the end. Then she turned and, walking more briskly, moved directly towards a man near the middle, touched him quickly on the arm before hurrying back to the detective-inspector without a backward glance.

Macleod gave a deep sigh of satisfaction. 'She's a bonny lassie,' he cried. 'Oh, she's a bonny wee lassie!'

In a matter-of-fact voice the detective-inspector confirmed Biddy had pointed to the same man arrested in London by a police officer and Mr Peregrine whilst Donald the Force declared it was the man he had seen in a village bar on the night before the attack on Cluny. As the parade was dismissed Morrison caught sight of the expression on Macleod's face and thought it probably fortunate the man was under police protection. Then it was all over.

Macleod elected to buy them all a celebration lunch and, with characteristic thoughtlessness, failed to notice that Biddy wasn't sharing his satisfaction with the morning's work. Carrie did, however, and as the men strode out towards the restaurant she dropped behind with the girl.

'All right?' she asked quietly.

'Did that man really push Cluny over the cliff?'

'It will have to be proven in court but Cluny *was* pushed

and the man *was* there.'

'I don't understand how anyone could do a thing like that.'

'No, it's difficult, isn't it. It's to do with priorities; that is, what seems most important at the time. The man thought that not getting caught was more important than hurting someone else.'

'He killed him, didn't he?'

'Cluny might have died as a result of the fall.'

'Why are you messing about with words?'

'Because sometimes it's very important to say what you mean.'

'I mean to say that that man killed Cluny,' Biddy muttered.

When they were all seated round a table Morrison asked Campbell, 'Where on earth is your friend Cornelius?'

'Man, I've no idea. He's disappeared from the face of the earth.'

'What happens to our plans? Our agreements?'

'If you'll take my advice you'd best forget them. And him.'

'And *her*,' murmured Biddy.

Morrison acknowledged the remark with a wink and then carried on. 'He's left me in something of a hole. Quite apart from anything I've lost my partner as a result of Bruce Cornelius.'

'No, darling,' corrected Carrie gently. 'You lost Sigmund as a result of *you*.'

'What do you mean?'

'It was your decision to start the fish farm and that decision was what Sigmund rebelled against.'

She wondered at her boldness for never before had he been taken to task for a careless statement, and in front of business colleagues. He looked at her across the table and saw calm honesty in the grey eyes. He nodded slowly. 'Yes, that's fair.'

He was impressed that by uncovering the kernel of his argument with Sigmund she had cut through the vexation of spirit he'd experienced since his talk by the boatshed.

Biddy commented, 'She's a great one for getting the words right, Morrison.'

'Yes, well you're all wrong,' said Macleod. 'You lost Sigmund Morhof because he's a strange man. Forty years in the country with never an attempt to understand the natives.'

'Explain that,' demanded Campbell gruffly.

'Och, laddie, it sticks out a mile. He's one for letting you know what his own feelings are, but then he forgets others might have a few of their own.'

'Why, what's he done to you?' Campbell persisted.

'I've had him off and on for as long as I can remember. All flashing eyes and enthusiastic smiles one minute and then, all of a sudden, he's beset with doubts whereupon you never hear from him again. Besides, he's a German!'

'What's that got to do with it?'

'We beat them in the war so what's he doing making his pile over here?'

Carrie smiled at him across the table. 'You're slow to forgive, Mr Macleod.'

'Forgive, are you saying? I've no even got used to him being here yet!'

'Macleod's factually correct,' Campbell told Morrison, 'although I don't go along with his sentiments. You're better off without Sigmund Morhof.'

That's all very well, thought Morrison, but you don't have to find £10,000 just when you thought you'd got things licked into shape. However it was Biddy who crystallised his real feelings into words.

'I like him,' was all she said.

'Mind you,' Macleod went on thoughtfully, 'I like the concept of fish farms. Either you go after salmon for sport or you catch them commercially; it seems to me your nets fall between the two extremes.'

'That's more or less what Bruce Cornelius said, but he was a bit short on answers when I asked him where the taste would come from. He seemed to think it didn't matter.'

'And what do you think, Mr Morrison?' asked Campbell.

'Me? I just want to earn an honest crust.'

'Then do that, David,' cried Carrie with sudden passion, 'do exactly that. The world is full of people knocking taste for six in favour of size, quantity, convenience, and profit. It's not just fish farms and battery hens, it's vegetables, meat, and everything else you can think of. Why, the Common Market even bans whole ranges of foodstuffs in the interests of so-called community efficiency, so nobody gets to taste them at all.'

'Well said,' muttered Macleod.

'If earning an honest crust means preserving the plain truth between supplier and customer by selling them exactly what they think they're buying then there's not many of you left.' Carrie made a slight head movement towards the police station they'd just left. 'You're as much an endangered species as Biddy and Cluny's golden eagle.'

'You can't stop these people,' Morrison pointed out to her. 'You can't stop progress. There comes a time when persevering with old-fashioned methods is nothing more than obstinate lunacy.'

'It all depends what you're in business for, laddie,' declared Macleod. 'You have to ask yourself how much money you really need, and so long as you earn it you're entitled to preserve any traditions you like.'

Morrison shook his head at him in smiling wonderment. 'Mr Macleod, you never cease to amaze me. I've known you eight months and you can change sides in an argument quicker than anyone I ever met.'

'It's a national characteristic, laddie. It's what keeps Scotland independent.'

The conversation switched to light matters and for several minutes Carrie heard none of it. In the moment David Morrison had looked at her she knew he saw her and nobody else. He'd only said 'Fair enough', but she was aware that in his eyes she had become an individual incomparable with anyone he'd known previously. She watched him as he listened to something Campbell was saying, switching his glance to Biddy when she chipped in, laughing suddenly as a turn of phrase amused him. Then she became aware that Macleod's eyes were on her and, when he gave a small smile of approbation, she blushed.

The Nottingham Conference was a very considerable success. The standard of debate was excellent, Parkinson-Small's own address to the combined executive staffs was sharper than in previous years, and a follow-up impromptu speech at the final dinner was witty, pointed, and pertinent. Debbie listened to the laughter and applause her father drew from the assembled delegates and, for the first time in a long while, consciously felt a pride towards him. Then, when the band took the stage and the dancing began, she knew the final part of her duties had been accomplished and she could herself relax and enjoy the last two hours. She found no shortage of partners; some admittedly because she was the chairman's daughter, but mostly because she was young, charming, and beautiful.

The following morning being Saturday the delegates had departed by 10.30. Debbie checked and signed the bill, then climbed into the chairman's Daimler. Parkinson-Small sat back in his corner, feet barely touching the floor, and looked at her.

'Well done,' he said.

'Well done you too,' she replied. 'Everyone was greatly impressed.'

'I'd intended they should be. High time they were reminded their chairman had muscle.' He looked out of the window and added quietly, 'Which of late has been growing somewhat flabby.'

Debbie checked quickly that the glass partition between themselves and the driver was closed. 'What brought this on?' she asked.

'You knew it. My secretary knew it. Everybody could see I was letting things slide. Too many assistants, too many opinionated managing directors, too many people making sure I was only told what I needed to know or wanted to hear, too many meaningless lunches, and too much booze.' The girl said nothing, waiting for it all to spill out. 'You asked what brought it on. I'll tell you. Scotland.'

'It wasn't important.'

'They made me feel an idiot. When I returned to my bedroom I looked in the mirror and *saw* an idiot. A red-faced, overweight, inebriated idiot. I don't mind telling you I stared at that reflection and wept.'

Debbie reached across and took his hand. 'It wasn't like that. I know the men involved. They were trying to impress you. You were important to them.'

He shook his head. 'No. It was my position that was important to them. They wanted to impress the influence I can bring to bear. It's all right,' he added before she could speak, 'I'm not feeling sorry for myself. I rose to the top of this company because people knew I was a man to reckon with; well, they're going to do so again.'

'After your performance these last three days a few tough memos will have them come running.'

'Instil a bit of fear, eh? Nothing like fear as an incentive. I should know, that weekend I frightened myself to death!'

He sat silently for several miles and Debbie too thought back on her last two visits to the Cornelius mansion. She squirmed with unspoken embarrassment as she forced herself to recall the occasion she invited David Morrison to take her to bed. She did not match up to the cliché about a woman scorned; this one just wanted to crawl away and hide. Then the abject disillusionment as she witnessed the pathetic scene which followed the explosive break-in of Mrs Cornelius. She had stood there and watched her millionaire knight, fallen from his horse, crawling abysmally beneath the torrent of the woman's abuse. What had all those wasted weekends been about? How had she become a part of that weak-faced group? If any good had come out of it at all it was that she had learned to see them for what they were.

Her father interrupted the thoughts. 'What about you? Will you stay with the company?'

'If you want me to.'

'I don't think you should.'

Debbie's eyes widened. 'Are you getting into practice on

me?'

'Not at all. Quite the reverse.' He turned directly to face her, his leg curving on to the seat, a hand around his ankle. 'I think you should go to the market place and rub shoulders with hard experience. Then, when I go, I'll leave you enough shares to come back and make your play in the take-over battle. You'll not last five minutes until you've learned about fighting for survival.' He saw a smile spread slowly across her face. 'What's up?'

Debbie shook her head at him and actually laughed. 'Because you will never know just how squarely you hit the nail on the head.'

'Do you want to tell me?'

'Not especially. He's not worth grieving over. What's funny is my own failure to make any impression. There was me, rich heiress, sophisticated, attractive; there was he, poor, straightforward, and devastatingly good-looking. You'd have thought he was a pushover but, do you know, he is the first man who *would not come* when I called.'

'Stunned annoyance!' murmured Parkinson-Small sympathetically.

'Wait till you hear about the girl who beat me. A *school-teacher* yet!' She laughed again but without rancour. 'Okay, Dad, I'll take your advice and go to learn all about in-fighting.'

They drove the rest of the way home in comfortable silence, each occupied with their own thoughts. If Morrison had known of the effect he'd had on the father and daughter he might have felt a little better.

As it was the season ended with so poor a catch it was an anti-climax. Morrison did his sums. He had managed to re-pay £3,800 of the bank loan but nothing towards Sigmund's investment. The German had received a salary of course and he had taken a weekly wage himself. Buzby and Bobo were well satisfied and he'd thought it right to pay £250 into a savings account for Biddy – set against the work she'd done it was a pittance. Then on the credit side the renovations, renewals, and the fact that Skerrymor Fisheries was once again a going concern rendered the house and equipment worth something nearer £50,000 than the £32,000 purchase cost. In the normal way it would represent an extremely creditable first season performance, and the following year promised even better when one took into consideration lower maintenance costs, a cheaper crew member now that he could skipper himself, Carrie and Biddy looking after the shore side of things, and no new purchases. Nevertheless the fact remained that he was in debt to the tune of £16,200 which, by the start of the new season, interest would have increased to about £18,500. It was a disheartening prospect and a far cry from the ambitious, anticipations he'd set before Carrie only a few weeks earlier.

He did not allow financial burdens to colour his enjoyment of the 'end of season' dinner Carrie prepared and to which they invited Bob MacPherson as well as Sigmund and his wife. Biddy thoroughly enjoyed these dinner parties and loved watching her father effortlessly steer his guests into their favourite stories. Carrie also fitted well into the team and she herself felt a security among them which allowed her to forget for an hour or two the enmity shown towards her outside. She was relieved that everyone had the good sense to make no mention of fish farms or other past differences, even when the factor called for silence in order that he might propose a toast to the new owner. 'A number of us have been "makin' our winnin's" at this game for monie a year but Mr Morrison is no man for hangin' aboot.' With heavy humour he added, 'Aye, and he's shown hissclf as one who can mek a catch ashore as well as afloat!' Carrie laughed politely and when they raised their glasses to Morrison she noted that Sigmund added his congratulations with every appearance of sincerity.

However, when an hour or so later she walked with him to his car, he presented a grimmer picture. Carrie asked directly, 'Your money, Sigmund, are you in a hurry for it?'

He made no objection to her blunt question and replied reasonably enough. 'I need the interest it can earn.'

'In that case could it stay with Skerrymor Fisheries for a while?'

'Does David know you are asking this?'

'No.'

'Then I can answer you in confidence. I'm afraid it has to be "no".'

'Very well.' She neither questioned nor argued, causing him to feel bound to offer an explanation.

'I am not optimistic about the future.'

'You know he's abandoned the fish farm project?'

'Only because his backer disappeared in a puff of wind. But, anyway, that's no longer the point. I find myself increasingly depressed by everything I see along this coast. I've worked hard all my life and, if I'm careful, will end my days in tolerable comfort, but a big question mark hangs over the wisdom of standing by the grave of traditionalism.' He gave an apologetic smile. 'I never said David was wrong in his assessment of fish farms, I merely stated I wanted no part of it. Mercifully I shall be dead before avarice finally takes over and buries the honest craftsman.'

'It won't happen, Sigmund. You underrate David, you underrate all of us.'

'I hope so.'

'These big combines will find their market, but David will find his as well. People will seek him out because they'll be given good value. You'll see.'

'With you behind him I've no doubt he will succeed.' His words hung in the evening air – they were not going to be backed up with his investment. 'Thank you for inviting me.'

'Goodnight, Sigmund.'

She watched him drive away, a man who was never at a loss for the right phrase but fell short when it came to pitching into a crisis. She walked slowly back to the house.

The following morning Biddy was walking back to the white house from the village when the post office van pulled up beside her.

'Are you on your way home, Biddy?' asked Postie.

'Yes.'

'Will ye take these along wi' you? It's a rare bumpy route that track of yours.' He handed out an overnight telegram and a letter which she shoved into the pocket of her anorak. She seemed to have heard the short conversation before.

272

Later in the day they saw Buzby and Bobo off at the station in Mallaig. 'Good luck, Buzby,' said Morrison. 'I hope your fortunes take a turn for the better.'

'They already did, David. Thanks to you.'

'I hope we'll be back next year,' Bobo added.

'You can count on it,' Morrison assured her. As the train pulled out of the station Buzby stuck his head out of the window to wave goodbye. Morrison shouted, 'When are you going to make an honest woman of her?'

'There's a cliché about the pot calling the kettle black,' came back from the young man. Unconsciously Morrison put an arm round Carrie and the three of them waved until the train was out of sight.

'It feels like an ending,' commented Biddy. 'Nothing seems to ever *settle down*.'

Morrison shook his head thoughtfully. 'D'you know something? I reckon we just bottomed out.'

'What makes you say that?' demanded Carrie.

'Optimism.'

'What does "bottomed out" mean?' Biddy wanted to know.

'It means from now on it can only get better.'

'Oh.' The girl was quiet for a moment. Then, as she opened the car door, 'I hoped it meant people might stop *going away*.'

It was late when Mrs Burgess arrived in Glasgow. For a moment she imagined she caught a glimpse of Buzby and Bobo, and half thought about hurrying after them to seek their advice, but she hesitated and when she looked again the young couple had been swallowed up in the crowd. She put down her two cases and handbag in order to pull on the mackintosh, it would be easier wearing it than carrying it. Then she pushed her hand through the handle of her handbag so that it hung from her wrist and picked up the smaller suitcase before lifting the heavier one with her other hand. She walked uncertainly towards the exit and held everybody up at the barrier whilst she put everything down to rummage through the bag for her ticket.

She felt too tired to even think of doing anything about buying a cruise ticket that night; apart from anything else she had not the foggiest idea how to do it. A bite to eat and a night's rest would clear her brain for the morning.

The sign above the door said 'Hotel' but really it was more of a boarding house, and a very shabby one at that. She had been walking a full half-hour before she came across it and decided it would just have to do. When she asked for a room the slatternly woman behind the counter looked surprised and a younger woman with too much make-up grinned broadly. The bedroom was positively dirty but Mrs Burgess told herself she could not expect others to maintain her own standards of cleanliness. When she asked for food the woman sniffed and said there was no restaurant but she could manage a sandwich if that would suit. Mrs Burgess declined and, after she'd washed in the small handbasin, went out in search of a meal taking the smaller case with her.

It was a noisy hotel, people coming and going until the small hours, and Mrs Burgess slept badly. She felt distinctly nervous and kept the suitcase in bed with her. It was nothing like she'd imagined, not like a holiday at all, but there was no doubt things would be very different once she was on the high seas. In the middle of the night she made up her mind on exactly what she would do. Trains left from stations, therefore big ships must leave from docks. She would go to the docks, find the ticket office, and board a ship that was going round the world.

She had no conception the docks would be so big. She could neither see where they started nor where they stopped. As the bus drove away she stood utterly helpless for several minutes, totally bewildered by their enormity. She actually felt like giving up, and would have were it not for all those years of dreaming and waiting for this moment. Taking a firm grip on her belongings she walked through a large iron gate, avoiding some railway lines which went through it as well. Almost immediately she saw a ship and her morale soared. It was a long way off but, rounding a corner, she discovered more of them tied up against wharfs which, she realised, must be like station platforms. She chose the nearest and struggled with her belongings to the foot of a gangplank. She studied the vessel more closely and decided it was not a particularly nice ship. Parts of it were very rusty and the whole thing could do with a lick of paint. She knew exactly what she was looking for because she'd seen pictures on her husband's television set. There should be ballrooms, sundecks, and swimming pools. She straightened up and firmly set off in search of a nicer one. Somewhere, she thought, there must be a large notice board announcing which countries the ships were visiting, what time they departed, and the number of the wharf.

'Can I help you?'

At first she could not make out where the voice had come from. She looked all around but when it repeated its question she realised suddenly the man was speaking through an open porthole right before her eyes. 'Oh, thank you. I was looking for the ticket office.'

'For the where?' The man seemed to be cooking toast in a kind of kitchen by placing slices of bread directly on to an electric hotplate.

'The ticket office,' she repeated. Then, because the man seemed to be staring at her open-mouthed, she went on to explain, 'I want to buy a ticket.'

'Where to?'

'All round the world.'

At this another face peered over the man's shoulder. Mrs Burgess did not like being stared at and, because they both appeared lost for words, she began to move away. 'Wait a minute.' The first man brushed his companion aside. 'I'll be up and give you a hand. Don't go away.'

He appeared at the top of the gangplank a few moments later and hurried down to her. He was tall and good-looking, a shabby white jacket over thick navy trousers. He spoke English with an accent – he could have been from anywhere.

'What's all that again?' he asked.

'I want to buy a ticket for a cruise,' she said distinctly.

'All round the world?' he repeated.

'That's correct. I'd be grateful if you'd direct – '

'How did you get in here?'

'I walked through the gate.'

'Good God!' She appeared shocked and he went on quickly, 'Look mum, I think you need taking in hand and looking after.' He reached down to take her suitcases but she clung on to the smaller of the two. 'Come with me. We don't have ticket offices here, not as such,' he explained. 'You buy your tickets for cruises from agents who have big offices, you don't pay on the boat like it's a ferry.'

'Can you take me to one of these offices?'

'I can't personally 'cos we're away in a couple of hours. But I tell you what I'm going to do. I'm going to sit you down in front of a cuppa tea, find out exactly what it is you *do* want, 'n' see if I can help.'

'I wouldn't want to presume.'

'Listen mum, you're not going to get anywhere on your own. I'm surprised you even got this far.'

She felt secure walking beside this confident young man. He shepherded her out through a different gate from the one she'd entered and she saw they were facing a line of decrepit shops. He chose a reasonable looking café and soon they both had cups of strong, tan-coloured tea poured from a monstrous tin teapot.

'Now then, where exactly do you want to go?'

'I keep telling you, all round – '

' – all round the world, right. Then it's going to cost you a pretty penny. Have you got a pretty penny?'

'I've enough.' Unconsciously her eyes went down to the smaller suitcase and he followed her look.

'You've not got it in there?' he whispered, horrified. She nodded sheepishly. 'Good God!' the man exclaimed again. 'How much?' She hesitated. 'All right, I don't need to know. You must've robbed a bank or something.'

'I've done no such thing!' She decided she liked him. She'd met enough rough and ready men off the boats in Mallaig and knew at once which were trustworthy. She watched him rub a hand across his face while he pondered on the best course of action.

'Okay,' he said at last. 'I'm not going to ask any questions about what you been up to, mum – '

'I've not – '

He held up a hand. 'Whatever you say I believe you. People turn up around these parts with a caseful of oncers every day of the week, don't they?' She didn't know if he was being sarcastic so said nothing. 'Here's what we do. I'm going to make a phone call to an agency I know and have someone come down and fix you up with whatever you want. It'll take me a while – have you had breakfast?'

'As a matter of fact – ' Mrs Burgess had taken one look at the tray the woman had brought to her room and decided she couldn't stomach it.

'Good God!' the man said, 'doesn't nobody love you?' He went to the counter and ordered bacon, eggs, and toast before slapping a pound note down.'

'Oh, I must – '

'Forget it, mum. You're the most novel lady I ever met.'

'You've been very kind.'

'I'll be as quick as I can.' He made to leave but turned back. 'Do me a favour, will you? If I'm going to leave you alone in this den of vice let's at least put that bloody suitcase somewhere it's safe, eh?'

'It's under the table,' she whispered.

'How's about behind the counter? Mick there is bigger'n you are.' He swept up the case and handed it to Big Mick who stuffed it out of sight under a shelf. Then he left.

The bacon and egg was delicious and Mrs Burgess was hungry. Big Mick brought her a cup of coffee and refused payment because, he said, the pound had covered it. Then he disappeared through a door at the back and she took advantage of his brief absence to surreptitiously cross to the side of the counter where, by standing on tiptoe, she could check on her case. It was there, safe and sound.

Twenty minutes later, a car drew up outside and a well-dressed man carrying a leather briefcase entered the café. His eyes came to rest on Mrs Burgess and he crossed to the table with an enquiring expression.

'Are you the lady . . . ?'

She nodded to him and he pulled out the other chair.

'May I?' he asked politely. She nodded again and he sat down opposite her. 'This is rather unusual,' he murmured.

'I only want to buy a ticket,' she said defensively.

He laughed at this. An open, frank laugh. 'Of course. You only want to buy a ticket.' It clearly amused him. 'Now, where do you want to go?'

'All round the world,' she said for the umpteenth time.

'I take it Liverpool or Southampton are not readily accessible to you?'

'I don't want to go to either of those places,' objected Mrs Burgess.

Once again the man gave his ready laugh. 'Very good,' he said appreciatively. He had dark brown eyes, a mass of wavy hair, and a well-trimmed beard. When she looked at him she was surprised to receive an amused wink. 'When do you want to leave?'

'As soon as it's convenient – maybe the next ship.'

'Ah, it's like that, is it?' She didn't understand but, anyway, he leaned across the table to ask, 'May one ask how much you have to spend?'

'Two-thousand, five-hundred.'

'I see.' He pursed his lips thoughtfully. 'Well, two-thousand, five-hundred won't get you quite round the world, but it'll take you a fair long way.'

'How far?'

'Rio?'

'Where?'

'Rio de Janeiro.'

She'd heard of Rio de Janeiro and certainly it sounded very nice.

'Will the ship bring me back?'

'You want to come back? I'm very glad to hear it.' He laughed again and, snapping open his briefcase, pulled out a bundle of brochures which showed resorts, hotels, entertainments, restaurants, and all manner of diversions. For half an hour they were engaged in deep conversation and Mrs Burgess loved every word of his exotic descriptions of places she could visit while she was 'away'. He gave the word special emphasis and several times she caught him looking at her with open admiration.

'Fine,' he said eventually. 'I've got the picture and I think we can handle this for you. The money, it's – ah – in cash, I understand?'

'Yes.'

'Good. Then I'll get away now and return with your – ah – ticket as soon as possible.'

'Should I come with you?'

'At this notice I need to rush around a bit,' he pointed out. 'Have you a passport? Er, no, I suppose you haven't.'

'Do I have to carry on sitting here?'

'Do you mind?' he asked apologetically. 'Have you had lunch?'

'I couldn't eat another mouthful.'

'Then I'll have to get back as quickly as I can,' he smiled. 'The money is – ?' She indicated the counter.

'I'll let you have it when you hand over the ticket.'

'That will be perfectly in order.' He winked again.

She watched the car drive away and she passed an hour reading every word of the brochures he'd left on the table. It struck her as being an odd way of going on holiday perfectly pleasant and the people were nice, but not at all what she'd expected. At some point she heard a ship's siren but it meant nothing to her. She drank another cup of coffee and toyed with the idea of eating a light lunch, but Big Mick was no longer behind the counter. She could not resist checking the suitcase.

It had gone.

She was simultaneously transfixed and engulfed by a great wave of panic. When Big Mick returned she was clutching the counter in a near faint. 'I gave it him through the back door,' the main explained innocently. 'We usually do that, it's quieter.'

Mrs Burgess stared at him wildly then, grabbing her other case, fled from the café. She ran through the iron gate back into the dock but was immediately lost. Then she seemed to recognise a great stack of packing cases and got her bearings. Breathlessly she reached the berth where she'd . . . the ship had sailed.

Suddenly she was sick. It was her most humiliating moment, heaving up into the murky water before lying sweating across a bollard. She knew the young sailor had been an honest man, she just knew. And she'd *thought* the well-dressed man had been straightforward enough. She slowly gathered together her case, mackintosh, and handbag. She mopped her face with a handkerchief. Then she walked away.

She'd been accurate in her assessment of both men. The well-dressed man delivered the 'ticket' at teatime but she'd disappeared. A canary must have sung somewhere. Hard luck. These things happen. He'd hang on to the cash, less his own commission, because she was just the type of cool customer who'd turn up for it when you were least expecting it. 'I helped enough taury-fingert folk out the country,' he mused, lapsing into the local term for thieves, 'but I ne'er came across a lady like that one!'

He was leaning far over the side of the workboat and hauling up the net. He was alone and the catch was a heavy one. The massive boat began to rock dangerously, something he had always feared, but at last he heaved the net inboard and began to count the teaming heap of salmon. It was difficult to concentrate, they moved about so much, and he was sure he'd counted the same fish three times. Suddenly they were flying all around him, taking to the air like a swarm of bees, and attacking with an angry buzzing sound like a petrol-driven model aircraft. It was too much; there were so many of them, salmon with seagull's wings . . . he needed Biddy to get him out of this . . .'

'Darling!'

Morrison climbed slowly from the heavy sleep and found himself in Carrie's arms. For a second he thought the fish were in the bedroom and he moved his arms to defend himself, but they receded and he was awake.

'Did I shout?'

'No. Generally threshing about. What was it?'

'I was being –' He tried to drag the picture back. 'I don't know.' He was relieved to be awake and began to laugh. Carrie laughed with him until moments later he was relaxed and peaceful.

'All right now?'

'Mm.'

'If you only half wake up it sometimes comes back again.'

'I'm awake.'

She pressed herself into his back, hugging him tightly, before releasing him when he turned over to face her. Then she kissed him, long and soft. She knew she was arousing him, she wanted to, because she was in love with him. She felt his hand around her waist, it slid down her body to return underneath her nightdress.

'Darling,' she whispered, 'I want to marry you.'

'*Wonderful!*' It was all he needed to say.

The next morning they lay dozing until nine o'clock. After months of rising with the dawn it was a luxury he consciously enjoyed although it was not within him to allow it to become habitual. This day they lay beside each other in a relaxed hour-long silence which he broke by continuing the conversation as if it had never been interrupted.

'Will it be a quiet wedding?'

'Yes.'

'Where?'

'Here. Skerrymor Bay is my home. All right with you?'

'Of course. It's my home too.'

'Keep it small though, eh?'

'Absolutely. The village doesn't deserve a spectacular. Just invite those who stuck by us.'

'I want a honeymoon,' she said. 'May we have a honeymoon?'

'Yes.' There was silence for a full five minutes. Then Morrison spoke again. 'Although there could be a snag about that.'

'We'll just have to take her with us.'

There came a crash from downstairs. It was followed by several more as if furniture was being moved.

281

'Darling,' said Carrie with studied calm, 'there is somebody moving about downstairs.'

'Biddy?'

'Not Biddy. Didn't you lock the back door?'

'I don't think so. I never do.' He jumped quickly out of bed, but then stopped as the sound of violent sweeping came from the hall.

'You needn't worry,' he said. 'I recognise the fairy footsteps.'

'Mrs Burgess!'

'Our housekeeper has returned to the fold.'

'It sounds like she's smashing the place up.'

'No, she's only cleaning it.' Then as she too climbed out of bed, 'Which comes to more or less the same thing.'

He tied the girdle of his dressing gown. 'The thing is I'm not sure we can afford her now the season's finished.'

'Let's worry about that later. First we'd better find out why she isn't sailing the seven seas.'

It was midday before they discovered the reason for the woman's return. Up until then she went about her work as if neither the conversation outside the church nor the aborted cruise had ever taken place. Then, over a cup of tea, it spilled over, the words tumbling out and punctuated by racking sobs. Morrison and Biddy were in the boatshed so Carrie took the full brunt of the housekeeper's distress. The woman had lost everything; the money no longer seemed important, it was the forfeiture of dreams and pride that hurt so much.

In the boatshed Morrison told Biddy he intended to marry Caroline. He saw the girl pale slightly before listening to his every word with total concentration.

'When?' she asked when he finished.

'We don't really know yet. Quite soon.' She nodded and continued coiling a long length of rope. 'Darling, this is something I want very much. I'm not going to find reasons, make excuses, or apologise.'

'I understand, Morrison. Truthfully, I do. I didn't at first, but I do now.'

'It doesn't alter anything between you and me, you know

282

that.'

She put the rope down and picked up the end of another tangled length. Then she put it down and turned to him, a child reaching for adult comprehension. 'It does, Morrison. It changes *everything*. When I think how much I want to cry.' She nearly did and he crossed to her quickly, but she held up a hand and fought for composure. 'The bit I understand is that it can't be the way I thought. It was to be you and me together but it's never been that, not ever once. Cluny said I was selfish and everything you did was for me, but *this* isn't for me, Morrison. This is for you.'

'Yes it is,' he admitted.

She nodded, relieved he wasn't going to pretend otherwise. 'Well, he said I was to allow that too.'

Morrison knelt in front of her and took both small hands into his, looking directly into her unhappy face. 'Since Cluny died you haven't thought about him every minute of every day. You've worked and played, laughed and cried, been good and been bad; but you've never forgotten the things he said, and you try to live by them. Well, as time passes it gets easier, things like identification parades are finished with once and for all and – ' he reached up and touched the hat, her hand still in his, ' – wearing his hat will seem less important. It's the same with me, darling. The days with Mummy were good and nothing can ever change that. What I've discovered is that other days can be good too. You're still the most important person in my life but now we're back to where we were before – there's someone else who's become important too.'

The emotion had become greater than her resistance could contain and now the tears coursed down her cheeks. 'I *understand*, Morrison, I keep telling you.'

He grinned and stood up. As he returned to the task of clearing the end of the season debris he said, 'Anyway, when we go on our honeymoon, you're coming too. You have to agree that's a bit original.'

She shook her tousled head and brushed aside the tears with the back of a grubby hand. 'No, you two go off together. I'll go stay with Grandpa.'

283

She had no conception of how neatly she had turned the tables. It was said without provocation. She had enjoyed her grandfather's visit and no longer dreaded the thought of two weeks in his company, even Grandma was bearable now she realised he could see her shortcomings as well. However, the effect on Morrison was electrifying. He experienced the identical surge of unjustified jealousy that flooded Biddy when first she saw him standing close to Carrie. He'd never minded her affection for Cluny but her willingness to spend a fortnight with his in-laws came as a surprising shock.

Fortunately he hid it from his daughter and Carrie did not share his concern when he told her later. 'If you ask me;' she commented, 'it could improve relations all round.'

In their private sitting-room at The Last Resort, Macleod was becoming increasingly irritated with his wife. He enjoyed his half-hour with the newspaper last thing before going to bed but here she was biting deep into the time sermonising in that self-righteous voice. Sometimes he was able to pull a mental switch and shut it into the background, uttering an occasional grunt and acknowledgement, but tonight she kept breaking through. After he had gone back to the beginning of one news story for the third time he lowered the paper and suggested with painful politeness, 'Why don't you go and have your nice bath?'

'So you're not interested then?'

'I am heedful of your every word but just now I would quite like to read my paper.'

'I dare say her marrying him makes it all right in your eyes.'

He blinked with surprise as he realised more than he'd thought had passed over his head. 'Eh?' he enquired.

'It's what I've been talking about.'

'I must have missed that bit.'

'Alistair Macleod, you've not listened to one word I've been saying.'

'So tell me what you're on about.'

'Caroline Kelso is planning to marry the Morrison man.'

'But that's wonderful news.' Macleod seemed genuinely pleased.

'I'm not so sure the village will see it in the same light. She has sinned before God and before society.'

He folded the paper and rose to his feet. 'Ah, we are still sitting in judgement, are we? We're still adopting standpoints born out of the Middle Ages. What must we do to absolve her sin – cut all her hair off?'

'Try not to be stupid, Alistair.'

'Ha-ha, it's me that's stupid, is it? Well, I'll tell you what we could do, shall I? We could give a reception after the wedding!'

'Give a – ?'

Macleod walked over to his desk and rummaged through a heap of mail. 'The Reverend Kelso canna be a rich man and I've no doubt he wouldna be above accepting a spot of help. We could invite the whole village and make a real occasion of it.'

'Are you in your right mind?'

He found the letter he was looking for and carried it to her. She saw the letterhead *Town & Country Tours Ltd*. 'You needn't bother reading it 'cos I'll tell ye what it says. They have reserved two rooms to the end of September and would like to discuss terms for the whole of next year.'

'What's this got to do with the wedding?'

He stood right over her, something she disliked intensely. 'This letter spells out to me that we'll be making a pound or two next year, and you'll be spending your fair share of the take. Very well,' he continued before she could answer, 'I'll worry about what the good Lord thinks when I meet him, meanwhile I have every intention of repaying my debt to the man who helped make it possible, and to his plucky wee girl who showed us the man who killed Cluny.

'I'm sure I – ' She wavered into silence as he raised his hand with solemn dignity.

'And now, if you don't mind, I'd prefer not to talk about it any more.'

He returned to his chair and, with every sign of satisfied

enjoyment, re-opened his newspaper. After a moment Mrs Macleod said, 'I'll be away upstairs to my bath.'

'Excellent,' he murmured.

Macleod was nothing if not influential within his own circle of acquaintances and, by using his own bar as a communication centre, he ensured that within a day or two most of the village was aware of the news and the forth-coming marriage had his and Mrs Macleod's blessing. The church was an equally effective means of dispensing in-formation and the gatherings outside the doors when services were ended frequently became hotbeds of gossip. In this respect Mrs Macleod was less helpful towards Morrison and Carrie than her husband, but the couple had a surprising ally in Mrs Burgess.

'Aye, I *was* thinking about a cruise,' she assured her friends. 'Indeed I'd even made plans. Then, of course, with the news of their engagement I could hardly leave them to look after themselves.' The bold statement was far from the truth. With Mr Burgess's disability pension dying with him the unfortunate woman was teetering on the verge of poverty and Morrison had thought long and hard before reluctantly agreeing to keep her employed through the close season.

Janet Mahoney was not convinced. 'It was my under-standing you were away *because* Caroline had moved in with him.'

'How could you think that, Miss Mahoney? I've known Miss Caroline all her life, and I reckon I know Mr Morrison and young Biddy better than anyone. They all need each other, they all love each other, and it's my belief such unions are arranged in heaven.'

In this way the village's stand against permissive immorality ended as quickly as it had begun and Mrs Burgess found temporary solace in scrubbing, polishing, washing, and ironing all that she could find in first the white house and, later, in her own. On Mondays she would crash through every room in the house collecting dirty clothes, towels, sheets, pillowslips and almost anything else that was soft and movable in order 'to give it a good clean'. On the first occasion Biddy's anorak was swept up during her round, and whilst clearing the pockets of coins, sweet-papers, bits of string, and miscellaneous unidentified objects picked up from beach or countryside, she came across a crumpled but unopened letter and telegram.

'How long have they been there?' asked Morrison when Carrie handed them to him.

'Look at the postmark.'

'Five days, for heaven's sake. That child is the living limit.'

He tore open the telegram, read it, and passed it to her without comment. The letter was from Patrick and when the opening sentence clearly showed it to be more than a bread-and-butter 'thank you' note he sat slowly on the upturned dinghy to read it carefully.

Dear David,

I am writing this while Martha is whooping it up at a Conservative coffee morning because, thus far, I have not discussed with her what I'm about to say. The habits of your friend Bruce Cornelius appear to be infectious! Needless to say I will talk to her but, by the time I do, this letter will be in the post and my mind made up.

Having said that I'm not exactly sure what I'm proposing or why I'm doing so. Let's just say you and Biddy have awakened a yen to return to the free life of my youth.

Writing simply how much I enjoyed myself last week is a considerable understatement. I have unstinting admiration for your enterprise and courage in carving a new life for yourself and, in bringing up Biddy the way you're doing so, you are keeping alive for me at least all the fine qualities of our daughter. For this I thank you.

To say more would be less than fair to your Caroline. You've found yourself a good woman there, son-in-law, and if you've an ounce of sense in you you'll not allow this one hesitation in your present life of bold decisions.

It was typical of you not to mention your money

problems having met unacceptable conditions at your first approach, and equally typical of my grand-daughter to spill the beans! I only hope you'll find this idea more to your liking.

I made my pile from hard graft, not all of which was enjoyable. It's there to buy me contentment in my old age and it won't do that sitting in Treasury Stock. (It has to buy my Martha happiness as well and I mustn't forget that.) My cup was filled and slopping over in the days I pitted my wits and strength against overwhelming Irish odds. I won then and I'll win again, even if neither the wits nor strength are what they were. You're a good skipper and if my money will buy me a place alongside you in that workboat of yours, and a partnership in your fish farm project, then we'll sell up here and move to where life still happens like it used to.

Well, I've said it. Now there's only one sentence more – I don't like it but it has to be written. If you consider this is the pipe-dream of an old fool who's past it, or if Martha shows genuine *distress when I tell her, then the money's there for you anyway – I liked what I saw at Skerrymor Bay and I want it to continue*

Yours,
Patrick.

Carrie was looking down, waiting for him to finish. She raised an enquiring eyebrow and he moved over to make room for her to sit beside him. She took the letter and he read it a second time over her shoulder. When she came to the reference to herself she squeezed his hand slightly. She reached the end and asked, 'What will you do?'

He pursed his lips. 'It's wonderfully generous, but not an idea to rush into.'

'Why not? The poor man's been waiting an answer for five days already.'

'I'll telephone him this afternoon.' He paused and then added, 'He seems to like you.'

She nodded, pleased, and then said, 'I think he wants

you to tell him when we're getting married.' She looked at him with a quizzical smile. 'When will you say?'

He kissed her gently. 'As soon as possible.' He rose with a sudden excitement. 'There's one thing about this place – you never know what the next day's going to bring.'

'What'll you do about this?'

He'd forgotten the telegram. It was terse and to the point:

PLEASE MAKE IMMEDIATE DELIVERY SEA DANCER MACGRUERS YARD CLYNDER.
REGARDS CORNELIUS

CHAPTER ELEVEN

THAT AFTERNOON the wind dropped to a dead calm.

Most townspeople seldom notice the wind. They become aware of it when strong gusts take hats away or squalls blow rain against trouser legs, but for most of the time they walk unaware of the feel of a breeze on their cheek and make comment only when a sudden deflected draught round a street corner affects a hair-do.

Along coastlines where people earn a living from the sea, or enjoy the sport of sailing, the wind takes on a special significance whilst perversely blowing less predictably. To a sailor the windstrength is relative to the size of craft he is aboard whilst the meteorologist relates it scientifically against measurements on the Beaufort Scale. This applies windspeeds to their effect on the sea from Force One, where light airs of three knots barely offer steerageway, to Force Eight where a forty-knot gale can raise eighteen-foot waves, and on to Force Twelve at which velocity a full hurricane performs the indescribable.

A dinghy sailor can be kept very busy in the moderate breeze of a Force Four, with three-foot waves showing white crests, at the same time as a cruising man still carries a full suit of sails and revels in a fast passage through, for him, a still-calm sea. At Force Six the forty-footers are tucking a reef in the mainsail and changing down to a working jib while longer waterlines hang on with genoas but heel over until gunwales are awash. By Force Seven the dinghy sailor has long been in the clubhouse and if the cruising member is not with him then he's pretty uncomfortable. The wind is coming at him around thirty-three knots, he's surrounded by heaped seas with foam running in long streaks, his mainsail is showing only five foot behind a storm jib and the bows smash down into troughs.

By this time all the skippers will have logged galeforce winds although the Beaufort Scale has still a further point to go before it agrees with them, with Severe Gale, Storm, Violent Storm, and Hurricane yet to be registered. They are right to do so, however, because the officially accepted measurement is of mean wind velocity, an average between gusts and lulls, and it follows that a Force Seven blow must be punctuated by galeforce gusts. The small cruiser sailor, huddled in oilskins and secured by lifeline within an open cockpit, is inclined not to notice the lulls; after all, if his craft is to be knocked down and capsized it will be by a gust and not a lull.

In the normal way weather forecasts are available with sufficient frequency and accuracy to render it inexcusable for the amateur sailor to be 'caught out' by a gale. It is equally true that whilst far out to sea a true and steady wind may be blowing, inshore this wind becomes affected by topography and land-heating. Moreover, shallow coastal waters susceptible to tide rips and funnelled winds produce overfalls and toppling seas, which unforecastable dangers can be as serious as anything thrown up by windforce alone. These factors produce so many club bar tales of threshing into Force Six breezes and running before Force Eight squalls that the true picture becomes confused; generally speaking, gales which blow around the club bar are in reality well down the Beaufort Scale.

Nevertheless, on the September day when 1500 hours saw only a mirror-like sea Coastguard stations reported that at 0200 hours the following morning there blew briefly a 'pocket gale' where shortlived Force Eight gusts caused spindrift and foam to streak downwind in long banners.

Biddy had spent that afternoon exploring with Andrew Campbell but returned to the white house in time for tea. She ran noisily into the room as Morrison was dialling Bruce Cornelius's office number for the third time.

'No, Mr Morrison,' the secretary said with pained

patience, 'he hasn't come in and we're really not expecting him this afternoon.'

He waved the girl to silence and she saw the telegram in his hand. 'Uuh-huh!' she commented.

'Would you tell Mr Cornelius that although I regret the delay in delivery of his telegram I just can't drop everything to fall in with his every whim. Then, for the hell of it, you might ask him who the hell he thinks he is.'

Biddy sank quietly into a chair to await her turn for his anger to be directed towards herself.

'I rather think, Mr Morrison,' the secretary replied, 'that Mr Cornelius hoped you would kindly help him out, having enjoyed free use of *Sea Dancer* for several weeks.'

'His telegram read less courteously. Does anyone there realise it's a helluva long haul to Clynder?'

'May I tell him you'll do your best?'

'I'd prefer to talk to him myself.'

There was a pause and he heard the woman sigh. Then she spoke again, quieter but very firmly. 'Mr Morrison, I am prepared to tell you that Mr Cornelius is not taking any calls at the moment. I'm sure he'll want to discuss everything with you in due course but –' she took a breath. '– MacGruers might have a customer willing to buy the boat and, Mr Morrison, he *needs* it there by Wednesday.'

'That's the day after tomorrow!'

'Will you try?'

'It's impossible.'

'Please.'

The encounter with his wife, witnessed by all, had obviously developed into a more ominous explosion. For once in his life Bruce Cornelius was a man who needed help.

'I'll call you back,' he said briefly and hung up.

'I'm sorry, Morrison,' began Biddy.

'There's no time for that now,' he said. 'What the hell are we going to do?' He turned back to a heap of charts and sailing directions on the table.

'Where's Clynder?'

'In the Gareloch.'

Biddy came up behind him and put a small arm round his shoulder as he stooped over a chart. 'That wasn't a terribly helpful answer, Morrison. Where the hell is the Gareloch?'

'Don't swear. I've told you before.' He was studying an Admiralty General Chart of Scottish Coastal Waters and pointed a finger for her to trace the course. 'Here we are in the Sound of Sleat so we begin by rounding Ardnamurchan Point before sailing the length of the Sound of Mull to Oban and the Firth of Lorne. Past all these islands until we reach Luing and Scarba, then we save ourselves an eight-mile haul round the Mull of Kintyre by using the Crinan Canal into Loch Fyne. Now we wiggle through the Kyles of Bute into the upper reaches of the Firth of Clyde, past Loch Long, towards Helensburgh, into Rhu Narrows and we're in the Gareloch.'

'Phew!'

'That's more or less what I was trying to tell that woman on the telephone.'

Biddy moved round the table so that she could look directly into his face. Her eyes shone over a captivating, dare-devil grin. 'Come on, Morrison, you and me, eh?'

'When?'

'Now. Tonight.'

'That's crazy.'

'But terrific fun.' She came back to him and jabbed a finger at the chart. 'We'd make Crinan by dawn, Tarbert by lunch, sleep in the Kyles of Thingumajig and sail triumphantly into the Gareloch on Wednesday to the sound of bands playing and Mr Cornelius muttering gruffly "Thanks, Morrison" whilst concealing tears of gratitude.

He allowed a slight pause. 'Have you quite finished?'

'Yes.'

'Darling, it's not as easy as that.' He shuffled through the charts and produced several large-scale, detailed sheets. 'For openers a night passage through the Sound of Mull tacking into a south-easter could be pretty hairy, but just take a look at the little lot we have stacked up here.' He pulled out a chart marked Craignish Point to Ardluing Point. 'This, my darling, is the Dorus Mor. It's a channel between this point here and Garraeasar Island where the tide sets through at eight knots with only fifteen minutes of slack tide when it's possible to pass through. One mistake and we can be carried into the Gulf of Coirebhreacain.'

'What are all those black squiggles?'

'Overfalls. They're caused by the tide rushing across an uneven bottom. The Admiralty Pilot warns against attempting the passage without local knowledge and the Clyde Cruising Club Sailing Directions consider it to be the worst gulf in the West Highlands.'

The girl looked up into his face and saw the excitement he'd been attempting to hide. 'Hey, how long have you been reading up on this?'

'All afternoon.'

'You want to do it,' she accused, 'just as much as I do. Come on, Morrison, we could make it by Wednesday night.'

He flicked through the pages of Sailing Directions. 'Look at the Crinan Canal, six locks up and eight down again. That's an awful lot of hanging on to warps after a night passage.'

'We can tie up against the bank and go to sleep if we want.'

Carrie's quiet voice came from the door behind them. 'Why don't you try?' They turned and saw her smiling gently. 'It's not the end of the world if you arrive late, and isn't it the kind of sail you've always talked about?'

'Yes, but it needs *planning*.'

'Then plan it. Biddy and I will sort out fuel and food.'

'Will you come with us?'

She saw Biddy's eyes on her, willing a refusal. The girl wanted desperately to share this one adventure alone with her father. 'Better yet, MacGregor and I will take the car to Clynder and drive you home again.' Still he hesitated, a thousand doubts ringing warning bells.

'Come *on*, Morrison.'

'Okay,' he decided.

Biddy whooped for joy and leapt at him in a brief excited hug before running across to put her arms round

Carrie. Over the child's head the woman gave him a small wink which was followed at once by an enquiring frown. 'You'll be all right?'

It was his last chance to point out the absurdity of treating a sailing yacht like a car and stretches of tidal water like roads; you don't simply jump into a boat and drive it, but his eyes went to his daughter who, typically, had at once transformed childlike excitement into adult concentration towards condensing daylong preparation into a few hours. He had become trapped by her regret that the two of them had not worked on anything together and it was no use crying wolf now.

'Yes, of course,' he assured Carrie.

He stepped outside and studied the sky. Light streaks of cirrus high above, no movement of air, the early evening sun hot on his face. The landmass of Skye obscured the horizon and prevented him seeing the distant build-up of turbulent cumulus cloud; not did he notice an almost eerie metallic quality to the light. The BBC Shipping Forecast promised a Force Four increasing to Six later for the area but, looking across the Sound, there was every indication they would be starting their passage under engine. He did not hear a local warning for fishermen put out by Oban Radio.

He sat down again with the charts and Admiralty Pilot to prepare himself a set of sailing directions. These cards noted light buoys, landmarks, leading lights, and compass bearings along their route together with tidal rates and set which would help or hinder their speed through the water. Then he noted a series of 'funk-holes', natural harbours they could run into if the weather turned suddenly foul.

Biddy and Carrie ferried supplies to *Sea Dancer* under the suspiciously watchful eye of MacGregor who stood protectively in the bows of the dinghy on each of the several journeys. Carrie put a cooked chicken, butter, milk and eggs into the galley fridge but filled a large Thermos flask with bubbling porridge and another with scalding coffee to ease the night passage and their first breakfast. Then she prepared a light supper before they set sail.

During the evening a light breeze sprang up from the north-east and as the sun set this freshened to a Force Three. They were ready to depart by ten o'clock and, once aboard, Morrison hoisted the mainsail but sensibly chose a working jib for the night in favour of the big genoa foresail. The final faint glow of the setting sun had faded from the western sky as they let go the moorings. They could just make out the shapes of Carrie and MacGregor on the beach and respond to her farewell wave. In the dark eastern sky massive cloud banks heaped several thousand feet into the air.

They sailed a fast broad reach for ten minutes until they were well clear of the land before altering to a south-westerly course with the black blotch of Eigg on the starboard bow and already the faint loom of the Ardnamurchan light on the horizon dead ahead. The breeze blew from directly astern and, with an extra experienced crew member, Morrison would have set the giant spinnaker without hesitation. As it was he steered a couple of points to starboard of his course to prevent the mainsail boom crashing across in an unintentional gybe. He noted the compass reading and time in the log before handing the tiller to Biddy.

'That's our course for at least two hours. You can take first watch until bedtime. Whatever you do don't allow the wind to get behind that mainsail.'

'Right.' She set a cushion and took up her customary kneeling position by the tiller while he sat comfortably to rest after the exertions of preparation. The sea had yet to respond to the freshening breeze and was still perfectly calm. Their run before the wind was practically silent with just a satisfying swish of water thrust aside by the bows and bubbling into a wake behind. The night air carried a chill which was in such contrast to the heat of the day that after half an hour Biddy found herself shivering. Morrison went below and threw her up a thick pullover then, whilst he was in the saloon, began to make things shipshape by preparing her berth with sleeping bag and pillow.

'If you pick up any lights other than those you can see

already, give me a yell,' he instructed.

'Right.'

Biddy's initial excitement had settled into deep contentment. There was nothing to compare with the sheer satisfaction of conning a sailing cruiser through the night. She felt as one with the vessel, it was alive beneath her, rushing through the darkness to where she and Morrison would be alone in the whole world. She could just make out the black water in the glow of their navigation lights and, looking up to the masthead, she saw a bright star situated precisely in the point of the triangle formed by mast and shroud. Suddenly she understood the line in the poem from English class – *and a star to steer her by*. She had only to keep the star in the triangle and she wouldn't have to bother concentrating on the compass. Her legs were getting pins and needles so she re-positioned the cushion, put her feet up, rested an arm along the tiller, and put her head back.

The windstrength was Force Four.

The most difficult thing for the novice helmsman to detect when running before the wind is an alteration of windstrength. As it blows harder the vessel simply increases speed without there being any noticeable difference of air movement in the cockpit. The waves are slow to respond to the new condition and until the hull reaches its optimum speed through the water it takes an experienced ear to pick up the myriad sounds caused by a marginal increase of speed. A hull's optimum speed is the result of a mathematical formula controlled by its waterline length – in the case of *Sea Dancer* this was approximately eight knots. Once that speed is reached it takes a disproportionate amount of energy to force it to move any faster. When the wind builds up sufficient strength to do so there will be a tendency for the boat to yaw, which magnifies as the waves grow higher and the speed increases. For quite a while, however, the inexperienced helmsman will instinctively correct the motion without consciously wondering what is causing it.

The truth was that down in the cabin Morrison *should*

have noticed it. There were plenty of clues. Apart from the water rushing past only fibreglass thickness away there was the rumble of the propeller revolving freely in its shaft and a kind of hum as rigging and fixings took the additional strain. Novice or not, Biddy *should* have noticed she was kneeling on the cushion again and her left hand had come round to assist her right hand on the tiller. As it was, more than half-an-hour passed before Morrison decided to check 'up top'. Before doing so he poured a couple of mugs of coffee from the flask and a sudden yaw caused him to spill a few drops on the cabin sole. Simultaneously his daughter's voice called down to him.

'Morrison, we seem to be going helluva fast.'

By then it was blowing at Force Five.

He climbed the three steps of the companionway and sat beside her. 'Let me take her for a while.' She ducked under his arm as he took the tiller and sat close up to him to drink her coffee.

'I nearly gybed just then,' she admitted.

He could feel the boat creaming through the water, the bows shouldering aside building waves in smothers of foam, the dinghy astern planing through the wake and bucking uncomfortably on the towline. It was exciting sailing, the darkness enhancing the sensation of speed.

'We seem to have found ourselves a land breeze. We'll make the most of this while it lasts.'

'Where are we?'

He pointed. 'That's Muck on our starboard beam.' His eyes were unaccustomed to the dark and although he looked carefully all round the horizon it was Biddy who announced, 'Two new lights.'

He followed her pointing finger. 'Got them. Thanks.' They had appeared from behind the island. 'It's a ship – a fairly big one, I fancy. We'll keep a *very* careful watch on her!'

They watched the lights for several minutes, noting they were moving comfortably from right to left across their field of vision, indicating the ship was crossing their course some two miles ahead. The red sidelight was plainly visible below the two masthead lights. Then the two lights began to draw closer together and merge into one. Morrison stood up quickly, peering ahead with enormous concentration.

'Biddy,' he said, 'line up the light with the pulpit and stand quite still. Tell me if it moves.'

After thirty seconds, 'No,' she reported.

'That's what I think too. Can you still see the red light?'

'Yes. And a green one now!'

'Christ, so can I!' The ship was heading directly towards them. 'Stand by to gybe,' he called.

He hauled hard on the mainsheet to bring in the boom and lessen its swing when they turned before the wind. Biddy moved to free the jibsheet from the winch on his order. 'Gybe ho!' he called and leaned on the tiller whilst hanging on to the mainsheet with both hands. Suddenly the wind caught the other side of the sail and, despite being ready for it, the force all but jerked the rope from his grasp. He managed to control the gybe whilst Biddy let fly the jibsheet and winched in on the other side of the cockpit. The manoeuvre was handled well and soon they were staring again at the approaching lights. Slowly, so slowly, the red light became masked and they knew the ship would pass them to starboard. They held the new course and watched the two pinpoints of light as they grew wider apart and higher. It was like an express train approaching from a distance which for ages grows slowly larger before seeming to accelerate at the last second. The lights hung apparently motionless for minutes on end before suddenly they developed haloes, light spilt from portholes, they saw deck lights and the terrifying black bulk of the superstructure. The next instant the ship became a vast, reeling, shimmering mass of movement and engine noise lighting the surface of the sea with its reflection as it passed them less than three hundred yards away. Then it was gone.

'I'm glad we missed hitting that,' commented Biddy.

'Hang on, they've not finished with us yet,' he warned. It was ages before the ship's wake hit them. Then *Sea Dancer* was lifted into the air like a cork, tossed and rolled three or four times, before the movement lessened and they sailed normally once more.

'So much for "ships that pass in the night",' Morrison observed. 'I doubt he even saw us.'

When they gybed back to their correct course Morrison realised they were running before a strong blow. The boat no longer felt comfortable as the hull was strained beyond its optimum speed. This was no land breeze, it was a wind with a ruthless strength.

In fact, it was then blowing Force Six.

'I think we'll shorten sail,' he said calmly. 'I'd rather be prepared for rounding Ardnamurchan sooner than later.'

'Are we all right?'

'Sure we are. Now, go below, climb into your oilies and throw mine out to me, fix yourself a lifeline and bring me one, and fetch out the number two jib.'

'Right.' She took the coffee mugs and disappeared below. Left to himself Morrison decided he wasn't happy about the wind rising so rapidly. The barometer had dropped like a stone and he had committed the cardinal sin of finding himself at sea, virtually single-handed, and ill-prepared for a blow. In the cabin Biddy found that putting on oilskins in a confined space that was pitching about was rather frightening. She began to feel distinctly queasy and when she passed her father's heavy-weather gear to him she grabbed several deep breaths before feeling her way to the forward cabin and delving into the sail locker.

By the time she returned to the cockpit she was very green about the gills. Morrison was ready in his oilies with the lifeline harnessed in place. 'I'm going to turn into wind and tuck a couple of reefs into the main, so we might get a bit wet.' Biddy nodded, her enthusiasm for the night sail was tending to wane. As they came about the boat heeled wildly for a few moments before there came the deafening slatting of sails. The girl hated the ear-splitting clatter which demonstrated so clearly their fragility against the elements. Her father fastened the lifeline snap-hook to the coachroof railing before lowering the mainsail several feet with the main halliard. Then he hauled hard on the roller reefing gear, causing the boom to revolve and take up the slack sail neatly. The job was accomplished quickly.

'Okay,' he shouted back to her. 'You can bring her back to course again.'

He hung on to the shrouds as she obeyed. She felt better up top and working although she would be jolly glad when Morrison had completed the task and was safely back beside her in the cockpit. She watched him move right forward and become swallowed up in the gloom. She saw the foresail come down and could just make out his figure in the faint light from the masthead as he removed the sheet and halliard shackles, made them fast, and began unhooking the sail from the stainless-steel forestay. Without the steadying jib the boat plunged through the water in an ungainly fashion and Biddy was forced to make massive corrections with the rudder. After five tiring minutes she saw the smaller sail being hoisted and a moment later he was back in the cockpit winching in the sheet. The boat felt balanced once more and sailed easier.

'I'm glad that's over,' she said, relieved.

'So am I,' he agreed. She watched him sit heavily and realised the effort had tired him considerably. He rested a while then took over the helm. 'You'd better turn in,' he advised.

'I don't think I fancy lying flat in that cabin, Morrison.'

'You must try. I need you fresh as a daisy tomorrow.'

'Do we have to undress?'

'Just your oilies and boots, then snuggle into the sleeping bag as you are.'

'I'll try.' She pulled off the oilskins, hanging on to him in the cockpit before entering the cabin with considerable misgivings. It was no surprise to him that she was asleep within minutes.

He was abeam of Ardnamurchan light just before one o'clock. He didn't know it but it was then that the Coast-guard station logged a local Force Seven. Morrison was in very real trouble because once again he was carrying far too much canvas. With the wind astern *Sea Dancer* smashed top heavily through the waves, every fitting straining to redress the imbalance between windforce and water resistance. As he came into the leeward of the land there was a blessed half-hour's respite and during it he resolved to put into the first of his plotted 'funk-holes' which was the harbour of Tobermory. He would need the sailing directions to swot up the leading lights but there was time enough before waking Biddy.

Suddenly the wind slammed into them with tremendous force. The yacht lurched violently, then went right over. There was a frightening noise of rushing water and a loud report as though the hull was cracked in. Morrison was thrown across the cockpit taking the tiller with him. The inadvertent movement brought the bows into wind and desperately slowly, as if in great agony, *Sea Dancer* righted herself, water cascading from the deck and pouring from the self-draining cockpit. From down below he heard Biddy scream out in fear.

'It's all right, darling,' he shouted. Then, because he was too stunned to think straight, he added with mindless stupidity, 'Go back to sleep!'

'You're joking!'

Morrison worked out what had happened and his heart sank. They had rounded the point and run straight into one of the most perverse factors of coastal gales. The wind that had blown from astern down the Sound of Sleat was now deflected by the mountain ranges of Moidart and Ardgour causing it effectively to veer until it came directly out of Loch Sunart. His course to Tobermory would be a beat to windward and this was simply not on in the prevailing conditions.

Biddy slid back the hatch and pulled out the top board. 'If that was your way of telling me it's time for my watch . . .' He laughed at her, admiring the spirit which dredged up a joke at this hour.

'Listen, darling, we've got to get these sails down. Can you bring up the storm jib?'

They went through the entire manoeuvre again, this time rolling the complete mainsail around its boom and changing the foresail for the tiny, canvas, triangular storm

302

jib. Then Morrison announced his change of plan. 'We're going to have to carry on running before this lot until it blows itself out. So we'll head south to Iona then cut across the Mouth of Lorne to Scarba and Crinan.' He would telephone Carrie from the hotel there to advise Cornelius of the delay. 'Now finish your rest, darling. I promise not to tip you out of bed again.'

At the moment of his setting the storm jib the half-gale had passed its peak. He had no idea of the precise wind strength – in a small cruiser sailing at night conditions tend to seem worse than they really are. On a bright sunny day the beat to windward in the same wind would have been less daunting and the storm jib could still have been bagged up.

His principal concern now was fatigue. He really felt desperately tired and wondered whether the doctor would still agree with the idea of ceasing to take the tablets. *Sea Dancer* was sailing steadily under the tiny foresail, he put his feet up, and made himself as comfortable as possible on the revised course.

By three o'clock the wind had lost its brutality, an hour later it had slackened to Force Four, and as the first glow of dawn lightened the eastern sky to port, it was no more than a gentle breeze. He was unsure of their precise position, dead reckoning suggested that daylight should reveal the Staffa Islands and he was confident he could find himself a positive fix from one of many clues. Blackness changed to grey as the sky brightened and he felt his sailing pride would suffer a reverse if any passing ship caught him sailing in a Force Three breeze with only a storm jib showing. He roused himself and left the boat to sail on its own whilst he hoisted the mainsail. The additional weight of unfurling the sail wrapped around the main boom was strength sapping after his night without sleep and it was at this moment he began to feel unwell. He went below to collect the sailbag containing the large genoa. Biddy stirred and her eyes flickered open as he passed her but she didn't waken properly.

Crouching on the foredeck it struck him that something

was wrong but his mind refused to analyse the feeling further. He lowered the storm jib and released the sheets. He stood up then, hanging on to the forestay and shook his head in an attempt to clear the spell of dizziness. He heard a sound and through the greyness he thought he saw a figure walking towards him from the cockpit . . . it was Biddy come to assist . . . no, wait . . . it was Wendy . . .

He regained consciousness the instant he hit the water, he'd passed out for less than two seconds. Too late he realised what had seemed so wrong – he'd failed to snap on his lifeline. He was practically abreast of the boat's stern and paddled desperately to catch the dinghy behind. He was hampered by flotation jacket and sailing boots and watched with despairing horror as it bucked away from his grasping hand.

Sea Dancer sailed on and Morrison stared after it in dumb disbelief, praying someone might waken him from this living nightmare, but knowing nobody could. Then he was alone.

Carrie had lain in bed and listened to the wind. She knew nothing about sailing and was not an alarmist by nature, being perfectly happy to leave such things to the experts. David had assured her he could manage and she accepted this as being so. However, the wind that shouted and screamed around the white house after midnight seemed awfully strong and she became deeply concerned about the speed at which they'd prepared and hurried away.

It was MacGregor who worried her most. He'd climbed the stairs to Biddy's room for all the world as if he'd forgotten they'd seen her off from the beach. He'd whined and sniffed outside her own bedroom door before crashing downstairs where she heard him wandering disconsolately from room to room. Then he'd climbed the stairs again and repeated the sniffing and whining routine until she'd opened the door and allowed him into her room. Still he gave her no peace. He lay at the foot of the bed for a few minutes, came round and peered into her face, then asked to be let out again. Eventually Carrie went downstairs and found the dog with his paws up on the living-room window-sill staring out towards the sea. She tried to remain calm but there was something very weird about his behaviour, almost as if the conditions around the house aroused memories of that earlier storm.

She returned to bed and managed to sleep fitfully until a great crash of wind made her sit up in bed, suddenly convinced that something had happened. It sounded to her like a hurricane was blowing out there and, as MacGregor at once sensed her fear, she put her arms round the animal and said, 'I know, old chap. I'm worried too.' It was exactly two o'clock.

There was nothing she could do so she set about persuading herself that David would have long since put into a harbour or found shelter of some sort. Doubtless he and Biddy were sleeping while the gale raged and she sat wakeful and frightened. She made herself a cup of tea and an hour later, when the noise appeared to have lessened, she went back to bed. She was awake again at first light by which time it was all over. However, on looking out at the sea she could see waves which still bore evidence of the night's blow.

She decided to telephone the Coastguard Service.

The sails were slatting again. It was the sound Biddy hated most. The wind noise had dropped and Morrison was probably changing the jib again; yes, that's right, she thought she remembered seeing him pass through the cabin. The slatting continued and she couldn't hear the sound of his feet on the deck above her head. The boat was pitching uncomfortably too, it seemed they were no longer under way. Perhaps he'd dropped anchor and was snatching a rest in the cockpit.

She slid out of her sleeping bag and opened the hatch. The cockpit was empty. She peered round towards the foredeck but there was no sign of him.

'Morrison!' she called. She climbed into the cockpit and

looked all round, a sudden fear tightening her stomach. She jumped down the companionway and ran needlessly to the tiny forecabin, looking also into the toilet compartment. There was no sign of him and she panicked. 'MORRISON!' she shouted. Her scared voice was loud in the confined space and she rushed back into the cockpit 'M-O-R-R-I-S-O-N!' she yelled. This time the cry was taken away by space, no echo, no resonance, nothing. Tears sprang to her eyes and a terrified sob broke from her. She tried to search the endless sea but the tears blinded her, and this immediate practical disadvantage caused her to take a grip on herself. She wiped them away and looked carefully as far as the eye could see. It was half light and the grey sea merged quickly into gloom. On deck the sail was hoisted but its boom swung uselessly in the breeze. The storm jib they'd set during the night now lay in the water several fathoms from the boat, still joined by its halliard.

Biddy ran forward and tried to pull it in. The waterlogged sail was too heavy for her and an unexpected lurch caused her nearly to fall in herself, so she released the figure-of-eight knot at the base of the mast beside her and allowed the halliard's tail to run up and through its masthead block and become lost overboard. Then her initially mindless actions were over and she pulled herself together.

Morrison was somewhere in the sea and she had to find him. She and Carrie had done this very thing once during a maths class. She was going to be able to think better if she could stop that damn sail from slatting. She released the halliard and, because she'd forgotten to take up the topping lift, it all came down in a rush and the boom crashed into the cockpit. No matter, she bundled the sail around its length and fastened ties more or less as she'd seen Morrison do. At least it had kept it quiet. She returned to the cockpit, this time moving carefully and hanging on to the coachroof rail. She turned the ignition key of the diesel engine, pushing it against the spring-loading for the battery to turn it over and over until at last it fired. Biddy felt she was getting somewhere. She pushed the gear lever forward and opened the throttle whereupon the engine roared comfortingly and the boat lost its purposeless pitching.

It was growing lighter by the minute and her range of vision had increased enormously during the last five minutes. She knew she must work out some kind of search plan to avoid covering the same stretch of water twice whilst overlooking the likely areas. But where to steer first? She stared again at the endless water and felt another surge of panic flood her body before subduing it with conscious physical effort. She left the tiller and ran below to find Morrison's logbook. The last entry had been at 0230 when he'd noted the compass course to Iona. She returned to the steering compass and carefully placed a finger over the degree number before reading off the figure *exactly opposite to it*. This would be the reciprocal course and she grabbed the tiller to pull on it until the number had revolved directly beneath the marker line. She noted the time from the cabin chronometer – 5.45; right, she'd search on this course until 6.15.

Her next problem became one of sightlines. Even standing up her view forward was blocked by the boat's length, the mast, and the pulpit. Her clearest vision lay to either side. God knows this gave her plenty of water to look at but she carried the absurd impression that she might run her father down without being aware of it. Another snag was the extremes of light to her right and left – the western sky remaining fairly dark with the sea beneath it a featureless mass, whilst to the east bright sky reflected off the water with confusing brilliance which, when suddenly the sun itself appeared over the horizon, became hopelessly dazzling. By 6.15 there had been no sign of Morrison and, something that was almost equally frightening, no sign of land. This gave rise to her third difficulty, the fact that she could not avoid massive sobs developing to occasionally engulf her chest and break from deep inside her throat. She knew she must keep icily calm but it was a desperately difficult thing to do.

It was time to go about. She had resolved to sail at right angles to her course for five minutes before going back along her track for another half-hour, then the opposite right angle for ten minutes, and so on. She looked long and hard over the stern, remembering a trick her grandfather had taught her in the workboat. The wake was bending ever so slightly to the right of the boat which meant that a current was setting her to port. Therefore Morrison must be drifting slowly westward. She decided to make her first right angle to starboard, that is *into* the current, to cover that side of the box search just once before concentrating on the westward side.

She found it mentally difficult to make the turn – there seemed greater security in continuing straight for reasons she couldn't define. However, gritting her teeth, she pulled the tiller into her tummy and watched the compass until exactly ninety degrees had crossed the marker line. Already her eyes ached from staring and now she was headed directly into the rising sun. Five minutes later she turned again and began to motor along the course marked in the log.

At 6.45 she saw him! Five hundred yards away on her starboard side. She couldn't believe it at first because the round blob appeared briefly on the crest of a wave before becoming immediately lost in the trough. Then she just made out the green and white of his woollen hat and, with an exultant shout, she pulled over the helm.

She was still over fifty yards away when she realised it wasn't Morrison at all. It was only his hat.

Morrison had been in the water for less than thirty minutes when he thought he heard the sound of an engine. He'd tried to work out the likelihood of being rescued and, in all conscience, he thought his chances were pretty remote. The worry which overwhelmed his thoughts was what Biddy would feel when she found herself alone. That she would sooner or later be saved he had no doubt, but he pictured the sight of her petrified little face as the great loneliness hit her and he became very upset indeed.

Then came the distant engine sound. He stopped the gentle swimming motion he'd maintained for warmth and

308

listened carefully. The noise grew more distinct and, as a wave lifted him, he saw the boat. It was way off to the west and only when they were both simultaneously atop the waves could he see lower than the mast. Then briefly he caught sight of his daughter. She was standing on the seat, hanging on to the backstay and steering with her foot, looking carefully out to both sides. He felt proud of her. God, he felt so proud. The kid wasn't just lying in a sobbing heap on the bunk, she'd got the mainsail down (bundled in a mess he smilingly noted next time she came into view) and was actually searching for him. Quite extraordinarily he wanted his daughter to find him more for *her* sake than for his! And, somehow, he knew she was going to.

When *Sea Dancer* became once more lost to view he experienced acute loneliness. He guessed that Biddy would be making an orderly search because she was that kind of girl but would her next leg be to the east, where he was, or to the west? It was a fifty-fifty chance.

Nearly an hour passed before she came back by which time he was extremely cold and had given up hope. He heard the diesel rumble and almost immediately the vessel came into view. *It was heading exactly towards him.* He resisted the temptation to shout until she was much closer, apart from anything else the engine noise inside the cockpit would certainly deaden his cry. He dared not work out the odds against the possibility of her finding him . . . but here she was.

Fifty yards away she made a definite turn to her *starboard*. He saw Biddy climb again on to the seat to stare fixedly at something in the water. But she was looking in the opposite direction.

Now he shouted. He waved and yelled. *Sea Dancer* headed off on its inexplicable new course and Morrison experienced heartbroken despair.

At eight o'clock Carrie managed to get through to the Coastguard station. She felt rather foolish as she voiced undefined fears supported by scant information but the man was courteous and helpful.

'You say they set sail from the Sound of Sleat at about ten o'clock last night. Where were they headed?'

'Down the Sound of Mull to Oban, and then to Crinan.'

'Okay, I've got that. What's the name of the boat?'

'*Sea Dancer.*'

'And the sail number?'

'Oh.' She racked her brains, trying to recall the large number stitched in black on the mainsail. 'I think it's thirty-eight.'

'Can you describe the boat?'

'It's a white one.' She heard the man laugh and went on quickly, 'I'm sorry to be such a dummy. Wait, it's about thirty feet long, one mast in the middle, and two sails!'

'Okay, she's a masthead sloop – that will do us fine. And the skipper's name?'

'Morrison. He has an eleven-year-old girl with him.'

'Right-ho, Mrs Morrison. We'll keep an eye out for them. I wouldn't worry, they probably holed up some-where. We'll call you if we see them pass one of our look-outs.'

'Thank you.'

Carrie hung up, feeling much better for the stranger's steady confidence. She also quite liked being called Mrs Morrison.

The water was no warmer than about 56°F and Morrison's aimless paddling had long since ceased to aid his circulation. By nine o'clock he was shivering violently and he knew that when that ceased he would be suffering severely from exposure. His lifejacket was no longer supporting him as it had at first and now the occasional wave slopped nastily into his face. His mind was working sluggishly but he realised that when first he'd heard the engine it was probably Biddy *starting up*, and, in fact, *Sea Dancer* had stopped sailing at more or less the same time he'd fallen overboard. It was on the cards that for half an hour the boat had been relatively close but swallowed up by

310

darkness and that he was adrift on the extreme end of each of Biddy's beats up and down the course. Anyway, it had become clear she was not conducting a box search but was moving as it were in rows steadily to westward. He rated the chance of her nearing him a second time as nil.

Something white caught his eye, quite near at hand. He swam towards it and discovered the storm jib. It was something of a find because by lifting its centre out of the water he could create a pocket of air which gave him added buoyancy, secondly it was white and could possibly attract somebody's attention, and thirdly it provided an excuse to stop swimming.

At ten o'clock Biddy was nearing the end of her seventh leg. She was neither frightened nor tearful and her initial panic had been replaced by a grim determination to find her father however long it took and however much her eyes ached. It occurred to her that the aching void in her stomach was hunger and, sensibly, she hurried below to snatch a chicken leg from the fridge and empty the remainder of the lukewarm coffee from the flask into a mug. She stirred in two heaped teaspoons of sugar and was about to run back to the cockpit when her eye went to the bunk. Lying beside the tousled sleeping bag was Cluny's hat. She reached across to pick it up. Then, slowly and deliberately, she pulled it firmly on to her head.

Back in the cockpit she stood up on the seat, both hands grasping the backstay, right foot on the tiller. She panned across the limitless stretch of water with scrupulous care and spoke aloud her first prayer in months. 'Please God, please Mummy, please Cluny – help me find Morrison.'

She didn't know which one of them replied but their answer came so quickly, and so loudly, that it frightened the girl out of her wits. The naval jet fighter flew thirty feet above sea-level at some 250 miles per hour with the mighty roar arriving at almost the same time as the aircraft itself. Biddy's sudden terror changed instantly to delight but by the time she waved the plane was half a mile away. To her relief she saw it turn slowly and head back towards her only a few feet above the water. It waggled its wings at the boat and Biddy caught a quick flash of the pilot's face looking at her as the jet shot past with a thunderous roar. She tried to think of some way to let the man know she was in bad trouble but then watched spellbound as he began an extraordinary manoeuvre. First he made a climbing turn, then she saw flaps come down from the trailing edge of the wings as the plane slowed and looked as if it was going to land on the water about three miles away. At the very last second before he seemed bound to splash down into the sea the engine roared and he climbed again. Then, still with his flaps down, he flew towards her and, flying comparatively slowly now, circled *Sea Dancer*. She could make out the pilot, he was waving and pointing. Once again he flew to the same position and went through the pretence of landing. This time something fell from the aircraft before he accelerated into a climb and seconds later brilliant orange smoke rose up from the sea.

Biddy pulled the tiller to her, kicked the throttle fully open, took a compass bearing on the smoke, and headed straight for it. The aircraft circled high overhead for fifteen minutes before coming in and dropping a second smoke flare. Then it made a final pass of the boat, the pilot gave Biddy a wave, raised his flaps, waggled his wings and was gone. The second flare, like the first, expired after about five minutes but by then she could see the patch of white about a hundred yards from where it had fallen.

Then she saw Morrison.

The voice on the phone asked, 'Mrs Morrison?'

'Er – yes?' answered Carrie.

'We've found your husband and daughter, Mrs Morrison. They were a long way from where we expected and there'd clearly been a spot of trouble but, so far as we can see, they're both okay and a rescue boat is on its way to them.'

'Oh my God!'

'Now I wouldn't worry yet, if I were you,' the voice said firmly. 'One of the chaps out of Lossiemouth spotted them on a routine patrol and he hung about until his fuel ran low but by the time he left he was satisfied the girl had everything under control.' The man must have bitten his lip over the indiscretion because he continued hurriedly, 'Could you wait by the telephone for a couple of hours and we'll let you know where they're being taken.'

'Yes, of course, but what exactly – ?'

'We don't know until we get there, Mrs Morrison.' The man rang off. He wasn't going to break the news that her husband was in the drink and, from what they could see, the kid girl was trying to find him. Not yet, at any rate.

He looked half dead and was very weak. She tried to con *Sea Dancer* so that the cockpit fetched up alongside her father but she feared she'd run him down so settled for heaving to as near as possible and throwing him the lifebelt. She saw him reach for it with great difficulty and waited until he'd hooked an arm through its centre before hauling him across to the side of the boat. She pulled the companion steps from the cockpit locker and hung them over the side from the coaming but, although he tried to grasp them his hands wouldn't close on the rings and he was too exhausted to climb unaided. This was a major setback because there was no way the girl could find strength to lift his deadweight from the water. His face carried the look of a beaten man and the expression would remain in her mind forever.

She looked around desperately. The tail of the portside jibsheet lay loosely across the cockpit seat.

'Just hang on, Morrison. Save your energy until I shout.'

She grabbed the rope, passed it under his shoulders and through the lifebelt, and tied a bowline. She lifted it over the top of the collapsed boom before taking three turns round the portside winch on the opposite side of the cockpit, and winched in the slack. When she felt his weight she called, 'Now, Morrison!' She pulled on the handle as fast as she could and heard him gasp in pain as he tried to help. His shoulders came over the side and she quickly made fast to a cleat before hurrying back to him. His weight heeled the boat slightly and she was able to lean out and grab the seat of his trousers. She summoned a last effort from somewhere and heaved with all her strength. Cluny's hat fell from her head into the water but there was nothing she could do to save it. Suddenly his point of balance was below the waist and he crashed in a heap to the cockpit sole. He was aboard. Biddy shot a brief glance towards the hat but it had drifted out of reach.

She began to remove her father's waterlogged clothing. She kissed him quickly.

'Hello,' she said.

'Cold!' he whispered.

She stripped him of every stitch of clothing and grabbed two large towels from below. She gently dried him, too scared to rub the white, puffy skin. She put his arms round her neck and hauled him to a sitting position to dry his back.

'You must help me get you into the cabin, Morrison.'

'Okay.'

They made it somehow, he was shivering now, but eventually she collapsed him on to the bunk. She finished drying him, took the last dry towel and wrapped him in it, before tucking two blankets around him. She unzipped the sleeping bag down its entire length and hauled it round him before zipping it up until only his head was showing. He was still shivering.

She boiled water on the galley gas-ring and made a mug of hot, sweet, chocolate. She pulled him up again, put her arm round his shoulders, and held the mug to his lips. Minutes later the first hint of colour began to improve his ghastly pallor. He achieved a shaky smile.

'Thanks, darling.'

She couldn't answer. No words would come. She laid him down again, trying to hug warmth into him, until he fell asleep.

At midday a fast, heavy, sea-going launch came alongside and a cheery man called out, 'D'ye need a hand?'

'Yes please,' said Biddy.

They put them ashore at Kilchoan where Carrie was waiting on the jetty. A man had remained aboard *Sea Dancer* to sail the yacht into Calgarry pending further arrangements. Morrison was improving rapidly but they carried him to the hotel where a doctor advised an overnight stay under his supervision. Biddy, extraordinarily, seemed perfectly fit but Carrie knew the child's personal and private reaction would come in its own time.

Before leaving the launch the skipper had asked, 'How old is your daughter, Mrs Morrison?'

'Turned eleven. Why?'

'Good heavens,' the man had said.

They were all back in the white house by lunchtime on the Wednesday. During the afternoon Morrison busied himself on the telephone calling, amongst others, Bruce Cornelius and Patrick. Cornelius came on the line himself to thank him profusely for the effort he'd made but carefully avoided any reference to the other business. On the other hand Patrick was speechless; first at the news of the rescue but then by his son-in-law's invitation to join him in Skerrymor Bay.

When they sat down to their evening meal Biddy said to Carrie, 'I hope you're going to be able to handle Granny.'

'I handle you, don't I?' she replied smiling.

'That man thought I was your daughter.'

'Did you mind?'

'No. Like I said to Morrison, you can't be forever living in the past.' The two adults exchanged glances across the table as Biddy carried on. 'I said a prayer when I was trying to find you,' she told him. 'I prayed to God, to Mummy, and to Cluny. It was Cluny who answered, because later on he took his hat back.'

HOW GREEN WAS MY VALLEY
by Richard Llewellyn

In the beginning were the green mountains and the fertile valleys and the people were happy.

Then below the meadows they discovered coal. And the men of the field were transformed into people who laboured in darkness. People who fought, loved, drank and sang in the shadows of the great collieries. People who lived with danger and disaster — who had forgotten how green their valley had been.

'Vivid, eloquent, poetical, glowing with an inner flame of emotion . . . To write from the heart, to measure experience in love and sorrow, to bear witness to nobility or the idealism of men — this is not the sort of thing a serious novelist tries to do nowadays. It is what Mr Llewellyn does, however. His story makes a direct and powerfully sustained appeal to our emotions . . . deeply and continuously moving.' —
The Times Literary Supplement

'A work of fiction which enlarges for us the whole bounds of experience . . . I say with all my heart: read it. It is a most royal and magnificent novel.' —
Yorkshire Post

NEW ENGLISH LIBRARY

THE STARS LOOK DOWN

by A. J. Cronin

This is a book about LIFE — ugly, beautiful, ironic, heroic, and despairing . . . A book about PEOPLE, the story of miners — their land, their lives, their loves, their fights, and their scars. A book, deep in human sympathy, to stir the conscience of a nation.

'His women are as brilliantly painted as his men. The wretched Janny who pines for the genteel and comes to so miserable an end, the Laura who gives Joe his first big chance and permits herself to become his mistress, her sister whom the war so subtly changes, and the Sally whom a lesser novelist would have transformed into a second Gracie Fields — all of them are wonderfully good. It is a rich and rare panorama.' — *Sunday Times*

NEW ENGLISH LIBRARY

HATTER'S CASTLE
by A. J. Cronin

A soul-stirring novel of pride and greed, and its terrible retribution.

When her father forced her to leave school, and cut off all her contact with the past and future, Mary Brodie's whole life became the narrow compass of her family's cold, comfortless house in a small Scottish town. Her mean and ambitious father tyrannised his timid, obliging wife, his cowed, overworked younger daughter, and his spineless son. Four people were held in Brodie's merciless grip . . .

Until, like a breath of the outside world Brodie so much despised, came the young Irishman in whom Mary found a forbidden love and freedom, and who brought to her mother and sister the only release.

NEW ENGLISH LIBRARY

NEL BESTSELLERS

All The Rivers Run	*Nancy Cato*	£1.95
Brown Sugar	*Nancy Cato*	£1.50
Forefathers	*Nancy Cato*	£2.50
North-West By South	*Nancy Cato*	£1.75
Adventures in Two Worlds	*A.J. Cronin*	£1.75
The Citadel	*A.J. Cronin*	£1.95
Grand Canary	*A.J. Cronin*	£1.75
Hatter's Castle	*A.J. Cronin*	£2.25
Keys of the Kingdom	*A.J. Cronin*	£1.95
Shannon's Way	*A.J. Cronin*	£1.75
The Stars Look Down	*A.J. Cronin*	£2.25
Women's Work	*Anne Tolstoi Wallach*	£1.95
Acts of Kindness	*Charlotte Vale Allen*	£1.50
Believing In Giants	*Charlotte Vale Allen*	£1.75
Daddy's Girl	*Charlotte Vale Allen*	£1.75
Hidden Meanings	*Charlotte Vale Allen*	£1.75
Love Life	*Charlotte Vale Allen*	£1.50
Meet Me In Time	*Charlotte Vale Allen*	£1.25
Moments of Meaning	*Charlotte Vale Allen*	£1.50
Perfect Fools	*Charlotte Vale Allen*	£1.50
Times of Triumph	*Charlotte Vale Allen*	£1.25
Almonds and Raisins	*Maisie Mosco*	£1.95
Children's Children	*Maisie Mosco*	£1.95
Scattered Seed	*Maisie Moscoe*	£1.95

NEL P.O. BOX 11, FALMOUTH TR10 9EN, CORNWALL

Postage Charge:

U.K. Customers 45p for the first book plus 20p for the second book and 14p for each additional book ordered to a maximum charge of £1.63.

B.F.P.O. & EIRE Customers 45p for the first book plus 20p for the second book and 14p for the next 7 books; thereafter 8p per book.

Overseas Customers 75p for the first book and 21p per copy for each additional book.

Please send cheque or postal order (no currency).

Name ....

Address ....

....

Title ....

While every effort is made to keep prices steady, it is sometimes necessary to increase prices at short notice. New English Library reserve the right to show on covers and charge new retail prices which may differ from those advertised in the text or elsewhere. (8)